EYE OF THE STORM

Nick Cook completed his degree in sculpture and then moved into the computer games industry. For more than 21 years, Nick worked as a graphic artist and creative director, helping to produce over forty titles, including many chart-topping hits. Nick has a passion for science and astronomy, often blogging about the latest mind-blowing discoveries made in quantum physics. He once ever soloed a light aircraft, an experience he's tapping into now for the Cloud Riders trilogy.

To Noah,
Happy Cloud
Riding!

Nick Cook

Eye of the Storm

NICK COOK

THREE HARES PUBLISHING

First published in Great Britain in 2017

www.threeharespublishing.com

Three Hares Publishing Ltd Reg. No 8531198
Registered office: 17 Plumbers Row, Unit D, London E1 1EQ

ISBN 9781910153208

Printed and bound in Great Britain by Clays Ltd, Elcograf S.p.A.
Typeset using Atomik ePublisher from Easypress Technologies

*For Mike and Ione, who helped nurture that flickering flame
of creativity throughout my childhood.*

'Let us be silent, that we may hear
the whispers of the gods.'
Ralph Waldo Emerson

CHAPTER ONE

HUNTERS AND HUNTED

I hiked towards the summit of the steep dune, every breath burning my lungs, my mind weighed down. Mom, the Sky Hawks and all other life on my Earth would be killed if things didn't play out well for us in this desert world over the next few hours.

Angelique, silhouetted against the swirling sand clouds overhead, stood at the summit of the dune. Her white dress, especially chosen for the big reunion with her dad, flowed out in the desert wind. In that outfit, and with her long blonde hair billowing around her head, she looked like an angel fallen from the sky... an angel with a throwing knife who could kill a man at twenty paces.

She shielded her eyes and scanned the horizon.

'Can you see anything?' I called up to her.

Angelique glanced back and shook her head. She'd barely said a word since we'd landed. I could only begin to imagine the fear buzzing around her head – that we might be this close, but were already too late.

Behind us, *Athena*'s song wove around *Muse*'s and *Hope*'s, and

1

began to fade into the distance. We'd set off to search for the lost king while Tesla, the chief scientist of Cloud Riders, and the other survivors of Hells Cauldron had got started on the installation of the chameleon nets that would make our ships invisible during battle. I could see the first of the panels they'd started to stretch over the vast bulk of *Hope* sparkling in the distance.

I gripped my owl pendant that held *Storm Wind*'s Psuche gem. *Can you hear* Zeus? I asked him.

His telepathic ship-song focused into words. '*I can't sense my brother anywhere around here.*'

I reached Angelique at the summit. '*Storm Wind* still isn't getting anything,' I said out loud for her benefit. Ship-song she could hear, but the hidden words within she couldn't.

Angelique chewed her lip, countless emotions darting behind those jade-green eyes. 'I still do not understand why *Zeus*'s signal died on us.'

She had a point. An hour before we'd been flying through the Vortex wormhole with our small fleet of airships, all set for one big, happy reunion. Until that moment we'd been in constant communication with King Louis over the Valve Voice radio. He'd said something about a storm blowing up, and then, with a howl of static, the rest of his broadcast had died. Since then we hadn't heard a thing.

'What if Hades picked up his signal and got here ahead of us?' she continued.

I knew that idea would eventually surface because I'd already picked at it a hundred times. 'We would've picked up radio chatter if they had.'

'But—'

I raised my hand and spread my fingers wide to stop her. 'I'm sure your dad is fine, Angelique.' I did my best to make my words sound convincing.

Angelique wrapped her arms tight around herself and gave me a faint I-don't-believe-you nod.

I gazed down into the valley between the towering sand dunes towards the ruins of an ancient town sitting at the bottom. Long shadows stretched from shattered stone walls and sand drifts ran across what once must have been streets. The circular outlines of buildings, roofs long gone, stood like abandoned, broken seashells.

No people. No vegetation. No sign of life.

At the centre of the grid of streets stood a clear rectangular area surrounded by dead trees. In the middle a tall stone column had toppled over and broken into several large chunks. The arm of what had presumably been a statue on the top of the column was raised from the sand, like someone drowning and waving for help.

'What happened to the people who used to live there, Angelique?'

She raised a shoulder. 'They had a runaway climate change on this Earth. What people are left on this planet are clustered around the poles. No one lives at these latitudes any more.'

'Apart from your dad…'

Angelique gave me a look that said, *So where the heck is he then, Dom?*

I answered her silent question. 'Maybe he's hidden in those ruins somewhere – maybe he took shelter from the storm that blew up.'

She lowered her head. 'But what if—'

This time I put my finger to her lips. 'Don't think like that, Angelique.'

Her lips curled into a tiny smile beneath my fingers. 'Okay, my lord.'

But I could see the worry still churning away behind her eyes. And I knew exactly what that felt like. It had been less than twenty-fours since I'd last made contact with my own dad. In my imagination I could picture him trapped in one of the glass-topped coffins, part of the Hive mind that Cronos was using to run his monstrous warship, *Kraken*. Every waking minute since we'd last communicated, I'd been haunted with thoughts of what Hades were doing to him.

Angelique's gaze tightened on mine, reading me. She'd got way too good at it. Just like Mom…just like Jules.

Her hand rose to my shoulder and squeezed it. We didn't say anything more. We didn't need to. That gesture was a whole conversation in itself about a kiss back at Hells Cauldron that we couldn't talk about.

Jules's voice came from behind us. 'Hey, wait for me, guys.'

We jumped apart, as if we'd been doing something wrong. And maybe we had. The problem was that now any affection between us, however innocent, felt like a betrayal to Jules.

Neither of us said anything while our gazes to each other said everything, knowing but not going there. We turned together to see Jules clambering up the slope towards us.

I called down to her, 'I thought you were helping Tesla fit the chameleon net to *Athena*?'

Jules didn't respond straight away and instead glanced between us.

What did she think she'd seen? My insides coiled into a ball. But Jules's dimpled smile appeared, and that only came when she was happy. I relaxed a fraction.

She reached us, barely out of breath after the thousand-ffoot climb. 'I needed to stretch my legs after being cooped up and, anyway, Tesla and the others seem to have everything covered. Besides, I didn't want to miss the big reunion.'

4

Angelique shook her head. 'I'm afraid that's not looking quite so likely at the moment.'

Jules pursed her lips at me. "You still can't hear *Zeus*?'

I shook my head. 'Not even a murmur.'

'Oh my…' Her gaze tightened on Angelique. 'I bet there's a simple explanation. Maybe *Zeus*'s Valve Voice blew a fuse.'

Angelique shook her head and pointed at the Tac on her wrist, the watch-like device that linked into *Athena*'s sensor net. 'Even if that was true, according to the coordinates that Papa gave us, *Zeus* should be sitting somewhere in that ruin down there.'

'But something as big as an airship can't just vanish,' I said.

A slight tremble passed through Angelique's expression. She breathed through her nose.

None of this made any sense. The king knew we were on our way to find him, so where was the big reception party thrown by a man who'd been marooned in a desert for the last year?

'Let's go and check it out to see if we can find any clues,' I said.

'Sounds like a plan,' Jules replied. She gave Angelique's shoulder a squeeze, her gesture mirroring exactly what the princess had done to me a moment ago.

My heart lurched. Was Jules making a point to her…to me?

Angelique's gaze skated away across the landscape. 'Let's get moving before the sun gets any higher and we're baked alive.' She turned and set off down the dune towards the ruined town.

Jules, avoiding my gaze, began to descend after Angelique, slipping and sliding. I followed her, sending small sand avalanches skittering down the slope ahead of me.

I pulled my T-shirt from my chest. Through the murky haze, the heat of the dawn sun, even though it had only just cleared the horizon, was already barbeque-hot. How on Earth had King Louis managed to stay alive for so long in this godforsaken place?

Compared to the ascent, the descent seemed to take only minutes and we soon neared the bottom of the dune.

Jules let out a squeal.

I whipped round, half expecting to see a Hades airship floating in the sky overhead.

Instead she pointed a trembling finger down at the ground. 'Rat!'

I gazed at the brown furry creature with yellow eyes that watched us. 'That's a serious overreaction, Jules.'

Angelique shook her head. 'And that's not a rat, it's a dirtjack.'

The rodent's ear twitched and it tipped its head to one side.

'He's kinda cute,' I said. I shoved my hand into my pocket and withdrew a small green fruit that Angelique had given me during the flight. According to her, it was some sort of exotic fruit found on some jungle Earth or other. All I knew was that it smelt of pears and tasted like strawberries, which kinda messed with my head.

I broke off a segment and held it out for the dirtjack. 'Come on, fellah.'

Jules's lips pinched together. 'It still looks like a rat to me.'

I ignored her and made a clicking sound with my tongue.

The dirtjack's nose twitched and it took a couple of hopping steps on its long back legs towards me.

I stayed as still as I could. 'That's it – you can trust me, buddy.'

A rustle came from somewhere close by.

The dirtjack froze and started to turn. Angelique's gaze sharpened too.

'Hey, don't run away. I won't bite,' I said.

The rustling grew louder and something pungent filled my nose.

'That smells like sandalwood,' Jules said, sniffing the air.

The dirtjack stiffened, head jerking left and right, nostrils flaring.

The patch of sand beneath the creature had started trembling. 'Hey, what the…' The words died in my throat as the ground erupted around the rodent.

Before it even had a chance to move, a round grey mouth crammed with hooked teeth burst from the ground.

Jules and I tumbled backwards as the enormous snake, at least ten feet long, flew up from the sand and, with a snap of jaws, swallowed the rodent in a single gulp. Its body arched over and it dived back beneath the surface like a disappearing sea serpent.

'What the heck was that?' I asked.

'A slipknife. They live beneath the surface of the dunes and feed on dirtjacks,' Angelique said.

Jules shuddered. 'Seriously gross.'

'Just dirtjacks right?' I asked, watching the sand slide down the sides of the depression left by the snake.

'Normally…although there have been reports of a few people vanishing over the years.'

Jules paled. 'Just how big can those critters get?'

'Rumour has it that snakes up to a hundred feet long have been spotted by passing airships.'

I imagined thousands of creatures roaming the dunes beneath our feet, looking for their victims before pouncing like sharks. The safety of our ships suddenly seemed further away than ever. 'That's so not what I wanted to hear.'

Angelique shrugged. 'It's just a myth to scare children at bedtime. I've certainly never seen one that large.'

'But what if it isn't just a story,' Jules said. 'What if that's what's happened to your dad—'

I nudged her hard in her side, but it was already too late – the idea was out there.

Angelique's expression crumpled. 'It's only a story.'

Jules glanced at me and grimaced.

Her bad. I gave Angelique my best attempt at a reassuring smile. 'Of course it is.'

She took a deep breath and strode away.

We followed her long strides across the sand, Jules shooting me guilty looks the whole time.

Sand slopped over my trainers and my feet became clammy as I imagined what was lurking just beneath the surface.

But in contrast, Angelique was a woman on a mission and she wasn't going to be distracted by any slipknife, however big. She glanced at her Tac and pointed at the empty square in the middle of the ruined town. 'According to the coordinates, *Zeus* should be right there.'

'But all these dunes look alike,' I replied. 'Maybe the king made a mistake and he's actually in the next valley.'

Angelique stood taller. 'Papa's a skilled Navigator. He wouldn't have made a basic numerical error like that.'

Not if he's dead, I thought to myself. 'Of course he wouldn't,' I replied.

Jules frowned at me, obviously sharing my unspoken worry.

As we walked in silence the rest of the way towards the town, the sun inched up into the sand-filled sky.

The few hundred yards felt like several miles and I only relaxed when we eventually reached the outskirts of the ruins. We began to walk over one of the buried streets and I spotted a few more dirtjacks watching us from cracks in the broken stone walls. Made sense for them to take cover here from what lay in wait for them beyond the town's borders.

Sand spilled from doorways and glassless windows, lining the streets. As we headed towards the square we'd seen from the top of the dune, the wind moaned through the holes in the broken walls. Eerie would have been a serious understatement.

As we passed the perimeter of dead trees surrounding the square, I realised the sheer size of the toppled stone column we'd seen from the top of the dune. Each chunk was at least the size of a large truck. Even the statue's arm rising from the sand was at least three times my height – the rest of buried stature had to be huge.

I spotted a rope tied to one of the fingers, disappearing down into the ground. Probably a last-ditch effort by the townsfolk to secure it before they had abandoned the town…a lot of good that'd obviously done.

Jules peered around us. 'Hey, what's that noise?'

A distant whooshing came from beyond the brow of the dunes ahead of us. At that same moment Angelique's Tac emitted a chime.

She glanced at it and scowled. '*Athena*'s sensing seismic wave activity beneath the surface.'

The sound – like a tumbling ocean wave – grew and seemed to be coming from beyond the ridge ahead of us.

'Follow me!' Angelique shouted.

She turned and sprinted back towards the ships.

'What is it?' I called as we ran after her.

'Sand quake – we'll get buried alive unless we get back to the ships!'

Despite the sand sucking at our feet, we all increased our speed.

Suddenly, dead ahead, a large dip began to form. We all skidded to a stop and stared down into the growing basin directly in our path.

'Slipknife?' Jules asked, her voice trembling.

9

'If it is, it's a massive one,' Angelique replied.

'So much for it just being a story,' I said. My gaze hunted for any cover – anywhere to shelter till the sandstorm had passed. The roofless buildings didn't look as though they would give us any protection from either a giant slipknife or the sandstorm.

'What do we do, guys?' Jules said.

I spread my hands and Angelique gave us a blank look.

Maybe this was how King Louis died…

The basin deepened into a ravine that reached right across the square. The sand sloped away beneath our feet and the head and torso of the statue began to reveal itself – a man in a toga, holding a scroll in his hand. The rope tied to his arm led down to the middle of the funnel, buzzing and humming as if the guy had caught himself a fish.

A wild idea crashed into my head. 'Maybe a slipknife got itself snagged on the other end of that rope, like a rabbit in a snare?'

Jules covered her hands with her mouth. 'I think you're right – look.'

A hump appeared at the bottom of the growing crater. We all stumbled backwards, our legs scrabbling to get purchase on the steepening slope.

Was this it, the only one choice left which way to die: swallowed whole by a monster or buried alive by a sand quake?

A tingle itched my scalp and ship-song began to form. *Athena*? No…this definitely wasn't any ship's voice I'd heard before.

Angelique stared at me. 'I'd recognise that ship-song anywhere – it's *Zeus*…my papa's alive!'

The song started to focus into individual words. *'Whisperer… coming…'*

Angelique shot me a questioning look. 'What did he just say?'

10

'I think they are on their way.'

Jules's eyes widened. 'Wherever they are, they better get a move on before that slipknife decides we're breakfast.'

The back of the snake broadened and rose from the ground, sand tumbling away… My mind caught up with what I was actually seeing. The skin of the monster was made from rippling, green-bleached canvas, a faded picture of a swan on its side.

Angelique clapped her hands together. 'Papa hid *Zeus* underground.'

'No wonder you guys couldn't hear him through all that sand,' Jules said.

Zeus's gondola finally emerged from the sand and he floated free from the ground. The line tethering it to the statue slackened as he rose a few feet into the air.

'That ship is one big fellah,' Jules said. 'He has to be least twice the size of *Athena*.'

'*Zeus* is dreadnought class,' Angelique replied.

A bank of swirling orange sand crested the top of the dunes and rushed down towards us, thundering like a dirt tsunami.

A door flew open in the gondola and a man with a bushy beard waved at us. 'Get yourselves in here, now!' he shouted.

'Papa!' Angelique cried out. She sprinted down the slope towards him, as the airship strained on its tether to the statue's arm.

We ran after her, the bellow of the sand quake growing at our heels.

Angelique reached the gondola, now several feet off the ground. Without breaking stride, she leapt up and into the cabin. Jules took a flying jump after her and dived straight through the doorway, but before I followed, the gondola surged up another foot above my head.

I stared up at the doorway, too high for me to make the jump.

The king stretched his arm down towards me. 'Come on, before you are cut to shreds.'

It wasn't as though I needed any extra motivation. I gathered my legs and leapt.

His hand clamped around my wrist and he lifted me in one swift movement into the gondola. He was broad-shouldered and, going by how he'd lifted me as if I weighed nothing, real strong too. If he was half the fighter his daughter was, he'd be a dangerous opponent in any battle.

King Louis threw the door closed behind us, muting the deafening bellow of the storm to a roar. He rushed to the ship's controls.

Through the windows, the boiling bank of sand rushed over the lip of the ravine and down towards *Zeus*.

'Hang on,' the king shouted.

The swirling sand smashed into the airship and the floor tilted, throwing us all to the ground.

The sand thundered over the ship like storm waves breaking above us. With a whip-snap crack, the rope that been anchoring *Zeus* to the statue broke free, and the ship was swept sideways by the sand tsunami.

Through a glass window in the floor, I saw the walls of the ruined town rush by.

The king clambered back to the controls, but instead of reaching for the burner leaver to float us clear of the quake, he hit the gas release valve. We started to sink back into the sand.

I stared at the surface of the sand as it drew level with the gondola's windows. 'What the heck are you doing?'

'Getting us to somewhere we can ride out the rest of the quake in safety. The sandstorm thrown up by the quake will have reached thousands of feet up into the air by now. If we try to fly through that, it will rip *Zeus* apart in seconds.'

We bobbed for a moment on the surface, like a bottle in a raging, stormy sea. Then, with a shudder, we started to descend.

The king pulled a red handle and *Zeus*'s song faded in my mind. He caught my surprised expression. 'I cannot run *Zeus*'s Psuche gem for long without draining his AI matrix completely. Ever since the Hades attack, I have only been able to run him for brief periods.'

We dropped beneath the surface and the view of the outside world disappeared. The gondola filled with the darkness of a tomb. The roar of the storm faded away, replaced by the vibration of sand quake sliding past the gondola.

With a hum, a glass chandelier flickered on. After all the chaos, the sudden calm seemed unreal as everyone looked at each other.

The king opened his arms wide. 'My beautiful daughter.'

Beaming at her dad, Angelique rushed over and hugged him hard. 'Oh, Papa!'

The king kissed his daughter's head again and again, as tears filled both their eyes.

I could only begin to imagine what Angelique was feeling right now...

Without a word, Jules crossed to me and held my hand. Yeah, she knew exactly what I was thinking.

'*Next time it will be your turn,*' *Storm Wind* whispered into my thoughts.

It seemed everyone was on my case.

I watched dad and daughter hold onto each other as though the world had stopped spinning for a moment. And for them it probably had.

But unless we were able to dig ourselves out, despite *Storm Wind*'s positive words, there'd be no chance for my own big reunion with my dad. I turned away and stared out through the windows at our sand tomb.

14

CHAPTER TWO

REUNION

Angelique and King Louis hung onto each for a long time, to the point where it felt as if Jules and I were intruding. The problem was, there wasn't exactly anywhere else for us to go while we were buried underground.

There were tears, plenty, especially when Angelique told her dad about how Bella, her mother and the king's wife, had been murdered by Ambra. But gradually their smiles caught and finally began to linger. Despite their roller coaster of emotions, the old pain behind Angelique's eyes began to lift. It was a relief – she so deserved this moment after everything she'd gone through.

It was finally the turn of me and Jules to fill in the gaps about what had happened while King Louis been marooned. We told him about *Kraken*, the capital ship Cronos had built, and Cronos's plans to invade our Earth and destroy it with his secret weapon called Fury. When Angelique told the king how Duke Ambra had fallen into the lava of the eruption at Hells Cauldron, the king gave her a grim nod and simply said, 'Good.'

A massive wave of emotion hit me when I told him about my own dad being one of the enslaved Navigators onboard *Kraken*. I almost lost it in front of everyone. But as Jules rubbed my back and Angelique patted my arm, the king looked me straight in the eyes and said, 'I will do everything in my power to help you, Dom Taylor.'

Just hearing him say that meant a lot, most of all because I knew he meant it, and if anyone was in position to help it was him.

Eventually we were all talked out, only the hiss of the gas jets lighting the candelabra filling the gondola. I became aware of the strong smell of sandalwood again, so thick that the air seemed sticky with it…the smell of the slipknives burrowing unseen through the sand around us.

The king topped up our water beakers, then sat in the cockpit seat. He leant back, fingertips pressed together, and narrowed his eyes on me, looking as if he was asking himself how a lad from Oklahoma had ended up with a gift that might control the fate of countless universes.

Exactly the same question I'd been asking myself a lot recently.

Trying to distract myself from his blue-eyed interrogator's stare, I took a sip of water. My throat still felt as though I'd swallowed most of the dunes outside, but as the cold water slipped down my throat it tasted like the best drink I'd ever had.

The king interlocked his fingers together. 'So you are the Ship Whisperer, Dom Taylor.'

I shrugged. 'It would seem your…um…' *How should I address this guy?*

Jules filled the gap in for me. 'Your Majesty?'

He shook his head. 'After everything you've both done in helping my daughter and my people, I think we can dispense with titles in these less formal times. Please call me Louis.'

Angelique twirled her lightning pendant in her fingers. 'Whisperer ability may give us a tactical advantage, Papa, and at the moment Cronos has no idea about it.'

Louis sat forward. 'Which could make all the difference in the coming battle with Hades.'

So there it was. The king saw me as some sort of military secret weapon. Not that I was necessarily going to argue with that if it meant saving our Earth.

'There may still be a problem though,' Angelique said.

'Such as?' I asked.

'Even with the strongest will, your ability is fairly erratic at best, Dom.'

I wished she was wrong, but she wasn't. 'Tell me about it. Even though I can speak to *Storm Wind* easily now, it still feels as if I'm talking to the other ships in a foreign language.'

'And that's exactly what worries me. If your ability to communicate fails at a critical point...'

'I'm sure Dom can do it,' Jules said, smiling at me.

I smiled back, grateful for her vote of confidence, even if I did share Angelique's worry. One slip from me at the wrong moment and we could lose everything.

A vibration ran through the cabin and *Zeus*'s ship-song called out in response.

My hand rose to my lightning pendant. *Storm Wind*'s song started to weave around the other ship's.

'Something is coming, Whisperer.'

What?

'You will find out for yourself in a moment.'

I caught the amused tone in his voice as a tremor ran through the gondola again and the water began rippling in our beakers. Outside, individual grains of sand had begun to shake, sparkling like tiny jewels in the gas light.

'Judging by the strength of this sand quake, it must be a slipknife passing close by – and a big one at that,' Louis said.

Jules slopped her water over the edge of her beaker, onto the floor. 'Are we safe in here?'

'Perfectly. They seem quite fond of *Zeus*. My belief is they probably see him as some sort of honorary snake – he does spend most of his time singing to them telepathically.'

I sucked air in through my teeth. 'Just as long as those snakes don't see us as a tasty gondola-wrapped snack.'

Louis chuckled. 'I've survived here with *Zeus* for over a year, so I think by now it is safe to assume that they do not.'

In all the talk of our adventures I'd almost forgotten that this man had been marooned in this desert, like some sort of modern-day Robin Crusoe. My mind filled with dozens of questions.

'So how have you managed to survive all this time? What have you done for food?'

Louis scratched his bushy beard which, combined with his dusty, ripped clothes, more than completed his castaway look. 'That has been the least of my problems. When I crash-landed on this Earth I had the stores for *Zeus*'s crew of a hundred men to live on, more than enough to keep me going. However, as you can probably imagine, a diet of canned food quickly becomes tedious, although in the last few months I have supplemented my stores with fresh meat whenever I have had the opportunity.'

Jules narrowed her gaze on him. 'What sort of meat? It strikes me there's not a whole lot of chickens and such like wandering around these dunes.'

'Actually, it is funny you should mention chicken, because that is exactly what they taste like.'

'What do?' I asked.

'Dirtjacks – I set traps for them.'

Jules pulled a face. 'Seriously gross.'

'At least water wouldn't have been a problem with supplies for so many on board,' Angelique said.

'In fact it has been,' Louis replied. 'Unfortunately, during our last battle with Hades, and unbeknown to me at the time, *Zeus's* water tanks were holed. My provisions ran out months ago.'

Jules shot a guilty look at the puddle of water she'd spilt on the floor.

'So how have you survived?' I asked.

'The sand quakes,' Louis replied.

'Come again?'

He gestured out at the wall of sand shifting around us. 'That is what is happening above us, right now. During the quake season on this world, the dunes can shift by thousands of feet.'

Angelique's eyes widened. 'Is that why we lost contact with you?'

'Precisely. *Zeus* was buried by the last storm.'

'But if your ship was underground, how come you were able to get back to the surface to rescue us?' I asked.

'I learnt that trick from the slipknife snakes…at least the big ones. You see, during a quake the sand loosens up enough to allow the giant worms to rise from the deep to the surface to hunt.'

'You mean like liquefaction during an earthquake,' Jules said.

I stared at her. 'Huh?'

'I read a blog about cars that disappeared in a parking lot during an earthquake because of it. Liquefaction happens when the ground is shaken really hard by a quake and it turns it into a sort of fluid. It means things start to sink into it.'

I shook my head. 'You really are a walking version of the internet.'

She grinned back at me. 'I do my best to keep surprising you.'

'It is an excellent explanation, Jules – the sand effectively turns it into a liquid,' Louis said. 'And when that happens the snakes can use their enormous lungs as flotation bladders to rise to the surface.'

'Flotation bladders? You mean like the hot air ones our airships use to maintain height?' Angelique asked.

He smiled. 'Just so, my daughter.'

It all fell into place in my head. 'So you're saying you're using the same technique and have turned *Zeus* into a sort of sand submarine?'

His smile widened. 'Very well deduced, Dom.'

'But I don't understand how a sand quake can help you with finding water,' Angelique asked.

'Neither did I until the storm season started. Things had started to look rather perilous by that point and I was relying on my final bottle rations.'

'So where did you find this water?' I asked. 'The desert looks bone dry from what I've seen of it.'

'And it is most of the time. But luckily for me, during a storm it is not only snakes that head to the surface. The sand quakes also force water up from deep underground reservoirs. It gushes to the surface through sand volcanoes – thanks to those temporary lakes I have been able to replenish my water supplies.'

Jules pointed upwards. 'It sounds as if the surface is a pretty dodgy place to be. If you don't get buried alive, you could end up drowning…' Her eyes widened. 'What about Stephen and the others?'

With everything that had happened, I hadn't even had a chance to think about how the rest of our party would be doing. But as the fear spiked inside, it wasn't lost on me that the only person Jules had mentioned by name was Stephen. Ever since he'd helped her escape from Hells Cauldron, the two of them seemed to be together at every opportunity.

The king sat back in his seat and glanced to the ceiling. 'I just pray that they managed to get airborne before the sand quake hit.'

'And if they didn't?' I asked.

He frowned, but didn't answer.

Despite the heat in the gondola, my blood chilled. 'We've got to get to the surface and start looking for them straight away.'

Louis glanced at the Tac on his wrist. It was similar to Angelique's, but bigger, with more dials and lights spinning beneath its watch-glass surface. 'The quake is starting to settle down. We should be able to surface in about another ten minutes.'

'Why can't we surface now, Papa?' Angelique asked.

'If we try to surface too soon we will be destroyed by the sand storm still raging up on the surface. However, if we leave it too late we will be stuck here when the sand solidifies again. And if that happens we will have to wait for the next quake, and that could take weeks.'

Jules clenched her hands together and Angelique fiddled with her lightning pendant. No one said anything, everyone lost in their own thoughts for a moment.

I couldn't hear the murmur of *Athena*'s ship-song beyond the chorus of *Zeus* and *Storm Wind* and the unseen, prowling slipknives. Dark images of our friends' deaths flooded my mind. I took another gulp of what had been sweet water, but now tasted bitter on my tongue.

CHAPTER THREE

SURVIVORS?

Grains of sand tumbled past the windows with the whoosh of a cement lorry dumping its load. With a shudder, *Zeus* rose clear of our underground hiding place and we settled onto the peak of a massive dune.

There wasn't any sign of the derelict town.

'Has the town been buried?' I asked.

'Just so,' Louis replied. 'Sometimes that town remains buried for months.'

I nodded as I started to take in the rest of the scene around us. Light glimmered in the spaces between the dunes... The breath caught in my throat at the impossible transformation.

Lakes stretched away in every direction, mirror surfaces reflecting the scudding orange sky. Just like that, the desert had been changed into a watery oasis and the tall dunes had become individual islands.

Angelique stared out through the windshield and pointed. 'Isn't that where we left our ships?'

Only lakes met my eyes in that direction. My gaze darted to the sky but it was empty.

Jules's face paled. She slammed her hands onto the cockpit controls. 'No!' She rushed to the cabin door and yanked it open. 'Stephen!' she shouted.

No answering cry came back, doing nothing to slow the fear creeping through my veins.

'It doesn't mean they're not safe,' Louis said.

Jules leapt from the doorway and raced down the dune in bounding steps.

Angelique gave me a grim look as we all followed.

Outside, the air tasted fresh, scrubbed clean of the scent of sandalwood.

Angelique scrunched up her brow and shut her eyes. '*Athena?*' she whispered.

No welcoming song echoed through my mind.

Angelique's eyes flickered open. After everything she'd been through, I knew that losing her ship would destroy her.

Louis rested his hand on her shoulder. "I'm sure they are alright, my daughter.' But his tight expression told me a different story to the one he was trying to spin us.

We all headed down the dune towards Jules. She'd already reached the bottom and had waded out up to her knees into the aqua-blue, clear water.

Part of my mind felt as if it was growing numb. Our plan, what there was of it, was already falling apart. Even though we'd only known the Cloud Riders we'd rescued from Hells Cauldron a short time, they already felt like friends – and whatever was going on between Jules and Stephen, that still included him, the guy who'd saved Jules from a volcanic eruption. For that I'd always be in his debt.

23

We reached the base of the dune. I shielded my eyes from the burning light with my hand and scanned the lake.

Jules let out a sharp breath. 'What's that?'

Our gazes snapped to something splashing far out on the water, sending out ripples in concentric circles. One by one, other points began to appear, until there were thousands.

Whatever was causing the splashes was too far away to make out. 'Survivors?' I asked.

King Louis shook his head. 'I am afraid not.'

Jules wrapped her arms around herself and started to shake.

Not for the first time I wished that Jules was back home and safe, not having to witness any of this. Before Ambra had abducted her, she'd led a normal life and, perhaps more importantly to me, a safe one. But being with the Cloud Riders meant that every day was a matter of life and death. Every person lost was another cut deep inside.

I waded out to Jules and wrapped my arms around her waist.

She huddled into me, shaking as I held onto her.

'So what are those things then?' Angelique asked Louis behind us.

'You will all see soon enough…'

I concentrated on a group of splashes heading in our direction. As they neared, I made out what was causing them: small creatures, their front legs clawing at the water as they made for the shoreline.

'Dirtjacks,' Jules whispered.

'They must have been caught out by the floodwaters,' I said.

We stood in silence, watching the creatures swim as fast as they could for the safety of the dunes. Considering how at home they were in the water, there seemed to be a lot of urgency to their paddling.

Then I spotted the reason. At first glance I thought it was just the shadow of a passing cloud on the lake, but then I saw the dark shape sliding beneath the surface, heading straight towards the group of rodents nearing us. The long, dark silhouette, at least the length of a school bus, rushed up towards the dirtjacks from the depths of the new lake.

'I have seen this a hundred times before – all part of the circle of life on this Earth,' Louis said.

The thing accelerated, its grey body becoming clearer as it rose like a torpedo towards the fleeing rodents.

Angelique gasped. 'That slipknife is gigantic.'

It burst through the surface in an explosion of foam. For a moment it hung poised, a shining, grey column of death rising from the water and towering over the dirtjacks. The creatures swam away from the slipknife's shadow, their frantic movements pulling at my heart. I knew there was only one way this could end.

Jules buried her head into my shoulder, hiding her eyes. 'I can't watch.'

Almost in slow motion, the slipknife dipped its eyeless head towards the rodents. Then, like a toppling tree, it started to bend back towards its prey and opened its hooked jaws wide. With a massive splash, both the snake and its prey vanished beneath the surface in a swirl of water.

My eyes darted to the remaining dirtjacks splashing towards the shore.

Angelique clenched her fists. 'If any of the Cloud Riders are out there…'

Jules put her hands to her mouth.

Louis shook his head. 'Trust me, the slipknives won't be interested in them.'

'Why not?' I asked.

'Because, unlike dirtjacks, and at least as far as I am aware, Cloud Riders do not taste like chicken.'

How could he be joking at a time like this? I let go of Jules and waded back to him. 'For all we know, our friends, your people, are out there. They could be drowned, or torn to ribbons by the sand quake!' I clenched my fists.

Louis's gaze hardened on me and he shifted his stance, his legs planted slightly apart. I knew from my Sansodo training that, although he still appeared relaxed, he'd taken up a combat-ready pose. Did he really he think I'd fly at him?

My anger pulsed inside me like a hot coal. And I did want to punch something. Maybe Louis had just read me better than I read myself?

Angelique waded out to me and her hand touched mine. 'If I know Tesla, Papa's right. That man will have everything under control and our ships will be safe.'

I could see in her eyes she wanted to believe that Tesla had it covered. But belief was one thing and reality could be another.

I breathed through my nose and unclenched my fists.

'Dom, I'm certain everything's going to be okay,' Louis said, his tone more gentle.

But I couldn't even bring myself to reply. Problem was, I'd already seen far too many people die in the war with Hades to last several lifetimes.

'Hey, something else is happening out there,' Jules said, pointing to the middle of the lake.

A big patch of water foamed outwards in a large ring. Another monstrous snake rising from the depths of the desert?

The largest slipknives began to swim around it, their cries echoing across the lake, like cows calling out to each other at milking time.

A familiar telepathic tingle crept under my scalp and my fear was swept away in an instant. I didn't know whether to laugh or cry.

Angelique clapped her hands and beamed at me as *Muse*'s voice appeared as a faint murmur in my mind.

The king's shoulders dropped and he smiled at us. 'Thank the gods.'

So he'd been putting a brave face on it. Of course he had, just like Angelique on countless occasions when things had been hanging on the edge. Like father, like daughter.

Jules peered at me. 'You can all hear them singing?'

'Just *Muse* at the moment,' I replied. I scanned the sky. 'So where the heck are they?'

In answer, the boiling patch of water grew wider across the surface of the lake.

Jules peered at it. 'You don't suppose…?'

Angelique clapped her hands together and nodded.

In a flash, I realised what they were getting at. If we could hide under the sand then…

An explosion of foam was followed by the saucer-shaped gas envelope of *Muse* and its copper-clad gondola breaking the surface. Her ship-song sang out, strong, clear and full of joy, answered in kind by *Storm Wind*'s and *Zeus*'s. The slipknives started to circle her, echoing the ships' welcome to each other.

Louis smiled. 'I told you the slipknives like to sing to our ships.'

'What about the others though?' Jules asked, although I knew she actually meant, *Where the heck is Stephen?*

'Look now!' Angelique pointed to two fresh boiling patches of water.

The one nearest us was about the same size as the disturbance caused by *Muse* surfacing, but the other foaming patch of water further out was as least twenty times as large. And there was only one thing that could cause that big of a wake.

Jules clapped her hands together and jumped up and down. 'I might not be able to hear the ship-song like you guys, but tell me that's not *Hope*.'

Not for the first time I thought how well she'd named that ship.

Hope's and *Athena*'s voices grew around the other ships' chorus.

Angelique beamed at me as *Athena*'s gas envelope broke through like a surfacing whale, followed moments later by her gondola. *Hope*, as huge as the biggest dunes around us, erupted from the lake, showering water down over the circling slipknives like a sudden monsoon.

As the vast vessel rose from the lake, King Louis shook his head. 'By the gods, you captured Cronos's flagship.'

'Oh, I didn't mention that, did I?' Angelique said with a broad smile.

'No, it seems it slipped your mind.'

Angelique grinned. 'I wanted to keep at least one surprise for you, Papa.' She gestured towards Jules. 'It's thanks to Jules's and Stephen's bravery that she's now part of the Cloud Riders fleet.'

The three airships started scudding over the water towards us.

'No way I'm taking the credit,' Jules replied. 'I lost it for a moment, but Stephen kept a level head and got everyone to safety. He was the total hero.'

I batted away a pang of jealousy. Jules and Stephen had gone through a lot together. But where did that leave us as a couple? Although, after what had happened between Angelique and me, what did that *us* mean any more? Had I blown our chance of a future together before we'd even a chance to begin?

Storm Wind murmured into my thoughts. *'Whisperer...'*

Yes? I replied in thought only.

'You need to open your heart to her.'

This was my life now. I no longer had any thoughts of my own. My own private mentor, on call 24/7. *I'm not sure I'll ever be brave enough to tell her about it.*

'*The truth has a way of coming out, whatever you might intend.*'

So that was it. Cursed if I did, and cursed if I didn't. Brilliant.

Louis's brow knotted as he gazed at Jules. 'Are you talking about Stephen Telphid, Danrick's son?'

Angelique turned to him, her mouth a tight line. 'Yes…and I also need to tell you about Danrick…'

My mind returned to the moment the head of the Cloud Riders spy network had been shot by the dove automaton. Another victim of this crazy war.

Louis breathed out through his nose. 'He's dead, I presume?'

She gave a sharp nod. 'He was helping us escape a Hades spy in Floating City when it happened, Papa.'

'Yet another friend lost.' Louis's gazed tightened on his daughter. 'I tell you this, my love. When this war is finally won, we will commemorate all our fallen. But for now we have to concentrate on honouring their sacrifices in the best way we can.'

'And how do we do that?' I asked.

'We prepare for battle…' Louis looked between Jules and me. 'And we prepare to defend your Earth.'

The old fear wove through my anger. 'But how can we stop them? You haven't seen the size of *Kraken*. What with that and their Fury weapon that can destroy a planet…'

Louis gripped my shoulder. 'Dom, I tell you one thing that we have and Hades do not.'

'What?'

'People like you, Jules and my daughter.' He smiled at the three of us and gestured towards the airships closing on our position, the slipknives swimming ahead of them like an escort of dolphins. 'We have the Cloud Riders – those who will always fight against oppression and defend everything that is good in this and every other universe.' He slapped his fist into his palm. 'With you as my witnesses, I swear to you that, whatever Hades do to us, we will never give in to the darkness that stains the hearts of monsters like Cronos.'

I saw his fierce belief burn deep in his eyes and felt it slow the spin of my fear. Under that desert sun, I knew exactly where Angelique got her strength from.

Angelique nodded. 'You see, Hades don't stand a chance against the Cloud Riders, however big they build their ships.'

I thought of the Fury that Hades would be making operational right now in one of their shipyards in a parallel world…a weapon that could tear a world apart. I just hoped that the belief of a father and daughter would be enough to turn things in our favour.

But one thing Louis was definitely right about was that, like them, I would sacrifice my life to defend our Earth and all the people who lived there. Family, friends, the billions of people I would never meet. I might not have been involved in starting this fight, but I would sure as heck help the Cloud Riders to end it.

Angelique gestured towards *Hope*. 'I have been thinking about the best way we could use that ship. It obviously has a lot of firepower at its disposal, but it's also big enough to carry hundreds of platoons of our lightning marines.'

'You mean turn it into a vast troop ship?' I asked.

She nodded. 'That would make a difference in any battle, especially if we equipped all our marines with fly-dive suits.'

'Have you got that many soldiers left?' I asked.

'We won't know until we see how many Cloud Riders ships make it back to the rendezvous point here,' Louis replied.

Angelique nodded. 'But in the meantime we could go ahead and refit *Hope* as a marine carrier. It's got a huge cargo bay that can be used for strike ornicopters.'

'For what?' Jules asked.

Angelique flapped her hands. 'They are a type of flying ship with wings, highly manoeuvrable and very effective in battle. For short durations they can even outpace the swiftest airship.'

'But won't Cronos have those sort of ships as well?' I asked.

Angelique stood taller. 'He may do, but our pilots are far more highly skilled. They can outfly any Hades ones.'

It wasn't the first time I'd heard her make that claim. Thing was, through experience I knew it wasn't an idle boast either.

'They will need to,' Louis said. 'Even if it turns out that most of the Cloud Riders fleet is intact, Hades forces will still outnumber us by ten to one.'

Angelique's expression hardened. 'That will almost make it a fair fight then.'

'If I could bottle your confidence, I reckon I could make a fortune,' Jules said.

Angelique smiled at her, but to me those still sounded like tough odds.

Stephen waved to us from the cockpit of *Hope* as she neared the shore.

Jules chewed her lip, the look in her eyes far away.

And I knew her well enough to know that she was thinking of home and her dad, Roddy. And like me she was weighing up the odds in her head.

'Never give up, Whisperer,' Storm Wind said into my thoughts.

Never… I'd cling on by sheer determination as long as I could because, apart from anything else, I couldn't get my head round the alternative – my planet being blown into a billion bits of rock, all life on it snuffed out in a heartbeat.

I welcomed the drift of spray from the airships that enveloped us, distracting me, if only for a moment, from the dark images flooding my imagination.

CHAPTER FOUR

THE FIRST ARRIVAL

While Tesla repaired *Zeus*'s systems, King Louis, who'd been fussing and managing to get in the way along with the rest of us, had been ordered out of the gondola so Tesla could concentrate.

The king used the opportunity to seek out each and every Cloud Rider. He shook countless hands as he thanked his people for everything they'd done. And as he did that I saw the hope etched in those faces and the spark of belief that glowed brighter.

Word spread like a forest fire that the airship *Celeste*, captained by Lady Samantha, had Valve Voiced in to say she was starting her final jump to rendezvous with us. Her ship was one of the first ships I made contact with, the first fruits of my ability to break Hades' jamming with my Whisperer ability.

Celeste's arrival would mark the first of many Cloud Riders converging on our location. It was an event that everyone was looking forward to with an almost party-like atmosphere.

Stephen, wearing a captain's uniform, headed over towards us. I caught both Jules's and Angelique's gazes snag on him. Even I had to admit, he looked pretty sharp, the good-looking guy who, while Angelique and I had been a bit preoccupied escaping Hells Cauldron, had helped save the day by capturing Cronos's flagship that had now been renamed *Hope*.

He snapped a salute. 'My king.'

Louis reached out, took his hand and shook it. 'It is good to see you again, Captain Stephen.'

Stephen nodded, a broad smile filling his face.

Louis's expression softened. 'I heard what happened to your father and I wanted to offer my deepest condolences. Danrick was a brave man, a close confidant and, I am honoured to say, a good friend.'

Stephen's gaze dropped to the floor, his beaded dreadlocks hanging either side of his face.

A memory filled my mind of Danrick helping us back at Floating City and how he'd been killed with a poison dart for his troubles.

Angelique and I traded haunted looks.

Stephen kept his eyes on the ground. 'He died in the line of duty.'

'I know he did, Captain. You should be proud of him.'

'I am, my king.'

'And I know that he would be so proud of you if he were standing here today and could see everything that you have achieved.'

Stephen's gaze flicked back up to the king's eyes. 'Do you think so?'

Louis gestured towards *Hope* towering over us. 'I think your accomplishment speaks for itself.'

Jules smiled at Stephen. 'That and a whole lot more. For one thing I wouldn't be standing here now if it wasn't for you. I'm not sure any of us would be.'

He gave her a small smile back.

'And it won't be long until you're reunited with your sister, when *Helios* turns up here,' Louis said.

Angelique gently touched her father's arm and shook her head.

'I didn't even know you had a sister, Stephen,' Jules said.

'And I don't remember a ship called *Helios*?' I added.

A pained look crossed Stephen's face. 'My sister, Captain Roxanne, commands the crew of *Helios*. We lost contact with each other at the start of the war. She and her daughter, Isabella, who always flew with her, are my last living relatives.'

So that was why I hadn't recognised the name. *Helios* wasn't one the ships I'd made contact with.

'I am sorry, Stephen. I had no idea,' Louis said.

'Maybe it's something simple such as they suffered a Valve Voice glitch and are now unable to communicate,' Jules said.

'Or maybe I just need to face the truth,' Stephen replied, breathing through his nose. 'Permission to be dismissed and continue *Hope*'s preparations for battle, my king?'

'Of course, Captain Stephen,' Louis replied.

Stephen turned and headed away at a brisk walk towards his ship.

I gazed at Angelique. 'Why hasn't he said anything about this till now?'

'It's his way of coping,' she replied.

King Louis sighed. 'I am afraid that, like most Cloud Riders, he carries far too many personal scars from this awful war with Hades.'

Jules wrapped her arms around herself as she watched Stephen walking up the ramp into the belly of *Hope*. 'I'm going to talk to him.'

'Just give him a bit of space, Jules,' I said.

'No, the worst thing he can do is to keep it bottled up.' Jules tucked her chin in and headed off after Stephen.

King Louis raised his eyebrows after her.

'Yeah, she's hands on in situations like this,' I replied.

Tesla appeared in the doorway of *Zeus*'s gondola behind us. He flicked up a magnifying monocle device that'd been covering his eye.

'How bad is it, Tesla?' Louis asked him.

'We will find out in moment.' He beckoned to us to join him.

The interior of the gondola had been transformed, with wiring looms hung out of the walls like electrical spaghetti.

Louis put his hands on his head. 'What have you done to my beautiful ship, Tesla?'

'It is not as bad as it looks, my king, as you will see when you reboot *Zeus*.'

Louis arched his eyebrows at the scientist, crossed to the cockpit and pushed in a recessed red handle.

With a hum, steam started to vent from the Eye and the metal lids opened like petals to reveal lit glass planets glimmering inside. *Zeus*'s ship-song whispered into my mind with a sigh like someone waking.

'You will find *Zeus*'s systems are once more all in perfect working order,' Tesla said.

'Thank the gods.'

'And I have better news, too. It would seem this Voice Scream weapon created an overload in *Zeus*'s auxiliary support systems, which is what caused the electrical short. Fortunately, we now have Dom and his Whisperer ability to counter the effects of this during battle.'

Louis's gaze lingered on me. 'That is most welcome news.'

I could almost physically feel his expectation building up like a weight on my shoulders.

Tesla screwed the panel back into the floor as *Zeus*'s voice continued to grow stronger.

Storm Wind sang out in response, warmth radiating from his Psuche gem inside the medal hanging around my neck. But something about his song felt different – more like someone mumbling in their sleep than his usual wide-awake tone.

Storm Wind, *are you okay?* I asked.

His voice pulsed in time to my own heartbeat. The cabin started to fade around me and I gasped as a man's face began forming in my mind.

Grandpa Alex, the Cloud Rider who'd crash-landed on my Earth, seemed to be looking directly at me. '*You, my descendant, are being played this message because the correct cyphers have now been received by* Storm Wind's *Psuche gem. This indicates that you are currently standing onboard the king's ship. It is imperative that you now relay the information you about to learn directly to the current monarch.*'

'Dom?' Angelique asked.

I opened my eyes that I hadn't even realised I'd closed. '*Storm Wind*'s Psuche gem has some sort of secret message from Grandpa Alex, for Louis.'

The king's expression widened. 'He has?'

Tesla tapped his fingers on his wand. 'How very intriguing. Please carry on.'

I closed my eyes and once again Alex's image swam back into focus. '*Since being shipwrecked on Earth DZL2351, somewhere that I have made my new home, I have dedicated the final years of my life to studying* Storm Wind's *Psyche gem in extensive detail. Specifically, I have concentrated my efforts on his rose matrix and have discovered something that may be significant.*'

'He says he found out something about the rose matrix,' I said aloud.

'Now that is even more interesting,' Tesla said.

'Why?'

'The rose matrix is a crystalline pattern – resembling a flower, hence the name – that lies at the heart of all Cloud Rider and Hades Psuche gems. Some people believe that the pattern contains a message left for us by the ancient race of Angelus. Please continue…'

I tuned back into *Storm Wind* and the message started up again as if I'd hit play. *'I believe there may be a way to unlock this program. This is why I have been working on the Whisperer ability. It is my belief that within you, my descendant, is the key to deciphering the message that has been left for us.'*

'He thinks my Whisperer ability may be able to unlock the rose matrix,' I said, keeping my eyes shut.

I heard Tesla's sharp intake of breath.

'Although I have been unable to ascertain what the purpose of this program is, I have been able to decode sufficient of the Angelus algorithms to decipher their name for this program was…'

A word formed in my mind and I repeated it out loud. 'Sentinel.' Alex's image smiled and then he vanished. I opened my eyes to find everyone staring at me.

'Sentinel – why name the program that?' Angelique asked.

'Maybe the Angelus deliberately left the Psuche gems behind to be some sort of guardian?' I replied. 'Hence the name?'

Tesla rubbed his chin. 'An interesting idea, Dom. And it would seem that you are the only one among us who has a chance of finding out the answer to that particularly intriguing question.'

'But I can barely control my Whispering ability as it is, Tesla. At best it's hit and miss. And I don't know about you guys but I'm anxious to get home and defend my planet.'

'Which of course we can all understand,' Louis replied. 'However, as we gather the fleet together there is going to be a natural pause.

And I can think of no better use of that time for you than spending it perfecting your Whisperer ability. I believe it is something that Angelique can help you with.'

Angelique shot him a questioning look. 'But how, Papa?'

'Long before the Cloud Riders performed automated jumps, as you know they had a specific device to help train new Navigators…'

Angelique sat up. 'You mean Dom should try using a Theta Codex?'

'I most certainly do,' Louis replied. 'And with my passion for collecting curiosities, I happen to have an antique pod stored here onboard *Zeus*.'

'Sounds good to me,' I said.

Angelique flashed me a smile. 'In that case I'll be more than happy to help you try it.'

The door to the outside flew open and Jules rushed into *Zeus*'s gondola. 'Stephen wanted you to know that *Celeste* is about to arrive.'

Louis leapt to his fleet. 'I better go and welcome them in person. A whole year alone and suddenly I have all this company.'

'Like buses,' I said.

The Cloud Riders all gave me blank looks, but Jules grinned at me.

'Pardon?' Angelique said.

'You know, you wait for one, then three arrive at once?'

Their blank looks continued.

I spread my hands wide. 'It really doesn't matter.'

Jules snorted and grabbed my hand. 'Come on, let's go meet and greet.'

* * *

In the distance, a vast column of sand spiralled around the forming twister. Strobes of blue light pulsed down the length of the spout.

We'd all gathered outside *Zeus* to meet them, the Cloud Riders ranged across the dunes all whooping and clapping. This was the moment they'd all been waiting for – the first arrival – and a huge step in the right direction to turn things around in the war against Cronos.

Even Stephen looked as if he was catching the party mood and had started smiling again. No doubt the private pep talk from Jules had helped too… She was good with people like that. And right now she was bouncing up and down on her feet, every bit as excited as each Cloud Rider around us.

The wind howled around us as *Celeste*'s song, pure and beautiful, rang out across the sky, the tornado beginning to unravel around her. The cloud thinned to reveal four wings running the length of her body.

Angelique hooked her arm around her father's as the wind died away. 'I'd forgotten what a magnificent ship she is.'

'She is even more impressive when you see her in battle,' Stephen replied. '*Celeste* may be the size of a frigate, but with Lady Samantha at the wheel they deliver the punch of a dreadnought…much like you with *Athena*.'

Angelique beamed at him.

For the briefest moment I caught Jules narrow her eyes towards the Cloud Riders captain. If I hadn't known any better I would have sworn she looked jealous.

'The human heart is a complicated thing,' Storm Wind whispered into my thoughts.

'Yeah, tell me about it.'

Jules shot me a questioning look. I hadn't meant to say it out loud. 'Sorry, just chatting to *Storm Wind*.'

'Oh right.' She frowned and looked back to *Celeste*.

Storm Wind was definitely right about one thing – this was getting more complicated by the second. Fighting Hades seemed simple compared to the emotional mess I'd got into with Jules and Angelique.

I felt a sense of relief as *Celeste*'s greeting, filled with joy and echoed by our ships' chorus of song, swamped out all my other thoughts for a moment.

Blue pendants fluttered from her wingtips and she swooped down towards us in a descending turn. The Cloud Riders surged forward, clapping and cheering, to meet her and her crew. The first arrival… but would we be able to gather enough ships in time to give Cronos a serious fight?

CHAPTER FIVE

THETA TRAINNING

The moment I saw the thing that Angelique had dragged out of a storage hold in *Zeus*'s cabin, I thought it was exactly the sort of mad gizmo that Tesla would invent. It was a sort of lidded copper bath with a riveted hatch set into it. Inside, wires had been woven together to form a skullcap. But it was what it was connected to on the outside that had me more than a little bit freaked out. On top of the pod sat a control panel with a large car-like battery and a round display. That combined with the two circular switches – one green, one red – gave the panel an uncanny resemblance to a face with its mouth locked open in a scream.

Angelique had hooked up the pod to a valve and was filling it with water.

'That thing looks like some sort of torture device crossed with a bath.'

'Let's just put it this way, no one has ever died from the training. Well, not counting…' Her voice trailed away.

I frowned at her. 'Don't leave me hanging.'

She gestured at a key switch near the base of the control panel. 'This particular model is an antique – it must be at least a hundred years old. And back then they built in a brain-boost function.'

'Sounds useful.'

'You don't understand. It was an experimental feature that was quickly withdrawn in later models.'

'Because?'

'Because it ended up killing most of the Navigators who attempted to use it and lobotomising many of the rest. Even the lucky ones who survived only saw a marginal increase in their theta activity. Eventually the feature was deemed to not be worth the risk.'

'But if we don't use the boost function it's safe, right?'

Her mouth curled at the corners. 'Stop worrying. Can you please lie down inside the pod?'

I gestured towards the water. 'But I'll get soaked.'

'Then keep your pendant on so you can communicate with *Storm Wind*, but take your clothes off.'

I gave her a look.

'Don't worry, I won't look.' She smirked and turned away.

I quickly stripped down to my boxers and clambered through the round hatch. Above my head a round display identical to that on top of the pod had been mounted.

As I lay down I began to float in the warm water. 'Whoa!'

'There's a lot of salt to suspend you so you're not touching anything and the temperature is matched to your body's,' Angelique said, her back still to me.

'It's kinda relaxing.'

'It's all part of the sensory deprivation that will help you achieve a theta state. Now, please put the skullcap on.'

I pulled it down over my head. 'Done.'

Angelique moved to the side of the pod and pressed the green switch on the control panel.

The pod started humming faintly around me. A tingle of static itched over my scalp too, but when no jolt of electricity spiked through my skull, I let my breath out.

Angelique gazed at me through the hatch. 'See, I told you it was safe.'

'And I thought you weren't looking.'

She shrugged.

A green phosphorescent spot on the round screen over my head started trailing a green line across it. It began to rise towards the stop of the display, the machine beeping along in a regular rhythm.

'What's that display showing?'

'Your alpha wave activity.'

'And that's important because?'

'It's measuring the alpha waves of your conscious mind which get in the way of communicating with a ship's Psuche gem. Think of it as interference.'

'So how do I get past that?'

'By falling asleep.'

'Come again?'

'Well not quite literally, but right to the edge of it. Theta wave activity is what you want for ship communication and it's at its peak when you dream, but also at the moment just before you fall asleep. So you're basically aiming to enter a deep trance state without the sleep part.'

'That's it?'

'That's it. But I promise you it's harder than it sounds and that's what the Theta Codex was designed to help with.'

Outside, the howl of a distant twister began to build again, the theme tune of another Cloud Rider ship about to appear in this desert world.

Celeste's arrival had already been followed by three more ships. Step by step, the idea that we were assembling a fleet to take on Cronos was beginning to feel real.

Angelique settled into the red upholstered seat by the pod. 'Okay, Dom, I want you to telepathically link into *Storm Wind*'s Psuche gem.'

'No problem.' I clasped my hand around my lightning pendant.

At once *Storm Wind*'s voice strengthened to a rolling chorus of whale-like song. His words focused from the melody. '*You are doing very well, Whisperer.*'

I saw a blue phosphorescent dot had joined the dance of the green one.

'That blue line is the current theta wave output of your brain,' Angelique said.

'Okay...' But as I watched the hypnotic movement of the line, it started to drop to the bottom of the screen and *Storm Wind*'s voice faded back to only song.

'What's going wrong?' I asked.

'Your conscious thoughts are getting in the way of you entering a deeper trance. Try to ignore the display and concentrate on *Storm Wind*'s voice, like you do when you communicate with him normally. I'm going to close the pod up and it's going to get very dark, but it will help.'

'Okay, you're the boss.'

She smiled and closed the hatch. The screen display dimmed and almost pitch-black surrounded me.

The sound of my breathing filled the pod as I focused on the murmur of the song coming from *Storm Wind*'s Psuche gem. His song slowed as I felt his attention switch back from the other ships to me.

'Your ability to control your gift is improving, Dom.'

You have never called me by my actual name before, I replied.

'Well, this is a momentous moment.'

I laughed.

'What?' Angelique asked through the pod's walls.

'Nothing important.'

I could hear Cloud Riders shouting instructions to each over the building wind. Probably loading *Hope*. I felt the usual stab of envy... What I wouldn't have given to have had my own ship like Stephen.

'Your theta waves are dropping again,' Angelique's voice said.

My bad.

I tuned back into *Storm Wind*'s song and let the other sounds, other thoughts, fall away. His song gradually became words.

'Our voices glow across the golden clouds, like fire storms burning the sky with their light...'

In response, the chorus of the surrounding ships' songs echoed his words like an orchestra.

'You're doing much better – your readout is halfway up the display now,' Angelique whispered.

Was that all there was to it? 'But this is only the level I usually communicate with *Storm Wind*.'

'Which, trust me, is already exceptional. The display indicates that you are a Level Five Navigator.'

'That's good then?'

'Only the highest ever level recorded. The previous record holder was a Level Four and they still sing songs about him.'

'Cool.'

'But we're playing for higher stakes here, Dom. I'm hoping that by the time we've finished your training, you'll hit the top of the scale.'

'Which is?'

'Level ten.'

'So how can I turbo-charge my theta waves to win the big prize?'

'Like I said before, I want you to almost fall asleep, but don't lose focus on *Storm Wind*'s voice.'

'I'll try my best.'

I relaxed my body in the water. The regular beat of the beeps from the machine seemed to fill the gondola and drown out *Storm Wind*.

Angelique sighed outside.

I didn't need to open my eyes to know my theta wave level had dropped again.

I took a deeper breath. *Okay, Dom, just chill.*

The beep of the machine now sounded like a demented drummer doing a solo at a concert. I did my best to ignore it.

Jules's face filled my mind with the look she'd given Stephen in his captain's uniform—

The machine warbled.

'Dom!'

My attention snapped back.

'I can see from your alpha wave output you're thinking about something.'

Or someone… I felt a squirm of guilt. 'Sorry…'

'Just empty your mind.'

Jeez, what was my problem? This time I tried not to think about anything apart from *Storm Wind*'s murmuring voice. His song started to grow stronger in my mind and I relaxed into the flow of its rhythm.

'Our souls span the universe, gossamer threads of life woven together...'

As I concentrated on his words, warmth grew in my body. My tight neck muscles started to let go and now I could hear only his haunting words as I floated in the warm water. The relaxation spread through my body and my thoughts fell away. Only darkness...warmth... comfortable darkness...

A burning pain surged through my scalp.

I yelped and snapped awake as the electrical jolt fizzed away.

Light flooded the pod and Angelique gazed at me through the open hatch, shaking her head.

'What the heck?'

She withdrew her finger from the red switch she'd just pressed. 'I told you to concentrate.'

I glowered at her. 'You deliberately zapped me?'

'Of course I didn't, but the machine did. I was just turning it off.' She narrowed her eyes. 'It must have detected you had fallen asleep.'

As the fogginess lifted I realised she was right – I'd blacked out for a moment. Frustration burned through me. I massaged my aching temples, any sense of relaxation long gone.

I slipped the skullcap off and clambered out of the pod, my embarrassment forgotten.

Angelique handed me a towel.

I started to dry myself off. 'That's one hell of an alarm clock...and I thought you said this training wouldn't hurt?'

'It was better you didn't know what might happen. I knew it would only make you tense up.'

I pulled my clothes back on. 'Maybe, but whose bright idea was it to give someone an electric shock to help them focus?'

'Unfortunately, it's a technique that's been proven to work.

Eventually your subconscious learns the lesson it needs to and stops you falling asleep. And besides, there's no need to exaggerate…that was only a mild shock.'

'Didn't feel that *mild* to me.' I rubbed my hands that still tingled from the shock that had travelled right through my body. I gestured towards the display. 'How did I do anyway?'

Angelique scowled. 'You managed to boost your theta waves to about halfway to the next level of six.'

'But that's nowhere near good enough. So let's get back to it.'

She shook her head. 'You need a break, Dom. With this sort of training, the harder you try, the more it slips through your fingers.'

'But we haven't much time and—'

Angelique put her finger to my lips, like she'd done when we'd been alone on the dune, and my heart jolted. She withdrew her hand, the warmth of her finger still lingering on my lips.

We gazed at each in silence. It felt as if things had shifted between us ever since that kiss, but what could we say to each other?

Angelique was the first to blink and just like that the spell was broken. The world rushed back in.

'What will be, will be, Dom. This isn't something we can force the pace of.'

I wondered exactly what she was talking about. Her and me…or my training? But didn't we both know that it was Jules who I was meant to be with?

'Come on, let's see how the others are getting on,' she said.

I followed her outside, confusion churning inside me.

* * *

In the golden light of sunset I wove with Angelique through the growing maze of airships. What a difference a day had made. From sand quakes in the morning, to the watery oasis of the afternoon, to now, when the landscape resembled a large sprawling airfield.

But as large as some of the new arrivals were, particularly the dreadnought class vessels with their hundreds of weapon turrets, *Hope* towered over all the other ships like a canvas mountain.

Angelique and I walked among the craft in silence, soaking up the buzz of Cloud Rider crews who hadn't seen each other in over a year.

But it wasn't just their happiness that was getting to me. All around us, the gathered ships had settled into a chorus packed with pure joy at their reunion. Their songs flooded my mind, often so overwhelming that I'd found myself having to wipe away tears. I caught a sparkle in Angelique's eyes, too.

As the sun dropped towards the horizon, the desert heat was very slowly letting go of the day and it was still blisteringly hot. We skirted a twelve-engine dreadnought and clung to its long shadow. Above us green Cloud Rider pennants fluttered from its wings in the wind.

I pulled at the T-shirt stuck to my chest.

'I think I preferred it when we had the lakes,' Angelique said with a small smile.

'Yeah, even though that sun is setting it feels as if it wants to make up for lost time by roasting us alive.'

Beneath our feet the sand was tinder-dry, no hint of the water that had lapped over it only a few hours before. I imagined the giant slipknives returning to the depths beneath us, bellies full of dirtjacks, slumbering till the next sand quake released them back to the surface to feed again.

We rounded the nose of the destroyer to see *Hope*, *Athena* and *Muse* directly ahead of us, the hub of the gathering fleet.

From within *Kraken* came a group of Cloud Riders in dark green uniforms, carrying things down a ramp and dropping them on a large bonfire, its smoke swirling into the sky.

Angelique followed my gaze. 'Those are our Lightning Marines detachment, assembled from the new arrivals. They are the bravest soldiers in any universe.'

'I'm sure they are, but right now they look more like removal men.'

Her mouth twisted at me.

I spotted Jules suspended by a rope halfway down the side of *Athena*'s gas canopy.

'What are you doing to my ship?' Angelique asked as we approached.

'Oh, you've spoilt the surprise. Tesla and I were hoping to get the chameleon net installed before you finished Dom's training.' Jules tugged a fine mesh of shimmering fabric which dropped down the side of the airship. The fine translucent cloth already wrapped the gondola and its windows.

Inside the cockpit Tesla waved at us through the windshield.

Jules pulled the rope out from her karabiner and dropped down the side of the airship, as if she'd been abseiling rock faces all her life. It seemed I wasn't the only one who'd picked up a lot of new skills recently. She landed, unhooked herself from the harness and grabbed the edge of the net that flapped in the breeze.

'I can't wait to try this out,' Angelique replied.

'And you can in a moment, but first give me a hand looping the net underneath.'

'We're on it,' I said.

Angelique and I positioned ourselves either side of Jules and she gestured towards the cords dangling from the edges of the net. 'Pull the fabric tight so I can connect the two seams.'

We leant back with our full weight hauling on the fabric to draw the edges together. Meanwhile, Jules clambered onto the gondola and started threading a cord along the seam. The wind sent a swirl of sand into my face, the fabric billowing like a sail in the breeze, and Angelique and I were dragged across the sand.

'Need a hand with that?' Stephen called out, jogging over to us from *Hope*.

He was now wearing the same dark green outfit as the marines. The difference between him and them was that he had gold epaulets on his shoulder to indicate his new rank of airship captain.

'Please,' Angelique said with a smile that lit her face up.

'And once again don't you look the part,' Jules said, beaming at him.

I scowled before I could stop myself. Whatever Stephen had, if he could bottle it, I knew plenty of jocks back home who'd sell their grandmas, family pets and probably even their wheels to have that sort of X factor with the ladies.

Jules caught my expression and red blossoms stained her cheeks. She quickly buried her attention back in looping the chord.

Oblivious, Stephen gave us a brief smile and took hold of the seams, helping us tighten the fabric against the wind.

I gestured with my chin to the line of soldiers ferrying stuff out of his massive ship. 'So what are those marines up to?'

'Stripping *Hope* of all of Cronos's things and burning them. By the time we've finished she's going to look every part a Cloud Riders ship, inside and out. I've got a team about to start dying his red canopy green, too.'

'Much more fitting,' Angelique replied.

For a moment I would have sworn she batted her eyelashes at him. Seriously? What had got into her and Jules? It was as bad as seeing the cheerleaders swoon over the football jocks. Personally, I couldn't see what all the fuss was about. He was a bit taller and older than me, and okay, he was now wearing a smart uniform, but he was still just a guy.

Jules pulled the cord tight and knotted it off. 'We're all good.'

We stood back to admire our work and Jules gave Tesla a thumbs up. Inside the gondola he reached towards a gleaming new chrome lever which had been installed in the cockpit.

With a slight hum and a ripple in the air, *Athena* shimmered and vanished. The view of the dunes through where she was still sitting shifted slightly, like the way water distorted a view by looking through it.

Angelique clapped. 'The chameleon net is working perfectly.'

Stephen shook his head. 'By the gods, I know we've witnessed this before, but it's still extremely impressive.'

'And going to make such a difference in battle,' Angelique added.

'It is quite remarkable,' Louis's voice said from behind us.

I turned and almost didn't recognise him. The straggly beard had gone and Louis's dark hair had been slicked back. He was wearing a grey uniform with nothing to indicate his kingly status. I remembered Emperor Cronos's outfit in contrast, dripping with medals. A puffed-up man, with a puffed-up ego to match.

'Oh, Papa, you look so handsome,' Angelique said.

'I don't know about that.' He smiled and drew his hand across his chin. 'However, you would not believe how good it feels to have a fresh shave. I ran out of razor blades months ago.'

'That wild-man look really didn't suit you,' Jules said.

He laughed and his gaze settled on me. 'So how's the theta training going, Dom?'

'Not well. Either I can't settle my mind, or I just fall asleep and get zapped.'

'You'll get the hang of it eventually,' Angelique said with a smile.

'Rather you than me,' Stephen said. 'I have never understood why anyone would be electrocuted voluntarily.'

Jules stared at me. 'Pardon me?'

I raised a shoulder. 'Yeah, it's a regular riot.'

Tesla emerged out of the gondola, staring at his Tac and shaking his head. 'I was hoping this wouldn't happen.'

'Problem with the chameleon net?' Jules asked.

'No, nothing like that. Hades have managed to increase the power of their Quantum Pacifier jamming signal.'

The Quantum Pacifier – a name that still made me shudder. Somewhere out there, in one of the countless parallel universes, was the Hive mind broadcasting that signal from onboard *Kraken*, a Hades war machine for which my dad was one of the mental cogs powering it.

Louis frowned. 'But the majority of our fleet are still out there and will be stranded again.' His gaze tightened on me. 'Looks as if we are going to need your Whisperer ability once more to break through it, Dom Taylor.'

I raised a shoulder. 'At least that's one thing I can get right.'

Angelique shook her head. 'If you are talking about your Theta Codex training, will you please be less hard on yourself?'

'But I need to be at the top of my game going into the battle with Hades.'

Jules rolled her eyes at Angelique. 'Same old Dom.'

'What's that supposed to mean?'

'Just because you've got into the habit of being a full-time hero, it doesn't mean that even you can't have an off day.' She gave me her pixie grin.

I snorted. 'I guess.' Jules had a knack of being able to lighten up the mood, even when things seemed darkest. 'Okay, let's go and take radio Hades off the air again.'

'Now that's the Dom we all know and adore,' Angelique said.

A glance passed between her and Jules and they smiled at each other. What was that about?

Tesla nodded towards Jules. 'So is our other surprise ready?'

She shot me a wide grin. 'Yes, it most certainly is. And I can't wait for Dom to see it.'

'Why me in particular?'

'You'll see.' Jules nodded and beamed at Stephen. 'And I couldn't have got it done without your help either.'

'I didn't have a lot of choice, did I? You can certainly be very persuasive when you want to be.'

She bowed. 'Why thank you, kind sir.'

'What sort of surprise are we talking about here, Tesla?' Angelique asked.

'One that I promise you'll approve of, too.'

I looked between them. 'Will you tell me already?'

Jules's grin reached her ears. 'Patience.'

A young, blond-haired Cloud Rider guy jogged over to Stephen and snapped a salute.

'What is it, cadet?'

'You're needed back on the deck, captain.'

Stephen turned to Louis. 'Permission to be dismissed?'

'Permission granted,' the king replied.

Stephen saluted Louis and headed off with the cadet towards *Hope*.

'It would seem, once again, that we are in your hands, Dom Taylor,' Louis said.

'I won't let you down.'

He patted my shoulder. 'I know you won't.' He glanced at *Zeus*. 'I'd better get back for the next war council meeting. They are a lot of things that my advisers insist only I can decide. I had forgotten how much work it is being a Cloud Rider king.'

'I'm sure you are already back into the swing of it, Papa,' Angelique said.

'Unfortunately, I am.' He kissed his daughter's head and headed towards *Zeus*.

Tesla pulled his sleeve back down over his Tac and gazed at me. 'We'd better go and get you set up with a ship's Eye, Dom, so you can you communicate with the stranded fleet.'

I took a step towards *Athena*.

Jules grabbed my arm and shook her head. 'Not that way. Follow us.'

'The surprise?'

'Exactly.'

Angelique shot me a questioning look as we followed Jules and Tesla away from the fleet and up the steep sand dune ahead.

CHAPTER SIX

STORM WIND

Jules and Tesla walked away from the squadron of gathered ships, towards the top of the dunes. Angelique and I followed as the last rays of the sun faded away and the stars started to appear.

I glanced back at the view behind us. At least forty ships had now gathered in the basin, but that was still nowhere near enough to give us anything like a fighting chance against Hades.

We were almost at the top of the dune when I heard the familiar burble of a burner ticking over. I scanned the area but couldn't see a ship close by. 'Hey, can you hear that, Angelique?'

She nodded. 'Have you got a cloaked airship parked up here, Tesla?'

Jules tapped the side of her nose. 'That's for us to know and for you both to find out.'

'Why all the secrecy?' I asked.

She pulled an imaginary zipper across her mouth and smirked.

It couldn't be, could it? The thing that had always filled my dreams since I'd been a child… My heart sped up. To own my own plane, just like Dad had. But of course, being Cloud Riders, this would be an airship.

My heart accelerated to overload as we reached the summit. Dunes carved from blue moonlight stretched away like a frozen, rolling, midnight ocean, but there was not a ship in sight. So, okay, Angelique had been right – it had to be cloaked.

Tesla turned to us, smiled and pointed his wand gizmo to an area of air that I could just see was rippling in the darkness. But hang on, the patch was only thirty feet across, way too small to be an airship.

'Tesla?' Angelique asked, gesturing towards the cloaked vessel.

He smiled and pushed a button set into the handle of his electronic wand. The patch of air started to grow opaque.

The breath caught in my throat as I took in a brass sphere slung under what looked like a converted Hades scout balloon. The device had been mounted in a frame from which four propellers pointed in different directions.

'Isn't it a beauty?' Jules said. 'I did all the mechanical work in one of *Hope*'s holds during the flight over here and Tesla sorted out the electrical side. We put it together from spares we raided from the stores.'

'I've never seen anything like this in my life,' Angelique said.

'I don't want to appear dense, but what's it for?' I asked.

Jules crossed her arms. 'Oh come on, it's obvious. And even if I say so myself, it was a genius idea of mine to build it.'

Tesla nodded. 'It was certainly an inspired flight of fantasy.'

So this thing was Jules's idea…

From the sphere hung a telescope on a geared mount. The whole device reminded me of a larger version of the little flying robots I'd seen back in Floating City.

'Is it some sort of automaton spying device?' Angelique asked.

'Oh so warm, but no prize quite yet,' Jules replied. 'Come on, guys, you see something like this every day on Cloud Rider airships.'

So it could be found on an airship... There *was* something very familiar about the round shape. I spotted the hinged mechanism that could split the top half open...and an idea sneaked out from the back of my mind. 'You've made a flying Eye?'

Jules clapped. 'He gets there in the end.'

'But why would you want to do that?' Angelique asked.

Tesla pointed with his wand at the lightning pendant hanging around my neck. 'Because *Storm Wind* needs a new home.'

I grasped my pendant. 'You built this to house his Psuche gem?'

'Just so.'

I gave them a blank look. 'I still don't get it.'

'It must be all this theta training that's making you a bit dense today,' Jules replied with a smile. 'Dom, think what happens when you put the Psuche gem into an Eye navigation system.'

'It enhances the Psuche gem's abilities so a Navigator can communicate with it and enables it to control the ship so it can jump between realities.'

'Exactly, but what does it specifically enable you, Dom Taylor, and no one else to do?'

'I can communicate directly with the Psuche gems and hear their real voices.'

'Exactly,' Tesla said. 'And of course with *Storm Wind* installed into his own Eye, you can communicate with the whole fleet, whenever you want.'

'You mean rather than use *Athena* to do that.'

Tesla nodded.

'But Dom is almost part of the family now,' Angelique said.

'That may be, Princess, but *Athena* is also your ship. And after everything that Dom has done for the Cloud Riders, don't you think that he deserves his own vessel?' Tesla replied.

Angelique's brow furrowed at me. 'Of course I do.'

'This is really kind of you,' I said. 'It's fantastic that you've done this for me, and it means a lot, it really does, but to be honest it wasn't quite what I had in mind when I pictured myself commanding my own ship.' I gestured back towards *Hope*. 'I don't want to sound ungrateful, but I can't see me making a huge difference with a ship this small.'

Angelique nodded. 'I see Dom's point. It only looks big enough to support the Eye, so to start with, where's he meant to sit?'

Tesla chuckled. 'Perhaps it's my fault for saying this was *your* ship, Dom. It would be more accurate to say this is *Storm Wind*'s vessel.'

'Come again?'

'Once his Psuche gem has been installed, this craft has been designed to be autonomous. *Storm Wind* will be able to fly himself but still communicate with you via ship-song at distance. However, when you physically touch the Eye, you can speak to him, or through him, to the rest of the fleet.'

I dragged my hand through my hair. 'So really you're saying that we're giving *Storm Wind* his own set of wings?' The murmur of his voice became sing-songy. He sounded happy, but wasn't saying anything else just yet. It seemed he wanted me to work this one out for myself.

Angelique tilted her head to one side. 'A Psuche gem that controls its own vessel...' A slow smile filled her face.

'He will be your own eyes in the sky,' Jules said.

'Okay, that does sound useful in battle.' I ran my fingers over my pendant. 'But there's something even cooler about this ship.'

'What's that?' Angelique asked.

'It will mean that *Storm Wind* can fly again.'

In response his song strengthened and I heard the other ship-songs behind us echoing him.

'*You are correct,*' he said. '*It will mean everything to me, Dom, to be able to fly once more.*'

So there it was.

Angelique beamed at me. 'His song sounds really happy.'

I smiled at her. 'He is. And in which case, so am I.'

Tesla patted my shoulder. 'Excellent. Now we need to prepare the craft so you can begin guiding in the rest of the fleet to us.'

'Okay, let's make a start,' Jules replied.

* * *

The final preparations for the flight test took some time as the moon slowly floated higher in the sky. While Jules helped Tesla work on the craft, Angelique grabbed the opportunity to help me practise my Sansodo, the Cloud Rider martial art. She said it was as good a way as any to mentally prepare for the gruelling marathon of guiding the rest of the fleet in. After an hour of that, when Tesla nodded towards me, I was feeling completely chilled.

'Are you ready, Dom?' he asked.

'As I'll ever be.' I slipped off Grandpa Alex's medal from around my neck and released the hidden catch. The moment the hidden compartment opened to reveal *Storm Wind*'s Psuche gem, his light blazed out as bright and clear as the stars above us. His crystal was warm to the touch as I plucked it from the medal.

Jules bent closer to gaze at his blue luminance dancing inside. 'It's incredible to think that the life force of an ancient Angelus is in there.'

'Isn't it?'

She narrowed her gazed on me. 'I've often wondered what you guys talk about in secret.'

I shrugged and avoided her eyes. 'Just stuff.' Stuff I couldn't speak to her about, the conversations you had with a best buddy... I found myself clasping the crystal in my fingers and not wanting to let it go. What would I do without the friend who'd recently guided me through the fog that filled my thoughts 24/7?

'*We will still be able to communicate with each other via ship-song, Dom,*' Storm Wind said.

I nodded as the others watched me in silence. *I hope so, my friend.*

Jules pressed a button in a control hatch on the bobbing craft and the sphere split like a pair of eyelids. A metal pillar rose up from the open device.

'You know the procedure, Dom,' Angelique said.

'Yep...'

As *Storm Wind*'s song sped up, I placed him gently in the jaws of the metal clamps. They locked his gem into place, and a deep ache filled me. I felt as if I was losing a chunk of myself.

We all watched in silence as, with a hiss, the pole descended into the bed of blue glowing coals that would interface his Psuche gem with the mini-ship's systems.

My skin prickled as the eyelids closed and shut the light of the Psuche gem away from view, almost like a jail door slamming shut on its captive. But *Storm Wind*'s voice wrapped tighter around me, comforting, and maybe understanding me better than I did myself at that moment.

'Why the long face, Dom?' Jules asked.

'Guess it feels as if I'm losing him.'

Angelique shook her head. 'I completely understand, Dom. You've been carrying *Storm Wind* around your neck for days now, and wearing a Psuche gem next to your skin creates a very powerful bond.' She tapped the side of her head. 'But he'll always be part of you up there from now on.'

'I guess.' In the darkness I hoped none of them could see the sense of loss threatening my eyes. 'So what happens now, Tesla?'

'Unlike a conventional craft, *Storm Wind* has full access to this ship's controls. Just give him a moment as he explores his new home and integrates it into his sub-systems.'

The small balloon vessel hung stationary, not a whisper of activity from any of its props. The only sound was the ticking of the burner's pilot light.

'I didn't do anything wrong, did I, Tesla?' Jules asked.

He shook his head. 'No...aha...'

A prop whirred up and slowed down again to edge the craft a few feet to the right.

'Here we go,' Tesla said. 'That was *Storm Wind*'s equivalent of stretching his fingers.'

Despite the sense of heaviness weighing down on me, I smiled. 'I can sort of imagine him running around inside his new home and trying out all the levers.'

Jules frowned. 'But what if I wired one of those levers back to front and he ends up crashing into a dune?'

Tesla shook his head. 'I have every confidence in you, Jules. You have a natural gift for engineering.'

'That's high praise indeed coming from Tesla,' Angelique said.

Jules nodded but chewed her lip. She stood a little bit closer to me. 'Promise me you'll forgive me if something goes wrong, Dom.'

I squeezed her hand. 'It won't.'

With a blast of the burner that sent blue light blazing across the sand, the props roared up and the craft shot into the air, curving away from us.

Angelique clapped. 'And we have lift off!'

Storm Wind's voice babbled in my head, less like an ancient being, more like an excited toddler who'd taken the wheel of an expensive supercar.

The vessel shot across the sky, banking and turning. I could have sworn I heard him laughing as he threw in a few bombing runs that had us all diving for cover.

Jules pointed at my head. 'Tell me he's not saying "Wheeee!" in there?'

Storm Wind's joy was infectious and the heaviness of a moment ago evaporated. I grinned. 'Pretty much.'

'Which may be, but we have a job to do,' Tesla said. 'Dom, can you call him down so we can contact the fleet?'

Jules winked at me. 'Time to whistle him in.'

'Oh, I think we can do better than that.'

I closed my eyes and focused my thoughts. The effort seemed alien to me, compared to the effortlessness of talking to him when he'd been hanging around my neck.

Storm Wind, *time for both of us to get to work. Can you come back here now?*

His voice replied in a lowering choral note. I opened my eyes as he began to bank back towards us in a slow descent and came to a hovering stop just before me.

Jules blew the air out of her cheeks. 'Very slick, Mr Whisperer.'

I reached out and put my hand onto the copper dome. At once the eyelids opened and *Storm Wind*'s song sharpened into his voice.

'*Thank your friends, Dom. This new craft is wonderful.*'

'He says thanks,' I repeated.

Jules beamed. 'Tell him he's very welcome.'

Tesla nodded towards me. 'Now the hard work for you both really begins. When you make contact you will need to keep the link open until the last ship arrives. With the strengthened Hades Quantum Pacifier signal they are now broadcasting, if you break contact, even for a moment, any ship in transit will be lost in the Void.'

In my mind, *Storm Wind*'s euphoria swept away, replaced by the familiar weight of other people depending on me. 'I understand.'

'Dom, do you want me to help you contact my brethren now?' Storm Wind said.

I do.

'Alright, my friend, let us begin our song together.'

With a faint hiss he released hot air from his balloon envelope and his ship settled onto the dune.

Maintaining my hand's contact with the Eye, I dropped into a cross-legged position on the sand. I took a deep breath as *Storm Wind*'s voice began to ebb and flow in a slow, hypnotic chant.

At first I felt the others' gazes on me as I mimicked *Storm Wind*'s voice with my own, but gradually I forgot them. It might as well have been just *Storm Wind* and me on top of that dune, our voices joined together and sang out across the landscape under the steady watch of the stars.

The desert scene, with my friends watching us, shimmered and faded away, replaced by snatched glimpses of parallel universes blinking past in a blur of shapes and colours too fast to catch. But then the racing realities slowed and came to a stop.

'My brother, Pythagoras, is here...' Storm Wind said.

I found myself gazing out at a green sea that stretched to the horizon in every direction. I heard whale-like song and caught a glimpse of something in the swell and for a moment I thought it was an island. But as I focused on the shape, I took in the large flight rudders sitting at the back of a green airship, the gondola beneath floating like a tanker in the sea.

Pythagoras.

I concentrated on the craft and my consciousness swept out towards it and its crew, as they waited to be reunited with their king.

CHAPTER SEVEN

THE LOST CREW

I felt like an overworked air traffic controller. Every sinew in my body ached as though someone had trampled over it and, for good measure, used my brain as a football. But none of that mattered now. I gazed out across the dunes at my handiwork…the massed remnants of the Cloud Rider fleet: ninety-nine ships parked up across the desert.

We'd watched from our high dune vantage point as Louis had personally met each and every landing airship. Angelique had paced up and down as she'd watched, obviously desperate to be doing the same. Finally Jules had waved her away, saying she could maintain the vigil with me until all the ships had arrived. The princess hadn't needed to be told twice and, all smiles, had bounded off down the dune to join the king.

Tesla had continued to tweak *Storm Wind*'s ship for several hours, but when he was finally happy that all the systems were functioning correctly, he'd headed off too so he could continue fitting chameleon nets to the latest arrivals.

Now, I sipped the last of my coffee, trying to gather my mental energy for the final push.

'I don't know about you, but I so need to sleep,' Jules said, stretching her arms, hands interlocked, up towards the sky.

'I feel shattered, but we still have that one ship left to guide in.'

She rolled her shoulders. 'I know, I know.'

The first rays of dawn began to creep up over the dunes, kissing their peaks with gold. The valleys between were still deep in shadow, the lingering gloom punctuated by the glow from thousands of portals.

I wrapped the thick blanket, which Jules had found for me during the night, tighter around me against the deep chill biting into my bones. The burner above the Eye pulsed several times, bathing my skin with warmth – *Storm Wind* doing his best to look after us.

Jules, teeth chattering, held up her hands to the flame. 'I'm frozen.'

'Me too, but the sooner we get this done, the sooner we can collapse into nice warm bunks.'

'That sounds like utter bliss.'

I stifled a yawn and jiggled my empty cup towards her. 'Any more coffee to help me keep sharp?'

She grabbed the flask and frowned. 'Sorry, Dom, we're out.'

'Just make sure I don't fall asleep.'

She shot me a smile. 'I'll have to pinch you then.'

I smiled back at her. 'Stick a pin in me if that's what it takes.' I placed my hand on the Eye.

At once *Storm Wind*'s voice spoke inside my head. *'Ready, Dom?'*

As I'll ever be.

In answer, *Storm Wind*'s song swelled for over the hundredth time that night. Although my throat felt as if it'd been scratched by a hundred claws, I joined my voice to his.

Jules wrapped her arms tight around herself and watched me in silence, like she had all night. She and the desert began to disappear around me, her weary smile the last thing to disappear.

The final ship that we were looking for seemed to be having some sort of problem transmitting. On the previous two attempts to make contact, all we'd got was a location broadcast, intermittent at best, but no ship-song to identify which vessel it was.

Tuning out the Hades roar of jamming static, I felt the steady pulse of energy in my mind, the beat of a ship's emergency beacon calling out across countless dimensions. I locked onto the thread as realities blurred past. The signal was growing in strength. At last I was closing in.

A world of green vegetation flashed through my mind and the signal became crystal clear. That reality sped past to an alpine scene and the pulse dropped back to a murmur. I jammed my mental brakes on the flicker book of realities and backed up.

The alpine landscape rippled away and was replaced by a thick jungle. Colourful birds flitted between the palms and a troop of orange monkeys – parents and babies – fed on yellow fruit hanging from the branches. I looked around at the scene which played out as a silent movie. Not for the first time I wished I could hear as well as see these new worlds with my Whisperer ability.

Nearby, a grey-striped four-legged creature, a bit like a horse with longer legs, had its head lowered to a forest pool, a purple tongue scooping up the water into its mouth.

The homing beacon pulsed again, but this time way stronger. I focused my attention in the direction the signal seemed to be coming from.

Bathed by dappled light, a long, narrow, green oval shape covered in creepers stood in a clearing.

Relief surged through me. We'd found them. I zoomed towards the craft.

Around the airship, men in faded Cloud Rider uniforms worked plots of dug soil filled with rows of tall plants. Strung from green branches, canvas awnings had been rigged up and under their cover meat was being spit roast over glowing log fires, slowly turned by small steam engines. Piles of yellow fruit had been piled up by the ship's gondola. The whole place had the feel of a pioneer homestead set up by the stranded crew, a regular Little House on the Prairie, Cloud Riders style.

Around the edges of the clearing stood small domed structures sculpted from baked red mud, draped with flowers of every colour.

I noticed movement through the windshield of the gondola. Inside the ship, a beautiful woman with a crewcut hairstyle gazed at the cockpit instrument panel. Behind her a young girl sat cross-legged by the ship's Eye and was playing with a teddy bear covered with long fur. The child had the same sharp cheekbones as the woman… Maybe mother and daughter?

An impossible idea burst into my head. *Roxanne and Isabella?* Was this the lost ship – *Helios?*

Excitement mounting, I moved my bubble of consciousness inside. Sure enough, the woman had epaulets of a captain on her shoulders. She was scowling at the blink of a green light which matched the pulse of the beacon still sounding in my mind.

I tried reaching out to her with my mind.

Roxanne, can you hear me?

There was no reply. So she wasn't a Navigator. But I'd got well used to the routine with the other ships I'd already brought in without a Navigator. Make contact with the ship first and then, through the ship, make contact with the crew.

I concentrated on the closed brass sphere. Helios, *can you hear me?*

A slow murmur. *'Yes, Whisperer…but my systems are severely degraded.'*

It always spooked me how all the ships seemed to know of my title, even the ones who'd been out of contact. Another mystery of how ship consciousness worked.

The child put down her teddy bear and stared at me. *'Are you a ghost?'*

You can see me? I replied.

Solemn-faced, Isabella nodded.

So she was a Navigator. That would make this bit a heck of lot easier, especially if *Helios* wasn't firing on all cylinders.

Isabella said something to her mother in the silent movie of their reality.

Roxanne turned with a questioning look. Isabella pointed at where I was standing, but her mother looked straight through me and shook her head. Her lips moved but of course I couldn't hear her.

Isabella, you need to tell your mom exactly what I'm about to tell you.

'Okay, Mr Ghost.'

I started to tell Isabella about the king and about all the ships waiting for *Helios* to join them. And as I talked and Isabella relayed the information to Roxanne, a look of pure joy filled her mother's face.

* * *

I fed the coordinates of the jumps required to bring *Helios* to us. While I worked with the ship, he quickly brought me up to speed with everything that had happened to him and his crew. *Helios* had been badly damaged during a dog fight with a Hades destroyer, but despite being heavily outgunned the ship and his crew had managed to take out their larger opponent. Before enemy reinforcements could arrive, they'd managed to jump away and had crash-landed on this planet, Earth TLZ4268. Ever since then they'd been cut off from the rest of the fleet. The crew, however, had proved resourceful and had repaired most of the ship with scavenged supplies from the friendly locals in the surrounding villages. The only thing they hadn't been able to mend was a fluctuating power loss that was affecting *Helios*'s systems, but he'd still had enough juice to run with his auxiliary systems turned off.

And I knew all this in less time than I could've blinked.

I communicated my own history with the ship: meeting Angelique and *Athena* for the first time, discovering that I was descended from a Cloud Rider, the battles with Hades, and meeting *Titan* to discover that I was a Ship Whisperer. All that and more – as my memories became his, and his became mine. At last the coordinates flashed past and lights began blinking on a control console. Time to get *Helios*'s journey under way.

I'd ducked out for a moment and found myself back on the dune.

Jules gazed at me. 'Everything okay?'

'Better than okay. I found the missing ship and it's *Helios*.'

She clutched her hands together. 'You mean Roxanne and Isabella are alive?'

'Yep, and I can't wait to tell Stephen,' I replied.

Jules's expression sharpened. 'Oh, I've a way better idea... Let's not tell him quite yet.'

'But why?'

'He's flat-out busy with the refit of *Hope* and won't be able to concentrate on anything else once we tell him this. So what if the first thing he knows about any of this is when *Helios* materialises above our heads?'

I turned the idea over in my mind and nodded. 'It's worth doing if only to see the look on his face – it'll be priceless.'

Jules beamed at me. 'Exactly.'

Storm Wind's song grew louder again. I placed my hand on his ship's Eye.

'*It is time,*' he murmured into my mind.

Jules nodded at me. 'Go and do your stuff.'

I closed my eyes and shifted to find Isabella holding her teddy bear. Her serious expression transformed into a wide smile as she saw me. '*Hi, Mr Ghost.*'

Hi back at you.

The view outside the gondola had been transformed. Hundreds of golden-skinned people wearing highly coloured rainbow cloths draped over them watched *Helios* with wide-eyed fascination from the edges of the clearing as the ship was prepared for flight by his crew.

Plumes of white smoke drifted up as the cooking fires were doused and canvas flapped in a gentle breeze as the awnings were taken down.

I gazed across at Roxanne, deep in conversation with her silver-haired officer, as they checked every dial in the cockpit twice and wrote down numbers on a glowing slab of crystal.

After I'd finished working with her ship the first thing I'd let Roxanne know, via Isabella, was her brother being alive. There'd been some serious tears and smiles at that particular piece of news. Still, I just couldn't bring myself to tell Roxanne about her dad. That was a job best left for Stephen and a conversation best had away from the eyes of others.

Helios's song flooded my mind.

'*That's so pretty,*' Isabella said to me.

He can't wait to fly again.

Isabella hugged her bear harder. '*I can't either.*' She spoke to Roxanne and the flight crew all turned and listened to her silent words. Everyone started clapping and I could tell there was a lot of whooping going on, too, even though I couldn't hear it.

Roxanne reached up and pulled down the burner lever. Outside, the villagers began to wave and smile as the last of the crew rushed aboard. The captain pushed the throttle forward and at the far end of the stern a single massive prop whirred up.

With a gentle shudder, the creepers that had started to grow over the canopy broke free and *Helios* began to climb into the sky. His song soared as fast as his rapid ascent and soon the rich, green jungle began to stretch away below the ship in all directions. Red domes, larger versions of the ones built around the edge of the clearing, lay dotted across the landscape.

What are those buildings? I asked Isabella.

'Mama says they are the temples for the local people.' She grinned. *'They believe we're some sort of sky gods fallen from the heavens. Every morning when we wake up we find loads of nuts and berries in the small ones they built around the clearing.'*

I could imagine the villagers would be making up stories about the Cloud Riders long after they'd departed.

Wisps of cloud sped past the ship and the sky deepened to a darker blue.

I glanced across towards Roxanne.

Isabella, ask your mother – is she ready to jump?

The child repeated my message to her.

Roxanne nodded with a broad smile.

I opened my consciousness to the other signal that had been continually hissing in the background throughout the night. At once the crackle of the Hades Quantum Pacifier jamming static filled the cabin. The glass planets inside the Eye started to flicker.

Roxanne's expression closed up again.

Tell your mother not to worry – this is where I come in…

In a universe countless realities away, my physical voice joined to *Storm Wind*'s voice, and *Helios*'s wove around both of ours.

Isabella's eyes widened.

You can sing too, I said to her.

She nodded and her voice, pure and clear, rang out.

All around her the crew stopped what they were doing and turned to stare at the child singing with all her heart.

Roxanne's eyes suddenly filled with tears. She crossed to Isabella and held onto her, as her daughter began to turn translucent, her body etched out in a series of faint lines.

Our song rose together, human and ship-song, each voice reinforcing each other over the hiss of the Hades static.

The attention of the crew focused on the spot where she'd begun to vanish. I could see the hope burning in their eyes, the same expression I'd seen in the faces of hundreds of air crew throughout this long night, the haunted look of people who'd been marooned too long, but had still managed to cling on despite everything.

Isabella kept her ghostly eyes on mine as the ship and the crew began to dissolve around us as parallel realities sped past.

'I'm scared,' Isabella whispered.

Don't be – I'm here to protect you…

As I had so many times before that night, I brought my attention back to the desert world where my physical body was sitting. It had become so burned into my brain that I could almost do it without trying now. The blurring worlds slowed to a stop.

I hovered over the dunes with Isabella's glowing ghost. Below us on the summit I could see Jules and my physical body sitting cross-legged by *Storm Wind*'s craft. I could hear the chant of my own voice drifting up and echoing the chorus in my mind. Although I should've been used to it by now, I still felt a little twist of vertigo inside at being in two places at once.

Isabella gazed down at all the ships.

Your uncle is down there somewhere waiting for you.

She beamed at me. *'I can't wait to see him.'* The air shimmered and she dissolved into nothing, returning to the deck of her ship.

For the final time that night, I focused on *Storm Wind*'s voice and returned to my body, immediately feeling the sand beneath me again.

I sang out with *Storm Wind* and heard *Helios*'s and Isabella's replies as a distant harmony. This would never get old for me.

A tingle swept over my skin. I was communicating, Whispering, with another being countless dimensions away. I took a deep breath and once again raised my voice to match theirs to help guide *Helios* and his crew back through the Void and to a big reunion.

* * *

Someone was crying.

'Oh, Dom, I'm so sorry,' Jules said between sobs.

Something gritty pressed into the side of my face. My mind was full of velvet and soft darkness, so quiet and peaceful without any ship-song to disturb me. I lay on the dune, tucked into a foetal position. Jules knelt over me, tears streaming down her face.

Cobwebs clung to my mind and my limbs felt like stone. I pushed myself into a sitting position. 'What's wrong?'

'We…' She took another shuddering breath. 'We fell asleep.'

My thoughts rushed in and ice crawled up my spine. 'But Isabella was jumping with *Helios*.'

Jules nodded, her tears sprinkling like raindrops onto the dry sand.

A woman was climbing the dune towards us. My mind felt so numb it took me a moment to register that it was Angelique.

'Shouldn't the last ship have arrived by now?' she asked as she reached us. She took in our expressions and her brow furrowed. 'And why aren't you chanting with *Storm Wind*?'

Jules's voice shook as she spoke for both of us. 'We fell asleep.'

Angelique's pupils became pinpricks. She rushed to me and grabbed me by the shoulders. 'Do you understand what you've done?'

I didn't have the words, didn't have the excuses. But most of all my brain didn't even want to go there, to look her in the eyes and see the shadow of my stupidity.

'It wasn't Dom's fault, it was mine,' Jules said. 'It was my duty to keep him awake and the last thing I remember is him chanting and then...' She wrung her fingers together as if she were trying to wash them free of a stain. 'I must've fallen asleep first.'

I stared at my best friend trying to take the bullet for me. I shook my head. 'This isn't down to you, Jules. This is my mess.'

Angelique glowered at us both. '*Mess* doesn't begin to cover the extent of what you've both done. Because of your negligence, a crew are dead. Dead, because you couldn't stay awake. And which poor ship was it whose crew's lives you threw away?'

Her fury cut into me like a sharp knife, but I forced myself to answer her, my words burning in my mouth. 'It was *Helios*.'

She gaped at me. 'Roxanne's ship?'

I nodded, wishing a slipknife would rise up and swallow me whole. 'Isabella was onboard too...'

'Oh by the gods, no.'

A mother and daughter who right now should be rushing into Stephen's arms, if I'd done my job right.

I stood, hands on my head. 'I'm so sorry, Angelique.'

'Sorry?' She balled her hands into fists and hurled her words at me like bullets. 'Is that what you're going to say to the people who knew the Cloud Riders on that ship – to the people here who knew someone onboard? To Stephen?'

I turned from her fury, away from the Cloud Rider fleet, and stumbled down the opposite side of the dune.

'Dom!' Jules called out.

But I didn't stop, couldn't stop; my stomach felt full of acid, my mind too full of people screaming as the Void consumed them. But most of all full of a child's smile, so full of hope that it burned me more deeply than any of Angelique's words could have ever done.

Isabella...

CHAPTER EIGHT

CONSQUENCES

I didn't know how long I'd sat with my back to the sandstone boulder, staring out across the desert, or when the tears had stopped streaming, but now all I felt was an emptiness as big as the rock I was slouched against.

A shadow fell across me and I had to shield my eyes as I gazed up at the silhouetted figure.

'There you are,' Louis said. 'We have been searching for you everywhere, Dom.' He passed me a canteen.

I swigged the cool water from it, taking some of the sting from the sandpaper lining my throat. 'I didn't mean to cause any more fuss by going off like that.'

'I'm afraid that's exactly what you have done. Jules and Angelique are frantic with worry about you.'

'Angelique?'

'Why would she not be worried?'

'The last time I saw her she looked ready to rip my head off my shoulders, and I utterly deserve it.'

Louis shook his head. 'I heard about what happened.' He sat down next to me. 'She was upset and said some things that I can assure you she now regrets. In the heat of the moment and all that.'

'But she was only saying the truth. Because of me, all those people are dead.'

The king shook his head. 'Look, Dom, I understand that you feel you are carrying everything on your shoulders at the moment and that everything is your personal responsibility. But it really is not your fault, it is all of ours.'

'That may be true, but in this I'm the one who was meant to bring Roxanne and…' My voice caught on the next name, but I forced myself to continue. 'And Isabella, and the rest of *Helios*'s crew safely here.'

'I understand your feelings, but you need to ask yourself what actually happened.'

Wasn't it obvious? 'I failed because I couldn't keep my eyes open.'

'Yes, but why couldn't you keep your eyes open?'

'Because I was exhausted.'

'Precisely. Now will you please get to your feet?'

If the king was about to strike me across the face, I more than had it coming. Part of me wanted the punishment, needed it even. My body ached on the outside as much as it did on the inside. Limbs stiff, I got up, arms hanging by my side. I wasn't going to begin to defend myself, mentally or physically.

But instead Louis gently took hold of my shoulders and turned me back towards where the fleet had moored up.

'Tell me what you see?' he asked.

'All the Cloud Rider ships that made it here okay.'

'Just so, and what name do you think they keep repeating, again and again?'

I shrugged. 'Yours…Angelique's?'

He shook his head. 'No, it's Dom Taylor. In nearly every conversation I've heard, it's your name that's been praised for bringing our people back together.' He swept his arm to take in all the ships. 'To them and to me, you, the Ship Whisperer, have been our saviour, when all hope seemed lost.'

I dropped my gaze to the floor. 'That's because they probably don't know that I messed up yet.'

'Actually, they do know that you lost contact with *Helios*.'

I groaned. 'So much for being a hero to them.'

Louis shook his head. 'It is quite the opposite. All my people understand how hard you pushed yourself to reunite the fleet. The only problem was that, on this occasion, you pushed yourself a step too far.'

'But can't you see that's still my fault? It all loops back to me.'

'No, it's mine, Dom. I should have kept a closer eye on how you were getting on. Angelique is blaming herself for that too. We should certainly never have let you work straight through the night, especially after all the theta training you did. Tell me – when was the last time you had a proper sleep?'

I cast my mind back. 'I'm not sure to be honest. Certainly not since I left my Earth.' It was funny how quickly I'd got used to qualifying which Earth I was talking about.

'So please understand that what happened to you could have happened to anyone who'd had so little sleep.'

'But it didn't happen to them, it happened to me. And I'm the one who's going to have to live with that particular guilt trip for the rest of my life.'

Louis sighed and slowly nodded. 'I understand…more than understand. In some ways we are more alike, Dom Taylor, than you can probably guess.'

I stared at him. 'What do you mean?'

'Can you begin to imagine the number of things I feel directly responsible for that led to the deaths of my people? The number of nights I could not sleep because Cloud Riders, the people who looked to me to guide them with wisdom, have been lost in the battles with Hades?'

'But that wasn't your fault – if anything it was Cronos's.'

'That is as maybe, but I still felt responsible for each and every one of them.' He peered at me. 'Regret has its place in our lives, but you must never let it overpower you, Dom. Learn the lesson from what happened and allow yourself to move on. I can assure you that's what Captain Roxanne would have wanted.'

'I'm not sure it's going to be that easy.'

'I am not saying it will be, but that is exactly what you need to do, for your own sake. You need to forgive yourself, Dom.'

I doubted that I could ever do that because every time I closed my eyes at night it would be Isabella's innocent face staring back at me.

Louis gestured towards the fleet. 'Come on. Let us get some food inside of you and, even more importantly, some rest.'

I slumped into my steps and followed him back towards the bustle of an encampment readying itself for war.

* * *

I'd been right. The moment I'd tried to sleep, Isabella's eyes burned at me from the darkness. Hours had slipped past as the horror show of my imagination played out what had happened to her and the others.

I heard a gentle tapping and my eyes opened to sunlight pouring into the gondola.

Angelique stood in the doorway, her green eyes framed with concern. 'How are you doing, Dom?'

I swung my legs over the bunk and sat staring at the floor. I couldn't bring myself to look at her. 'Awful.'

Angelique sighed and sat next to me. 'I can imagine…' She picked at her skirt. 'Look, Dom, I'm sorry for how I reacted.'

'You shouldn't be. I deserved everything that you threw at me and a whole lot more.'

'No you didn't. By the gods, you're only human.'

'But at the moment I need to be more than that. Everyone is depending on my Whisperer ability, which right now feels like a curse.'

Her ice-green stare became so sharp that I had to look away.

'Any one of the Navigators I know would trade places with you in a second to be able to talk with their ships like you can, myself included,' she said.

'And I would gladly trade places with any of them right now.'

'Well, you can't and we need you. So stop feeling sorry for yourself, and to use a phrase that those on your Earth like so much, you need to get off your ass.' A small smile broke her frown.

I found myself, despite everything, almost smiling back at her. 'What happened to the sympathy approach?'

'That didn't seem to be working and, besides, I ran out of patience dealing with Jules over exactly the same issue. If you think you're feeling awful, you should try talking to her. She not only blames herself for *Helios*'s loss, but she also utterly believes she completely let you down when you needed her.'

I sat up. 'Jules has got that so wrong. She just fell asleep and that could have happened to…' My words trailed away as Angelique raised her eyebrows.

'Exactly. And isn't it easier to get a sense of perspective when you're talking about someone else, Dom?'

'Maybe…'

'So *maybe* you can go and talk to her then? She needs her best friend right now.'

'Of course. Where is she?'

'Working with Tesla to install the last of the chameleon nets on the fleet.'

'They're nearly finished? Exactly how long have I been out for?'

'Two days.'

I stared at her. 'Come again?'

'You needed the rest, Dom. And you should also know that Jules has kept checking in on you, even though she hasn't slept at all since the accident.'

'But she must be shattered?'

'She is moving like a human automaton with a broken piston. The problem is that nobody has been able to persuade her to stop. I think she's trying to make amends by driving herself into the ground.'

'I'll talk to her.'

'Please do. I think you're the one person she'll listen too. Even Papa couldn't get her to stop and he's normally, as you know, very persuasive.'

'Leave it to me.' I stood up.

* * *

I spotted Jules hanging down the side of *Hope*'s gas envelope. Despite the size of the ship, making Jules look like a tiny ant riding an elephant, I could see that most of the ship was now covered with chameleon nets. They caught the sunlight and sparkled like a sea of gemstones.

As I neared I could see how Jules fumbled to draw a seam together, her body half slumped against the canvas as she tried to pulled the cord tight.

I waved up at her. 'Jules.'

Her head snapped round in my direction as if she'd been slapped. Jules looked way beyond shattered. She turned away and bent her head back to her work.

Angelique hadn't been exaggerating about the mess she was in. I walked to a spot directly beneath her. 'Jules?'

She didn't look down at me this time.

'Are you seriously going to give me the silent treatment?'

Her shoulders slumped. Her voice drifted down as barely a whisper. 'No…'

'Good, because we need to talk.'

She responded with a slow shake of her head. 'What's there to say apart from the fact I let you down, Dom?'

Even fifty feet above my head I could see that she was shivering despite the heat. 'You get yourself down here right now, Jules Eastwood, so I can set you straight on this.'

'But it's my fault!' Jules shouted. She shifted her position to glare at me and started to slip from her suspended bench seat.

'Watch out!'

Jules grabbed hold of the chameleon net as she started to tip backwards, but it ripped in her hands. My senses switched into slow motion as she tumbled backwards off the platform and dropped towards me, her safety line shooting out behind her.

My instincts kicked in and I started to move. From nowhere Stephen blurred past me, grabbed a rope unravelling on the ground by my feet and shot upwards towards the pulley. The rope burned his hands as he held onto it and leant backwards.

With a snap like a whip, Jules jerked to a stop on her line.

Stephen turned to me as he hung onto the rope, fire in his eyes.

'Just how many more people are you going to kill, Whisperer?' He grimaced as he strained to hold onto the rope.

His words cut through my shock. 'Here, let me help you.'

He gritted his teeth as blood dropped from his hands onto the sand. 'I don't need your help.' The rope slipped a few feet through his hands. He hissed through his teeth and his knuckles stood out as he clung onto the line. It slowed and Jules jerked to a stop again as Stephen braked her descent.

Anger coiled through me and I glowered at him. 'I'm not having my best friend break her neck because you can't take the weight.'

He gave me a hard stare back, but growled and nodded.

I took position behind him and wrapped the end of the rope around myself. Even with us both taking her weight on the line, my muscles ached as we started to lower her foot by foot.

Jules hung her head and twirled on the rope as she descended, reaching us like a broken puppet. Her legs buckled and, with a whimper, she slumped to the ground.

Stephen and I reached her at the same moment.

My heart raced as I bent over Jules. 'Are you hurt?'

She opened her eyes and shook her head.

Stephen crossed his arms, his bloodied hands staining his uniform.

Tesla raced over from *Hope* and joined us to stare at Jules. 'What happened?'

'She fell because his Lord Highness, the Ship Whisperer, distracted Jules from her work,' Stephen replied.

I stared at him. 'Thanks for the guilt trip, buddy.'

'Oh, you've got plenty more than this to be guilty about,' he replied, menace dripping from every word.

His words struck home, but heck if I was going stand there and take it. 'Yes, I know I do, and I don't need a jumped-up newbie airship captain to remind me of my shortcomings.'

Jules choked back a sob. 'Will you two just stop.' She half rose to her feet, but started to fall again.

Tesla grabbed onto Jules to steady her.

'Let me go – I've got to get finished here.'

Tesla shook his head. 'You have done more than enough, young lady. I can find another pair of willing hands to help me finish the installation of the final panels.'

Jules gave him a pale look. 'But…'

I shook my head. 'You heard the man – no arguments – and when you've had a chance to sleep, we are so going to have ourselves a little talk.'

She blinked, her pupils growing to saucers. 'You don't need to say anything, Dom. I know I messed up.'

I stared at her. 'You've got it all wrong, Jules.'

Tears flooded her eyes and she looked away.

Stephen took her by the arm. 'I'm going to take you to your bunk so you can get some proper sleep.'

A stab of irritation shot through me and I stood in his way. 'I'll take her.'

'Oh, I think you've already done more than enough, Whisperer,' he said, spitting the title at me.

Jules looked between us, tears flowing over her cheeks. 'I can't take any more of this attitude from you two.'

The anger uncoiled inside me and guilt rushed into its space. 'Sorry, Jules.' I stood aside. Stephen shoved me as he guided her past. I let it go…for her sake.

I felt a hand patting my shoulder and turned to see Tesla gazing at me.

'Give Stephen time, Dom.'

I nodded, but a huge part of me wasn't convinced that all the time in the universe would be long enough for Stephen to look at me again without hatred in his eyes. But wouldn't I have hated someone's guts too, if I thought they'd been responsible for the death of people that close to me? Yeah, I probably would have.

'Come on, you need to keep yourself busy, which is fortunate as I find myself in need of an assistant,' Tesla said. 'Do you think you could help me finish off installing the last chameleon nets on *Hope*?'

With the mess that my head was in, I felt pretty certain I'd be useless trying any theta training at the moment. And maybe lots of physical activity was exactly what I needed so I couldn't rattle around my own brain any more…probably exactly the same reason Jules had thrown herself into work to the point of exhaustion.

'You've got it,' I replied. For a change I'd get something right. Then I'd tackle Jules and make her see sense.

I took hold of the harness, slipped it on and clipped myself into the rope. My fingers travelled to my empty pendant out of a force of habit. I could have done with *Storm Wind*'s wise words at that moment. Instead his distant ship-song washed over me as he flew somewhere high above in the desert sky. Even so, the notes of his song were filled with warmth and compassion, which made me feel worse than ever, under that blazing sun.

CHAPTER NINE

MESSAGE FROM HOME

Tesla, his hands clasped behind his back, gazed out through the glass of the round observation dome at the summit of *Hope* at the 360-degree view of the fleet parked up around us. The big moment had finally come. As long as this worked, we'd be able to set out for my Earth straight away.

I stretched my fingers that ached from the installation of the final chameleon nets. I felt exhausted and I'd only been at it for a few hours. How Jules had kept going for so long was nothing short of a miracle, but also, knowing her, a combination of pure stubbornness and raging guilt would have powered her through. But everything was my fault, a fact that I saw every time I ran into Stephen and he glowered at me. Far worse was seeing Isabella's features in his – that was the deepest cut of all.

Storm Wind floated outside *Hope*'s observation blister in his new ship. He had his observation telescope trained on us like some sort of over-familiar drone. But despite the mess I felt inside, I smiled at him. Since his new-found independence, for someone who was an ancient sentient being he'd been acting more like a dog let off the leash. At every opportunity he'd taken himself off for joyrides to carve up the sky and then had appeared unexpectedly back by my side. All he needed was a tongue lolling out and he'd be set.

Angelique and Louis emerged from the corkscrewing stairwell. I just wished Jules was here to share something she'd worked so hard on to make a reality.

'Are we ready?' Louis asked.

'Everything has been prepared, King Louis,' Tesla replied.

Angelique crossed over to me. 'I can't wait to see this in action.'

I did my best to smile back at her, but only managed a tight grimace.

Tesla unclipped the wand device from his belt and pointed it out towards the fleet. He held it still for a moment with his arms outstretched like an orchestra conductor waiting to begin, and then in a sweeping circle he pressed the button in the wand's handle.

Storm Wind began to hum beyond the dome, the wasp-like noise echoed by the hundred ships around us. The sound rose slowly in pitch to beyond my hearing as the air started to shimmer around each and every ship. Then, just like that, the entire fleet became rippling patches of air and vanished, leaving an uninterrupted view of the dune landscape.

Angelique clapped. 'What an amazing sight.'

Louis slapped Tesla on the back. 'I think we can call that a resounding success.'

Tesla's shoulders dropped and he looked round with a wide smile. 'It would seem so.'

'And this is going to give us a huge tactical advantage against the Hades fleet,' Angelique replied.

But I was finding it hard to catch their enthusiasm. Now this hurdle was out of the way, the next target had come into sharp focus: a vast Hades fleet heading for my home world.

'How many ships have Hades got?' I asked.

Angelique's gaze sharpened on me. 'Around a thousand. Why?'

'That means we're outgunned ten to one – and those are lousy odds in anyone's book.'

Angelique shook her head. 'Dom, a Cloud Rider ship is worth ten of theirs.'

'So you keep saying.'

Speakers on a pillar in the middle of the round room burst into life. 'My king, we are receiving a Valve Voice broadcast,' Stephen's voice said.

'From the fleet? Is something wrong?'

'No, it's from a parallel world – Earth DZL2351.'

Confusion pulsed through me. That was the Cloud Rider code for my Earth.

Stephen's voice crackled through the speaker. 'It's a woman who says her name is Cherie. She's demanding to talk to the Whisperer straight away.'

I ignored Stephen's clipped tone as he referred to me by title rather than name. 'Cherie from the Sky Hawks?'

Angelique stared at me. 'But how can she be contacting us? We didn't leave her a Valve Voice set.'

I nodded. Until now, back home was a sort of compartment I'd walled off in my head, a place that seemed less real the more dimensions I'd crossed away from it. But now somehow that other life was reaching out across all those parallel dimensions to talk to me.

King Louis unhooked a mic from the pillar. 'You better patch her through to the observation deck, Captain Stephen.'

'Yes, my king,' Stephen replied.

My heart hammered as Louis handed me the mic. The radio hissed for a moment.

'Hi, Dom, you there?' Cherie's faint voice said between the hisses and pops of static.

I cradled the mic in my hand, a lifeline to back home. 'Cherie, is that really you?'

Whooping came over the radio's speaker.

'Dom, Dom, you're okay?' came a new voice. Mom.

It was almost too much, the sound of her here in this alien desert world. Suddenly I felt like blubbing. I rested my head against the pillar, trying to hold it together.

'Dom?' Mom's voice repeated.

Where to begin? How could I tell her about Dad being alive, then losing him again; about the invasion force about to tear our Earth apart? I felt Angelique's hand on my back.

'Start by telling them that Jules is alive,' she said.

She was right. When I'd last seen Mom and the others, we'd been heading off after Jules who'd been abducted by Ambra. That seemed like a lifetime of experiences ago now.

'Tell Roddy that we rescued Jules from Hells Cauldron and she's okay.'

More whoops crackled over the radio.

'Oh, thank goodness,' Mom said. 'And you're okay too, my love?'

With everyone listening in I could hardly tell her what an emotional car wreck I was right now. 'Yeah, I'm good, Mom.'

'That's so wonderful—' Sobbing filled the speaker.

'Sorry, Dom – your mom has ducked out for a moment,' Harry's voice said. 'She's just a bit overwhelmed, you know?'

Yeah, I knew. 'Give her a hug from me, Harry.'

'You've got it.'

Tesla tapped me on the shoulder. 'Do you mind if I ask your friends something, Dom?'

I nodded and handed the mic over to him.

'This is Nikola Tesla. I'm chief scientist of the Cloud Riders and I'd like to ask you something.'

'Go on, shoot,' Harry said.

'How is it that you have been able to contact us?'

'That would be my doing,' Cherie said. 'I came across this burned-out Valve Voice radio in the gondola of *Apollo* after he crash-landed here. The radio was badly damaged and it's taken me one heck of an age to get my head around fixing it.'

'Well, it's quite an accomplishment,' Tesla replied. 'Even a skilled Cloud Rider master technician would have had trouble achieving what you have managed to.'

'Oh, I'm pretty handy when I need to be. By the way, is your name really Nikola Tesla?'

I noticed his expression tighten a fraction. 'Yes, why?'

'It's just you've got yourself quite a famous name there.'

A strange look that I couldn't quite read crossed his face. 'Really?'

'Yeah – there was this cutting edge scientist on this Earth during the last century called Nikola Tesla. He was a major player and responsible for all sorts of amazing discoveries, but ended up dying penniless and alone.'

'What a tragic story,' Tesla said, his gaze distant as he handed me back the mic.

'Hey, Cherie, Dom here again. I can't believe I'm talking to you.'

'Yeah, we've missed you too, kiddo,' she replied. "But before this all gets too mushy, we've got something real urgent to tell you and your friends. It's also the reason I've been working flat out to get this Valve Voice fixed up.'

'Which is?'

'I'll let Harry tell you as he's as twitchy as a jackrabbit since he started tracking it.'

'Hi, Dom. Yeah, we've got a feeling that bad news is coming our way,' Harry said.

A sliver of cold ran up my spine because I knew exactly what he was about to say.

'You've detected a pressure drop, haven't you?' I said.

'You're right. It first started near the Jackson airbase a few days ago, but nothing to raise any eyebrows initially. However, a few hours ago – *bam* – it dropped off the edge of the cliff, but not a storm cloud in sight. And we all know what that means, right?'

My stomach hollowed out. 'Yeah…'

'At first we thought it might be you guys coming home, but this is a way lower pressure than anything we've seen before. It's now at twenty inches and still heading south.'

Tesla shook his head and took the mic again. 'There is only one thing that would cause that level of disruption to atmospheric pressure – a massed fleet jump.'

I stared at him. 'You mean we're going to be too late to stop them?'

'No, I am not saying that. Just let me check my calculations.' He picked up a glass tablet and started scribbling glowing formulas on it with his wand.

But this was it – the start of a full-blown assault on my world. Nightmare images flooded my mind: fractures snaking out across the surface of the Earth from Oklahoma; the planet breaking apart like an egg; the shattered remains imploding into the massive wormhole that Fury would unleash. I didn't have an emotion big enough to even begin to cope with any of this, just an overpowering sense of numbness.

Everybody on the observation deck traded tight looks and their eyes skipped back to me. How do you break the news to someone that their planet is about to be blown out of existence?

'Let me tell them,' Louis said.

I shook my head and took the mic back from Tesla. 'No, they need to hear this from me. After all, it's my world we're talking about.'

He nodded. 'Of course, Dom Taylor.'

Everyone looked at me in silence. I could see what was replaying in their heads written across their haunted faces – the moment their own world was destroyed. In that moment something hardened inside me. Yes, the loss of *Helios* was a disaster, something I'd never ever forgive myself over, but like every Cloud Rider around me who'd found the strength to fight on, I would somehow do the same.

Harry's voice crackled over the speaker. 'Are you guys still there?'

Time for the truth – and not a sugar-coated version either. I owed them all that.

'Hi, Harry. You're right, the entire Hades armada, complete with a vast capital ship called *Kraken*, will be turning up on your doorstep any moment. And it gets worse.' I took a deep breath. 'On that ship they have a weapon they intend to destroy Earth with…'

At the other end, I heard voices all talking over each other at once.

Cherie cut through the hubbub. 'Will everyone quieten down and let Dom finish?'

The voices hushed again.

'But there's better news too. We've managed to get the Cloud Rider fleet back together and…' I gazed at Tesla, who'd finished scribbling some serious-looking maths calculations, and he nodded and gestured for the mic.

'According to my calculations, it will take a minimum of forty-eight hours for *Kraken*'s Vortex to power up sufficiently to allow Hades to jump the fleet in one go to your world,' Tesla said.

'You mean we still have a chance to outrun them and get there first?' Angelique asked.

Tesla nodded. 'With our smaller fleet we can jump far more quickly.'

'Thank the gods,' King Louis said.

'Looks as if we're going to be home before the bad guys turn up, Cherie,' I said.

She shouted over the whoops in the background, 'Now that sounds more like it!'

I turned to Louis. 'We need to launch right away.'

He gave a sharp nod. 'Captain Stephen, have you been listening in to all of this?'

'Yes, my king,' Stephen's voice replied.

'In that case, signal the fleet that we take off in five minutes.'

'Cherie, tell Mom to wipe away those tears and to get the coffee on – we're coming home,' I said.

'In that case you can give her that hug yourself,' she said.

A fierce ball of joy filled me. 'Roger that – over and out.'

CHAPTER TEN

FORGIVENESS

Deck twelve...at last. Angelique had told me this was the level in which I'd find Jules in the cabin, hiding herself away from the world.

I headed down a long, bending corridor, passing porthole after porthole, the views through them continually catching my attention. Tiny ant figures swarmed over each and every airship, pulling canvas covers off gun ports, carrying green ammunition crates into ships, others fitting battle blades to the airships' noses. The Cloud Rider fleet getting ready for war.

I reached the end of the corridor and pulled open a heavy, squealing bulkhead door. I walked out onto a metal walkway that ran just beneath the curving roof of one of *Hope's* numerous hangers.

Below me, lightning marines, already in their fly-dive suits, had stretched their drag chutes out onto the deck as they checked the control lines and fabric. Beyond them, dozens of small black craft, the ornicopters that Angelique had mentioned, squatted like black dragonflies on mechanical legs. Technicians in blue coveralls filled those ships' spherical fuel tanks from hose lines hanging down from the ceiling like creepers.

I spotted Stephen among the craft, directing the unfolding of transparent wings that shimmered with rainbow patterns under the numerous arc lights. He turned and his gaze snagged mine for a moment. Even at this range I could see the anger in his eyes. He turned his back to me like a wall.

Storm Wind's song thudded into my mind. Going by his tone, he sounded worked up.

Is there a problem, Storm Wind?

His voice pulsed and an image of *Helios* flooded my mind.

What?

His ship sped through the open door of the hangar, watched by everyone inside, including Stephen. He sped to a stop right next to me on the raised walkway.

I placed my hand on his Eye and his voice rushed into my head.

'Dom, I can hear Helios.*'*

But he's dead.

'It would seem not, my friend. His signal is faint but I have a definite lock on his position on the Earth where we last saw him.'

Joy rushed through me. 'Stephen, *Storm Wind* has made contact with *Helios!*' I shouted.

As his eyes snapped wide, everybody else stopped working to stare at me.

'Isabella, Roxanne…the rest of the crew?' he called back.

'Let me find out…'

I focused my attention on *Storm Wind* and closed my eyes as his song swelled in my mind.

I joined my voice to his and flowed away from my body, out from the hangar, from the fleet, from this reality, and headed back to the jungle world. The kaleidoscope of images started to slow and I recognised the pattern of neighbouring dimensions. Yes, it was the next one…

Pitch-blackness wrapped around me, far beyond normal night-time. What the heck was going on? I had to be in the wrong place. But *Storm Wind's* song strengthened and sang out into the darkness.

'*I am are here, my brother,*' *Helios* replied from somewhere in the gloom.

'*Mr Ghost, is that you?*' Isabella's voice said.

My heart leapt. She was alive – she really was alive!

Are you all okay?

'*Yes…but I'm very frightened.*'

I risked quickly opening my eyes to find Stephen now standing next to me on the walkway, his hands clenched together. 'They're all okay!'

Everyone apart from Stephen cheered. Instead he blinked once, twice, three-times – a hundred emotions flickering across his face in those few seconds.

'You're sure?' he asked.

I grabbed his shoulders. 'I am.'

He breathed through his nose fast, fighting back tears. And, just like that, the hostility in his eyes was snuffed out. 'By the gods, Dom, do whatever you have to do to help them.'

'Oh, don't worry, I intend to.' I shut my eyes and tuned back in before I lost the link.

This time I gave myself a moment, allowing my eyes to adjust to the darkness. I could just make out the dark forms of the jungle that I'd last seen Roxanne in. But the world of beauty and life had been transformed. At the base of the trees, dead forms of birds sprawled over the ground and the horse-like animals floated dead in the pool. In the distance a vague outline of mountains seemed to be swaying as if it were being shaken by an earthquake.

Even though my physical body was still standing in the hangar, a chill rippled over my skin. Something was wrong, very wrong.

A movement on the floor drew my gaze. Dark, shadowy shapes slipped between the blades of glass, flowing like eels over the jungle floor. The shapes all seemed to be moving towards a low hill peaking over the jungle canopy. On it, golden points of light shone out in the darkness surrounding the silhouette of *Helios*. Above the ship, the faint wavering form of a twister spun sluggishly in the air. I locked my consciousness onto it and sped towards *Helios*.

Helios, his engine pod shattered and with feeble sparks of blue energy jumping between his Vortex electrodes, lay stranded on top of the hill. The golden points of light I'd seen in the distance were coming from lanterns that had been anchored to the ground in a circle around the ship, as the wind whipped the grass flat around them. But it was the dark forms swirling beyond the perimeter of light that seized my attention. My heart rose to my mouth. It couldn't be them – not here, not in this world… Shadow crows, thousands of them, swarmed around the ship.

Isabella, where are you?

A figure in the darkened cabin waved at me and I zoomed towards her.

Isabella, trembling, put both hands back onto the Eye. Inside, the navigation glass globes flickered. Panels had been ripped from the floor and wiring looms had been pulled out.

Roxanne and several other Cloud Riders were busy with small gas soldering irons, reconnecting several severed wiring looms.

Isabella turned towards me. *The Shade have been trying to get us, Mr Ghost. Mama and the others set up the lights for protection.* Her sob filled my mind.

What happened, Isabella?

'I managed to bring us back to this world when I lost contact with you. But Mama hasn't been able to shut down our Vortex drive since we crash-landed and the Shade came through it, and into this world.

I looked at the shadow crows massing beyond the lanterns. *If I guide you, can you still take off?*

Isabella looked at me and shook her head, tears filling her eyes. She pointed out of a porthole to the wrecked engine.

Roxanne stared across at her daughter and said something to her that I couldn't hear in the silent movie beyond her daughter's words. Isabella nodded and pointed to where I was standing.

She grabbed a glass tablet and started writing on it, then held it up to me. It read:

'We've been able to hold the Shade off with the gas lanterns, but for some reason their light is getting dimmer. And when they go out…'

My imagination filled in the rest. There was no way I was going to let that happen.

Isabella, tell your mom that we're going to get you out of there somehow. I'll be back with help, just hang in there.

She gave me a terrified look but nodded. *'Yes, Mr Ghost.'*

With a rush of blood to my head, I heaved my consciousness back into the hangar.

Stephen stared at me. By him now stood Angelique and King Louis.

'You've really found *Helios*?' Louis asked.

'Yes, but they're in trouble. They crash-landed back on the jungle world, but they haven't been able to shut down their Vortex drive. Somehow the Shade broke through to the world and I don't think the crew can hold them off for much longer. To make matters worse, they've bust up their engine.'

Stephen stared at the king. 'We've got to go and help them.'

Louis's face became lined. 'Do I need to remind you, Captain Stephen, that we have a deadline to keep? Miss that and Dom's whole world could be lost.'

Stephen stared at him. 'Please…'

I felt as if I were being torn in two. 'We can't leave them to die.'

Angelique nodded. 'We could take the fleet via their position, pick them up, and then head on to Dom's Earth.'

'And that would also delay our arrival,' Louis replied. 'What should be a twenty-four-hour advantage would be cut down to twelve. And that may not give us enough time.'

'May…' Angelique said.

Louis rubbed his temples. 'Any delay is risky and I don't feel this a decision I should make. This is your world, Dom Taylor, so you should decide.'

Their eyes turned towards me. And not just them. Every Cloud Rider in the hangar seemed to be listening in, waiting for my response. This was an impossible decision. Could I risk everything I knew and loved because of one ship and his crew?

Stephen's pleading gaze burned into me. 'Dom, they're my only living relatives.'

I knew deep down I didn't have a choice. Not really. I certainly knew I would never be able to live with myself if I turned my back on Isabella and Roxanne at this moment. I knew that if Mom, Harry, Cherie or any of the others had been standing here, they would have agreed too. My resolve strengthened. It might not have been the best tactical decision, but it was the right one.

I stood taller, looking Stephen straight in the eyes. 'We'll make enough time to rescue them.'

In two steps Stephen closed the distance between us and pulled me into a tight hug. 'I don't know how I'll ever thank you.'

I pulled away and held him by the shoulders. 'We'll just have to make sure we kick Cronos's butt when he dares to show up in my world.'

He shoved his hand out. 'There, you have a deal.'

I grasped his hand and shook it. And, just like that, all the tension between us evaporated.

As the Cloud Riders in the hangar whooped and cheered, fresh hope flowed through me. Somehow we'd rescue Roxanne and I'd also nail my theta training. Even though the enemy heavily outnumbered us, they were no match for the spirit of the people inside this hanger and in the rest of our fleet. Cronos had no idea of the storm that he'd unleashed and that was headed his way. But best of all I couldn't wait to see the look on Jules's face when I told her the news.

CHAPTER ELEVEN

GONE

The Vortex energy walls shimmered past *Athena* as we travelled along the wormhole. Angelique sat in the captain's seat deep in conversation with King Louis over the Valve Voice set. They'd been talking Cloud Rider tactics, tactics and more tactics for the coming battle. But just as important for me was the plan we'd agreed before departing the desert world.

The main Cloud Rider fleet was going to head straight to my Earth in case Cronos had sent any ships ahead of his main attack group. Meanwhile our mission onboard *Athena* was to rescue *Helios* and her crew en route.

Jules spun her co-pilot chair towards me and gave me a wide smile. The broken girl of earlier had been swept away by the news that Isabella and Roxanne were alive.

For what felt like the hundredth time since we'd left the desert world, I wandered over to the Eye and placed my hands on it.

Isabella, can you hear us?

A low tone beeped in my mind. *Helios*'s carrier signal and nothing more. Voice contact with Isabella had gone dark after they'd lost power to their main systems. My initial euphoria had ebbed away, replaced by a knot of fear growing inside me. What if we didn't make it in time? What if we were already too late?

I opened my eyes to see Jules standing over me.

'Anything yet?' she asked.

'Still nothing.'

Angelique hung up the Valve Voice's mic and gazed at us. 'Just because *Helios* has lost his main power supply, doesn't mean they're not okay.'

'You didn't see the way the Shade were swarming around them like vultures.'

Jules nodded and bit her lip. 'Angelique, have the Shade ever broken through into a parallel dimension before?'

'Until now, the Shade have only existed beyond the Void in our fairy tales as nightmare creatures.'

'A nightmare that has somehow escaped into the real world,' I said.

A troubled look filled Angelique's face and she gazed past me at the Eye and the lit planets of our fleet.

I headed to the rear of the gondola and gazed out through a clear panel in the ornate glass window.

Around us, the wormholes of the rest of the fleet carved their routes like a hundred glowing silk threads through the emptiness of the Void, all headed one way – Earth DZL2351. My Earth. My home.

The largest trail rippled behind *Hope*. Stowed onboard him for the journey was *Storm Wind* in his new ship, which didn't have its own Vortex drive in order to travel.

Jules wandered over to sit by me and gazed out at the fleet. Her home too…

I pictured Mom rushing out from the diner and gazing up at the twister waiting for us to emerge from it. But my imagination kept the movie running… The sky kept growing darker, the Vortex twister bigger. Then, instead of *Athena*, it was *Kraken* that edged out from the tornado, lightning playing around it as the Fury weapon got ready to—

A nudge in my side pulled my thoughts back.

Jules gazed at me, eyes questioning. 'What are you thinking?'

'You mean you can't tell for once?'

She tilted her head to one side. 'Maybe I can, or maybe I can't. But I'm pretty sure that either way you need to talk about it.'

Yeah, Jules was right – I did, I really did. 'I'm just thinking of home…' My words trailed away.

'You're worried we may have a very short homecoming, right?'

She'd nailed it in one. I tipped my head back and pressed it against the glass. 'Exactly.'

'Dom…' She reached over and placed her hand on mine. 'We can win this.'

I dropped my voice to a whisper so Angelique wouldn't hear. 'You mean, we *have* to win this. You do realise just how stacked against us the odds are?'

'I know, but…' Jules gestured out through the windows at the luminous threads of the fleet all around us. 'If anyone can stop Cronos, it's going to be our friends out there. But perhaps the key reason that I'm so confident team Cloud Riders will kick Cronos's butt is…' she reached over and wrapped her hand around mine… 'because of you.'

I concentrated on the flecks of amber in her brown eyes, trying to ignore the dark images threatening my imagination. 'I hope I can live up to your belief, Jules.'

She flashed me a smile. 'I know so.'

I appreciated her vote of confidence, even if I didn't share it in myself. 'We'll see…'

She tilted her head to one side. 'Anyway, enough with me being nice. I should still be furious with you about letting me sleep through all the excitement.'

'Hey, I woke you eventually and told you.'

'S'pose.'

'And you did need to catch on your beauty sleep.'

She flashed me her pixie grin. 'You think I'm beautiful then?'

I knew she was trying to lighten the mood and I appreciated it… I needed it. I smiled at her. 'Stop fishing.'

Although Angelique had her back to us, I could tell she was listening into this conversation. I knew I would've been.

But the thing was, when Jules looked at me like that, her eyes so wide and clear, I did think she was a beautiful person in every sense of the word.

The buzz of my mind slowed and I felt like a guy who'd just made it through the fog to the top of a tall mountain and was seeing the incredible view for the first time. Everything seemed clearer. The confusion Angelique had stirred up in me was just noise, nothing more.

I gazed at the princess's golden hair flowing down her back. Yes, she was an amazing person – my friend, a truly great one – but it was Jules Eastwood, and her pixie smile, who was my everything and would be all my tomorrows – if we had them.

Jules peered at me? 'What?'

I bit back a smile. 'Nothing – I'm good.'

'Okay…' She gazed out at the shimmering void walls skimming past *Athena* and a frown creased her forehead.

'Now it's my turn to ask what you're thinking.'

'I'm just glad I'm off the hook for messing up.'

I shook my head. 'It wasn't your fault, it was mine.'

She chewed a nail. 'That's not how I see it.'

A chime came from the control console.

We all exchanged glances. This was it – we were about to reach the rendezvous point.

'See you on Earth DLZ2351,' King Louis said over the Valve Voice.

Jules gestured to the mic. 'Do you mind if I use that, Angelique?'

'Be my guest.'

She took it and pressed the button on the side. 'Please send everyone back home our love, won't you?'

I knew what she was doing: a final message in case we didn't make it.

'Of course we will,' the king said.

I felt a surge of love for Jules. Despite her fear, the guilt that had eaten her up, she was one of the bravest people I knew.

'May the gods fly with you,' King Louis said.

Angelique took the mic from Jules. 'And with you, Papa. Over and out.' She placed her hands on the wheel. 'Okay, Dom, get ready to shut down our Vortex field.'

I nodded and crossed to the lever.

The ships' chorus grew stronger, singing in duet with *Athena*.

Angelique smiled at me. 'The ships are saying *au revoir* to us.'

Jules peered between us. 'That's French for "till we meet again", right?'

'Yes – another one of the few phrases I know.'

I remembered how the first time we'd met Angelique she'd tried to convince us she was French rather than a visitor from a parallel dimension. Innocent moments that seemed a lifetime ago.

Our glowing wormhole thread started to curve away from the

rest of the fleet and their collective song faded as we sped away until *Athena*'s voice sang out alone into the Void.

An alarm sounded in the cockpit.

Angelique gazed at the control console and frowned. 'That's strange.'

'What is?' I asked.

She pointed towards a series of numbers spinning down to zero on the console. 'According to Athena's instruments, we're rapidly approaching the exit, but I can't see the event horizon into their reality.'

I peered out through the windshield, but a lack of exit wasn't the only thing that looked wrong out there. The walls of the wormhole, which a moment ago had been strobing with brilliant light, were now little more than a faint cobweb of energy.

Jules scowled. 'It looks like our Vortex field is collapsing too.'

Angelique shook her head. 'But that's impossible. In theory, nothing can affect it.'

The warbling alarm grew shriller.

'Whatever the theory says, something's definitely wrong with our Vortex field,' Jules said. She peered ahead. 'Hey, Angelique, can you kill the lights for a moment?'

Angelique shot her a questioning look, but flicked a switch. The chandelier blinked out and plunged us into darkness.

Then I saw it dead ahead of us: a perfect circle of nothingness with not even a hint of light. I gestured towards it. 'There's your exit.'

But as I studied it I realised something was wrong… It looked more like a black hole than the exit to another Earth. Before I could voice my concern we rushed it and the air locked in my throat. Instead of a jungle world, all I could see beyond the flickering walls of the Vortex was unbroken darkness.

'Kill the drive, Dom,' Angelique whispered.

I pressed the red switch and the crackle of our lightning died away. We all stared out into the nothingness.

Angelique flicked on some large arc lights on *Athena*'s nose. Their beams stabbed out into the gloom.

'Guys – did we take a wrong turning or something?' Jules asked.

Angelique scanned the readouts. 'No, these are definitely the right coordinates.'

I rubbed the back of my neck. 'But how can it be so dark out there? Even if it's night, shouldn't there be a bit of sky glow or something from the surrounding villages?'

Jules nodded. 'This looks more as if we've just dropped down into a deep mine.'

A new warbling alarm joined the first as ice began to build up on the gondola's windows. Angelique stared at a panel that had started flashing red. 'We are bleeding our cabin air rapidly. The indicators would suggest that we've jumped into a vacuum.'

'As in space?' I asked.

'That's what the numbers are telling me,' Angelique replied.

Jules's scream made us both jump.

'Look out there.' She pointed a shaking finger at the beams of our search lights.

We both stared at the spot. Something dark sped through the beam, sparking as it passed through. It was followed by another and another.

Shadow crows – hundreds of thousands of them – swarmed around *Athena* and raked the beams with blazing claws.

I gasped. 'We're still in the Void!'

'But how can that be even possible?' Jules asked.

Angelique flicked the lights back on. 'I have no idea, but we've got to get out of here while we still can.'

My mind stuttered. 'But what about Isabella, Roxanne and the others?' I pointed to the green light on the dash. 'And *Helios* is still broadcasting his carrier signal.'

'An automated distress beacon,' Angelique replied.

I shook my head, not wanting to confront what was staring me in the face. The only song I could hear was *Athena's*... I balled my hands into fists.

Jules stared at us. 'But surely we can spare a few minutes for Dom to scan for them through *Athena's* Eye.'

Angelique sucked her cheeks in and slowly nodded. 'Alright, but if we're going to do that we're going to have to put pressure suits on, otherwise we'll be dead in minutes.'

I shot Jules a grateful look. 'Done.'

Angelique and Jules crossed to the locker and started hauling out the flight suits.

I pressed my palms to the Eye. *Okay*, Athena, *we're on the clock here. It's down to us to find your brother*. My brain started to tingle as her voice appeared among my thoughts.

'I am afraid the Void is blocking my sensor net, Whisperer.'

Please try... My fingernails clawed onto the metal surface of the Eye.

Frost had already started to creep across the inside of the windows. I shivered as the warmth leached away from my body. I screwed up my eyes, trying to ignore the freezing cold, and wove my mind around *Athena's* sensors.

In a rush of light, I found myself floating outside the cabin. Thousands of shadow crows flocked around *Athena*, weaving between the needle beams of her spotlights, their abstract shapes forming and breaking apart as they flew past. Inside the gondola, a lonely golden sun in this abyss, I could see Jules and Angelique pulling on their pressure suits, as the other Dom knelt by the Eye.

Where are you, Helios?

A nearby single shadow crow started to turn in a slow circle. It pulled its wings in and dived straight towards where I was hovering in the Void.

Breathing fast, I instinctively ducked, readying myself for the slice of its claws, but instead it sped straight past me and headed onwards to attack one of the beams of our searchlights.

As a sense of relief flooded me, I saw the other Dom inside the gondola drop his shoulders. I was obviously invisible to the Shade out here.

Angelique and Jules now had their helmets on and were pulling out a third suit for me. If we could survive in the Void by wearing pressure suits, maybe *Helios*'s crew could too…

I drifted away from *Athena,* like an astronaut on a spacewalk. The suffocating darkness clamped around me and the ship's drumbeat song grew quieter. The further I travelled, the more the Void felt as if I were wading out into black treacle.

Helios, *are you out here?*

Nothing.

Isabella, if you can hear me, we're here to rescue you.

Athena's voice faded into silence as I drifted away from her. Everything about this place shouted wrongness to me, somewhere that something alive was never meant to be in. I was alone. It would be so easy to let go and drown in the Void…

Come on, Dom, concentrate. I breathed deeply, like I learnt to with my theta training, and a sense of peace started to roll my fear away. I felt myself slowly expanding, as if I were growing into a giant within this sea of blackness.

Isabella?

My bubble of consciousness pushed outwards and then... It was the barest smudge in the dark far below me. Could it be? I concentrated and started to make out a faint oval shape...

Helios! I plummeted towards him like a diving hawk, but glided to halt when I saw the gondola's cabin was dark and his propellers were motionless. A ring of lanterns floated around him, casting a feeble light over the ship. A vast swarm of shadow crows circled lazily around him, the *vultures* waiting for their dinner.

My pulse amped. Please, god, let them be alright. I hurtled into the gondola.

Inside, the crew, all wearing pressure suits, were slumped in their seats. Dead? But then I spotted their chests barely rising and falling. No, not dead – unconscious. Then a small figure with a hand on the Eye slowly raised her head towards me.

'Mr Ghost...'

Isabella! My heart felt as if it would burst. *What happened?*

'Mama left this message for you...' She pushed a glowing tablet across the floor towards me.

I read Roxanne's scrawled words:

'The Void has consumed the planet around us. If you read this in time, if you can do nothing else, please save my daughter. I have topped up her oxygen supply but she won't last much longer.'

None of them would... My mind whirled. The Shade had done all of this. Destroyed a whole planet.

Isabella's eyelids fluttered behind her faceplate and her head slumped back onto the floor.

No! I yanked my consciousness back to *Athena* and opened my eyes. The freezing air in the gondola burned my lungs as Angelique's and Jules's helmet-framed faces peered down at me.

'I've found *Helios*. He's drifting directly below us. The crew are alive but, apart from Isabella, all unconscious and running out of air.'

Angelique blinked and gave me a sharp nod. 'Okay, suit up before you freeze to death, and leave the rest to me.'

My breath billowed and my hands shook as Jules helped me put the suit on, her face smoothing with relief.

'Dom, you keep seriously impressing me,' she said.

'I try my best,' I said, teeth chattering.

Angelique shoved a button on the console. Two eyepieces extended up from it and a screen lowered from the roof. With a hum, a green phosphorescent target appeared with a view of the nothingness outside. Angelique pulled a lever and all our spotlights converged. In their beams the faint shape of *Helios* appeared on one side of the screen.

'What are you doing?' I asked as Jules pulled the gauntlets over my frozen hands.

'Giving them a tow.'

Angelique scooped her hair back over her shoulders and placed her head to the eyepieces. She took a deep breath and took hold of a joystick, then became very still, the only movement her fingertips finely adjusting the control.

'Steady, steady...' she whispered to herself.

Gears whirred beneath the gondola as the target reticule crawled towards *Helios*.

Angelique extended her thumb forward over a trigger, as still as a cat about to pounce.

I found myself holding my breath as she pulled the trigger.

A loud hiss came from below us. On the screen a grab claw shot away from *Athena* like a harpoon, trailing rope behind it.

Jules lowered the helmet over my head, cutting out my view of the screen for a moment.

'Seven hundred feet, eight hundred feet, nine…' Angelique said.

Jules turned a knob on my suit and air hissed into it, making my ears pop.

The claw smacked into *Helios*'s gas envelope with a shudder.

I let the air out of my lungs in a rush. 'Nice shooting,' I said into my helmet's mic through chattering teeth.

Angelique beamed at me. 'Now let's save the lives of every soul onboard that ship.' She pressed a button in the cockpit.

I heard a whine from beneath us and saw the line snap taught on the monitor. A slight shudder passed through *Athena*'s gondola.

'Looks as if we caught ourselves a whale,' Jules said. She reached for a control on my suit's right arm. 'Now let's get you defrosted, Dom. We can't have our hero getting frostbite.' She turned the knob and heat washed over my frozen skin.

'Yeah, I'm rather attached to my fingers and toes.'

She leant in and gently bumped her helmet against mine. 'Yeah, so am I.'

Minute by minute, and accompanied by its circling flock of shadow crows, the ice-covered gas envelope of *Helios* crawled towards us, beginning to fill the monitor screen.

'Three, two, one…' Angelique whispered. Another gentle shudder and *Athena*'s voice soared. *Helios* echoed hers with a feeble response.

Angelique rushed to the Eye and placed her hands on it. 'Dom, power up the Vortex.' With a shimmer of air she started to become transparent as she shifted.

I grabbed the lever and shoved it down. With a dull clang the ring of electrodes shot out around the gondola and at once blue lightning began to arc between them. I couldn't help noticing that they looked really feeble compared to normal. The Shade swarmed around us like angry wasps.

'Our Vortex field looks kinda unstable,' I said.

'I'm on it.' Jules dropped into the captain's seat. 'Increasing the power to overload.' She spun a dial on the cockpit.

With a boom of thunder the lightning blazed around us and burned the Shade close by to ashes. The gondola shook as the wormhole walls around us started to grow stronger.

I pressed my face to a window and peered down to see *Helios* safely docked beneath us, our Vortex field extended around both ships.

Angelique raised her transparent eyebrows towards Jules. 'When did you learn that particular trick?'

'Oh, you'd be surprised what I've picked up from Tesla. That man's a regular genius.'

'You have your moments too,' I said.

Jules flashed me a smile through her visor. 'Oh, you do know how to sweet talk a girl.' Her eyes widened. 'And now we're going home, Dom.'

Mom's smiling face filled my imagination. 'Yes – yes we are, Jules.'

But as the Void disappeared beyond our twister walls, a thought struck me. The Shade had destroyed an Earth teaming with life, and if that could happen there, could it happen to other worlds too? The sense of unease took hold as we started to speed away from the dark world towards Earth DZL2351, also known as home.

CHAPTER TWELVE

ARRIVAL

With *Helios* lashed securely below us, we sped down the cascading tunnel of light. We'd all watched the monitor feed from the gondola of the other ship like an unfolding TV drama...

Angelique had fired an air hose into *Helios's* gondola and transferred our oxygen reserves through it. As the fresh air had been pumped into their ship, Roxanne, the first of the unconscious to wake, had gradually been able to rouse the rest of the crew. Although some needed treatment, the bulk of the Cloud Riders seemed to be okay, particularly Isabella, who kept waving at the camera, her face one enormous smile.

I noticed Jules's gaze fixed on the Vortex walls shimmering past. She looked a million miles away.

'A penny for them?' I asked.

She locked her hands behind her head and slowly spun in her chair. 'Just thinking about what happened back in that reality we rescued them from.'

'You mean, how can a whole planet simply disappear like that?'

She nodded.

'Yeah, that's been bugging me too.'

Angelique tore her gaze away from the monitor. 'I've never heard of anything happening like this before. Yes, the Shade have attacked our ships on occasion, but their territory has always been in the Void.'

'So what's changed that?' Jules asked.

I felt the answer itching at the back of my skull. I tried to pull the fragments together… 'The Void exists in the space between the dimensions, right?'

Angelique wound her fingers through her hair. 'Yes, and…?'

I needed to demonstrate what my mind was stumbling towards and noticed the wash basin in the galley. I filled it almost to the brim with water from the faucet.

'Thinking of freshening up?' Jules crinkled her nose at me. 'You could certainly do with it.'

'Thanks for that.'

She grinned.

'Imagine the Void is the water in this basin and the parallel universes are the sides of the basin keeping it in place.'

'Okay, still not with you…' Jules replied, frowning.

But Angelique had started to slowly nod. 'I think I understand where you are heading with this, Dom.'

I smiled. 'Imagine this bowl has sprung a leak.' I deliberately slopped some water over the side, but hadn't spotted Jules had stretched her legs out. The liquid splashed over her legs.

She leapt up and brushed her hands over her soaked jeans. 'Dom!'

I held up my hands. 'My bad, Jules.'

She dropped onto the bench seat at the rear of the gondola. 'Just as well I love you, isn't it?'

The expression on Angelique's face flickered for a moment, but held. Jules hadn't seemed to notice. Her attention was on me.

Once again I felt as if I was walking over glass shards whenever the three of us were together. This was getting crazy. I needed to man up and talk things through with Angelique to clear the air. The longer I delayed it, the more awkward moments like this would get.

I coughed. 'Yeah… So as I was saying… Imagine that the spilt water is the Void. It leaked into that universe because they couldn't shut down their Vortex drive.'

Angelique narrowed her gaze. 'That makes a lot of sense. And if the Void leaked into the universe, like boats in floodwater, it carried the Shade along with it.'

Jules drummed her fingers on the stained glass windowsill. 'Okay, if that's true, here's the thing. If it can happen there, who's to say it couldn't in any other universe?'

'Exactly what I've been worried about.' I peered out through a porthole at the wormhole walls. 'We haven't seen a single shadow crow beyond the walls.'

'No wonder, they were too busy with an *all you can eat buffet* back in the universe we left behind,' Jules said.

'The sooner we tell Tesla about this the better.'

Angelique pointed to the coordinates spinning down to zero. 'Which shouldn't be much longer.' She took hold of the wheel.

I joined Jules as a soft glow started to build outside, the light of my home world. I felt a hand on mine and glanced down to see she'd wrapped her fingers around mine.

'I'm excited and nervous, all at the same time,' she said.

'Yeah, me too.'

'After everything we've been through, I can't wait to see everyone. But...'

'But?'

She peered through a clear panel in the window at the pool of light that had become a framed circle of fields rushing towards us. 'What if we fail, Dom?'

I squeezed her hand and did my best to give her a reassuring look. 'We can't let ourselves fail...'

'No, I guess we can't.'

Twister walls billowed around the framed eye of the storm, with our Earth at the centre.

Jules bounced on her feet. 'Home sweet home.'

Angelique nodded. 'Okay, we're approaching the event horizon. Get ready to shut down the Vortex drive, Dom.'

I crossed over to the controls, barely able to believe that in a few minutes I'd been breathing sweet Oklahoma air.

We hurtled through into the glowing heart of the tornado spiralling around us. I pressed the red kill button of the Vortex drive and the crackle of lightning fizzled away from the electrodes ringing the gondola. At once, the twister started unravelling around us and, through the gaps in the spinning tornado, rays of sunrise bathed our cabin with amber light.

As the cloud unravelled, I took in the familiar pattern of fields, the reassuring flat landscape stretching away as if someone had run an iron over it. I felt myself welling up at the sight of my old house, the hangar and Twister Diner. But that building had been gutted by fire, a leaving present from Duke Ambra, and now had scaffolding all around it. It seemed Harry had made good on his word about helping Mom to get the family business back on its feet.

In our car lot, among the Sky Hawks vehicles, stood Harry's

motorhome and Cherie's bright-scarlet storm-chasing vehicle, the Battle Wagon Mark Two.

I scanned for the rest of the Cloud Rider fleet, but I couldn't see them. However, the chorus of a hundred ships told me they were there. Their voices wrapped around us in welcome and joy as *Helios* and *Athena* responded in kind.

The air rippled and something sped past the windshield like a meteor and then banked towards us.

Storm Wind looped and spun around us like a swallow soaring through the sky.

Angelique laughed as he buzzed within inches of our gondola, his song ecstatic. 'Looks as if the other ships have gone in cloaked to avoid drawing too much attention.'

I raised my eyebrows. 'As though arriving in a twister isn't a big enough advertisement.'

Jules snorted as the Valve Voice started to hum. She began to fiddle with its dial.

Stephen's voice burst from the radio set. 'You saved them!'

'Yep, and there's a certain sister and niece who can't wait to see you,' Jules replied.

The whoops and cheers were so loud on the radio that they threatened to break the speaker.

'I will never in a thousand lifetimes be able to thank you enough for this,' Stephen said. 'But first I have someone here desperate to speak to Dom.'

Jules smiled at me. 'Understood.' She handed the mic over.

'Dom?' Mom's voice said.

The tears I'd being trying to hold in broke from my eyes. 'Hi, Mom…'

I heard her burst into sobs at the other end. 'Yeah, I love you too, Mom.'

Roddy's voice cut in. 'Can I have a word with my daughter, Dom?'

'Sure.' I held the mic to her mouth.

Jules's eyes sparkled, happiness almost glowing through her skin.

'Yeah, Dad, I'm here…' She flapped her hand over her face as her tears started to spill too.

'Will you look at the two of you,' Angelique said with a wide smile.

'Yeah, tell me about it, one big mushy mess,' I said.

'So let's get you both down on the ground so you can carry on your family reunion in person.' Angelique crossed to the Eye and placed her hands on it. 'Okay, *Athena*, with all the ships cloaked you'd better take us in so we don't crash into them.'

Her ship-song swelled and the choir of the hidden fleet rose to meet *Athena*'s. She began to descend faster, banking hard enough to force us all to suddenly hold on.

Angelique's mouth twitched as the ship's wheel spun by itself. 'She's showing off to *Storm Wind* – making it clear he's not the only one who can carve up the sky.'

'Yep, part ancient beings, part regular teenagers,' I said.

Angelique and Jules laughed.

Below us a woman ran from the house towards the middle of the meadow… Mom. She was followed by a sprinting man in coveralls.

Jules squealed. 'There's my dad!'

As Roddy and Mom waved up at us, *Athena* steered us straight towards them.

'I think we have our landing zone.' I wrapped my arm around Jules's waist.

Angelique's gaze snagged on us, but not missing a beat she smiled. 'In that case, let's get this reunion under way.'

* * *

Mom and I hugged each other hard as Jules and Roddy did the same, but hanging onto each other as if they were never going to let go ever again. Harry and Cherie appeared with the Sky Hawks to form a ring around us. My back was slapped so many times, I felt sure it must be bruised and Harry's bear hug came pretty close to cracking my ribs.

Around us, Cloud Riders with medic insignias on their sleeves flowed past. I saw one pull some healing Chi stones out of a medical bag as they headed into *Helios*'s gondola. Stephen, Angelique and King Louis were already onboard, tending to the crew.

Mom pulled away from me and held my face in her hands. Emotions crowded her eyes, but most of all it was a fierce, burning love. 'I've been so worried about you, Dom. I've barely slept a wink since you've been gone.'

'I'm sorry, Mom.'

'For what?' She gestured to Jules hanging onto Roddy and sobbing into his shoulder. 'I'm so proud of you that I'm fit to burst.'

'Please don't – it would make heck of a mess.' I gave her my crooked smile.

She tussled my hair and laughed.

There was so much to tell her…to tell all of them. But where to begin? My visit to Floating City to meet *Titan* where I learnt that I was some sort of chosen one to the airships; the fight to the death with Duke Ambra in the basin of an erupting volcano; a thousand stories in between. But as I gazed at her I knew there was only one story that really mattered.

'Mom, there's something you need to know about Dad…' My throat choked up.

Over Roddy's shoulder, Jules's gaze swivelled towards me. She gave me an encouraging nod.

Tears filled Mom's eyes and she rubbed my cheek with her hand as if she were trying to rub away a mark. 'There's no need to, my love. King Louis explained what that monster Emperor Cronos did to Shaun. I didn't quite follow everything he said, but I understood enough to realise how awful it must be for Dad.'

A man in living agony, whose mind had been trapped in the Hive. Awful couldn't even begin to describe what he had to be going through. 'Somehow we'll free him, Mom,' I said.

Her gaze searched my face. 'You really believe we can, Dom?'

I caught the tight look that Jules shot me. I tried to arrange my face as though I really believed what I was about to say. 'Of course I do. Haven't you noticed all the help we brought home with us?' I gestured at the vague shimmering outlines of airships stretched out all around.

Mom almost managed a smile. 'You certainly don't do things by halves, do you?'

I shrugged. 'If you're going to do a job you might as well do it properly.'

She leant in and kissed me on the cheek.

Stephen appeared from *Helios*'s gondola with Isabella in his arms as he supported a limping Roxanne.

As they neared us Isabella raised her head to peek at me over her teddy bear. Her mouth curled into a line. 'Mr Ghost... But you're not a ghost any more.'

I reached out and cradled her face with my hand. 'No, I'm not. It's wonderful to finally meet you in person, Miss Isabella. You are one brave girl.'

Her serious look was swept away by a smile. 'Yes, I suppose I am.'

Roxanne kissed her daughter's head and gazed at me. 'If it wasn't for you, Dom, none of us would be alive.'

Mom looked between us, her expression full of questions.

Stephen raised his gaze to mine. 'Dom Taylor, I owe you an apology for my previous behaviour.'

'No you don't. I'm just sorry for the mess I caused in the first place.'

He shook his head. 'You shouldn't. I know you did your very best.' He reached out and shook my hand with both of his. 'If there is anything, anything, that I can ever do for you, all you need to do is ask.'

I returned his smile. 'I sure will.'

As he walked away with the others towards our house, which had apparently become a Cloud Rider field camp surrounded by tents and map tables, Mom looked on after them. 'What was that all about?'

Jules raised her shoulders. 'It's a long story.'

'One that you can tell us all about while we get you fed. I've got a slow-cooked lamb casserole on the stove with both your names on it. Of course, I've been having to fend Harry and Cherie off from eating it.'

Cherie wrinkled her nose. 'Hey, Sue, it's not our fault that it's flooded the house with gorgeous smells all day, and made me as hungry as a racoon.'

The thought of Mom's home cooking suddenly made me realise just how hungry I was too.

The look on Jules's face was as though she'd just been given the keys to the gates of heaven. 'I'm sure there'll be enough for everyone knowing Sue.'

Mom chuckled. 'How did you guess?'

The warmth of everyone settled over me like a comforting blanket. It wasn't just great to be home – it was fantastic.

I glanced up at the sky and watched the specks of swallows swoop and catch flies in the light of a new morning.

But how long did we have left till Cronos ripped up our sky with his war fleet? Pushing the dark thought away, I wrapped my arm around Mom's shoulders and we headed after the others towards the house.

CHAPTER THIRTEEN

COUNCIL OF WAR

Jules and I feasted on Mom's food as if we'd never eaten. Despite all the food I'd come across during my travels, hers still tasted the best.

As we ate we told our stories till our tonsils burned. Even so, we could've carried on talking forever, both of us wanting the buzz of the happiness of being back home to last, but it was King Louis and Angelique who eventually broke up the party. They summoned us all to a final war council and, just like that, our smiles were swept away.

We followed them to the middle of a room onboard *Hope* that I'd never seen before. It was a large circular auditorium, its stepped seating – packed with airship captains, friends and family – encircling a raised stage where Jules and I stood with King Louis, Angelique and Tesla, who fiddled with a control panel on a lectern.

Mom and Roddy sat in the front row, flanked by Harry and Cherie and the rest of the Sky Hawks. Mom kept giving me small window-wiping waves, as if I were six again and back in a school nativity play. I half expected her to whip out a camera at any moment.

Tesla turned a dial and a projector with lenses descended from the ceiling.

I wrapped an arm around Jules's waist and she tucked into me. I caught Mom and Roddy watching us. They quickly looked away, but smiled at each other. It seemed we had their approval at least.

The lights dimmed and a beam of light shot out of the projector. 'We should've brought popcorn,' I said.

The smile on Jules's lips died as a map of Oklahoma appeared over the round stage floor on which we stood. The reason we were all gathered here came back into sharp focus.

Tesla pushed one of the buttons on the lectern. With a hiss, holes started to open in the stage and glass planets, lit with green lights, rose on thin metal rods all over the map.

'It's a massive Eye computer,' I said.

Angelique shook her head. 'No, this an auxiliary battle computer used to plan war strategies.'

'Whatever it is, it looks awesome,' Jules said.

The green glowing planets slid into position. A much larger hole opened next to us and we had to step aside as a Cloud Rider ship marker, at least ten times the size of any of the others, rose into position high over the rest.

'That has to be *Hope*,' Jules said.

I looked around the room for Stephen, but couldn't see him. Probably still in the infirmary with his sister.

Tesla peered over the lectern at the audience. 'Based on our knowledge of Cronos's battle tactics, together with information we managed to retrieve from *Hope*'s memory archives, I've been able to decipher Hades attack patterns.' He leant across and pressed another button on the control panel.

The map zoomed in and, with a whir of hidden cogs, the Cloud

Rider ships moved further apart to compensate. Jules and I danced aside as the baubles of light moved past us.

I recognised the layout of the Jackson air force base down the road, which now filled the map.

'We know from our friends the Sky Hawks about the enormous pressure drop over this area. I am afraid this is indicative of the Hades enhanced Vortex drive building for a massed fleet jump to this world.'

Harry and Cherie nodded to the airship captains around them.

'And it can only be a matter of hours till *Kraken* jumps here with the entire Hades fleet in tow.'

Across the map, red spheres appeared from the copper plate and began rising on their poles. Although I'd known Cronos had ten times the number of ships that we had, seeing the thousand red, glowing glass globes massively outnumbering the sizeable Cloud Rider fleet in front of me stole the breath from my lungs. And if that wasn't bad enough, a massive sphere sat at the middle of the Hades formations with a marker at least three times the size of *Hope*'s.

Kraken.

Several of the captains around me gasped. It seemed I wasn't alone in being struck by the scale of the fight we were taking on.

'When Hades jump to this Earth, we will need to keep our vessels clear until the *Kraken*'s massive Vortex field has dissipated,' Tesla said.

The tight knot of Hades ships rotated around the large marker, like planets orbiting their sun. King Louis walked between the markers of both sides, tapping his lips as if he were considering a chess move.

The room fell silent. I knew what was decided in here would have implications for all of us...for my whole world.

Louis finally lifted his gazed back to his audience. 'As you can see, this will be the biggest battle that the Cloud Riders have ever faced.'

A female airship captain with red hair raised her hand. Louis nodded towards her.

'Are you planning to attack *Kraken* in a mass assault, my king?'

Louis shook his head. 'No, Lady Samantha, and here is the reason...' He gestured towards Tesla.

Tesla pushed a button. 'You described our alpha attack pattern, the first strategy we considered.'

At once the hundred Cloud Rider ships rushed towards *Kraken*. But the Hades ships were already responding in a choreographed dance move, closing their ranks around *Kraken* until there wasn't a gap to be seen. One by one, the Cloud Rider globes shuddered as they crashed into the Hades airship barrier and were taken out, dropping on their poles back into the floor. The action played out for another minute as the Cloud Rider ships smashed themselves like breaking waves onto a rocky shore. *Hope* was the final ship to be hit by a huge barrage of at least a hundred Hades craft.

Sweat trickled down my back as Jules's hand gripped mine. Game over. My world over.

Every captain craned forward to take in the view, their dark expressions saying it all. Opposite me, Roddy had his arm around Mom's shoulder as they both stared at the *Kraken* globe, grim-faced.

Louis's gaze swept over the audience. 'As you can see in this scenario, even though our fleet took out three times the number of Hades vessels with them, it still wasn't enough to break through their barricade and destroy *Kraken*.'

Jules shoved her hand into the air.

'Yes?' Louis asked.

'But what about our chameleon nets – surely they must give us some tactical advantage?'

'They do, but I'm afraid we have already factored in their effect and that is exactly what you just saw in this simulation,'Tesla replied.

'So what do we do?' I asked.

Angelique walked around the edge of the simulation until she was standing in front of me. 'I have discussed this at length with King Louis. We have run countless simulations that've led us to one conclusion.'

'Which is?' I asked.

'That we need to keep our ships spread out so we don't present easy targets, using the skill of our captains and ships to make constant rapid strikes at the Hades fleet.'

It sounded like one of coach's briefings for a football game – something I could get my head around.

Roddy stood. 'But what about this Fury weapon of theirs that we've heard so much about? What's to stop Cronos powering up that bad boy up straight away and blasting us all to kingdom come before you've had even a chance to fire a single shot?'

Tesla shook his head. 'After they appear, it will take them a while for their weapon generator to spin up to full power. That will give us a window of opportunity in which to destroy *Kraken*.'

Light briefly flooded the room from the doorway before the door was closed again.

Stephen, Roxanne by his side, walked down the steps into the auditorium. She looked way different to the woman I'd seen on the verge of suffocation. Bright eyed and standing tall, her gaze found mine and a smile lit up her face as she nodded towards me.

'Shouldn't you still be resting?' Angelique asked her as they squeezed into the seats by Mom and Roddy.

'That is what I tried to tell her, my Princess,' Stephen said, frowning at his sister.

'And as I told you, dear brother, we need every airship captain to make themselves available for this battle.'

He scowled at her but I could see the pride in his eyes. I just wished Danrick were here for this moment too.

Louis smiled and his gaze travelled on around the auditorium. 'You can all see for yourselves the futility of a direct assault. It would be doomed. Princess Angelique and I ran countless battle scenarios until we eventually arrived at what we are calling the Omega strategy. But I must ask that you do not divulge what you are about to see to your crews, for reasons of morale, until the battle starts.'

'I don't like the sound of this,' Jules whispered to me as all the captains exchanged questioning looks.

'Me neither.'

The king nodded to Tesla again. 'Please run the Omega pattern.'

The green planets rose back out of the floors and all the markers returned to their starting position. At first the battle went better…a lot better. This time the green pyramids swooped and dived as individual crafts, each striking at a single Hades craft, destroying it and then diving away untouched.

Stephen gazed at *Hope* which, once again, had been left out of the assault on the Hades ships and only floated high over the main battle. He raised his hand.

'Pause simulation,' King Louis said to Tesla.

The scientist pressed a button and the dance of distraction ground to a hissing halt.

'My king, there is one thing I don't understand in all these strategies. Why aren't you using *Hope* in the front line of our attacks, especially as she has so much available firepower at her disposal?'

Louis shook his head. 'You, Captain Stephen, will have the responsibility of keeping *Hope* out of the firefight for as long as possible.'

'But why, my king?'

'To maximise the impact of our ornicopter squadrons and lightning marines onboard *Hope*. Your mission is to protect *Hope* until the time to deploy them has come.'

'And then what?' Stephen asked.

King Louis exchanged a silent look with him that I couldn't quite decipher.

Stephen nodded. 'Of course, my king.'

Roxanne gave him a grim look.

Angelique gazed at her dad. 'And how do you propose we best use the ornicopter squadron, Papa?'

'Together with the lightning marines, their agility may be pivotal to the outcome in terms of whether we can take out *Kraken*.' His eyes tightened on her. 'And for that I need one of my most experienced captains to command them...'

Her mouth became pencil thin. 'But my place is onboard *Athena* during this of all battles, Papa.'

'But you are also one of the best ornicopter pilots we have left in the fleet.'

'But, Papa—'

He raised his hand to silence her. 'It is where we need your expertise most during this battle, Princess Angelique. This is all about maximising every edge we have over Hades and you are one of our sharpest edges.'

She opened her mouth to say something, but then closed it again and only blinked at her father.

Louis held his daughter's gaze, his expression softening. 'I need you to do this, my beautiful daughter.'

Suddenly it felt as if we were all intruding on a private family chat. But when I glanced around the room all the faces were filled with the understanding that this was massive thing Louis was asking of her. And I more than understood. To not be flying *Athena*, a ship that was part of her own soul, in what could be her last ever battle, was tougher than anything he could ask any of the other captains in here.

Angelique's shoulders dropped and she nodded. 'Of course I will, my king. But who will pilot *Athena*?'

Jules nudged me in the side.

'Huh?'

Angelique turned towards us. 'Of course.'

I looked between her and Jules. My brain finally caught up with what they were getting at. 'You'd really trust me to fly *Athena*, Angelique?'

'I can't think of anyone else I would rather have pilot her for this.'

I'd dreamed of captaining an airship since Angelique had first fallen out of the sky onboard *Athena*. I cleared my throat. 'In that case, it would be awesome.'

'And I'm going to be right by your side,' Jules said.

I gazed at her. If this was going to be the end I wouldn't have it any other way and, without saying a word, I caressed her palm with my finger.

King Louis nodded towards Tesla. 'Please resume the simulation.'

The war dance of glass planets began again. Hades vessels were taken out in twos and threes in the hypnotic spin of battle. But as the minutes ticked past I noticed that the movement of the Cloud Rider ships became increasingly jerky, while the enemy craft continued to glide effortlessly. The advantage of the battle swung back to Hades as their airship started to pounce and pick off the Cloud Rider airships one by one.

It was turn to put my hand up. 'I don't understand – what's going wrong?'

Angelique answered me. 'It's what often happens when a battle drags on. Ship-song fills the heavens, both from Cloud Rider and Hades ships, and that adds to the confusion of the fog of war.'

Tesla nodded. 'It was one of the reasons that we lost to Hades in the last major battle at our home world. For Cloud Rider vessels, it becomes increasingly difficult to maintain the chain of command during the fight. A lost order can be critical and what we are seeing now in the simulation is the consequence of that. Unfortunately for us, Hades lobotomised Psuche gems making them barely sentient and immune to its effect. And in this particular coming battle, it's a task made even more difficult by the fact that our ships will be cloaked so we won't have line of sight with each other.'

'Not to mention that awful Quantum Pacifier of theirs flooding the airwaves,' Angelique said.

As I knew they would, all eyes turned towards me. Talk about peer pressure. I stood straighter, feeling my face burn up. 'Thing is, I've hardly made a dent in boosting my ability.'

Louis frowned. 'I know, Dom, but just do what you can for us during the battle to suppress the Quantum Pacifier's effect. Do enough and we might even win this.'

Might… Like the odds stacked against our fleet, I was also going to be heavily outnumbered by the Hive mind, a hundred people, which included the remains of Dad's mind, screaming in my ears. How could I stand a chance?

I caught Mom's eyes, looking to me, the son she was so proud of, to make things right. That look was a lot to live up to.

I tried to keep the doubt out of my voice. 'I'll kick the Hive's ass for you.' The captains gazed at me and nodded their approval. Whether they believed I could or not was another thing.

Harry stood. 'Is there anything the Sky Hawks can do to help in all this?'

Cherie nodded. 'We'd rather not sit this one out on the bench.'

The Hawks around her murmured their approval.

The king gazed at them all. 'We need to send scouts out to detect exactly where the Vortex event horizon starts to appear so we can muster the focus of our force's response accordingly.'

Harry grinned. 'Now that sounds like the job for a bunch of storm chasers to me.'

Angelique smiled. 'Just so, my dear friends.'

'In that case, we're on it,' Cherie said and high-fived Harry and the other Hawks.

Mom fixed the king with one of her stares that was enough to make me feel guilty without any reason. 'If you are expecting me to hide in the storm shelter while this is all happening in the sky over my head, you've all got another thing coming.'

Shucks, I was so proud of her. I reckoned that even Cronos would flinch if he had to look her in the eye.

Harry gestured towards her. 'Sue, we're going to need someone coordinating the Sky Hawks when we're out on the road.'

Cherie nodded. 'We were wondering if you could help with the radio, like you used to for Shaun when he was chasing…'

She turned and beamed at them. 'Of course I will, and I even still have his old CB rig up in the basement.'

Roddy rubbed his chin and gestured around the room. 'And if anyone needs a mechanic, I'm pretty handy with a spanner.'

Roxanne raised her hand. '*Helios*'s main engine is still out of commission, so we could certainly do with your help, because, to use your world's expression, myself and my crew would rather not sit this out on the bench.'

'Then I'm your man,' he replied.

'Then it would seem that we have everything agreed,' Louis said. His blue eyes skimmed over the officers in the room. 'Airship captains, please return to your ships and load the tactics into your ships' Eyes.'

With a murmur of voices the officers filed out through the room, each taking a cog-shaped device from Tesla. Angelique took one and handed it to me.

'What this?' I asked, looking at the etched crystal with brass gear teeth around its edge.

'It's the automated Omega battle orders…just in case all communication fails.'

'You mean *in case I mess up*.'

'It's just a precaution, Dom.'

The crystal gear felt sweaty in my hand. 'I understand, Angelique.'

Louis tapped Roxanne on the shoulder as she was about to leave with the other captains.

'I need you for a moment longer, Captain Roxanne.'

'Yes, my king.'

Stephen gave her a questioning look as he disappeared out of the door.

Louis waited until the final officer filed out of the auditorium before turning his attention to Roxanne. 'We need to discuss the world you were stranded on.'

She gave him a grim look. 'You mean what happened with the Shade?'

'Yes,' Tesla replied. 'We need to know exactly what happened.'

A dark look crossed her face. 'It was one of the most awful things I have ever witnessed in my life and I just pray that my daughter isn't plagued with nightmares for the rest of her life. One moment Earth XLA500 was teeming with life, the next the shadow crows appeared and began feeding on the life in that world.'

Lines spidered around Tesla's eyes. 'I see…' He nodded towards me. 'Princess Angelique told me your theory, Dom, about the Void leaking into that world and carrying the Shade along with it.'

I shrugged. 'It was just an idea.'

'And a very good one. It is my belief that is exactly what happened.'

Cherie's eyes widened. 'When you say…' she used her fingers to scratch air quotes… '"leaked", you make it sound as if this Void has some sort of mass.'

The scientist nodded. 'According to my previous measurements, it does. Whenever we pass through the Void it exerts an infinitesimal gravitational pull on our craft.'

'It does…?' Cherie's eyes widened further. 'Holy cow!'

'What's the big deal?' Jules asked.

'I'll get to that… You call this stuff the Void, right?'

Tesla nodded.

'Then I think we have a name for it too. Actually two names. We call it dark energy and dark matter. It's the missing stuff of the universe. We've known it's there, have even been able to measure its gravitational effect on other galaxies, mapped it with computer simulations and the rest. But, although we've searched high and low for it, until now we haven't been able to find it.'

'Dark matter, dark energy…fascinating descriptions,' Tesla replied.

Jules waved her hand. 'So this dark energy, matter, whatever it's called, how do we stop it leaking into other universes too and bringing the Shade right along with it?'

King Louis steepled his fingers together. 'That is a very good question, Jules. And that is the reason I didn't want the rest of the officers hearing about this. They have enough to concern them with the coming battle without worrying about the further threat the Shade may represent.'

Tesla scratched his beard. 'Maybe we shouldn't worry too much about that for the moment. After all, this was a freak accident to do with a Vortex drive that couldn't be shut down. And if we all live through the final battle, it shouldn't be too hard for me to build a retrograde safeguard into our ships' systems to make sure that it never happens again. However, I do also feel it is a worrying development that warrants further study.'

Cherie sat up straighter. 'In which case I'll be more than happy to help you with that. I know a few astrophysicists who'd sell their grandmothers to be involved with anything to do with dark energy.'

'Then it sounds as if we have our priorities worked out for now,' King Louis said.

Tesla flicked a switch and the globes of the craft disappeared back into the floor.

I suddenly realised we hadn't seen the end of the Omega battle plan. 'What about the rest of the simulation.'

Angelique gave me a tight look. 'You've seen everything you need to.'

By her expression I could tell I wasn't going to get any more information out of her, which couldn't be good. 'Right…' As the lights came up I caught the deep worry in Mom's face.

I stepped down off the platform and held out my arms to her.

She crossed to me and we wrapped our arms around each other, not saying anything, just hanging onto each other.

Mom was the first to pull away. 'I wish we had more time.'

'Me too, Mom…'

Her expression breaking like a rain storm, she quickly turned away and headed through the door with Roddy and the others.

Angelique circled back around the stage towards us.

'Dom, let's get you some last-minute training with the Theta Codex,' she said.

'Seriously? Surely you've got bigger priorities at the moment than nursemaiding me?'

She shook her head. 'You, Dom Taylor, even if you don't realise it, are the biggest priority in this entire fleet. If we manage to boost your theta waves, by even half a point, it could make the difference to us winning this war.'

Jules nodded. 'Like usual, she's making a lot of sense, Dom.'

I looked between them, the burden of their expectation weighing me down. I felt so out of my depth that I almost couldn't breathe, but I forced a smile anyway. 'Of course she is.'

'I'm glad we have that sorted out,' Angelique said. She crossed back to Louis deep in conversation with Tesla.

Jules rubbed my arm. 'Dom, I just want you to know…' Her eyes held mine and in them I saw our lives together: real happiness, love, the whole happily ever after thing. That was, if we had a world left to have a life together on.

'Yeah, me too.' I had the strongest urge to kiss her, but then I caught Angelique watching us and felt my thoughts cloud.

Enough of this already. I needed to go into this battle with a clear head, and although I'd have rather taken on an entire Hades armada than have this conversation with Angelique, that was exactly what I had to do… For Angelique's sake, for Jules's too. The future of a whole world might depend on me sorting out my guilt trip.

My stomach flipped as Angelique beckoned to me to follow her.

Jules brushed her fingers over my wrist. 'I need to go and get something sorted out, but I'll catch up with you onboard *Athena*.'

I felt my resolve strengthen. I could do this. I'd no other choice. I followed the princess out of the room for the toughest conversation of my life.

CHAPTER FOURTEEN

SECRETS

I floated inside the darkened pod onboard *Athena* where we'd transferred the Theta Codex so we wouldn't get in the way of the king onboard *Zeus* and his preparations for war.

I tracked my theta wave graph as it pulsed across the screen and stuck at a stubborn level five. 'Just one more try, Angelique.'

'I'm afraid we've run out of time,' her voice said from outside.

'But you said yourself that we need my ability working to its max.'

'And it looks as if your *max*, as you put it, for now at least, is a level five. Let's hope that's enough for the battle.'

But what if it wasn't? There had to be something I could do. I hauled myself out of the pod.

As I started to towel myself down, my gaze fell on the key switch in the control panel and a mad thought struck me. Why I hadn't thought of it before?

'We need to take a chance and use the mind boost,' I said.

Angelique gawped at me. 'There's no way on this or any other Earth that I'm going to let you try that. You know what the risks are.'

That my brain might end up being scrambled like eggs…but then again it might not be. 'Surely it's got to be worth the risk?' I said as I hauled my clothes back on.

'No – no it isn't. Besides which, I don't have the key, not that I'd give it to you even if I had.'

'But Tesla could take a look and bypass the lock.'

Angelique jabbed her finger at me. 'You're not listening to me, Dom. Not a chance. Never, ever. And the last thing we have time for is our chief scientist to be distracted by some idiotic plan of yours.'

I stared at her, frustration raging inside me, but part of me also knew she was talking sense. The problem was, I just couldn't accept it. We were talking about my Earth's future being on the line here.

'But, Angelique…' My words trailed away as her eyes became emerald hard. I knew there was nothing I could say to change her mind.

Angelique's expression softened. 'I'm sorry, Dom. Just do your best in the battle.'

My shoulders dropped. 'You know I will.'

'Of course I do.'

I could see in her eyes that she more than understood how I was being torn apart by this.

'And you're sure you're ready to fly *Athena* by yourself?' she said.

'With you teaching me, more than ready. You've been a brilliant teacher.'

'So have you, Dom, in all sorts of ways.' She blinked.

It suddenly struck me that this might be the last time we'd see each other. Her irises, as green as our meadow had once been, pulled at mine. We'd been through so much together; had taken on impossible odds and somehow got through.

She brushed her hand over the Eye. 'You look after him, *Athena*.'

The airship's song rose around us, heart breaking in its sorrow, in its love. A lost look filled Angelique's face and a lump rose up my throat. Somehow the distance evaporated between us as if we'd been pulled together by magnets and we hugged each other.

I breathed in her hair that smelt of flowers.

'We will show them, won't we?' Angelique said, her voice trembling on the edge of tears.

This felt more and more like a final goodbye. I swallowed past the lump crowding my throat. 'We'll show them what real flying is all about.'

She pulled away and I saw her eyes full of tears. 'Oh, we will.' She nudged my shoulder with her fist. 'And you make sure you bring *Athena* back to me in one piece, or I'll give you hell.'

I snapped her a salute. 'Yes, of course, my princess.' But as I saw her trembling smile, my arms dropped to my side. 'There's one last thing I need to talk to you about…'

Her gaze searched mine and she bit her lip. 'About what happened between us back in the prison cell?'

So she knew. Of course she knew. How couldn't she? My throat loosened a fraction and I nodded. 'I'm so sorry for what happened. I crossed a line with you that I shouldn't have.'

Angelique dropped her gaze to the floor. 'It wasn't just you who crossed it, Dom. It was me too. I just wanted to take your pain away about your papa, to stop your grief…'

'I know, I know… and if it hadn't have been for you, I would've lost it.'

'I'm glad if I helped you, even if it was for just a moment…' She raised her head, her eyes pooling with tears.

I reached up and gently touched the side of her face. 'I know I shouldn't say this, but it was one heck of a kiss.'

A smile broke through her tears. 'It really was. In another life—'
She stopped mid-sentence and stared over my shoulder.

I knew before I even turned who was standing there, could feel
her eyes burning into my back as I slowly spun around.

Jules stood in the doorway staring at us, the amber flecks in her
eyes drowned by her tears smudging the eyeliner she never normally
used. She was wearing new black jeans and a tiny rose-printed white
blouse that I'd never seen before. She looked beautiful.

'How long have you been standing there?' I whispered.

Jules breathed through her nose. 'Long enough.'

Angelique headed towards her. 'It's not what you think.'

But Jules glared at her. 'And what do I think it is, Princess? That
the first opportunity you had, you tried to steal Dom away from me?'

'You're not being fair, Jules,' I said. 'I was falling apart and neither
of us meant for it to happen.'

'But the problem is, it did happen, Dom, and worse still, you didn't
tell me about it.'

'I'm so sorry—'

She raised her hand to cut me off, anger chiselling her face. 'We
haven't the time for this. If we're lucky to survive today, then maybe,
Dom Taylor, you can decide what the heck it is that you do want.'

What did she mean? I knew what I wanted: her and everything
that came with it. But I knew by the set expression of her jaw that
she was in no mood to hear me out right now.

The Tac on Angelique's wrist warbled and she stole a glance at its
face. 'I've got to go and brief the ornicopter squadrons.' She tried to
catch Jules's gaze. 'I really am so sorry for any hurt that I've caused you.'

But Jules looked through Angelique as if she were glass. 'Not
as sorry as I am. I was stupid enough to think you were my friend.'

The battle-hardened princess blinked and fresh tears rolled down her face. That rocked me more than anything. None of us needed this heartache at the moment. If I hadn't been such a coward and had manned up before now, I might have got this sorted out before it had blown up in all our faces. Now I'd broken the hearts of the two people I cared about more than anything. And worse still, I might never have a chance to sort it out.

Angelique dropped her head and hurried out of the cockpit. I felt a tug in my gut, like an invisible elastic band between us being drawn tight to the point of breaking. What a stupid mess.

Jules crossed to the Valve Voice, her back to me.

I raised my hand to her shoulder but she stiffened without me even touching her.

I dropped my hand away and slumped into a seat by the Theta Codex machine. I ground my palm against my forehead as I stared at the key switch slot. I'd screwed my training up too – the one real chance the Cloud Riders had of beating Hades. What a complete and utter waste of space. I thumped the pod, making its control panel jump.

Jules winced but didn't turn.

I reached out to check I hadn't broken the controls, but it still quietly hummed away and all the lights remained lit. I picked at the lock with my finger. If only I had the key – after all, what did we really have to lose…? An idea burst out of the back of my brain. I pressed the button to kill the power to the machine.

'Jules…'

She didn't respond, but instead concentrated on spinning various dials on the Valve Voice.

I felt awful about doing this, but I had to tell Jules one final lie. 'The Theta Codex is broken.'

Jules glanced at me before her gaze skated away. 'What sort of broken?'

'It's this key switch. It's busted and the Codex won't switch on.'

'Oh, is that all...'

I nodded, hoping my racing pulse wouldn't show itself in my face. Jules needed to think this was her idea.

She squinted at the lock. 'It looks like a simple ignition to me.'

'And?'

'An ignition switch, as you get in cars.'

'You mean you can hot-wire it?'

'Yeah, probably...' she said, tone flat. She crossed to *Athena*'s tool locker and picked out a long, flat-headed screwdriver and a pair of pliers. 'Are you sure this is okay for me to do?'

I couldn't risk telling Jules the truth. If she even knew for a moment what I had planned, there was no way she'd let me go through with it. 'I just want to try to squeeze in a few last minutes of training.'

She nodded. 'Oh, I see...'

Guilt burned like embers inside me. Here I was throwing another lie at her. But even if she never forgave me, I'd take that chance if it meant she and everyone else would live beyond today.

My heart thumped hard in my ears as Jules pushed the tip of the screwdriver under the ring of the keyhole socket. With a sharp tap on the handle, she popped the lock mechanism out. It hung loose, trailing red, black and green wires.

'How's it looking?' I asked.

'For all the weirdness of some of the Cloud Rider technology, sometimes it's just so straightforward.' Jules held the tip of her tongue between her teeth as she cut the three wires.

I tried to lighten the moment. 'At least it didn't explode.'

Jules didn't even bother looking up, her hair forming brunette walls to shut me out. She wound the end of the wires together and blue sparks leapt between them. She dropped the key mechanism and sucked the end of her fingers.

I reached out for her. 'You okay?'

She flinched away. 'I'll live. Anyway, it worked.' She pointed at the screen. It read:

'Warning – mind boost mode engaged.'

Jules scrunched her lips together. 'What's that message about, Dom?'

'Just part of the boot-up sequence.'

'Right…' Her gaze moved away from me. 'If we're done here, I need to get back to patching the Valve Voice into the CB frequencies so we can communicate with your mom.'

'Yeah, I'm all good.'

She threw a vague nod in my direction and turned her back on me. The feet between us felt like miles.

I spun my chair away to gaze out of the windshield. Flight crews, soldiers and mechanics ran between the airships. It would be too risky to try the mind boost here…someone might enter the gondola at the wrong moment and try to stop me.

I unhooked the Valve Voice. 'Stephen, are you there?'

'Yes, just running some final diagnostics on the bridge. What can I do for you, Dom?'

I needed an excuse that he would buy into. 'I need to get some flight time in with *Athena* before the battle.' And I did. Although I'd clocked up quite few hours flying *Athena*, I also knew that dogfighting in combat would be a whole other level of flying.

I held my breath as Jules carried on her work, waiting for Stephen's response.

'Of course, Dom. And are you up to speed with *Athena*'s main weapon?'

'I know how Angelique activates it if that's what you mean.'

'If I were you I'd get some trigger practice in as well as the extra flying time.'

'Good advice.' Great, he was buying my cover story. 'Can you let the others know for me?'

'Of course and, Dom…'

My chest tightened.

'I just wanted to tell you it has been such an honour knowing you.'

The past tense wasn't lost on me. Jules's shoulders dropped, but she didn't say anything.

'You too, Stephen.' I heard the murmur of voices in the background.

'Princess Angelique has just appeared on deck. Would you like to have a word with her?' he said.

Jules stance stiffened again.

I couldn't risk Angelique sussing what I was up to. 'No, I'm good. Need to get on with things here. Kick their butts, Captain Stephen.'

'Oh, I intend to. Good luck to us all. Over and out.'

I gazed out of the windshield up into the golden dawn sky. *Athena*'s chameleon net buzzed quietly away in the background. We were invisible and good to launch. I pressed the starter and, at once, all our props growled into life.

From somewhere outside I heard *Storm Wind*'s song strengthen in my thoughts, his tone questioning. An image flooded my mind of the diner, house and hangar, viewed from above. Ranged around them, the faint shimmers of air and large depressions in the grass were the only hint of all the airships parked up across our meadow and beyond.

Just taking Athena *out for a spin,* I replied.

His song strengthened in response and I could feel the concern in it. He'd been part of my thoughts for so long, and knew when I was lying to him. I needed to speed this up in case he gave me away. I pushed the throttle wide open and with a long blast of propane flame we began to rise into the sky, *Athena*'s song climbing with our ascent.

The Valve Voice hissed and popped.

'We're getting an incoming message,' Jules said. She studied a dial. 'It's your mom's frequency.' She cast the briefest glance in my direction, such a hurt look filling her face that it took every fibre in my being not to reach out and hold her. Instead, I took the mic from her.

'This is Eye in the Sky, are you reading, over?' Mom's voice said.

My throat thickened. She was using Dad's old call sign. 'Hi, Mom. You managed to get that old CB up and working then.'

'With Roddy's help… And thank goodness I've been able to reach you.' She paused.

I knew what was coming. I had my own sixth sense when it came to Mom.

'Dom, you know how much I love you, don't you?'

'Of course I do.'

Jules had become motionless, her head still turned away from me.

'And I know that you may be facing an impossible decision in the battle… That you may…' Her sobs filled the speaker.

'Mom, speak to me.'

But it was a new voice that came through. 'It's Roddy here, Dom. Your mom needs a moment. But she was trying to say that she understands you may face a difficult choice when *Kraken* gets here.'

I stared at the back of Jules's head.

'What do you mean, Roddy?'

'With Shaun…'

Then I knew exactly what Roddy was getting at – that if it came to it I might have to destroy *Kraken* and Dad along with it, if it meant saving our planet.

I cradled the mic. 'I won't let it come to that, Roddy.'

Mom's voice cut in. 'But it might, Dom. And you have to do what's right for everyone's sakes, not just ours. Please know that Shaun would understand this most of all and would say the same to you if he could.'

What could I say to that? I stared at the mic, no words coming.

'Dom?' she whispered.

Bands of steel contracted around my chest. 'Okay, Mom…' I said with a voice that was barely a whisper.

'I'm so proud of…' Her voice trailed away into fresh sobs.

'Is Jules there with you?' Roddy asked.

I handed the mic to her in silence.

Her gaze brushed past mine and then down through the windshield to the fields dropping away below us.

'Jules?' Roddy said.

'I'm here, Dad…'

'You need to promise me something, my love.'

'What?'

'That if it looks as if everything's lost, then you and Dom will get yourselves to safety and build a new life on another Earth.'

Her hand clawed around the mic. 'But I can't leave you behind, Dad.'

'You may not get to have a choice in the matter,' he whispered.

Now Jules's eyes did seek mine out, her expression breaking.

In that moment I didn't care about what had happened between us. One hand still on the wheel, I reached out my other and pulled her close.

Jules slumped into me, her fight gone, and wept into my neck.

I gently unhooked the mic from her grasp. 'We understand, Roddy.'

'Thank you, Dom…'

'And tell my mom I love her.' I heard Mom's muffled crying in the background.

'She knows. And tell that gorgeous daughter of mine I love her too.' Jules's sob echoed Mom's.

'May the Cloud Rider gods protect us all,' I replied.

'Amen to that, son. Safe voyage. Over and out.'

I let the mic drop from my hand and held onto Jules with one arm as she shook.

With my free hand I pulled back on the wheel and we began to climb higher. Sunlight light glowed through the cabin and, despite the drone of the propellers, a sense of peace filled me up. Right here, right now, soaring into the sky of my Earth, with Jules, and with *Athena*'s gentle song accompanied by *Storm Wind*'s backing hymn somewhere in the distance, was a moment of utter stillness, and maybe the last peace we might ever know.

I gazed at Jules's reflection in the windshield and a fierce love swept through me. I would do anything for her. I eased the wheel forward to level out and pulled the throttle back until the engines idled. I glanced back at the Theta Codex. It was the best chance for everyone. I didn't have a choice, not really.

'Jules, can you take over for a minute.'

She stared at me. 'You want me to fly?'

'There's nothing to it. Just keep *Athena* level. I need to have another go with the Theta Codex.

'Okay…'

Athena's voice became keening, but the last thing I was going to do was place my hand on the Eye so she could talk me out of this.

Jules reached out her shaking hands and took hold of the wheel. I put my hands on hers to steady them.

'Believe in me, Jules.'

'I'm trying to, Dom.'

I swallowed hard and let my hands fall away from hers. Like a zombie I crossed to the Theta Codex.

The text still pulsed slowly on its screen, burning its message into my mind. *Warning – mind boost mode engaged.*

My finger hovered over the button as I watched Jules flying the ship. In the light streaming into the cabin she looked so gorgeous with her hair shining like autumn maple leaves. She'd dressed up for these final hours, with Mom probably throwing in advice on what to wear. Worst of all, I knew Jules had done it for me, the boyfriend who'd gone and broken her heart.

I stuck my fingernails into my palms. For Jules. For everyone on my planet. No turning back. With a deep breath I pushed the button on the Theta Codex and the machine hummed up. Palms slick, and not even bothering to undress, I clambered into the pod. As the warm water soaked through my clothes I slipped the skullcap over my head.

CHAPTER FIFTEEN

MIND BOOST

Fireworks exploded into my vision as a million needles pierced my skull. Molten metal burned my veins. My jaw jammed together and a yell squeezed between my teeth. *Athena*'s song roared in my mind, her tone desperate. The world around us began to tilt as the gondola angled towards the ground.

I focused on Jules's face hovering over me through the open hatch. She shook my shoulders. 'Dom, Dom!'

I tried to talk but my thoughts were too broken into pieces. My mouth wouldn't work. Sleep lapped through me. All I wanted to do was give in and float away into nothingness, to escape the pain that screamed through every muscle of my body.

Something glowed orange on the table above me...the screen of the Theta Codex. I became aware of the green line rising towards the top.

'What have you done?' Jules said. She started tearing the skullcap off my head.

But the line kept still. 'Theta waves: level 8, glowed on the screen. This was good, was what I wanted. I clung onto Jules's face with my eyes. If I kept going and made it to level ten, we might yet beat Cronos.

I grabbed her wrist with my hand. My head felt like a ten ton weight as I slowly shook it.

'You don't want to stop? But this is killing you, Dom!'

'Not yet...' I hissed through my teeth.

She let out a sob. 'Oh, Dom.' Her hands fell away from the skullcap and she knelt back on her haunches, tears streaming down her face. 'Level 9...'

My body felt as if it were being ripped apart. I thrashed around in the water like someone drowning.

Jules, sobbing, got hold of the wires in the key switch, ready to yank them apart.

I ground my teeth together and shook my head again.

She gazed at me, eyes pleading. 'Dom, please!'

But I couldn't give in to her. Not yet. This was way too important.

'Level 10,' flashed on the screen.

At once the impossible pain stopped dead. The noise disappeared from my thoughts and a deep sense of peace filled my body. Then, like a bird calling out from somewhere deep in a forest, the beautiful voice of a woman started singing to me.

Jules lapped in and out of view as the velvet darkness thickened in my skull. I so wanted to sleep. But the woman's song became insistent and rainbow colours danced through my head.

The song sharpened into words. Even though I wasn't touching the Eye, *Athena*'s words became clearer than I'd ever heard them before. *'You must warn Jules, Whisperer.'*

The words slipped through my mind as I tried to hang onto them. Warn her? Of what? I focused on Jules's blurring face so close to mine through the hatch. She dabbed a cloth on my forehead. When she took it away I saw it was covered in blood.

Her mouth opened wide. 'Dom, can you hear me?' she said, her voice the barest whisper. Her face swam above me, as if she were peering into a pool that I was drowning in.

I started to let go, too tired to do anything else, and drifted downwards into the deep darkness that sucked at my body.

Jules's face grew dimmer and turned into a series of smudges.

'Dom,' she said, her voice coming from a long way away. The sound of her weeping faded into the distance.

The colours in the darkness started to form into images: Dad, sitting on my bed when I was five reading a bedtime story to me about a caveman; the day Mom opened Twister Diner and we'd let off fireworks for most of the night; camping in my field with Jules when we were ten and getting so scared we ended up sneaking back into the house; the moment Angelique had arrived in *Athena* like some sort of storm angel…

The images spun faster and faster, one memory merging into another.

'You must stay awake, Whisperer,' Athena murmured in my mind.

Awake?

'Or you will both die.'

Both die… Jules? I stared up at her face as it hung over me, a dimming moon over the surface of the sea. She was going to die too?

I tried to pull my shattered thoughts together and, from somewhere deep inside me, my determination flickered and caught. I clung to it, fighting the fog swirling in my mind. I had to save Jules.

I started to thrash towards the surface of my thoughts, heaving on the darkness that pulled on my limbs as if someone had tied lead weights to them. But Jules's face had started to focus. Her mouth opened and closed as she cradled my head on her lap. She was speaking to me, but I couldn't hear her words.

Athena's song faded and a complete silence filled my mind. My skin prickled. My eyes might have been open, but what had happened to my hearing?

Through the windshield behind Jules I could see corn fields rushing towards us. And in the distance, the asphalt line of a runway ran next to a grid of buildings. We'd drifted all the way to the Jackson military airbase... I tried to pull myself up, but my body felt stuck by superglue.

Jules's eyes tightened on mine, her lips moving rapidly, but I still couldn't hear anything. Worse still, she hadn't noticed what was happening beyond the windshield, because her whole attention was focused on me.

I tried to lift my hand but it sat there as if it belonged to someone else. I concentrated everything I'd got and finally it twitched as if I were trying to lift a million tons. Pain screamed through my body as I extended a shaking finger to point past Jules.

She turned and her expression widened. In perfect silence she jumped up and dashed to the wheel. She yanked back hard on it. The brown cornfield still rushed towards us but, inch by inch, the nose of *Athena* started to rise.

Come on...

Jules heaved back on the wheel.

I felt the vibration running through the deck beneath me as the engines scrabbled to give us extra lift. But I'd had enough flight time to know that we were still going in too fast for anything but a crash landing. My stomach rose to my mouth as the corn field blurred towards us. I braced and cried out a silent warning.

The deck slammed into my body and my vision bounced around. Jules hurtled backwards and sprawled next to me.

In perfect silence the contents of the galley flew out and landed around us like shrapnel. *Athena*'s momentum still carried us onwards. Stalks of parched corn thrashed past the porthole windows. The gondola tipped forward and we started to spin, the horizon zooming past like a crazy carny ride. The whirling slowed and the earthquake tremor subsided as we skidded to a sideways stop.

The stillness after the chaos was almost shocking. A ghostly red light blinked somewhere in the cabin. My eyes sought it out and locked onto an indicator on our chameleon net controls.

Jules pushed herself up on her arms and stared at me through a curtain of blood streaming from a gash on her forehead. I felt like a puppet whose strings had been cut as she pulled me out of the pod and cradled me in her arms.

Through the gondola's windows above us, I saw specs appear in the sky. Maybe Angelique had realised we'd gone and had sent ships to search for us?

But my hope died as the dark outlines drew close enough to make out. Military helicopters – Black Hawks, going by the outline of them against the clear sky. And they were closing in fast, which could only mean our cloaking net had failed and that they could see us.

Jules had spotted them too and started shaking me. Her mouth opened and closed like a silent ventriloquist's dummy.

'What?' I tried to say, but nothing came out. I suddenly realised all I could hear in my mind was my own thoughts. There was no murmur backing track from the ship.

Panic gripped me. Athena, *are you there?*

The silence pressed into my skull. No reassuring song responded to sooth my chaos of thoughts. A coldness crept through me. If she'd died because of my stupidity…

I gazed at the two Black Hawks rushing towards us. All my fight drained away as they drew close enough for me to spot machine gunners in the doorways, their weapons trained on us as if we were the enemy. Yeah, a formerly cloaked airship that had crash-landed near their airbase would do that. There was no way this could end well for us. Even if we managed to convince them that we weren't the bad guys, it would take too long and we'd be too late – Cronos's invasion would already be in full swing.

Jules hauled herself to her feet and crossed to a locker. She threw open the gondola door. What was she doing?

She started to put on the chameleon stealth suit Angelique had once worn to take on a Hades scout.

Despite all that had gone wrong, I felt a huge surge of love for Jules. Everything might be falling apart, but she wasn't giving up so easily. Already in the suit, she rushed back to my side.

I spoke to her even though I couldn't hear my own words. 'I can't move, Jules. I'm not going anywhere, so just get yourself out of here.'

Her mouth became a thin slit. I knew that look and it meant she wasn't about to listen.

She pulled up the hatch in the floor and started to tug out boxes of provisions.

The corn whipped around us again as the two Black Hawks touched down. Troops poured out, their guns pointed at the strange ship that had appeared out of nowhere. One guy, ahead of the rest, made a chopping motion with his hand towards the gondola. His squad edged towards us in a tightening circle.

Jules grabbed hold of my shoulders and started to heave me towards *Athena*'s underfloor storage hold, as if I were one of Mom's sacks of bread flour.

Teeth gritted, she lowered me into it. Her eyes locked onto mine and her mouth moved slowly enough for me to make out the words: 'I love you, Dom.'

A portal shattered above us. A small cylinder shot through and smashed into the far cabin wall. At once smoke billowed from it and began filling the gondola.

This was like a textbook special ops move from every war movie I'd ever seen.

The smoke filled my lungs and Jules started to cough as red, glowing lines lanced the smoke – laser sights, the bullets with our names on them if we didn't cooperate. As I started to choke too, Jules grabbed a flight helmet from the locker and gently lowered it over my head. Oxygen flooded my nose and swept away the burning sensation from my lungs.

We had seconds left and I was as good as finished, but Jules still had a chance. This was one thing I could still get right.

I concentrated every last bit of energy I had and grabbed Jules wrist. 'Go,' I said.

Her hand brushed my face.

'I love you too, Jules…always.'

Tears filled her eyes as she clipped her face mask into place to cover her features. Her hand moved to the control built into the suit's sleeve. She shimmered into a ghost and vanished.

The hold's hatch was lowered back into position over my head by her invisible hands and I was shut into darkness. Through the cracks in the floor above me, I saw the boxes that had been in the hold being moved over the top of the hatch. She was doing her best to make sure I didn't get discovered. But what about her?

All alone, the fight drained away from me. I'd gambled and lost.

Darkness surged up around me again, and this time I let myself drift down into it as the world slipped away.

* * *

I tried to open my eyes, but they felt glued shut. Redness glowed through my closed eyelids as deep warmth sucked at my thoughts and softness filled my body like a cloud. All I wanted to do was rest.

The red light flashed. Something was vibrating above me.

My eyelids flickered open to see the hatch, outlined by a rectangle of light, just above my face.

I tried to marshal my thoughts. Where was I? What'd happened? I'd hooked myself up to the Theta Codex and then…

My memories tumbled back in an avalanche. We'd crashed at the military base and I'd blacked out, but for how long? Was Cronos already here? And Jules? Had she been captured, or mistaken for a spy and shot by a trigger-happy soldier?

Panic surged through me as the hatch vibrated again and a shadow flickered across the rectangle of light.

Even though I couldn't hear the source, they had to be footsteps. A soldier, or maybe Jules in the gondola? I needed to know what was going on up there, but how to do that without giving myself away? I scanned the crammed compartment in which I was trapped. Boxes filled the space around me. Off to one side I could see a large hose connected to the floor. A heating vent?

I tried to reach out to touch it, but it felt as though someone had syphoned all my blood out. My limbs remained stuck to the ground like they belonged to someone else. I fought the sense of panic spinning through me. I needed to keep it together. What would Angelique say if she were here?

Centre yourself, Dom, and think your way out of this…

I took a deep breath and tried to order my thoughts. So I couldn't move, but maybe it was a temporary effect of the brain boost…

I raised my trembling hand and breathed through my nose as bubbles of pain exploded through my fingers. It might hurt as if I were holding a boiling pan, but this was a start. But I needed more – a way to get my broken body to loosen up and work again. An idea hit me.

Despite the confined space, and battling the pain for every inch of movement, I forced my limbs to follow one of the Sansodo moves that Angelique had taught me. I felt like a rusty version of the Tin Man from *The Wizard of Oz*. I just hoped whoever was above me wouldn't hear my efforts to get some control back over my body.

The pain started to let go bit by bit and my movements gradually got easier. It seemed the paralysis was only temporary.

I worked through the rest of my body, slowly stretching every muscle. As I did so, my mind raced… Was the attack already underway? Were there distant explosions going off that I couldn't hear?

One thing was for sure, I needed to get out of my tiny cell and find out what was going on out there.

I examined the wide rubber pipe connected to the vent set into the floor above me. There was a simple hooked wire clip that locked it in place. I moved my hand carefully towards it so as to not make a sound, pinched the wire clip and slowly released it. The hose dropped away and I caught it just before it hit a crate. I gazed out through the unobscured vent.

A soldier in black combat gear, his goggles pushed up to the top of his head, gestured to a second soldier standing in the doorway. Just by the way the guy held himself, and even though I couldn't see any insignia on his sleeves, something told me that this dude was in charge.

I had a clear view of the gondola's windshield and through it I could see the stationary rotors of several helicopters parked around us – massive Chinooks by the look of them.

I tried tuning into *Athena*, but all I got was deafening silence. Despair tugged at my guts again.

The officer's head whipped round and he stared at something. From his line of sight I realised he had to be looking at the Eye.

Red light blazed through the gondola. The ship's Eye was working, which meant…

Athena, *talk to me.*

No itch of telepathic communication filled my skull. A fresh, slow trickle of fear seeped through me. But if *Athena* was fine that would mean…

It had been staring me in the face, the thing that everyone had warned me about. I'd gone and done it – I'd fried my brain. I'd gambled everything and lost. And our Earth would pay the ultimate cost for my stupidity.

A whirlwind of thoughts crashed around my head. What the heck could I do now? Open the hatch and give myself up? And how that would play out? Hadn't we just crashed a strange ship onto a US airbase? Wouldn't they treat me as some sort of spy? Even if they did eventually believe my story, by then it would be too late.

Jules's face filled my mind, the person I loved… Determination burned through me. No, giving myself up wasn't an option. For her, for Mom, for everyone else who was relying on me.

I checked over the rest of the hold. Cargo nets had been strung across to contain the boxes, and beyond that a network of wiring looms spiralled together like a nest of brightly coloured snakes. Then my gaze snagged on something else – racks with hundreds of green, fletched arrows with steel-barbed tips. They had to be the feed for *Athena*'s weapon system that I'd seen lowered through bomb bay doors beneath her gondola…

Doors!

I ran my fingers down to my belt and unclipped my Leatherman multi-tool, relieved that I now always wore it out of habit. I opened the tool and selected the blade. Although I still felt real weak, my muscles started to respond more smoothly. I edged myself towards the cargo net between me and the weapon system and took one last look through my vent spyhole at the soldier. He seemed to be talking into a mic mounted on his helmet. Was he being radioed to be told that they'd caught Jules?

At the moment, my plan, what there was of it, just consisted of getting out of *Athena*. I'd work out the rest as I went along.

I started to cut at the woven ropes of the cargo net and within seconds had created a hole large enough to crawl through.

I grabbed hold of the net and pulled myself through, alongside the weapon system.

If there'd been little room in the cargo hold, it was even tighter in here. Beneath me, the barrel of *Athena*'s steam powered-weapon gleamed, surrounded by polished gears. And beneath that I spotted two bomb bay doors. Okay, now to find a way to open them. With my body snug against one of the racks of arrows, I studied the mechanism. Four rods ran up from the doors to semicircular geared racks. A metal shaft sat between them and if I could manage to turn that…

I took hold of it with both hands. No good. My weakened grip just slipped on the polished metal rod. I looked again at the shaft. A third of the way along its length was a drilled hole. Okay, now I could use that. I closed the blade on the multi-tool and poked the nose of its pliers into the hole. I gripped with both hands and started to slowly pull, praying it wouldn't make any sound and give me away to the soldier above.

The multi-tool jerked towards me and a slit of light appeared between the doors. It was working!

Suddenly everything around me trembled. I waited for the hatch to be thrown open and the barrel of a gun to appear, but instead the seconds ticked past and nothing else happened.

I began to relax, only for the gondola to pitch slightly to one side and the ship lurched upwards.

I stared down through the gap in the doors to see the cornfield falling away beneath the ship as we rose into the air. Military Humvees were parked up around the scar of our crash landing.

Maybe Jules had somehow overpowered the guard and was flying us to safety? Fresh hope filled me and I crept back the way I'd come and looked up through the vent. My brief sense of elation crumbled away.

Through my view of the windshield, I could just about see three twin-rotored Chinook helicopters with cables running from them to *Athena*'s gas envelope. I knew from Dad that the military used these things for heavy lifting. And that was exactly what they were doing right now – raising the whole airship – but where to? And what about Jules? If she wasn't captured, was she back on the ground surrounded by troops and watching *Athena* dwindle to a point in the sky?

I pressed my head back against the floor of the hold, despair washing through me, as we gathered speed and were towed into the sky.

CHAPTER SIXTEEN

CAPTURED

We'd only been airborne for around five minutes when we started to descend. I looked back to the bay doors beneath me. Through a gap between them I saw squat concrete buildings and hangars skimming past. Of course the military would be bringing *Athena* back to their airbase, probably to tear her apart as they worked out where she came from. Next, they'd probably decide she was some sort of weird UFO. Then they'd ship her off to Roswell with the rest of the exotic tech our government pretended they knew nothing about…at least that was Jules's conspiracy take on it.

I tried to order my thoughts. Within moments we'd be on the ground and then it'd be only a matter of time before someone discovered me. I had to do something, but if I tried to make a break for it in a military base, I knew I wouldn't get far. Realistically I'd only one option.

I glanced up at the ceiling. The guy up there, as well as being the one in charge, was obviously a pilot too. If anyone might listen to me, maybe a fellow flyer would. And perhaps I stood a better chance of him believing me if I gave myself up while we were still in flight and got to say my piece before we landed.

Fear prickled through me as I placed my hands on the hatch. Here went nothing.

'Don't shoot – I'm coming out with my hands up,' I said, not hearing my own words. I prayed I wouldn't be history before I'd even cleared the hatch.

Muscles stinging I pushed up the lid, made heavier by the boxes Jules had stacked on top, and they tumbled aside. I wasn't surprised to find myself staring at the wrong end of the pilot's sidearm.

The guy's sharp blue eyes narrowed on me. His mouth moved but I wasn't receiving and I couldn't follow his lips well enough to read. Outside, beyond the Chinooks towing us, we'd also picked up a Black Hawk escort. A soldier sat in its open doors, his machine gun trained on *Athena*. It seemed they weren't taking any chances.

I switched my attention back to the pilot and pointed to my ears. 'I can't hear you – I've been deafened.'

The officer's eyes became slits and he jerked his pistol upwards. I was sure I would've acted the same in his position. I hauled myself out of the hold and raised my hands.

The guy crossed to me and took a plastic tie from a pouch on his belt. He forced my hands down my back, lashed them together and tied me to the railing surrounding the Eye. Red light blazed from an enormous glass globe near the bottom that spun faster and faster. *Kraken* had begun its jump and was on its way to our Earth…

The pilot gave the navigation system a suspicious look.

Time to try to convince him. 'Okay, I know how this all must look to you, but you've got to listen to me because we haven't got much time. My name is Dom Taylor…'

The pilot's mouth didn't move as he looked at me as though I were a puzzle he couldn't quite work out. He pressed a button on the radio strapped to his jacket, probably about to say he'd taken me prisoner.

I needed to convince this guy before he set the gears in motion that would almost certainly result in me being thrown into a cell.

'Before you do that, just give me a minute to tell you what's really going on here.'

The pilot's finger hovered over the button but he didn't press it. I had his attention.

I quickly carried on. 'You see this machine behind me with the red sphere in it?'

His gaze flicked over to the Eye and back to my face.

'It's the navigation system for this ship…' Okay, here went nothing. 'And any moment, a massive twister, bigger than anything you've ever seen, is going to hit. But here's the thing. It isn't a twister, but a wormhole to a parallel dimension…and that globe is a marker for an invasion fleet from another dimension that is going to appear from it.'

He stared at me. A slow grin crept across his face, followed by a headshake.

I could imagine his thoughts… *Great, I've got a wacko on my hands.*

'Look, I know how crazy all this sounds and I wouldn't believe me either. But one of these ships has a weapon powerful enough to destroy our planet.'

This time the guy actually laughed at me, not that I could hear him. And somehow that made it even worse.

With another headshake he pressed a button on his radio and started talking into it.

'You've got to believe…' I trailed off as I heard a scratching noise in my ears. 'Me,' I said. It was the faintest mumble but still clear enough for me to make out. My hearing was coming back!

I did my best to keep the joy off my face. If the pilot thought I couldn't hear what he was saying it might give me an edge that I could use.

The pilot turned away from me to look out of the windshield towards the Black Hawk.

'I've got a terrorist onboard,' he said into his radio, his voice the barest whisper in my still numb ears. 'But he's secure,' he continued. 'I'll need an armed escort ready to meet us when we land.'

'Affirmative, Major Daniels, we'll radio it in,' a woman's voice replied.

So I'd already been labelled as a terrorist. This was going real well. My mind raced. If my hearing was starting to return, what about my telepathic abilities? I extended my fingers behind my back and pressed them against the warmth of the open copper lid of the Eye.

Athena... *if you can hear me, just give me a sign.*

I listened to the swirl of my thoughts, but got nothing else. My psychic link with the ship was still broken... maybe forever...

I slumped back against the rail as the horizon outside the portals began to climb. We were coming in to land. Behind me the red planet spun faster and faster.

'Okay, you might not believe me at the moment, but just remember what I've told you when that enormous twister appears,' I said. 'Then you'll see for yourself that I've been telling you the truth.'

This time the guy glanced back at me and there was something else in his expression. What, I couldn't tell. But the laughter was gone. Maybe I'd started to get through to him. If anyone had any sway on how things panned out from here, surely a US air force major would?

Before I'd had a chance to say anything else, our descent slowed and a concrete taxiing apron came into view, far away from the main runway and any of the hangars or buildings. They probably weren't taking any chances, in case *Athena* turned out to be some sort of flying bomb.

We dropped towards our landing spot and another group of Humvees ranged around it in a circle. With a gentle shudder *Athena* settled onto the ground. Ground crew rushed forward and released the cables that had been securing us to the Chinooks. With a clatter of rotors they banked away, but our Black Hawk escort settled right alongside us, close enough for me to see the gunner chewing some gum as he kept his weapon aimed at the airship.

A squad of soldiers rushed towards *Athena* as Major Daniels opened the gondola door for them.

Then he gestured to me. 'The prisoner is secure.'

A blond man wearing an armband with 'MP', military police, on his sleeve stared at me from the doorway.

'Where was he hiding, Major Daniels?' the soldier asked, his nose turned up at me as if I were giving off a bad smell.

'In a hidden compartment under the floor. Transfer him to a holding cell.'

'At once, Major. Apparently every government security agency is on its way. Your prisoner has generated a lot of interest.'

The major nodded. 'I bet he has. It's not every day that someone crashes an advanced stealth vehicle into one of our military bases. And you wait till they hear his crazy cover story – he almost had me going for a moment.'

So he had started to believe me, the good that had done me.

The MP shrugged. 'I'm sure they'll drag the truth out of him, Major.' He crossed to me, unhooked a knife from his belt and cut me free from the railing. I extended my hands backwards and immediately felt the cold snap of metal around them. Handcuffs.

'Follow me, son.'

Daniels shook his head and pointed to his ears. 'The prisoner claims he is deaf.'

I didn't jump in to correct him.

'Don't try anything stupid,' the MP said, exaggerating each word so even I could lip read him.

I nodded as he hooked a hand under my left armpit and towed me towards the door.

As we left *Athena*, the soldiers cradled their guns, every pair of eyes watching me as if I were America's Most Wanted.

I turned back to Daniels standing in the doorway. 'Everything I told you is true. You need to release me so I can help the others fight the Hades invasion.'

His gaze sharpened on me. 'Others? So you're not alone?'

'No, I'm not. I'm with the Cloud Riders and they need my—' I realised my mistake but it was too late. I clamped my mouth shut.

'So you can hear me.' He shook his head. 'And everything else you've been saying has been a lie, hasn't it, son? But one way or another they'll get to the truth.'

'I promise you I haven't lied about anything else. My hearing only returned just now.'

The major shook his head. 'Yeah, right.' He nodded to the MP. 'Get this guy out of my sight.'

The soldier snapped a salute and shoved me away from *Athena*. I felt his pistol pressed into the small of my back.

'Don't give me a reason to shoot you, son.'

Among the Humvees encircling *Athena* stood a black van with darkened windows. The MP pushed me through cordon of soldiers towards the open rear doors and into a dark, cave-like interior, ready to swallow me.

A shadow raced over the tarmac from behind us. Everyone glanced up to see the swollen black storm clouds rushing out from a single point in the sky. I stopped dead and the MP's gun jammed into my back.

'Keep moving,' he hissed.

I ignored him. 'Major, look!'

Daniels came out from the gondola and nodded to the MP. 'Hang on a second.'

Everyone gazed up at the swirling knot of cloud growing fast across the sky.

'It's starting, Major,' I shouted. 'You've got to warn everyone that everything is about to kick off.'

'Okay, you've got my attention but you still have a whole load of people to convince yet.'

The cloud spun faster and a column started to head towards the ground about a mile away. A siren's wail echoed out across the base.

'Twister,' the MP said.

'That's not just a twister, it's a wormhole, and at any moment an invasion fleet is going to appear right over your stupid base!'

Daniels looked between the growing tornado and me. He held my gaze for the longest moment.

'You have to do something,' I shouted over the roar of the growing wind.

Lines spidered around his eyes and his finger moved to his radio. 'Put the base on red alert; we may have incoming hostiles.'

My shoulders slumped. At least it was a start. 'Thank you, Major.' I nodded towards *Athena*. 'You've got to let me get airborne again.'

He shook his head. 'I'm sorry, son. Even if I wanted to believe you, there are strict procedures to follow. You can't expect to land in a military airbase and just waltz away. Tell your story to the people who'll be interviewing you. Convince them and all sorts of things will become possible.'

'But there isn't time.'

'I'm afraid it's the only way it's going to play out from here.'

I stared at him, but could see from the set of his jaw that the conversation had ended. Behind him the tornado spout was expanding fast. It had to be at least a mile across already. The wind was whipping around us.

The MP, this time a lot more gently, pushed me in the small of the back. 'Come on, lad. The sooner you get interviewed, the sooner you may have a chance of getting someone to believe you.' I didn't resist as he guided me into the back of the van.

I took a last glance at *Athena* sitting on the concrete. I should have been soaring into the air with her to meet Cronos head on, along with the rest of the Cloud Rider fleet. Instead, I was going to be stuck in a cell as the invasion kicked off.

Frustration spun inside me as the MP shut out the howl of the growing storm with the van's doors. The guy thumped on a metal panel between us and the driving compartment. I heard the engine start up.

Through the barred rear window I watched *Athena* recede, framed by the flickering lightning around the storm spout. Everything was about to go to hell in a handbasket.

CHAPTER SEVENTEEN

ESCAPE

We pulled away from *Athena* in the van and any hope I had of making a swift exit from the airbase died. I dropped my head to stare at the painted metal floor.

'How long do you think it will take for me to see someone in charge?' I asked.

'With the base on full lockdown, it will be a while before someone gets round to you,' the MP replied.

'But it will be too late by then.'

'I'm afraid that's just the way it is.'

My gaze snagged on the baton on his belt, slowly sliding itself out of its clip and rising up into the air behind the MP's head, whose gaze was still on me.

It couldn't be, could it?

I tried to keep my expression neutral as the air became opaque behind him and the form of young woman dressed in a dark, tight-fitting chameleon suit appeared.

The MP started to turn. 'What the—'

Jules slammed the baton down onto his head. The guy sprawled forward as his eyes rolled up.

She peeled off the mask covering her face. 'Are you okay, Dom?'

I just stared back at her, trying to process what had happened. 'Better than that guard is doing.'

'He'll live.' Grim-faced, she gestured to my ear. 'You can hear again?'

I nodded. 'It started to come back when they were airlifting *Athena*. But how did you get here?'

'Hitched a lift in the back of a Black Hawk. Then I snuck onto this van and this was the first opportunity I had to rescue you. If I'd tried anything sooner they'd have caught me too.'

Jules ducked down to the knocked-out MP and started hunting through his pockets.

I stared at her, shaking my head. 'You're seriously amazing, Jules.'

'You're not the only one in this fight, Dom. You need to remember that sometimes.'

'Yeah, I do.' Outside the wind had begun to shriek and the van kept being buffeted. The driver, oblivious to what had happened back in this separate compartment, was having a hard time controlling the vehicle. But it couldn't be long until we got to wherever we were headed.

I gazed at Jules. 'Don't call me ungrateful, but I can see a small flaw in your plan.'

She pulled out a key from the MP's breast pocket and started fiddling with the cuffs behind my back. 'Which is?'

The cuffs sprang open and I rubbed my wrists. 'The moment they open the doors they'll grab both of us.'

A slow smile filled Jules's face. 'Already thought of that.' She unhitched a small rucksack on her back, took out a second chameleon suit and handed it to me. 'Put this on. When they open the van all they'll see is the knocked-out guard. Then all we have to do is to sneak back to *Athena* and get out of here and back to the others.'

I slowly shook my head, a smile spreading. 'You really did think of everything.'

'I can't let you steal all the limelight, can I?'

I undid my belt. 'Guess not.'

Her gaze sharpened.

I felt heat blaze across my face. 'Jules, do you mind?'

'Oh, you're no fun.' She crossed her arms and turned her back to me.

I quickly undressed and started to pull the suit on.

'So how's your head since you managed to zap yourself?'

My euphoria swirled away. 'I was trying a brain boost, but all I seem to have done is fried my Whisperer ability.'

Jules stiffened. 'You knew it was dangerous when you got me to hardwire that gizmo?'

I nodded, not meeting her eyes.

'So you lied to me about that too, Dom.'

Fresh guilt surged through me. 'I had to, Jules. You'd never have helped me if I hadn't. I thought it was worth the risk.'

'That you nearly kill yourself and now the Cloud Riders have no way to counter Hades Voice Scream weapon?'

'You don't need to tell me I've messed it all up.' I pressed on before my courage failed. 'And to top it all, I've gone and broken your heart.'

She looked at her feet for a long moment, gave a small head shake, then reached out and pulled me into her arms. 'Maybe, but we'll work a way through this, Dom. All of it.'

The kindness in her face was the last thing I'd been expecting. I sagged into her, saying nothing, as an emotional storm rolled through me.

Jules hung on, wrapping me in her warmth as she caressed the back of my head. 'Just remind me what your dad's pet saying is?'

'While there's breath in our bodies...' I pulled away from her. 'You really believe we have a chance?'

'In every way.' She gazed at me, eyes sparkling. 'What's happened has happened, Dom. Done. Finished. Do you hear me?'

I nodded, although I wasn't quite sure what we were talking about. 'It's what happens next that really matters now,' she said.

I gazed at her, losing myself in the gentleness of her eyes.

Her smile caught and lingered. 'You may be a stupid ass sometimes, and get yourself into all sorts of scrapes, but you are still a guy with a heart of gold.'

There were a thousand things I wanted to say to her, but somehow I knew I didn't need to, because Jules already knew them...and maybe even better than I did myself. Instead, I brushed the side of her face with my hand.

Jules tilted her head towards it and kissed my open palm, as the van's engine pitch changed to a lower note and the world rushed back in.

'Sounds as if we're about to arrive wherever we're headed,' she said.

I quickly pulled the chameleon hood over my head.

Jules reattached her mask as the van came to a stop. The engine died and the howl of the growing storm took over. It sounded close, real close, the scream of the wind growing to a high-pitched whistle. And as all storm chasers knew, if a tornado was getting louder it was a sure sign it was headed your way and you'd better take shelter immediately.

Footsteps approached the back of the van as the whole vehicle started to shake in the wind.

'Good luck, us,' Jules said. She touched the panel on her arm and vanished.

I saw the vague outline of Jules's ghost-like figure move to the back of the van. I pressed my own control and a faint hum filled my ears. Through the fine mesh covering my eyes, a green light shone steady as my chameleon suit powered up.

I joined Jules as the van doors opened to reveal a two-storey concrete building with barred windows. I instinctively held my breath as a broad-shouldered MP stared at the guy sprawled across the floor.

His eyes widened and he pressed a button on his radio. 'The prisoner has escaped. I repeat, the prisoner has escaped. And get me a medic, now!'

'Affirmative,' a voice said over the radio.

As we both stayed stock-still the scene played out before us in slow motion: the MP rushing into the van; him taking the pulse of his companion; the green military ambulance turning up in less than a minute with medics running out. All the while the wind screamed louder, shaking the van harder and harder on its shocks.

Finally the MP escorting the medics carrying the injured man off to the ambulance. Moments later, the vehicle pulled away with all of them inside, flashing blue lights slicing through the dimming storm light.

I heard Jules breathe out next to me.

'Oh thank god – I felt sure they were going to spot us,' Jules said.

'Yeah, me too.'

The van was rocking even harder on its shocks, tilting at a wild angle as the doors slammed open and closed.

'Come on, let's get out of here before we become twister debris,' I said.

We scrambled forward and jumped clear of the van.

A massive fist of wind punched into my body and I clenched onto Jules as we sprawled onto the hard concrete. I rolled over and looked up.

The breath locked inside my throat.

The twister had grown to something beyond a worst nightmare. A solid mountain of black cloud, at least five miles across, spun just beyond the base. Already, countless points of flotsam whirled around the massive spout. The runway led straight into it, its green and white lights disappearing into the gloom. A freeway to hell.

Jules gawped. 'My god, that thing is way bigger than even an EF5.'

I couldn't reply for a moment. The biggest storm in history, the storm to end all storms, and this was just the opening act. The enormity of what we were taking on slammed into me. How could we fight this? How could anyone?

The twister crawled towards us, its monstrous mouth devouring the land beneath it. With an ear-numbing crack, thunder split the sky and a barrage of lightning erupted around the tornado and struck a radio mast near the edge of the base. The wind monster bellowed as sparks erupted from the mast and it collapsed.

'We have to get to shelter!' I shouted.

Holding onto each other, we crawled with our bodies pressed flat against the ground to the wall and its protection from the claws of the tornado screaming over the building's rooftop.

I stared back to the opposite end of the airstrip. Off to one side I could see *Athena*'s gas envelope being buffeted by the wind. However, the military seemed to have done a good job securing her down and ropes held her fast. Even though I couldn't hear *Athena*, I knew she'd be singing her heart out right now, desperate to carve up through the storm winds to get into the fight about to kick off over our heads.

Jules, breathing hard, followed my gaze. 'That's going to be one heck of a long walk back through this weather.'

'We haven't got any other choice. *Athena* is our only ticket out of here. I might not be a Whisperer any more but I'm still a pilot. And even if we can only make a small difference in the battle, we've got to try, right?'

Jules squeeze my hand. 'Right.'

I nodded to her. We so got each other in every way.

In the distance the Black Hawk took off and circled back towards the abandoned van we'd been transported in.

I shook my head. 'Except they're looking for us—' Something hard smashing down into my shoulder cut me off.

Jules yelped and put her hand to her forehead. A thin trickle of blood had appeared. In a roar the clouds above us opened and hail-stones, some the size of golf balls, began slamming down onto the concrete floor around us. In the distance, the Black Hawk's rotors clattered as the frozen bullets from the sky shattered on them.

'We'll be cut to ribbons by these things,' I shouted. I stared around us, looking for shelter, but the van had already been peppered by three giant hailstones, holes now gaping in the metal. That wouldn't offer us any real protection. About three hundred yards away the open mouth of a hangar beckoned.

I grabbed Jules's hand and pulled her with me. With the wind at our backs we sprinted hand in hand towards the hangar. The air hissed around us as the smaller hailstones bounced off our suits with a hundred whiplash stings.

We'd got less than thirty feet when Jules screamed and fell onto the floor. She rolled over, clutching her shin. Blood dripped through the mesh of the chameleon suit.

'Get yourself to safety,' she hissed.

'No way I'm leaving you.' I heard the whistle of a large hailstone approaching and bent over Jules instinctively to protect her. It slammed into the back of my ribcage and every bone in my body juddered, but somehow I stayed upright as pain roared through me.

Jules stared past, up into the sky. 'Dom, look!'

I glanced up to see a round shape speeding towards us. For a terrible moment I thought it was the mother of all hailstones heading straight at our heads. Then I spotted the flicker of blue flame and the shimmering outline of a small balloon outlined by the hailstones bouncing off it.

'*Storm Wind!*' Jules whooped, as the ship rushed down towards us, battling to hold his position in the whistling wind. His canopy shuddered as the frozen projectiles bounced off it, shielding us from them.

The Black Hawk, also fighting for control in the storm, had already banked towards the small ship. *Storm Wind*, despite his chameleon net, was as good as visible as a clear space in the barrage of hale.

I didn't need to hear the radio chatter to know what the flight crew would do next.

'That helicopter will be on top of him at any moment,' Jules said.

There had to be a way out of this. *Storm Wind* dropped into the shelter from the wind of the concrete building and settled in to land. As his Eye, suspended beneath the balloon, grew level with us, a crazy idea rushed into my mind.

'Get onto his Eye!' I shouted.

Jules stared at me. 'Come again?'

'We can ride him out of here.'

'But look at the size of him – surely he can't lift us both?'

'We are out of other options and there's only one way to know for sure.'

She nodded. 'Another day at the fun house.'

We both clambered onto the Eye's dome, feet slipping for purchase on the polished metal surface, and grabbed the ropes connecting it to the balloon above. The hailstones started to ease, replaced by lashing rain so dense it was as if the air had become a waterfall. A roar blazed from the burner over us and we started to rise.

'Looks as if *Storm Wind*'s got the right idea,' Jules said.

The ship's props rotated upwards and scrabbled at the air to pull us skywards.

As we slowly cleared the roofline, the wind seized the balloon again and at once we slid towards the outer spinning scud wall of the twister. The Black Hawk also swooped down closer to us.

'Talk about between a rock and a hard place,' Jules said.

A tracer bullet sparked through the sky and whistled past *Storm Wind*'s balloon.

'And that was a warning shot,' I said.

The twister had seized us now and began drawing us in like a spider pulling in its prey on a silk thread. The airbase and *Athena* slid away from us, but the Black Hawk wasn't giving up and was still on our tail.

'We've got to land before we get either blown out of the sky, or torn to shreds by the twister,' Jules said.

I nodded and, with a silent prayer, pressed my hand onto the surface of the closed Eye. Whatever it took, I had to make contact with *Storm Wind*.

I ignored everything – the roar of the storm, the boom of the thunderclaps shattering the sky, the whine of the Black Hawk speeding after us – and poured all my concentration onto the copper surface beneath my palm.

Storm Wind, you've got to land.

Nothing happened.

I breathed through my nose, ignoring the spike of fear inside. *Work with me here...*

A tingle in my head and the faintest whisper filled my thoughts, but loud enough to drown out everything else for a moment.

'Yes, Dom...'

The flame hissed out and *Storm Wind* rotated his four props towards the ground. We began to drop fast.

Jules whooped. 'Way to go, Whisperer.'

Just inches beneath us, tracer fire blazed off the bottom of *Storm Wind's* Eye.

'Oh, come on, we're the good guys here!' Jules shouted at the Black Hawk.

The air started to ripple and *Storm Wind's* props screamed at maximum thrust, matched by the howl of the helicopter. The Black Hawk bucked like a wild stallion through the sky, but at least no more bullets were coming our way – its crew had better things to worry about right now.

But the spinning debris field gyrating around the tornado column was drawing closer too. A truck, defying gravity, sped past us as if it were dandelion clock caught on the breeze, and curved away into the growing blackness.

We dropped faster and the Black Hawk steepened its angle until its nose was almost pointed straight down.

The ground rushed up towards us and we slammed into it and

were thrown clear of the airship. Meanwhile, *Storm Wind*, now on his side, was being dragged towards the tornado.

I scrambled back to the ship and pressed my hand onto the Eye as Jules tried to hold onto him.

Deflate your balloon, Storm Wind!

At once the hot air hissed from the canopy.

The Black Hawk wasn't doing so well. Bits of grit slammed into the helicopter and it started to swing round as it slid backwards towards the twister.

'No, no, no,' Jules whispered.

I knew it was already too late for them…

The helicopter's engine screamed like a wounded animal as it fought an impossible tug of war. Then I spotted the tree stump hurtling along the outside of the storm wall straight at the craft.

In my mind's eye, the moment the stump smashed into the Black Hawk's cabin seemed to last forever. The world burned orange and the remains became a thread of flame that sped away around the massive storm wall.

Jules's numb gaze bumped into mine. 'Those poor people.'

'I know…' I looked past her at the vehicle headlights rushing towards us. It seemed even the storm wasn't going to stop the military taking us prisoner again. Misguided it might have been, but you would have to give these guys an A for effort.

The wind bellowed and the invisible outline of *Storm Wind's* balloon fluttered in the air like a mad flag. The debris field rushed towards us and, if that didn't kill us first, the massive spout behind it would finish the job.

Jules cradled my hand in hers as the sky dimmed to night. In that moment, as the tornado ate up the distance, and the headlights of the oncoming vehicle carved through the darkness, the brightest things I could see were her eyes.

She buried her head into my chest. 'Always…' she said.

'Always,' I replied and gently kissed her head. The rain tilted towards the horizontal and the tornado cry rose to an ear-numbing scream.

CHAPTER EIGHTEEN

EYE OF THE STORM

As the vehicle's headlights blazed towards us, I started to make out its outline through the blur of slanting rain. This wasn't a military Humvee. With everything overloading my senses it took me a moment to realise that the vehicle charging our way had a squat beetle shape. It also happened to be painted an unmistakable scarlet, fluorescing like a burning ember in the growing darkness.

Jules's fingers clawed into my arm. 'The Battle Wagon!'

'But how did they know we were here?'

She pointed towards the twister behind us. 'They're not after us, Dom, they're headed for that big momma.'

'But that vehicle's our best chance of surviving the next few minutes. Kill your suit's power before they run us over.'

Jules's ghostly figure nodded and the air shimmered as our bodies became solid.

Together we staggered upright against the wind, using *Storm Wind* to anchor us against the buffeting wind.

The Battle Wagon drew closer and I made out Cherie's and Harry's shimmering faces through the waterfall of driving rain on the windshield. But despite waving our arms like crazy, the Battle Wagon was almost on top of us before Cherie's expression widened as her gaze locked onto us. She swung the wheel hard over and the tyres started scrabbling through the shallow water that flooded across the end of the runway.

I sucked in my breath and braced, ready to leap aside as the Battle Wagon spun, sending out a huge wave of spray our way. The vehicle managed a complete 360 turn before coming to a complete stop less than ten feet away from us. I breathed out again.

Lightning split the sky over our heads as a hatch on the roof crashed open.

Harry stuck his head out. 'What the heck, guys, you nearly got yourselves killed!'

Jules pointed back at the huge twister chewing the world up and charging our way. 'We soon will be if we're outside when that monster hits.' She glanced down by *Storm Wind*'s invisible saucer. 'But what about him?'

I placed my palm onto his Eye.

'Get yourself to safety,' he whispered into my mind.

'But we can't just leave you,' I said out loud.

Jules nodded. 'We need to take him with us.'

'Who?' Harry asked.

I pressed my hand harder into the ghostly outline of his Eye.

Storm Wind, *kill your chameleon net*, I thought-voiced.

His form rippled through the rain as he appeared, the balloon's canopy sprawled away from him like a collapsed tent.

Harry's eyes widened and he jumped down from the Battle Wagon, followed by Cherie. They charged towards us as the air growled and a storm of fine dirt pelted us.

'We've only got moments before things get mental around here,' Cherie shouted.

'Then help me.' I grabbed *Storm Wind*'s saucer and the others followed my lead, heaving the dead weight of the craft between us.

For a ship that had been so nimble in the air, stuck here on the ground it felt as if we were trying to carry a baby elephant. We stumbled towards the Battle Wagon's headlights, only just visible through the building haze of the dirt storm.

'There's no room for him inside,' Harry shouted. 'We'll have to lash him to the roof.'

The strain on Jules's face echoed the scream of my arm muscles as we tried to lift him up. With a groan we all found impossible strength and somehow heaved *Storm Wind* up and onto the Battle Wagon.

Cherie and Harry lashed the small craft down with steel cables as the wind accelerated to rip at the ground beneath our feet and my nose filled with the scent of compost. The Battle Wagon rocked on its shocks as the debris storm grew to utter blackness.

'The outer storm wall is about to hit us – get in now!' Cherie cried out. She threw open the hatch and beckoned us over.

Jules sprang up and dropped down inside, with me and Harry right behind her.

Cherie slammed the hatch shut and bolted it shut. A second later, bullets of earth rushed past the windows and bangs and clatters echoed through the vehicle.

Jules hung her head and panted.

Harry shot us a grim look. 'We're not out of the woods yet. This twister is off the scale and I'm not sure that even the Battle Wagon can survive it.'

Cherie dropped into the driver's seat. 'Let's see.' She turned the ignition, gunned the engine and hauled the steering wheel hard over. The Battle Wagon surged forward and we turned back along the runway.

'Permission for takeoff,' Cherie said to Harry.

'Permission granted,' he replied.

She gunned the engine and we heard the tyres scrabbling for grip as we lurched forward. We only managed ten feet before we slowed to a stop. Then our eight ton vehicle started to slip backwards towards the tornado.

'Seems that monster doesn't want to lose its snack,' Harry said. 'Deploy the skirt, Cherie.'

Jules raised her head. 'The what?'

'The metal skirting around the Battle Wagon can be lowered to the ground so the wind can't get beneath us and flip us into the air,' Cherie replied. She punched a green button and a clonk came from outside as she killed the engine.

Harry reached up and thumped a red button. I heard a bang from below us and the vehicle bucked.

'What the heck was that?' I asked.

'Our latest upgrade. Anchors that are fired into the ground with an explosive charge. Hopefully the military won't be too annoyed with us at messing up their runway.'

Jules gestured through the window at the maelstrom of dirt swirling past the window. 'Something tells me they're not going to notice after all the damage.'

Stones, dirt and bits of goodness knew what struck the outside of the vehicle until the Battle Wagon's armoured walls began humming with the impacts.

A huge bang and a crack appeared in the windshield and started to craze across, as the world outside blurred away. Suddenly, bullet-proof glass and two inches of armoured plate didn't seem a heck of a lot to protect us from the predator outside.

'Oh sweet lord, we're into the storm wall,' Cherie whispered.

Harry patted the dash. 'Come on, old girl, you can ride this out.'

Jules pressed her hands over ears as the wind screamed so loud that my ears became numb. I wrapped an arm around her shoulder and squeezed. But outside I could actually hear *Storm Wind*'s faint voice soaring in my mind. He was born to ride storms. No doubt this was his idea of a fun day out.

All our faces were lit up with red from the vehicle's warning displays.

Harry whooped. 'This is fantastic. I'm reading gusts of over three hundred and fifty miles per hour.'

Jules grimaced. 'It's interesting what's some folks' idea of fun.'

'Heck, this is the first F6 tornado there's ever been and we're riding her all the way in,' Harry shouted over the roar of the wind. 'And yep, that's definitely my idea of a good time.'

The world thundered with shrieking demons too loud for any more words between us. Even Cherie looked real worried and grasped onto Harry's hand. I hugged Jules hard against me.

Shapes loomed in the fog and sped past. I saw a rotor blade zoom by…which had to be the remains of the Black Hawk. I shuddered. Even though they'd been shooting at us, doing their job as they'd seen it, what had happened to them still cut me up.

When a haze of light appeared ahead then vanished again, I thought it was my eyes playing tricks on me. But then the light flared once more.

Harry looked at Cherie and she gave him a sharp nod. He leant into us so we could hear him. 'We're almost through the storm wall,' he shouted.

I felt Jules's claw-like hands on my back release a fraction as the rocking in the Battle Wagon started to slow and the whine of the wind began to die. In a rush of light the cloud fell away and an impossible silence took the place of the storm's scream.

Harry started to speak but his voice was muted. For a panicked moment I thought my deafness had returned but then I swallowed and my ears popped.

Cherie pointed to her own ear, stretching her jaw wide. 'We just passed through a huge atmospheric pressure change, which is what's affecting our ears.'

We all looked out through the shattered windshield. The view outside looked surreal. We sat in a clear circle at least a mile across. Around us the walls of the twister spun towards clear blue sky framed at the top. The odd flash glowed outside the storm walls as the occasional ribbon of lightning leapt between the marble-smooth cloud walls of the twister.

'Holy cow,' Cherie said. 'That's one heck of an eye of a storm.'

Jules peeled her gaze away, back to me. 'At least there's no sign of Cronos and his posse yet.'

'It can't be long now,' I replied.

'We'd better warn the others we're about to receive visitors,' Cherie said.

Jules raised her eyebrows. 'With something this big, I suspect they already know.'

'They still need to know that you're here and alive and well,' Cherie said. She unhooked a CB mic from the ceiling. 'This is Scarlet Woman calling, over.'

Only static crackled from a speaker mounted on the ceiling.

Harry slapped the CB unit with his hand. 'Must be the wormhole messing with our equipment.'

'Don't suppose you've got that Valve Voice you fixed up with you?' I asked.

Cherie groaned. 'Nope, it's back in the hangar. My bad.'

'But we've got to get back to *Athena*,' I said. 'The military will have to believe us now they've seen the size of this twister.'

Jules nodded. 'Maybe if you take it real slow you could drive us out of here, guys?'

Harry and Cherie exchanged tight looks.

'I wish I could, but you saw how vicious that storm wall is,' Cherie said. 'If I raise the hydraulic skirts to drive through, the wind will be under us and we'll be airborne in moments.'

'Then we just wait it out until it passes overhead,' Jules said.

Harry glanced at the instruments and shook his head. 'If this were a normal tornado, you're right, we could, but unfortunately this is anything but and it's slowing to stop. We're going to be trapped bang in the middle of this twister until Cronos and his fleet get here.'

I stared at my friends huddled together in the vehicle. We'd be sitting targets when the enemy fleet arrived. But there had to be a way out of this. I scanned around for anything that might give me inspiration and spotted the shredded remains of *Storm Wind*'s balloon draped over one of the Battle Wagon's side windows. A crazy idea surged into my head.

'Harry, is it safe to go outside?'

'It will be as long as we're in the eye of the storm.'

'Good.' I reached up, unbolted the hatch and swung it open. At once ice-cold air bit into me and my breath steamed as Arctic temperatures flooded the cabin. I zipped my bomber jacket tight to my neck and started to pull myself up.

Jules grabbed my arm. 'What do you think you're doing?'

'Getting us out of here, that's what.'

She gave me a questioning look but let go.

I clambered through the hatch and felt a huge surge of relief when I saw that, although *Storm Wind's* balloon canvas had been shredded, his Eye saucer was still lashed in place.

Jules, who'd followed me out, frowned as she took in the damage. 'There's no way we can get him into the air again if that's what you're thinking.'

'Not quite, although you're along the rights lines. And I promise you that if I manage to pull this off we will be able to fly out of here.'

'How?'

'Leave that part to me.' I ignored a burst of lightning overhead and pressed my hand to the Eye.

Storm Wind, *I need you to do something for me.*

His voice gently sighed into my thoughts. *'What, Dom?'*

Can you contact Athena *and relay my words to her?*

'That may be difficult, Dom. The energy field generated by this Vortex wormhole is enormous and I cannot hear any of my kin currently.'

Just please try.

'Of course, my friend…'

Through my palm I felt a surge of energy as an image started to form in my mind. Suddenly I saw myself crouched on top of the Battle Wagon with my eyes closed, Jules just behind, chewing her lip and watching me – the view that *Storm Wind's* sensors could currently see.

Nearby I heard the soft whine of gears spinning and the view in my mind shifted as *Storm Wind* focused his scope on the black tornado walls that rose all around us to the top of the sky. Another whir and the view zoomed in on the wall of debris. And just on the other side of that was *Athena*…

'*My sister, can you hear me?*' *Storm Wind* said.

A pulse of lightning briefly flooded the view with light then faded away.

The faintest song, so far away that I could barely catch it, sang out. Athena? I asked.

'*Yes, Dom, it is her. But at this range the interference is so great, and your Whisperer ability is so badly debilitated, that you will not be able to communicate with her with words.*'

My mind raced. There had to be something I could do. Maybe, even if I couldn't talk to her, I could still show her what to do.

Storm Wind, *do you think you could relay images from my mind to* Athena?

'*That should be possible, Dom.*'

I concentrated with everything I'd got. I thought of *Athena* as I'd last seen her, surrounded by Humvees and soldiers. *Storm Wind*'s song sang out, pure and strong, a lighthouse beam pushing through the biggest tornado that the Earth had ever seen.

In response, *Athena*'s quiet, whale-like voice sang back, but so quiet it felt like the width of an ocean between us.

I threw in all the detail I could, trying to strengthen the connection: visualising the rain lashing down on her, the twister we were stranded inside towering over the far end of the runway, the wail of the storm sirens, the smell of ripped earth flooding the air…

Athena's song became louder as the ocean distance shrank between us.

'*She's receiving you, Dom,*' *Storm Wind* said.

My idea was simple enough. Show *Athena* what to do and maybe she'd get the idea and follow my lead. But now for the hard part.

I screwed up my eyes, doing my best to imagine I was actually sitting in *Athena's* cockpit. As I had done a hundred times in real life, in my imagination I reached up and pulled the propane lever above me. At once a blast of blue flame, visible through a window in the roof, blazed up into the canopy.

My imagination was running at full tilt now. Outside *Athena* I saw Major Daniels and his soldiers running towards the gondola. This was starting to feel so real it was as if I were actually there. Now to complete the movie with its big, dramatic ending…

I pictured pulling back on the throttle and could almost feel the smooth brass handle warm in my grip…just like it did in real life. Then I imagined the throttle moving forward and the airship surging and beginning to lift off.

Through *Athena's* windshield I saw Major Daniels staring up at the gondola. One of his soldiers raised his gun to take a shot, but the major reached out a hand to stop the man and shook his head.

Nice creative touch there, Dom, I thought to myself.

I visualised the wheel turning and *Athena* banking towards the twister. I pushed the throttle to maximum. *Athena* pushed forward, all three props spinning up to maximum. With another blast of flame I raised the airship above the altitude of the debris field that spun around the base of the tornado spout. The twister churned and boiled – grey walls, a sliding rock face.

The ship lurched as her nose edged into the twister. But *Athena's* song became exultant as her spinning propellers drove her into the storm wall. At once darkness clamped around the gondola as the ship tilted to the side. I pushed the wheel hard over to compensate as everything shook.

This had become so real, more like a vivid dream, and one I was no longer in control of…

I tipped the nose, using the steep dive to help drive *Athena* forward.

'Hey, I can hear something,' I heard Jules say.

I ignored her and concentrated on the mental film playing inside my skull. The view through her windshield was growing lighter.

'Look there!' I heard Cherie shout.

What now? I couldn't risk breaking my mental rehearsal with *Athena*. I needed to see this through to the end and then she would know what she had to do… I kept my eyes tight shut.

The cloud wall swept away and the airship surged into the clear air in the eye of the storm. From the cockpit I could see the bright scarlet Battle Wagon parked up, with Jules and me sat crossed-legged in front of the drone. Cherie was in the hatch and staring up at the ship. An English teacher had once told me I needed to work on my imagination with my writing. I wished she could be in my head right now. She'd definitely give me an A+.

Now for landing procedures… I released the hot propane air from the airship's release valves and turned towards the Battle Wagon in a descending circle.

I heard the whine of props getting louder as Jules gasped.

'What the heck?' she said.

Hey? I risked opening my eyes and a sense of vertigo slammed into me.

A thousand feet above and descending fast, *Athena* carved through the air towards us. She rolled back to level and started to head straight for the twister wall again.

Slack-jawed, Harry and Cherie watched her slide back towards the twister.

Jules stared at me. 'You've been piloting her, Dom?'

'I thought I was just imagining it.'

She shook her head. 'No, and whatever you were doing, you'd better get back to it, otherwise she's going to head straight back out into the tornado wall.'

'I'm on it.' I snapped my eyes off and pictured myself back in the gondola. Once again I turned the wheel and used a blast of burner to slow her descent. And in real life, from where I was sitting, I heard her props grow louder once more. I felt like two different people – one an airship, the other an Oklahoma lad. But right now we were both one and the same thing.

A final blast of flame and I floated *Athena* to the ground. In my mind's eye, Harry and Jules ran forward to grab the ropes dangling from the gas canopy, as Dom – me – sat on the Battle Wagon, my eyes still closed. I shivered and saw my mental twin do the same. There was no way I'd ever get used to this.

With a rush of light, and feeling as if I'd just stepped off the edge of a cliff, my mind flew back to my own body. I opened my eyes and saw *Athena* sitting on the ground next to the Battle Wagon. I lurched like I did when I dreamed I'd fallen and then suddenly woken up.

'Slick bit of flying there, Dom,' Cherie said, patting me on the shoulder.

'You'll have to be careful showing off skills like that around here – the military will want you for one of their drone pilots,' Harry said.

A high-pitched whistling grew above us and we all looked up.

Light started pulsing downwards through the twister walls and a tiny but growing black point appeared in the sky.

My stomach knotted into a ball.

'Cronos…' Jules whispered.

'Okay, Dom, what's the plan now?' Cherie asked.

All three of them looked at me as though I had all the answers. If only. I was thinking one step at a time, and any minute the biggest warship that had ever taken to the skies, in this or any dimension, would arrive with a massive fleet in tow. Then what?

I gazed up at the ink stain enlarging into a tunnel. And along that tunnel a tiny spec appeared and grew fast.

Kraken.

The hairs on my neck stood up. The beginning of the end game was about to kick off. An end game for which I'd crippled my Whisperer ability.

CHAPTER NINETEEN

WAR

Jules pointed up at *Kraken*'s spec rushing down and growing to the size of a baseball. 'We'd better get a move on before that thing lands on our heads.'

'Let's get the heck out of here on *Athena*,' Harry replied.

Cherie shot him a frown and gestured to the Battle Wagon. 'No way I'm leaving my baby here.'

Harry blew his cheeks out. 'Oh, come on, Cherie. It's just a vehicle and we've got bigger priorities to worry about.' He pointed up. 'Priorities which are growing by the moment.'

The dark silhouette of the flying citadel, Vortex lightning spinning around it, was growing fast. Behind it I saw hundreds and hundreds of red airships also plummeting towards us.

Cherie folded her arms. 'I'm not leaving her.'

'You're so stubborn, but if you're staying, then so am I,' Harry said.

I looked between them, frustration bubbling through me. 'I'm not going to argue you around on this, am I?'

Cherie shook her head. 'Sorry, Dom. You know how much the

airships mean to you? Well, it's the same with me and this bucket of bolts. Too much of my life has gone into her to just leave her behind.'

As much as that drove me crazy, I understood too.

Harry sighed. 'And we haven't got the time to try to persuade her otherwise. Dom, get yourself and Jules into the air. Meanwhile, I'll do my best to keep Miss Stubborn here alive.'

This was so not how I'd wanted it to play out. These guys were my friends and if anything happened to them… I glanced at the storm-chasing vehicle. The moment *Kraken* arrived, someone onboard was bound to spot a bright scarlet vehicle on the ground beneath them.

Harry and Cherie needed an edge… My gaze tore to *Storm Wind* lashed to the armoured car's roof.

'Jules, can you get *Athena*'s chameleon net working again?'

'Definitely. There's an automatic safety cut-off that kicked when we crash-landed, so all I need to do is reset it.'

'Great. But you'll need to power *Athena* down too. Better to be on the safe side and use silent running.'

'Good thinking.' Jules rushed towards *Athena*.

'Okay, guys, if you're going to insist on staying, help me to drape the remains of *Storm Wind*'s gas canopy over the Battle Wagon.'

Cherie stared at me and her gaze widened. 'Oh, that's just pure genius, Dom.'

Harry looked between us. 'What?'

Cherie grinned at him. 'We're going to give the Battle Wagon an invisible paint job, that's what.'

A slow smile filled his face. 'I like your thinking.'

The three of us started hauling *Storm Wind*'s canvas envelope and his attached chameleon net over the Battle Wagon.

The pulses of light streaming through the twister walls around us sped up. The air tingled over my skin as the static charge built.

As we lashed the last corners of the chameleon net down to the vehicle, each dot above *Kraken* had grown into a recognisable airship.

'Okay, all done,' Harry said. 'Best of luck, Dom.' He shoved his hand out.

I shook it. 'You too.'

Cherie hugged me. 'What will you and Jules do now?'

'I reckon we'll play it by ear. What about you guys?'

She shrugged. 'Help where we can, and try to stay alive, I guess.'

I nodded. 'As Angelique would say, may their gods be with us all.'

'Amen to that, brother,' Harry said. He clambered after Cherie into the Battle Wagon, but paused for a moment and turned back to me. He gave me a long look that said everything without any words – that maybe it would be the last time we'd see each other alive.

My heart squeezed and I raised my hand in farewell.

Harry tipped his baseball cap towards me and disappeared into the Battle Wagon, pulling the hatch shut behind him with a clang.

The lightning blazed into a solid corridor of light. That meant the enemy fleet was approaching the event horizon into our world.

I placed my hand on *Storm Wind*'s Eye. *Whatever happens, I need you to look after my friends.*

'I will do my best, Dom.'

Do his best…that was all any of us could do from here on out.

I pressed my palm harder onto *Storm Wind*'s Eye.

I need you activate your chameleon net and then shut yourself down so Hades don't hear you.

'Of course…'

See you on the other side.

The ripped remnants of his chameleon net hummed and the Battle Wagon vanished. Suddenly I found myself, for all the world, looking as if I were floating in mid-air. But at least now my friends just might stand a chance.

I withdrew my hand and jumped down as I heard the Battle Wagon's V8 engine roar to life. I sprinted back to *Athena* as she shimmered and vanished.

A shadow spread over me and grew fast. With a clap of thunder that shook my whole world, *Kraken*, travelling at hundreds of miles an hour, hurtled out of the wormhole and came to a dead stop a few thousand feet directly overhead. The sky boomed again and again as each warship with him blazed into our reality.

I rushed through *Athena*'s still visible gondola door and slammed it shut behind me. Jules sat back on her haunches in front of the red matchbox reactor that powered the chameleon net and wiped a bead of sweat from her forehead. The Eye was closed too.

Silent running.

I rushed to the wheel, blazed the burner and pushed the throttle hard forward.

I braced myself for a storm of bullets as we leapt into the air. But the moment stretched onwards and we continued to gain height without anything bad happening.

Jules dropped into the co-pilot's seat. 'Looks as if we got away with it.'

'Here's hoping.'

She nodded and crossed the fingers on both hands.

Kraken floated over us, a dark rock mountain of death.

'Looks like a mothership from an alien invasion movie,' I said.

'Complete with its planet buster, ready to fire up.'

Even without *Kraken*, the Hades fleet around it was very

intimidating. As each ship appeared, they fired up their propellers and began gliding into dozens of box formations around *Kraken*, the smaller frigates arranged around the larger battleships in each group – a well-oiled war machine kicking into gear.

Goosebumps prickled over my skin. If the idea of taking on Hades and winning had felt impossible before, now that I saw them with my own eyes, any hope of winning seemed like an impossible fantasy.

Jules chewed her lip and pointed to my head. 'Can you hear your dad?'

Dad… With everything that was happening I hadn't given him a thought. I shook my head. 'I'm not firing on all cylinders since I fried my brain.'

Jules scowled. 'Maybe that's a bit of a blessing at the moment. The last time you ran into the Hive they almost took you out.'

She was right. I'd only managed to hold it together when I'd been mentally fit. But at least right now I was being spared the screams that were filling the skies above us.

Around us the twister walls had begun to thin, revealing our world beyond them: fields ripped clear of dead crops around the sprawl of the airbase. All over the military complex, dirt had been thrown up like sand dunes. I could imagine the disbelief of the survivors down there, as they stared up at the Hades invasion fleet over their heads.

The final wisps of the twister unwound and I banked *Athena* over to join the tail end of a boxed formation of about thirty ships around a battleship. With a mechanical rumble, a huge weapon battery with hundreds of stubby gun barrels descended from the belly of *Kraken* and swivelled towards the airbase.

'No…' Jules whispered.

A blaze of light erupted from the weapon battery and a boom rattled our gondola.

A single massive shell sped away from *Kraken* towards the base, tracing a black contrail through the sky.

I found myself clawing onto the wheel as Jules hunched into her seat.

With a distant thump, the hangar disappeared into a ball of orange fire. Even with my broken Whisperer ability, the battle cry of every Hades ship roaring victory iced my blood.

We stared at the blazing fire where a moment before a hardened concrete bunker had been sitting. A boiling cloud of smoke rolled up into the sky. The specs of soldiers swarmed towards it, like ants whose nest had been attacked.

The war for our world had begun.

'We've got to do something,' Jules said.

'There's nothing we can do apart from getting away and joining up with the main Cloud Rider fleet. If we try anything by ourselves, we'll get shot out of the sky for our troubles.'

Jules's shoulders dropped. 'I know, but that doesn't make it any easier to watch.'

Not for the first time I wished Jules didn't have to experience any of this madness. But also a big part of me was grateful that, however this day turned out, she was by my side for this final battle.

I reached over and squeezed her hand. She gave me a broken smile.

A fighter jet hurtled along what was left of the runway, its afterburner blazing orange flame behind it. Already, other jets had begun taxiing, getting ready for their turn to take off. Our US military was about to crank into action, but they had no idea what they were going up against.

As the first jet sped up into the air, my pulse amped. 'Even if they can't beat the Hades fleet, maybe they can make a dent in their forces.'

Jules nodded.

With a burst of light, two missiles sped away from the first airborne jet, heading for *Kraken*.

'Come on...' I whispered under my breath.

The missiles ducked and weaved. No way could they miss a target so big.

But already hundreds of enemy gun batteries had swung towards the attacker. I felt the pulse of *Kraken*'s voice and the air filled with the blaze of tracer fire converging on the missiles. Both blossomed instantly into balls of light.

The tracer fire swivelled towards the fighter jet, which ducked every way it could through the clear sky and banked away. The pilot was skilled, way beyond good, but there was only one way this uneven fight could end.

Gunfire from the closest battleship sped through the air and sliced through the jet's wing like a knife.

My stomach clenched as the aircraft tumbled away, a broken bird falling from the sky. I continued to watch, unable to tear my eyes away, until the plane slammed into the ground and exploded. No parachute. No hope for survival.

'That poor pilot didn't stand a chance,' Jules said.

'I know...'

Dozens of fighter jets now raced towards the enemy fleet.

In my mind I heard *Kraken*'s muted dark song urging their fleet on with a beat of a war drum. The nearest battle block of airships turned to the fighters.

The sky filled with missiles, tracer fire and the blazes of explosions. Plane after plane was swotted from the sky, like so many annoying mosquitoes. The dead wheat fields started to fill with burning wreckage.

'Look!' Jules shouted.

A lone jet had reached the first lead battleship, which was at least three times the size of *Athena*. It sped towards the red vessel, dodging the tracer fire. But the fighter didn't return fire. No missiles sped away from it, no machine gun blazed a pathway clear.

I gripped the wheel harder. 'That pilot's got to be out of ammo.'

'So what's he doing?'

The plane hurtled towards a Hades frigate. The cry of the targeted warship grew louder, its panicked tone drowning out even *Kraken*'s booming voice for a moment as it started to turn away.

Then I knew exactly what the enemy airship was worried about.

These weren't just any old pilots they were up against, these guys were the best of the best, trained to do whatever it took to stop the Hades attack in its tracks.

'That pilot is going to ram that battleship,' I said.

Jules gasped. 'But he'll get himself killed.'

'I think he's already figured that part out…'

We watched in silence as the plane rolled and tracer fire skimmed past the blister canopy of the cockpit as he sped towards his target. I imagined myself in that cockpit for a moment, my hands locked onto the joystick, everything focused on the airship rushing at me…

My stomach dropped as the fighter hurtled into the Hades airship's midsection.

The panicked ship's cry disappeared from my mind as both craft vanished behind an expanding fireball and tumbled towards the ground.

An ache filled me. Even if this was a small victory, it also felt like a defeat.

Brave didn't even begin to describe the pilots of the remaining jets as they adopted the same tactics. They jinked around the sky, avoiding the enemy fire as they picked out their targets.

The drone of *Kraken*'s Hive song changed as the entire fleet converged its firepower onto one plane.

No pilot, however skilled, could avoid that and each was wiped from the sky. Plane after plane exploded.

With each fresh death, a hollow feeling grew inside me. By the time the last fighter spun away, that feeling had become a vast cavern.

Then *Kraken*'s war drum sped up. The fleet, with their combined hunting cry, sang out towards the airbase.

Dozens of points of light glowed around the airfield and rockets arced up and shot towards the Hades ships.

'Anti-aircraft missiles,' Jules said.

Kraken's Hive mind cried out its challenge, and hundreds of gun ports opened up in the bottom of the flying palace.

Machine-gun fire flooded the air like dark hail, and long before they reached the enemy fleet the missiles blossomed into fireworks.

'Just how much firepower are Hades packing?' Jules said.

'Too much for our military. This fight is turning into a massacre.' My hand moved towards the weapon control.

Ashen-faced, Jules stared at me. 'That would be suicide, Dom.'

I so wanted to do something – anything – but I also knew she was right.

'Where the heck are the Cloud Riders anyway?' she said. 'They should have spotted this Fourth of July display lighting up the horizon by now.'

'Good question. Let's go and find out.' With my heart feeling like a lump of stone, I banked *Athena* away towards Twister Diner.

Six Black Hawk helicopters started to lift off.

I dived directly beneath the vast flying fortress, the ultimate war machine that Cronos's scientists had created. Somewhere on that ship he'd be directing the attack. I imagined the Emperor laughing at our Earth's best efforts to stop him.

One of the battleships swivelled its guns towards the fleeing Black Hawks and a moment later the lead helicopter was ripped to shreds by an explosion.

Rage boiled through me. So many brave men and women dying and this was only the beginning of the war.

The capital ship's main gun roared and roared, again and again. All the might of a US military base had only managed to take out one Hades warship from a thousand. And this wasn't even the main event. When *Kraken* unleashed Fury, just like that our Earth would be torn in two to its very core, and billions of people would die.

'Not on my watch,' I muttered under my breath. I pushed the throttle to full.

Jules wrapped her arms around herself, and nodded. 'Mine neither. So let's go and find out what's happened to the cavalry.'

We sped away, through the smoking plumes of death drifting into the sky, and back towards Twister Diner.

CHAPTER TWENTY

DEATH AND DESTRUCTION

I felt shaken to my core, having seen so much death and destruction in such a short space of time. And Cronos had hardly broken into a sweat to win such a decisive victory. Could the immense bravery and skill of the Cloud Riders somehow stop the march of the Hades war machine in its tracks?

I gazed towards Jules standing by the Voice Valve with its headphones strapped over her ears. 'Any joy?'

She shook her head and lifted one of the earpieces. 'Nothing but static. Hades are completely jamming the airwaves with the Quantum Pacifier. I was kinda hoping that we might be able to contact the Battle Wagon, but zip there as well.'

'I just hope they're okay.'

'We are, aren't we? And I think with everything that was going on in the sky Hades would be unlikely to spot them on the ground, especially with *Storm Wind*'s chameleon net turned on to mask them.'

I just hoped that was true because I wasn't sure I could cope with losing close friends so soon in this battle. Without doubt this was going to be the longest day of my life…if we survived to the end of it.

Overhead, contrails threaded the sky. Fighters – bomber aircraft and drones – were now all heading towards the Jackson airbase. Along the highways beneath us, convoys of green military vehicles – tanks and Humvees – rushed to the frontline, every vehicle loaded with guns and troops.

This had to be a sign that our president had been informed of the invasion. He was probably in some bunker deep beneath the Oval Office, ashen-faced as the generals informed him about the attack on home soil.

'Yes, Mr President, the enemy fleet appeared from a tornado…'

Yeah, good luck with that conversation.

For the last ten minutes, flashes had lit up the horizon like an artificial dawn – the continuous thundering sound of explosions rolling past…and so far nothing had returned from that firefight.

I spotted three triangular aircrafts at high altitude. I grabbed Angelique's spyglass from the clip and gazed up at them.

Jules squinted at the sky. 'What are those?'

'Stealth fighters.'

Jules's eyes widened. 'Dom, watch out.'

Something streaked towards us.

Instinct kicked in before I'd had time to think. I banked hard to the left and the thing sped past close enough for me to eyeball the cruise missile as it tore beside our gondola. It shot along on its way, its single jet engine howling like a banshee into the distance.

Jules breathed fast. 'I thought that Hades had spotted us for a minute there.'

'Me too.'

'Our government really is throwing everything it has at them.'

'Not everything, although I expect it's only a matter of time before they launch nukes.'

She gave me a grim look. 'This is turning into a regular *War of the Worlds*.'

A chill ran through me. This was exactly what it was, but not a battle with Martians like in the movie, but one with crazed humans from a parallel world.

The cruise missile had already vanished into the distance. I counted the seconds off in my head. 'One, two, three, four...' The higher the number got the nearer the missile would be getting to the target. 'Five, six, seven—' A pulse of light blazed and slowly faded. Ten seconds later the boom reached us.

Jules slumped back in her chair. 'Something tells me that one didn't reach its target either.'

'I was kinda hoping it might have made it through because of its small size.'

Jules's shoulders dropped. She looked at me for the longest moment. 'Dom, I need to ask you something. And I want you to be absolutely straight with me. Don't dress up your answer just to make me feel better, okay?'

I had a strong hunch I knew what she was going to ask and my stomach flipped over. 'Okay...'

'Do you really believe we have a chance of winning today?'

So there it was – the same question I kept asking myself over and over. The person I'd crossed dimensions to save, who knew me better than I did myself, was voicing my own personal nightmare. No point in lying, not to her. She'd see straight through that in seconds.

'No. No I don't, Jules.'

She closed her eyes and took a long breath. But when she opened her eyes again, there weren't any tears, just a determined set to her jaw.

'That's what I thought too,' she said. 'But we're still going to try anyway, right?'

I felt a huge surge of love for her. She wasn't going to turn tail from this fight. Just like me.

'Too right, and at the very least I'm going to scratch the paintwork on Cronos's precious *Kraken*.'

Jules crossed over to me and pulled me into a hug. She smelt of summer meadows, of home, of countless memories. She buried her face into my neck, her warmth mingling with mine.

I held onto her with one arm as I steered *Athena* towards home, not wanting this moment to end. Time might be about to run out for our world, but right here, right now, in a frozen bubble of time, it felt as if we had forever.

She coughed and moved away, breathing through her nose. 'Thanks, Dom. I needed that.'

'Me too…'

She laced her arm through mine, as outside the grid of fields fell into a familiar pattern. We were nearly back at the diner – less than a few miles to go.

'*Athena*, are you there, over?' Angelique's faint voice crackled from the headphones connected to the Valve Voice.

I broke away from Jules. 'Oh, thank god.' I rushed over to the radio and flicked a switch.

Angelique's voice came through the cabin speaker. 'I repeat, *Athena*, are you there, over?'

I squeezed the button on the mic's side. 'We're about five miles away from your position, over.'

'Where have you been, Dom? The whole fleet has been waiting for you. We can't launch until you counteract the Quantum Pacifier that's stranded our whole fleet.'

Can't launch... I gripped the mic harder. With everything that'd had happened I hadn't even thought of it. And how could I tell Angelique that I'd now messed up any chance of that? I cupped my hand over the mic. 'What do I say, Jules?'

She brushed her fingers down the side of my face. 'The truth, Dom.'

I nodded, but my heart thudded so hard I thought it might break. 'Just give me a moment.' I handed her the mic.

'Sure...' She took it from me. 'Angelique, Cronos appeared with the Hades fleet over the airbase and he's already taken it out.'

Angelique sighed over the Valve Voice. 'We've been seeing the explosions. Textbook Hades tactics. Destroy any nearby tactical facilities that pose a threat.'

'But I don't get it,' Jules replied. 'They could've simply jumped in, pretended they'd come in peace while they powered up Fury, and destroyed our planet before anyone realised what was really happening.'

'I'm afraid it's arrogance. Cronos likes to test his captains in battle with live targets, especially when he knows the odds are stacked in his favour.'

Anger boiled through me and I snatched the mic back. 'Target practice. We've just witnessed hundreds of people losing their lives. And you're telling me this is just a bit of sport for Hades.'

There was a longer sigh at the other end. 'I'm afraid that's exactly the sort of monster that Cronos is, Dom.'

Jules shook her head. 'That jerk is like some sort of sick Roman emperor watching his gladiators take out the barbarians in an arena.'

My anger burned to white hot. 'I'll give him barbarians.'

'It's time to take the fight to him,' Angelique said. 'Time to use your ability, Dom.'

The fire inside me spluttered out.

Jules patted my arm. 'You have to tell her,' she whispered.

I took the deepest breath, my heart hammering harder than it had with any fight I'd ever faced with Hades. Nausea rose up through my gullet. 'I don't know quite how to tell you this, Angelique, but…'

Angelique's voice became sharp, almost as if she already knew. 'What is it?'

'There's been a problem.'

'What sort of problem?'

I swallowed hard. 'I tried the Theta Codex boost function…' I took a deep breath as the precipice rushed towards me. 'I seemed to have fried my mind…'

There was a moment's awful silence. I could almost feel my words detonating at the other end.

'You did what?' Angelique said so quietly that it was somehow way beyond anger. 'But how can that even be possible? That function is locked out on the machine you've been using.'

Jules grimaced. 'That would be my fault. I hardwired the machine for Dom so he could override the lock-out.'

Angelique's voice dropped to an even fainter whisper. 'Do you realise what you've both done? You have put the entire Cloud Rider fleet out of this battle.'

Guilt rushed through me. There was no way I'd let Jules take any blame for my stupidity. 'It wasn't Jules's fault. I asked her to do it but didn't tell her what it might do to me. I'm afraid this is all my doing.'

'I thought you would know better, Dom, especially when you knew everyone was depending on you. Why do you think that function was locked out?'

'As a safety measure.'

'Precisely, and that was because we quickly discovered that too many idiots, like you, thought they could try a shortcut.'

Her words stung me more than if she'd struck me around the face.

'I'll make this right, Angelique.'

'How? Just tell me how, so I can go and tell my father and all the Cloud Riders about your grand plan.'

'I…' My chest tightened. 'I don't know, Angelique, not yet at least.'

'That's what I thought, Dom. I'm going to let the others know about your utter stupidity.' The radio hissed into silence, turning the slap into a punch.

'Angelique?'

Only the hiss of static answered me.

Jules rubbed my back. 'She's upset, Dom, but she'll calm down eventually.'

'That's just it – there may be no *eventually* because of me. What have I done, Jules?'

She took my shoulders between her hands and made me look at her. 'Listen here. You knew that boost function might kill you, right?'

I shrugged. 'Yeah, and?'

'But you went ahead anyway.'

I shrugged. 'So?'

'That's just it, Dom. It took guts – real guts – to try what you did. You knew you could die, but you took a calculated risk because you thought it would help us win the war.'

'I guess…'

'You see, even when you get it wrong you still manage to do it for heroic reasons.' Despite everything, she actually smiled at me.

And impossibly, from somewhere deep inside, I found a smile too. 'What an idiot, huh?'

'No, just someone who should confide in his best friend more than he does.' She took my hands in hers. 'Look, Dom, what's done is done. The important thing now is to find out if there is a way to get your full ability back.'

'I don't know if—'

She pressed her finger to my lips. 'I'm afraid *don't know* isn't allowed at the moment. We need a bit more *can do* attitude from you, Mr Taylor.'

My smile broadened. 'Maybe you're right.'

'Of course I am. So let's stop stumbling around in the pit of despair and see if we can figure this out together.'

'Okay…' Somehow, however bad things were, just talking to Jules made my anguish loosen its grip a fraction.

'So let's think this through,' she said. She raised five fingers and bent the first one back. 'When you first tried that boost function you could barely move, not to mention you deafened yourself.'

'Yeah?'

'Stick with me on this…' She counted off the second finger. 'And you've started to recover some of your ability since it happened.'

'And?'

She closed the third finger. 'So who's to say you won't get your full ability back any moment now?'

'That's been my secret hope too, but right now it's as if my brain has been filled with fog. I can't even hear the any of the other Cloud Rider ships.'

She pulled down her fourth finger. 'But you spoke to *Storm Wind* despite the effects of the Quantum Pacifier and what you've done to yourself.'

'Yes...'

She lowered her final finger and gestured towards the Eye. 'So how about asking *Athena* if she can help you accelerate your recovery? I mean, she has to be the nearest thing we have to an expert onboard.'

I stared at her. Jules was making a lot of sense. 'It's got to be worth a go.'

She smiled. 'Of course it is. We've still got a few minutes till we land and we must be at a safe distance to boot *Athena* back up again... So why don't you try talking it through with her?'

Ahead, the diner had come into view, but the fields looked deserted, no sign of anyone anywhere. Probably all onboard their cloaked ships as the flight crews tried desperately to coax their vessels into life. And down there somewhere Angelique would be letting King Louis know how I'd messed up everything.

But I also knew that all my guilt was doing was adding to the noise in my head... and that wasn't going to help anyone. The most important thing was to make this right – everything else was secondary to that.

'Okay, let's try,' I said.

Jules patted my arm as she took over from me at the wheel. I opened the hatch in the cockpit and pressed the red button to boot up *Athena* again.

Lights twinkled across the cockpit as steam hissed from the Eye. I crossed over to it and with a deep breath placed my hand on the warm copper dome.

Please, dear God, let this work...

CHAPTER TWENTY-ONE

REBOOT

My brain felt as if it had been filled with sticky maple syrup that sucked at my thoughts as I tried to form them. *Athena*'s song still sounded as if she were singing to me down a long echoey tunnel.

Athena, *why I can't hear the other ships any more?*

Her voice was barely audible in the jumble of my thoughts. *'Some of your neural connections have been damaged, Whisperer.'*

My chest gripped. So there it was – brain damage. So now the real question was: how bad?

Permanently? I thought-voiced.

'No – as you have already discovered, your brain pathways are starting to re-establish themselves.'

But I need to stop the Quantum Pacifier right now or we won't stand a chance of defeating Cronos. There has to be a way, Athena.

There was a long silence in my thoughts.

Athena?

'There is a way, but there is also a huge risk, Whisperer.'

What sort of risk?

'*That you may, quite literally, lose your mind.*'

What?

'*To understand what has happened to you, you need to imagine the sum of your thoughts like a complicated pattern on a carpet. And based on that analogy, your mind's synapses – the threads of the pattern if you will – have been broken by the brain boost attempt.*'

So you're kinda saying that my brain – the carpet – needs to be woven back together again?

'*That sums it up very well, Whisperer.*'

And there's a way to do this?

'*Maybe…*'

I felt a glow of hope. *What?*

'*Sing with me.*'

The brain syrup was obviously getting into my mental ears. *Come again?*

'*If we can build our combined song to a sufficiently powerful level we may be able to reach some of the other ships. Then, each ship we can connect to will amplify your own song inside your brain. However, you will also experience extreme neural pain and I must warn you that if you break concentration, even for a moment, then the pattern of who you are will be lost forever.*'

I let *Athena's* words sink in… Get this wrong I might end up with my brain wiped. But I already knew what I had to do. I opened my eyes to gaze across at Jules.

'And?' she asked.

'*Athena* thinks there may be a way to reboot my mind.'

'Sounds great, but I'm sensing a "but" here?'

I gazed at her. No more lies, no more half-truths. She'd always deserved so much more from me than that and from now on, however many moments we had left together, she'd get it.

219

'There is… Apart from it hurting real bad, if I break contact with *Athena* during this, my brain will be wiped.'

'Oh…' She slowly blinked. 'But you've already made up your mind, haven't you, Dom?'

'I haven't really got a choice, have I, Jules?'

She tied off *Athena*'s wheel and the ship settled into a gentle turn. She crossed to me. 'Of course I understand,' she whispered.

And she did. I saw it in her eyes and I adored her all the more for it.

'Whatever happens, you're everything to me, Dom.'

'You too, Jules…'

She gazed at the Eye. 'I'm going to be right by your side through this. I'm here for you.'

'I know you will be…' I turned to the Eye and placed my hand on the dome. *Okay, let's do this*, Athena.

'Good luck, Whisperer, but you must remember not to let your song falter.'
I promise you, I'll try my best.

Her song began to reverberate along the tunnel between us and at once a deep pain spiked inside my skull and it began to throb. A groan squeezed between my lips. I felt Jules gently cradling my neck.

Whatever was coming, I had to get through it… I had to.

Athena's song strengthened and I slowed my breathing. The image of looking through the bars of a cot flashed into my mind, Mom and Dad gazing down at me, their faces full of love… The scene faded and agony rocked through my body. I gritted my teeth.

Now I was outside the house beneath the oak tree, my body covered with the dappled light of leaf shade. A young Jules, complete with pigtails, looked down at me from the branch she was sitting on. I felt a pain in my ankle and remembered I'd been climbing with her in a race to the top, but had fallen. We'd been eight. Jules leapt down, her expression full of guilt, and wiped away my tears... The scene faded.

My body burned as if I were being torn apart, muscle by muscle, but *Athena's* song grew stronger.

'You can do this,' I heard Jules whisper.

My hand clawed onto the Eye.

Another image flashed through my mind: skyscrapers rearing up to the sky around me. I gazed at a shop window filled with Christmas decorations so amazing that my heart wanted to burst at the sight of them. This was a family visit to New York when I was ten.

'This memory,' *Athena* whispered.

The image shifted. I was holding Mom's hand as we got off the subway in New York, Dad leading the way as always. Then we heard a woman singing, her voice so beautiful that we all stood still and listened... Pain blazed through the nerves of my body, worse than anything I'd ever experienced before.

I clung onto the memory in the sea of pain, knowing that I'd drown if I let go.

Her voice had been so clear, so full of joy...

I could hear someone whimpering in pain – me. But I could feel Jules's hands on me as she caressed me face. I hung onto the thread of memory with every ounce of energy I had left.

'It's the voice of a New York angel,' Mom said.

Dad chuckled and rubbed the top of my head. I pulled Mom by the hand as the voice got louder. We rounded a corner and there she was, a girl of about fifteen in tattered clothes, her hat lying on the ground in front of her, filled with a few dull coins...

Molten metal rushed through every nerve of my body.

'Do not let go...' Athena whispered.

I stuck my hand in my pocket and gave the girl all the money I'd been saving to buy a present for Mom and Dad. I remembered the pride that had filled their eyes as I placed the five dollar bill in her hat. But best of all was the biggest smile the girl had given to me as she sang out even louder.

Right then I'd decided that Mom had to be right – this girl was an honest to God angel. But now, looking back, I found myself seeing this memory in a new light. That girl might've been down on her luck, but the beauty of who she was had still shone through.

And then I knew exactly why Athena had chosen this particular memory. She was showing me that it was possible to be more than the sum of what had happened to you, just as that girl had proved by singing her heart out despite everything. And I may have messed up, as bad as it was possible to do, but that was the past and what really mattered was what I did next.

'Forgive yourself,' Athena said.

A lump came to my throat. Yes...

My determination started to build, growing like a mounting wave. It was down to me to stop Cronos. There were others like that girl out there on our Earth who were worth a million of what Cronos could ever hope to be. And I was going to save her and every other person in New York, San Fran, LA, London, Paris – all the cities – all of this whole beautiful crazy world that we all lived on and loved, even if we sometimes forgot that we should.

The pain hissed and roared, trying to break me, but I dug deeper than I'd ever gone before. Athena's song soared and I knew exactly what I had to do. I took a shuddering breath. My throat scratched as I breathed, but I forced myself to sing and my voice joined Athena's, her harmony altering to match mine.

A sensation like warm water ran through my body. The pain and fear started to ebb away, as our song began to climb together. We raised our voices to the sky, like soaring birds, and as we sang I realised her voice no longer sounded echoey, but now chimed with crystal clarity. Then I heard another ship's song, a distant backing track to our own duet but which also grew louder.

With a surge of joy I realised it was Tesla's ship, *Muse*. Her voice wove around *Athena*'s. And then other songs joined in, creating a chorus so loud that I felt it buzz through my chest.

My Whisperer ability was back and I could hear the Cloud Rider fleet clearer than ever before. But still our combined hymn climbed to beyond the limits of our sky, and I felt it sweeping out across the universe. Then I heard a second chorus of another orchestra echoing our hymn. But it couldn't be the Hades ships because these voices sounded at peace – full of love. A vision began to form in my mind…

I hung in space, surrounded by a million pinpricks of light against a black velvet backdrop. Ahead of me, a nebula glowed, lit up by the stars hidden within it. My mind whirled. This was Empyrean, the AI heaven, a simulation run by the slumbering minds of all the ships clustered at Floating City, which *Titan* had shown to me.

I found myself drifting towards the gas cloud.

Two small suns orbited me. The song of *Athena* came from one, and *Muse*'s from the other. The warmth of the nebula grew stronger as I neared it and within the hidden points glowed brighter. The scarlet cloud expanded until it rolled over me and I dropped into its soothing warmth.

The murmur of the combined ship-song began to fill my mind, rushing through my body and my thoughts like cold spring water, washing all the heat of my pain away with its touch.

Through the wisps of nebula, a point of light greater than all the others combined into a huge, blazing ball before me.

'Whisperer, it is time for you to awaken,' Titan's voice said from the massive star.

Awaken? I don't understand.

'Everything that you have striven for is now within your grasp.'

But how? And for that matter, how can I even be here when you're all the way back at Floating City?

'When you first visited this place, part of your consciousness was left here,' Titan replied.

What do you mean part of me was left there?

'An imprint of everything that you are was stored in the combined matrix of the ships' minds. You are part of us now, Whisperer, and we, you. And it is time for us to heal you.'

Heal my mind?

'Yes, we will restore your mind from the information that we have here.'

What, like a computer backup?

'More or less.'

I thought of the time I'd had to restore my laptop from a backup after it'd crashed. I'd ended up losing all the essays I'd been working on for an assignment since it had last been saved. A pang of worry swooped through me.

Hang on, this isn't going to wipe my memories of all the experiences I've had since I left you, is it?

'No, we will weave the neural pathways around the existing ones. I promise you, you will gain everything and lose nothing.'

The pulse of hope grew stronger inside me; the key to everything finally within my reach. *Okay, tell me – what do I need to do, Titan?*

'Just lose yourself within our song and trust in us completely.'

And I'd never been so certain about anything in my life. Without hesitation, I tuned into the chorus of ships, and sang out with everything I had.

Around me the points of light, the AIs, the souls of individual ship Psyche gems floated towards me, the chorus of their song vibrating every atom in my body. Like a swarm of fireflies they orbited around me.

It felt as if insects were crawling through my mind and leaving tingling footprints deep within my skull. The dull headache began to let go as my senses sharpened. I buzzed with energy like a battery fully recharged. I felt strong – so fit that I could run around the whole planet without stopping if I'd wanted to. I'd never felt so alive, so brand new. And most importantly of all, I felt ready to take anything on, even Cronos.

The ships' songs around me focused into human voices…and my voice became lost among theirs. They, me, one, and all the same, with no boundaries between us any more.

My senses multiplied by every ship, I could feel each of the Angelus within the nebula. As I concentrated, I could even pick out individual voices among them – *Athena*'s, *Muse*'s, *Storm Wind*'s, *Zeus*'s – any ship that I chose. And each time I did so my view shifted in the nebula and I found myself looking back at my own body hanging suspended in the crimson mist, glowing like some sort of human torch…the ships' view of me within Empyrean.

The huge star of *Titan*'s AI drifted towards my hovering body – a sun on a collision course. The smaller orbs began to spin around both of us, faster and faster until they became blurs of light, a storm of comets rushing past.

I switched back to my own body's perspective and watched *Titan*'s star boil towards me. But I didn't feel fear, just utter peace. As its outer golden wall brushed over my skin, no burning heat ignited my body, but instead the warmth of a summer's day. Whatever this was, it certainly felt like destiny – like something I'd been waiting for my whole life.

The ships' joyous song roared as I fell into *Titan*'s star and everything around me blazed with light.

Titan's voice boomed in my brain. *'Dom Taylor, it is time to awaken.'*

'Awaken,' the ships all cried out around me.

I felt a kick in the stomach and from the nebula I flew out and away from the sun, racing through the stars. A tiny blue dot appeared before me, in the vastness of space and I hurtled towards it at an impossible speed. The dot became Earth, growing larger fast, until the view centred on the North American continent...on Oklahoma... on a ship bathed with golden light heading for somewhere called Twister Diner with a hangar and a house nearby.

I hurtled towards *Athena* and shot into the gondola. With a jolt, I opened my eyes and found Jules crouched over me.

She smeared her tears away. 'I thought you were dead! You stopped breathing for a whole five minutes!'

'Not dead, just rebooted and all brand new.'

Her expression widened. 'Pardon me?'

'No time to explain, but I need to contact Angelique straight away. I've just got my abilities back, Jules, but better than ever. I can now hear the whole fleet – even the ships back at Floating City inside their AI heaven.'

Jules's eyes widened. 'That's fantastic, but...' Her expression broke.

'What?'

'While you were out...'

I could see bad news burning behind her eyes. There was something she didn't want to tell me.

A sense of dread washed over me. 'Go on, Jules, please...'

She took my hands in hers. 'I've been listening to the chatter on the Valve Voice...' She swallowed. 'Angelique's already set off to attack Cronos with a squadron of ornicopters, which weren't affected by the Quantum Pacifier because they don't use Psuche gems.'

'But they'll be slaughtered without the rest of the fleet to back them up.'

'I know... Angelique did too.'

'Then we've got to radio her and stop them.'

Jules shook her head. 'But we can't. The ornicopters are going to maintain radio silence during the attack. That way, Angelique hopes to hit Cronos before he realises what's going on...' Her voice caught and she took a deeper breath. 'And they've loaded the craft with explosives, Dom.'

There it was – the awful news Jules hadn't wanted to break to me. And suddenly I knew exactly how Angelique and the other pilots intended to bring the enemy airships down – they'd do just what our military fighter pilots had done...

'You mean they've turned them into flying bombs?' I said.

'Yes...'

I tried to push my panic away, to force myself to think clearly.

I grabbed Jules by the shoulders. 'Contact Louis on the Valve Voice and let him know our plan is back on track. Getting the Cloud Rider fleet airborne immediately is the only hope for Angelique and those with her.'

'You got it.' Jules rushed to the radio set and started spinning dials. I stared out at the horizon that still popped with explosions. Somewhere out there, Angelique was flying to her death if we didn't get to her in time.

CHAPTER TWENTY-TWO

LOST

The song from the ships, moored on the ground, bellowed in my mind with impatience. The news that I'd got my Whisper ability back had sped like wildfire throughout the fleet's crews. I could feel the hope of the ships and their crews reborn in the faster heartbeat of the fleet's song.

I was still getting my head around my enhanced abilities as we all waited for King Louis to launch the fleet. I'd quickly discovered that I could use my ability even when I wasn't touching an Eye to communicate. It was kinda liberating to no longer be tethered like that. Now, just by concentrating, I could tune up my supercharged vision into any of the ship's sensors.

At first, this new view of the world had been disorientating, almost enough to make me hurl Mom's Eye of the Storm breakfast. But as I'd experimented with it, I'd grown better at coping with the two views — one of the everyday world and one of the ship-sensor view of things that I could superimpose over the other at will.

I gazed down at the fields around the diner and, despite the airships' chameleon cloaks being turned on, I could see each ship as clearly as a glowing ghost. And at the heart of each vessel a blue star blazed – the Angelus within the ship's Psuche gems. I could even see the ship-song rippling through the air like a heat haze between the ships. My ability didn't stop there though. I also saw dozens of individual diamonds of light within each craft – thousands in the case of *Hope*. The ship's crews. It was mental, mad and exhilarating, all at the same time.

I gazed towards the Jackson airbase. The sooner we set off after Angelique, the better. I turned the wheel and banked *Athena* back towards her.

Jules glanced up from the Valve Voice – she'd been listening into the fleet's chatter. 'How are you doing, Dom?'

'It's taking me a while to get my head around it, but I just wish you could see what I could now, Jules.'

'You can tell me all the details afterwards.'

'You think there'll be an afterwards?'

She gave me a tight smile. 'We have a much better chance of that now, thanks to you.'

I appreciated her vote of confidence, but also knew that even with my supercharged abilities there'd only be a slim chance we could pull off a victory today. However, below us the ships strained at their mooring ropes to get into the sky.

'Will the king get on with it already?' I said.

The headphones crackled. Jules slid them back over her ears and flicked a switch. 'Your wish and all that…'

The gondola's speaker crackled into life.

'On my mark, be ready to lift-off,' King Louis said.

Jules jutted her chin out. 'Bring it on.'

'May the gods fly with us... Launch!' the king shouted.

Below us, *Zeus* was the first to leap into the air, his big single prop spinning fast at his stern with the urgency of a king going after his daughter.

Athena sang out above the entire fleet as they rose like a shoal of glittering green fish behind their leader. The last ship to ascend was *Hope*, her hundreds of props whirring in unison.

Pride rushed through me for each and every ship rising into the sky. This might have been a hopeless fight but there was nowhere else in this or any other universe I wanted to be.

'What an incredible sight,' I said.

Jules leant over and peered out of a porthole, her brow furrowed. 'I'll have to take your word for it.'

'Sorry, I keep forgetting they're invisible to you.' I gunned *Athena*'s engines to pull ahead of the ascending fleet.

'Shouldn't we be waiting for the others?' Jules asked.

'No way I'm waiting a moment longer than we have to – Angelique needs our help.'

Jules's gaze tightened on the horizon. 'How do you think she's doing?'

Dark images flooded my imagination. I gave Jules a helpless look, but kept quiet. If I voiced my thoughts for even a moment they would stick their claws into me and wouldn't let go. I found myself pushing the handle harder against its stops.

She just nodded, her expression mirroring my own concern.

Behind us the fleet had formed itself into an arrowhead formation with *Zeus* at its point. *Hope* followed at the rear, quickly rising to a position high above, and *Muse*, altitude balloons deployed, higher still. Tesla was going to have quite the view of the battle that was about to unfold.

With my enhanced vision, my gaze snagged on Jules's attention, intent on the Valve Voice. She looked so alive, so beautiful.

Jules stared at me. 'What?'

'Oh, nothing…'

'You sure? Because, if there's something you need to say to me that you may never get another chance to…'

What did I have to say to her? That she was my best friend…that she meant everything to me…that I loved her?

Without saying a word, Jules put down the headphones and crossed to me. She curled her hand through mine. 'Whatever you're thinking, you give me the shivers when you look at me like that.'

My body felt electric. If she stood any closer, sparks would start flying between us. Her eyes, pools of darkness, pulled at me.

'I…'

'Shhh.' Jules tilted her head up to me and I found myself leaning towards her, the remaining distance evaporating between us.

Our lips met and it felt like a firework display exploding in my head.

Jules let out a faint sigh, her body relaxing against mine.

Time stood still. I didn't want this to stop, but it was hard to ignore the fleet's song swelling around us, reflecting my own joy burning inside. I wondered how many Navigators were wondering what the heck was going on with their ships.

'Will you guys please cut that out? It's distracting!' I said into the air.

Jules rubbed my wrist with her thumb. 'Ship-song?'

'Yeah, and they're singing away like some sort of backing orchestra to a romantic film.'

She laughed. 'Perfect.'

I noticed how her hair framed her face, the freckles on her nose, how her eyes shone – all part of the complicated jigsaw that Jules was. And I loved all that and every part of her.

I leant in and kissed her again. When we finally broke apart it felt as though a fragment of my own soul had broken away with Jules.

She grinned at me. 'Mmmm. Who would have thought Dom Taylor would be such a fantastic kisser?'

I laughed. 'You're not so bad yourself.'

A flash of light came from the horizon.

My joy swirled away as my heart tightened. 'Looks like Angelique and the others have reached the Hades fleet.'

Jules, grim-faced, let go of me and crossed back to the Valve Voice.

Time for me to do my thing. Time to make a difference. For all the people I loved, all the people I knew, and even the people who'd never heard of Dom Taylor. Time to save them all.

Hundreds and hundreds of lit glass planets filled *Athena*'s Eye. On one side, the glowing green spheres of Cloud Riders, on the other, ten times the amount of Hades red planet markers. I breathed deeply and let my consciousness rush outwards across the fleet.

At once I had the eyes of a hundred Cloud Rider ships and could see everything that they could as prismatic overlapping images.

Where was Angelique among all of that? Was she even alive?

I centred myself on *Athena* and her viewpoint filled my mind. I gazed forward, using her optical scope to extend my own sight towards the horizon. The air squeezed from my lungs as I took in the view.

Hundreds of plane wrecks now littered the corn fields in raked scars around Jackson, a few discarded parachutes lying like oversized daisies among them. I swivelled the scope towards the airbase. The burning remains of destroyed tanks and Humvees crowded the rubble of the former airbase.

Heck, our military had to be running out of things to throw at the Hades fleet. Then what? Nukes?

In my mind's eye, I focused my attention to the sky over the airfield and the Hades ships. At the centre of their fleet the huge mass of *Kraken* hung like a mountain in the air, so vast that it dwarfed even *Hope*.

Something else snagged my attention. At first I thought it was a flock of crows, small black dots swooping between the enemy airships. The things ducked the tracer fire way more successfully than our own military fighters had. Then my heart leapt as I took in the shimmering blades of their flapping wings – Angelique's ornicopter squadron!

I watched a small group of the dark crafts dive towards one of the larger Hades airships. They spiralled around the incoming bullets as though they were doing their best to taunt the enemy. Then I spotted a craft higher than the rest. The lone ornicopter dived straight down like a hawk hurtling towards its prey. My heart shot into my mouth as the tiny craft struck the warship and it exploded with a bloom of light.

The other ornicopters swept away, almost in slow motion, as the back of the Hades airship broke in two.

Even though I was keeping the Hades fleet song suppressed in my mind, I heard the dying ship's fearful howl as it tumbled to the ground, its crew spilling from its broken corridors into the clear air.

With a tumble of giddiness, my consciousness snapped back into *Athena*'s gondola.

Jules lowered the spyglass from her eye. 'Angelique?'

I spread my hands. 'I don't know.' Were we already too late? A sense of despair tightened its grip around me.

'You have to try to make contact somehow,' Jules said.

'I'll try…' I shifted back into *Athena*'s sensors and scanned the swarming black dots. One of them had to be Angelique, just had to be.

Okay… If I were in her shoes, what would I be doing right now? In an instant it came to me – exactly what any badass warrior princess would do – go after the demon emperor himself.

I focused my attention on *Kraken*. Sure enough I spotted a group of ornicopters swarming around it, but up against *Kraken* they looked like mosquitos matched against an elephant.

A wall of bullets rushed out from the vast capital ship. Ornicopter after ornicopter disappeared in balls of explosion. But then I spotted that the Cloud Rider fighters weren't alone. A few F-15 fighters ducked and swooped right along with them… Their pilots had obviously recognised an ally in the air, even if they hadn't when on the ground.

I saw a single ornicopter avoiding every bullet hurled at it as it jinked left, right, up, down, as though the pilot could read the mind of the enemy ship. I knew to the core of my being that nobody else could fly like that, not with that sort of skill.

Angelique.

Kraken threw all it had at her – even its Voice Scream tinged with frustration at the princess who refused to die.

Angelique's ornicopter sped towards the battlements at the top of *Kraken*.

My feet felt glued to the floor. This attack run was on a one way ticket to its destination.

Athena's song faltered and her words shouted in my mind. *'Please stop her, Whisperer!'*

But how? The dot hurtled towards *Kraken*.

'Project the entire fleet's song into her mind and she might be able to hear us,' Athena said.

Less than a few hundred feet remained…

I expanded my consciousness to every single Cloud Rider ship, their thoughts becoming mine, and mine theirs.

A hundred ship voices shouted with mine. *'Angelique, stop!'*

The ornicopter stopped jinking for a second and a line of tracer fire almost hit it. Had she heard?

Two hundred feet...

Angelique, break off, we're almost with you.

The black flying machine started to pull up. She had heard me! But even at the extreme range I could see the ornicopter vibrating and shaking, wings tearing themselves apart under tons of G-force as she tried to pull up. Tens of feet left and the ornicopter's nose came up just enough for it to hurtle past *Kraken*'s battlements.

Elation surged through me. She'd made it—

My thought was stamped away by a gun battery swinging towards her craft. Its tracer fire ripped through the delicate wings. Then, in terrifying detail, I watched the small ship start to tumble away, end over end, towards the ground.

No! I couldn't breathe. This couldn't be happening.

Angelique, can you hear me?

The broken craft hurtled downwards and a cold sense of dread rushed through me. Maybe she'd blacked out, or a bullet had already found her heart, or—

'Princess Angelique, you must wake up,' *Athena* cried out, her voice echoed by the chorus of a hundred ships.

But the ornicopter continued spiralling, trailing smoke, with no sign of anyone bailing out.

The ships' song became frantic as though they were trying to halt her descent with their combined willpower and raise her back into the sky.

The ornicopter smashed into the ground and crumpled to nothing. A pulse of light was followed by an orange fireball rolling up into the sky. A ring of fire rippled out across the dry cornfield.

The craft had crashed.

Time stopped.

The song of the fleet fell silent, ship by ship, and for a moment there was only complete stillness.

The frozen moment stretched on.

Not a murmur or whisper was uttered, the sense of utter shock radiating throughout the fleet.

This couldn't be happening – it was impossible… Angelique was gone… She was really gone.

I opened my eyes, blinking back tears.

'What's wrong?' Jules asked.

My mouth fell open. The pit inside devoured my mind. 'Angelique, she…' I swallowed hard. 'She's…she's dead.'

Jules rocked back as though someone had struck her. She dropped the Valve Voice headset, rushed over and flung her arms around me. 'She can't be. Not after all this – not after everything we've all been through together.'

All I wanted to do was let out the pain splintering my soul, and howl at the sky.

The Valve Voice whistled. 'What is happening, Dom?' King Louis said from the speaker. 'Ship-song has fallen silent across the entire fleet. I cannot even get any sense from *Zeus*.'

Jules and I stared at each other.

'We've got to tell him,' she whispered.

'I'll do it.' The walk to the Valve Voice was the longest walk of my life. Every part of me felt dead as I picked up the mic.

Jules peered at the Valve Voice display. 'He's broadcasting on an open channel. The entire fleet is going to hear this conversation, Dom.'

'Best they should all know the truth. Angelique would have wanted that.' I took a deep breath, hands trembling. 'King Louis, Angelique's ornicopter just crashed into the ground.'

He gasped. 'No, it can't be – not my precious daughter.'

I forced myself to continue. 'There's no way she could have survived the impact.'

His pause pressed into my skull. I stumbled on, trying to fill the space. 'I'm so sorry. This is my fault. If we could have launched sooner we might—'

'Stop, stop right there, Dom,' he said, his tone becoming hard. 'You must not blame yourself. That's the first thing Princess Angelique would've said if she were still with us. There is only one person responsible for all of this and that is not you.'

'Cronos…' I whispered.

'Yes, the man who has murdered my daughter and so many innocent people on our journey to this moment.' The king's voice strengthened to steel. 'My people, what say you to avenging Princess Angelique's death, and the death of every other person that has been caused by Cronos's cruel heart. Do we turn away, or do we fight?'

'Fight!' Jules and I shouted, along with a hundred Navigators on the open comm channel.

The ships' voices swelled as one. *Fight!* the Cloud Rider ships thundered around us.

'Then let the final battle begin,' Louis shouted.

With a roar, the craft behind us dipped their noses and gathered speed, engines maxed out to take us all into the fight.

'Let's go and kick their murdering asses,' Jules said.

My heart hardened to stone and I gave her a sharp nod.

If it's war you want, Cronos, I'm going to ram it down your stupid throat...

I crossed back to the wheel, braced my feet and clung onto my anger, knowing that if I dared look into my grief for even for a second, my heart would shatter...and me right along with it.

CHAPTER TWENTY-THREE

VOICE SCREAM

Shock slammed into me as we neared the air battle. A squadron of over two hundred ornicopters had been cut down to the last fifty. The remaining craft wheeled and dived like bats between the Hades airships. But, unlike the US military, they'd made a significant dent in the enemy forces. I counted at least twenty large red airships burning on the ground.

The remaining mile between us crawled past, our relative positions tracked by the glass globes in *Athena*'s Eye. The problem was, these weren't just points on a map. I could feel every single ship as a living being and an extension of my own consciousness. And, despite all being cloaked, and even if Hades couldn't see them, it had to be only a matter of minutes before the enemy detected the approaching ships' songs. For the coming battle there could be no silent running if our fleet wanted to stay in contact with each other.

We rocked gently in *Zeus*'s prop wash who, with his engines considerably more powerful than *Athena*'s, had already pulled ahead of us. Meanwhile, Tesla had broken away from the rest of the fleet and taken *Muse* to the edge of the stratosphere high above us. I wasn't sure what he had planned from all the way up there, but something told me that didn't include sitting the fight out.

'Cloud Riders, rise to Zeta pattern attack altitude,' King Louis said over the Valve Voice. *Zeus*'s nose tilted up towards the sun. The chess pieces were being moved into their final positions.

I pulled back on *Athena*'s wheel and felt the vibration of our props churning through the air. She hadn't said a thing…a heart too broken to speak.

Jules, sitting in the co-pilot chair, scanned the dials. 'Oil pressure is looking good and all other gauges are in the green.'

We climbed high into the sky above the Hades craft. At this distance they almost looked peaceful as they floated gracefully through the air. But the burning airbase beneath told a different story. Those airships were killing machines.

The Cloud Rider fleet song rolled through me, the ships' chorus the most complex I'd ever heard. At one level the harmonies knitted together to form one voice, but as I listened in closer I could hear that the Angelus sang so many songs beneath it. One was a battle hymn to stir the soul – to loosen the grip of fear. Beneath that anthem the individual ships' voices were tinged with a million emotions. It was as if I were listening into the private thoughts of an army marching into war. A hundred stories; a hundred moments of reflection; a hundred souls trying to find peace before they met possible death. The cost of war and everything that personally meant to those caught up in it.

Angelique…

Jules flicked a switch and the crew chatter coming over the speakers from the Valve Voice fell quiet.

I realised she was talking to me.

'Dom?'

'Huh?'

'I said it's as if everyone is holding their breath.'

'I think everyone is probably lost in their own thoughts at the moment.'

She reached over and gently touched the side of my head, her expression gentle. 'And what is Dom Taylor thinking about right now?'

'Guess?'

Her expression broke. 'I know, me too.' She gripped my shoulder. 'We'll make Angelique proud of us, won't we?'

'That's the plan…' I took her hand and kissed her palm.

In front of us, the ghostly form of *Zeus* levelled out and I followed his lead with *Athena*. The rest of the spectral fleet drew into position, with *Hope* bringing up the rear. Hades had no idea of the storm that was about to come crashing down on their heads.

I hooked the seat harness over my body and buckled up.

Jules did the same. 'Okay, let's do this.'

'Bring it.'

The Valve Voice speaker on the instrument panel crackled back into life.

'Dom, you need to hold your position, along with *Hope*,' Louis said over the Valve Voice.

I flicked the mic switch. 'Pardon me?'

'Cronos will soon realise we are here and use the Voice Scream to try to cripple our systems. You're the only person who can counter that. If you are killed during battle then Cronos will have a free hand to destroy our whole fleet.'

'You mean you want us to just sit up here and watch while the rest of you risk your lives?' I scowled at Jules.

'I am sorry, Dom, I know how this must feel, but please understand this is the best tactical decision for us.'

I cupped my hand over the mic. 'But I want to get down there and fight.'

Jules scowled. 'I know...me too. But King Louis is also making sense.'

I let my breath out through my nose. 'Okay, I can't pretend I'm happy about this, but I guess we understand your reasons, Louis.'

'Thank you, Dom. See you on the other side of this.'

Zeus's voice started to beat out an attack song.

'Fleet, assume attack pattern Delta,' the king said. 'Cloud Riders, concentrate your initial attack on the Hades vessels protecting *Kraken.*'

At once, *Zeus* began to dive, all the Cloud Rider ships following, apart from *Hope* who held his position with his precious cargo of lightning marines.

The fleet's song locked into the beat set out by *Zeus* and became sweeping and powerful, the notes reaching deep inside and making me feel proud. Making me believe that we could win, that victory was within our grasp. They sped towards the Hades fleet, still doing their best to avoid the remaining attacking ornicopters and jet fighters.

A green light flashed on the Valve Voice panel.

'What's that?' I asked Jules.

'Private comms channel.' She pressed a button beneath the blinking light.

'How do they expect us just to watch?' Stephen's voice said from the speaker.

'Yeah, it blows big time being stuck on the bench,' I replied.

'Not for the first time, I have no idea what you are talking about, Dom, but I can still gather your meaning – waiting while others risk their lives?'

'Yeah, that's the one.'

'What makes it worse is knowing that *Hope* has serious firepower at its disposal. I know protecting the lightning marines is important, but…'

'But we didn't come this far to be spectators either, especially after what happened to Angelique.'

The radio crackled but no response came.

'Stephen, are you there?'

'Yes, sorry… I need to go.' The green light blinked out.

Jules shook her head. 'Poor guy.'

'What?'

'You mean, you don't know?'

I narrowed my gaze on her. 'I'm guessing that we're not talking about sitting out the battle here?'

She shook her head. 'No, Stephen is grieving. In case you hadn't realised, he was in love with Angelique.'

It was as if Jules had just told me down was up and up was down. 'Seriously?'

'Seriously. Stephen asked me for advice about what to do about Angelique. We had lots of little heart-to-hearts about her.'

'You mean, all those times I saw you together…'

Her eyes widened. 'Dom, please don't tell me you thought he was into me…and vice versa?'

I rocked back in my seat, feeling utterly stupid. 'Maybe…'

She made a mock swipe at my head. 'Honestly, for someone I adore, I could throttle you sometimes. There's only one man I want to be with, well apart from Dad, and he's sitting right next to me.'

If there'd been a hole nearby I would have gladly crawled into it. I dropped my gaze. 'I know I can be a jackass sometimes.'

'Yes, yes, you really can be.' She pulled my chin up to make me look at her. 'You great big fool.'

'Yep.' I gave her a crooked grin. 'So you were saying about Stephen…'

'He told me that although Angelique was the love of his life, he just couldn't tell her.'

'How come?'

'Apparently it's just not the done thing for a Cloud Rider officer to date royalty.'

'But that's just crazy if he was really into her.'

'It's worse than that. I'm as sure as my female intuition can be that Angelique was totally into him too.'

I tried to get my head around this new reality. 'But I thought she was just doing her man-manipulating thing with him like she does with guys.'

'You have got this all wrong, Dom.'

I shook my head. 'So I'm starting to realise.'

The Valve Voice crackled into life. 'On my mark, open fire,' Louis said.

We both peered down through the windshield.

'It's weird – all I can see is the Hades fleet down there,' Jules said.

I watched our invisible fleet speeding towards the enemy. 'Right now, our fleet is spiralling down, with *Zeus* at the lead, towards the massive battleships surrounding *Kraken*.'

Jules chewed her lip and nodded.

The ships' battle hymn roared through my mind. My muscles tensed before the first blow was struck. This was the moment the Cloud Riders could use the element of surprise to inflict maximum damage on Hades. What I'd give to see the look on Cronos's face when that happened.

'Fire!' Louis bellowed.

With a roar, the Cloud Rider airships broke formation and their gun ports lit up the sky beneath us. A stream of projectiles flew away from them to the Hades fleet like a sudden thunderstorm.

The animal cry of Hades warnings sounded all at once, the red airships aware at last of the approaching attack.

I gripped the wheel as the projectiles sped towards them. 'Come on, come on…'

The black rain of bullets smashed into the battleships surrounding *Kraken*. Several craft exploded into fragments and others began listing towards the ground like sinking ships.

The Cloud Rider ships dived down towards the enemy, keeping up their barrage. A noise like a truck gunning its engine filled my mind, as *Kraken* and the other Hades ships rose towards their attackers in a slow-motion aerial ballet.

'The cat is well and truly out of the bag now,' Jules said.

A cry crashed into my mind, jamming my thoughts and sending searing pain through every fibre as the Voice Scream scoured the skies, looking for its enemy.

'*Surrender!*' *Kraken* cried.

The mind-numbing power of the mental attack was overwhelming and the Cloud Rider war song faltered as the Voice Scream broke through our ships' battle hymn.

Someone was screaming. It took me a moment to realise it was coming from the Eye.

'*Athena!*' I shouted.

Jules gripped my arm. 'What's happening, Dom?'

I drove my fingernails hard into my palm. 'Voice Scream.'

'Dom, we need your help,' Louis said over the radio.

This was the moment I'd trained for, the moment when everybody was depending on me.

The Cloud Rider ships drifted through the air, their guns falling silent. The Hades fleet was climbing towards its invisible attackers and in a few moments our initial tactical advantage would be lost. If I messed this up it would be the end... There'd be no second chance this time.

Jules grabbed my shoulders. 'Do it, Dom. Do it for Angelique.'

Determination burned through me. 'Yes!' I shoved back against the mental attack with everything I had.

Kraken's Voice Scream – the cry of a hundred Hive minds that included what was left of Dad – started to falter. At once the pain began to ease in my skull and the logjam in my thoughts cleared.

Athena, *are you okay?* I thought-voiced.

Her trembling voice filled my mind. *'I will be, thanks to you, Whisperer.'*

I wrapped my thoughts around her mind, like hands protecting a flickering flame against the howling storm of *Kraken*.

Her voice grew stronger. Then, one by one, the other ships joined her, their battle hymn rising to challenge Hades.

I used my enhanced vision to gaze downwards again. The Cloud Rider ships' engines had powered up once more. We were back in the game.

Kraken's Voice Scream howled out with so much anger, so much hatred, that I had to strengthen my focus into a mental wall around the fleet.

'You can huff and you can puff but you can't come in,' I said.

'Huh?' Jules replied.

'Cronos is getting pretty worked up. He's turned the Voice Scream weapon up to max volume.'

'But you're on it.'

'Too right.'

A barrage of shells flew up from the Hades fleet and exploded around the diving Cloud Rider ships like fireworks heralding their arrival.

'Hades are firing blindly at them,' Jules said.

'But they are bound to get lucky eventually.'

Almost in answer, a Cloud Rider frigate blew up directly beneath us. I caught her voice wink out of our fleet's chorus. One less ship to counter Hades.

Zeus trained his guns on one of the Hades battleships and raked its flanks with fire. Two of the enemy craft's six engines blew up, props whirring away like Frisbees. Hades guns turned in the direction of the king's ship and shells exploded around *Zeus*, but he avoided all their fire as if it were nothing.

Jules chewed her lip as she watched the glass planets in the Eye spin around each other. 'I so wish I could see for myself what's happening. How's it going down there?'

'As well as it could, but this is going to be one long and tricky fight.'

I caught something change in the Voice Scream. A single voice focused from it. At the same time the Valve Voice crackled into life.

'Cowards!' Cronos shouted from the radio. 'Show yourselves and fight like real soldiers, or are you too afraid?'

'I am *afraid* I will not be able to oblige you with that request,' King Louis's calm voice replied.

A long laugh filled the cabin. 'As I live and breathe, it's the king who lost his honour and ran away.'

'If I were you, Lieutenant Cronos, I would worry about your own honour at this precise moment.'

'Emperor Cronos, you mean.' His cackle filled the speaker. 'And if it is honour you want to discuss, what honour is there in attacking us with invisible ships?'

'I do believe that if you had such a wonderful invention, you too would be utilising its abilities.'

Cronos laughed again. 'That may be true, King Louis, however you are only delaying the inevitable. As you are about to discover, we are going to adapt our battle strategy to take appropriate countermeasures.'

The Voice Scream's beat intensified, but rather than coming from all around me, it seemed to emit from just one part of the sky.

With my enhanced vision I saw the focused energy of the voices of the Hades fleet sweeping through the sky like a red searchlight beam. That spotlight locked onto a Cloud Rider frigate corkscrewing towards a damaged Hades battleship for the final kill. At once a note of fear crept into our ships' song.

Was Cronos trying to directly attack the Psuche gem in the ship?

I strengthened my mental wall around the vessel, shielding her with every ounce of my ability. But with a peel of thunder, every Hades gun seemed to open up at once, all of them focused on one point in the sky: that Cloud Rider ship.

With a starburst, the frigate exploded, ripped apart by the shrapnel from a thousand shells. Her voice howled into silence.

I stared at the falling debris, only a moment before an airship so alive with ship-song.

The radio whined into life. 'Dom, Jules, can you hear me, over?' Tesla said.

Jules flicked a switch. 'Loud and clear.'

'I've been monitoring the Voice Scream with *Muse*'s sensors. I am afraid to say that what just happened is an extremely worrying development. I have to give Cronos top marks for his twisted ingenuity.'

'That sounds bad,' I said.

'It is,' Tesla replied. 'Now he realises that the Hive's Voice Scream is having no effect, he's turned it into a powerful echo sounder.'

'An echo sounder?'

Jules was slowly nodding. 'Like bats… They send out a high-pitched signal and use its echo to navigate.'

'Just so,' Tesla said. 'And *Kraken* is doing the same with the Voice Scream. What we have just witnessed is what happens if the Hive hears one of our ship's positions echoing back from that focused sweep of the sky.'

'Then we have to shut it down and fast,' Jules said.

'But how?'

'The Hive is powering that thing. You reached your dad before – can you reach him again?' she said.

'You mean try to wake him?'

She nodded. 'Maybe he can do something to stop them.'

'That is certainly worth an attempt,' Tesla said.

Shut down the Voice Scream…talk to Dad… 'Okay, I'm more than up for it.'

I closed my eyes, trying to cut out everything else, and reached with my mind towards the building throb of the Voice Scream. Already its ruby beam was searching the sky for another victim.

CHAPTER TWENTY-FOUR

HIVE MIND

Jules frowned as she watched me. I could also hear Tesla's breathing at the other end of the Valve Voice. I screwed my eyes closed to try to sharpen my attention.

Even opening my mind a tiny fraction to the Voice Scream was like dropping straight into the middle of a nightmare. My skin grew clammy as its song's twisted notes washed through me: so much hate, anger and, as I'd picked up before, the pain of people enslaved inside the Hive. Dad was lost somewhere in that darkness.

I began to pick through the individual minds I could feel inside the Voice Scream. *Dad, are you there?*

One of the cries grew quieter.

Dad?

Within the mental storm, a thread of thought grew brighter and words started to form in my mind.

'Dom?' Dad's voice whispered.

A lump caught in my throat. The last time I'd spoken to him he was being spirited away by Cronos. Back then I'd thought I might never see him again. And I still might not if the Cloud Riders blew *Kraken* out of the sky.

Yes, Dad, it's me.

'But where am I?'

You're onboard Kraken. *Do you remember?*

The thread hummed as the link wavered between us.

'*Kraken…*'

Your mind has been connected with other people's to run the ship's systems.

'*Hive…*'

I could feel the fragments of his mind knotting themselves back together. *Yes. Cronos converted you so you could be part of the Hive mind that runs the ship.*

'*Converted—*' A mental gasp. '*Oh god, I'm starting to remember everything.*'

Dad was back – he was really back. I could feel the man I knew and loved at the other end.

You've been unconscious. But now you're back on our Earth and bang in the middle of a massive battle between Hades and the Cloud Riders. You should also know we're going all out to destroy the ship you're on because it has a weapon called Fury onboard it – a weapon that Cronos is going to destroy our Earth with.

'*What!*' Dad's tone became alert. '*Dom, I'm trying to wake up, but it's as if I've been drugged. My eyelids feel glued down.*'

I willed energy through the link to him. *You can do it, Dad.*

I heard a groan at the other end – the strain of a man fighting with everything he had. A sigh buzzed through our connection.

'*I've managed to open my eyes a fraction, but heck the light hurts. Anyway, I seem to be in some sort of pod with a glass lid covered in ice… I'm so cold.*'

So he was still in the pod I'd last seen him in back at Hells Cauldron. *What else you can see?*

'There's a clear patch in the lid. Heck, even focusing my eyes is like heavy lifting. Give me a moment…'

I could hear his ragged breathing vibrating through the tether.

'Okay, I'm starting to be able to focus. I'm inside a white room filled with displays. There are lots of other pods like this one around me. Looks like some sort of intensive care unit. And there are people in lab coats monitoring things. My skin is coated with black stuff.'

That's the carbon nanotubes, Dad. It was part of the conversion process so they could connect you to the Hive mind.

'Whatever they've done, it's paralysed me. I only seem to be able to move my eyelids and that's it.'

So he wasn't about to bust himself out of there and escape. But maybe there was something else he could try.

I understand, but we need to stop Cronos firing Fury up. If there's anything you can do to stop him, please try.

'Such as…'

Can you can talk to the others, get them to wake up like you have? Then, maybe together you can wrestle control of Kraken *from Cronos.*

'I'll do my best… Hang on, something's happening…people are shouting and there are red lights flashing everywhere… Holy cow, a technician has just dropped dead right next to my pod with an arrow though his neck. Now the others are trying to escape…'

Someone was onboard *Kraken* and fighting Hades? But who? Then an impossible but wonderful thought struck me. It couldn't be, could it? I didn't even dare voice the thought in my head in case I jinxed it.

Dad, can you see who's attacking the technicians?

'I can't, but everyone seems real afraid of whoever it is.'

The idea took root. *I know this sounds crazy, but might their attacker be invisible?*

'*Arrows keep appearing out of nowhere and taking people out, so yes, I guess they could be.*'

So it was a crack shot, a lethal trained soldier, and someone who had to be wearing a chameleon suit. All the trademarks of a certain ninja princess I knew. My heart raced as joy sped through my veins and I opened my eyes for a moment to stare at Jules.

'I think Angelique is alive and well, because all hell has suddenly broken out onboard *Kraken*.'

'She's alive?' Tesla said over the Valve Voice.

Jules put her hands to her mouth, tears filling her eyes.

'I'm certain of it,' I replied. 'She must've jumped clear when her ornicopter swooped past.'

'In that case I will switch this to an open channel so the whole fleet knows – this is exactly the sort of news they all need to know at a moment such as this…'

Several lights turned green on the Valve Voice. 'This is *Muse* calling. Dom Taylor had just made contact with his father onboard *Kraken*, and we now have reason to believe that Princess Angelique is alive and well, and is fighting her heart out.'

A hundred cheers burst from the speaker.

'She's alive – she's really alive?' King Louis said over the Valve Voice.

'Yes.'

'Oh, thank the gods,' he said.

Someone whooped over the channel.

'You have just made this day a million solar cycles better for me,' Stephen said.

A wide smile filled Jules's face.

'My king, are you there?' Stephen continued.

'Indeed, Captain Stephen,' Louis replied.

'Permission to dispatch the lightning marines immediately. Adept as Princess Angelique is with her combat skills, even she needs help taking on an entire army.'

'With my blessing.'

In *Hope*'s belly just above us, dozens of portals opened up. From each, a stream of marines in fly-dive suits leapt into the air and sped past us down towards *Kraken*.

Dom, something's happening, Dad said in my mind, his tone urgent.

I closed my eyes again. *What is it, Dad?*

A technician managed to pull a lever on the wall just before he was killed. And now thick metal hoods are lowering over the pods we're all trapped in—' His voice vanished from my mind.

Dad?

Nothing, not even the faintest murmur, just the continuing cry of the Hive mind. I tried to pull his voice from the others, but this time there were no individual notes that I could pick out, just the awful harmony of the Voice Scream.

My eyes snapped open. 'I've just lost contact with Dad after he told me that they were lowering metal lids onto the pods.'

Tesla groaned over the Valve Voice. 'I should have realised Cronos would do something like this. I suspect those lids will have a fine electromagnetic wire mesh built into them.'

A memory rushed into my mind. 'You mean like Hades used back in the processing plant at Hells Cauldron to block the Psuche gems' screams?'

'Just so, Dom. Which also means that there's now no way for you to be able to reach him.'

I clasped *Athena*'s wheel and stared down at *Kraken*, sitting like a vast spider in the middle of the web of battle raging around him. And Dad was now trapped in the belly of that monster.

'But there has to be, Tesla,' I said.

'There is one way, but it's too risky—'

'Just tell him already,' Jules said.

'Even with Dom's enhanced ability, the only way of breaking through the blocking effect of that electromagnetic shield is for him to be standing right next to his father.'

Jules paled. 'You're not saying Dom has to go onboard *Kraken*?'

'I am afraid that will be the only way for him to make contact. But that of course is far too dangerous.'

The Voice Scream boomed in my mind and the cabin shook. A thick swarm of arrows with round spheres at their tips struck a Cloud Rider battleship, green pennants flying from multiple wings. Its rear engine exploded as its chameleon net flickered off. It tilted towards the ground, trailing smoke.

My resolve hardened. 'Let me be the judge of that, Tesla. Even with me blocking the Voice Scream's effect, you've seen for yourself how Hades are using it now. Unless we do something, they'll continue to pick off our ships one by one until there's no one left to fight them.'

As the lightning marines sped towards *Kraken*, enemy fire raced up to meet them and many tumbled away like shot birds.

I glanced at the locker where the fly-dive suits were stored.

Jules followed my gaze and grabbed my arm. 'No way, Dom. What happens if you get yourself killed? Then there'll be no one to counter the Voice Shout!'

'And if I don't get my ass down there to make contact with Dad, there'll be no ships left to save. We both know what Cronos has next on his to-do list: destroy our planet.'

Jules crossed her arms. 'If you think—'

A cough over the radio interrupted her. 'You've been talking on an open channel all this time,' Stephen said.

Jules rolled her eyes. 'Can I please just have a minute alone to talk some sense into my boyfriend?'

'Actually, I may be able to offer some assistance to you both and increase Dom's odds for survival.'

'How?' I asked.

'Now my mother hen job has been fulfilled, and my precious cargo of lightning marines has been dispatched, the time has come for me, *Hope* and my crew to get ourselves into this fight.'

Hope's song strengthened in response and she sang out with impatience.

'I can clear a path all the way down ahead of Dom before he jumps,' Stephen said.

I reached out for Jules's arm, but she flinched away.

The first of the marines had almost reached *Kraken*'s battlements. 'Jules?' I said.

'Good luck in whatever you decide,' Stephen said. The radio clicked off.

Jules shook her head at me. 'At what point did I sign up to be a spectator? If you expect me to just watch you—'

'No, I expect you to fly the heck out of *Athena* and make a difference in this battle when the time comes.'

Jules stared at the floor. 'You're really going to do this?'

'I'm afraid I have to.' I gently grasped her shoulders and made her look at me. 'Everything depends on me making contact with Dad and shutting down the Hive mind. The lives of everyone, the destiny of our planet, hangs in the balance based on what I do next.'

She groaned. 'I just knew it was a matter of time before you'd decide to do something heroic. It seems hardwired into your DNA these days, Dom Taylor. What happened to the guy I used to know?'

'He worked out who he really was.'

A slow smile filled her face. 'Yeah, yeah he did.'

'You understand then?'

She dropped her arms and wrapped them around me. 'Of course I do. But if you don't get yourself back to me in one piece, I am so going to give you hell.'

I gave her a crooked grin. 'Deal.'

We closed the distance and held onto each other for a long moment. Was this goodbye?

Jules blinked and turned away first. She headed to the locker and handed me the fly-dive suit. 'Okay, let's get you suited and booted, Mr Hero. Then I'll fly you in as close as I can to minimise the risk when you jump.'

I started hauling on the suit. 'You're the best, Jules.'

She flashed me a smile. 'Yeah, I probably am.'

As I buckled on my boots, I gazed straight through the floor using *Athena*'s sensors.

Beneath us the first marines had touched down on *Kraken* and were engaging the Hades guards swarming the battlements. Explosions and small arms fire lit up the towers of the flying citadel.

Jules handed me my flight helmet. I pulled it down and looked into her brown irises flecked with gold. I could get lost in those eyes forever. Neither of us said anything, but in those few seconds was a silent conversation that said everything words could never get close to.

Athena sang quietly to me and broke the spell. Yeah, I had a job to do...

I opened the weapons locker and clipped a crossbow pistol, along with several clips of ammunition, onto my webbing belt.

I glanced towards the Eye. Athena, *please look after Jules.*

'I will do everything in my power to, Whisperer.'

I know you will…

As I hauled open the gondola's door, an icy wind howled into the cabin.

The vast, shimmering bulk of *Hope* surged past us, his hundred props driving him down towards *Kraken* at maximum speed.

I paused for a moment, took the Saint Christopher out from beneath my suit and kissed it.

From the depths of my memory I remembered a line from a Shakespeare play we'd been forced to study at school – one that I'd hated at the time.

'Once more into the breach…' a king had said as he urged his men into a final battle. In this moment I knew exactly what he'd meant by that: facing one's fear, knowing one could die, but doing it anyway because sometimes there were things that mattered more than that.

I tucked the medal away again and looked at Jules. Her eyes held mine. God, I loved her.

I tore my gaze back to the cold air outside, closed my visor, tucked my arms by my side and, before my resolve crumbled, leapt.

CHAPTER TWENTY-FIVE

BOARDING PARTY

In my fly-dive suit, I swept down towards *Kraken*'s battlements as the ship's gun emplacements welcomed me by spitting bullet fire. I pulled my arms up and sped into a shallow dive, ducking behind *Hope*'s ghost form as he descended in front of me. The spray of tracer fire broke apart on his armoured envelope. Nothing as trivial as a bullet was going to scratch the Emperor's former flagship.

I activated the radio in my suit. 'Stephen, I'm right behind you.'

'In that case, let's see what I can do to help improve your odds of not resembling a piece of Talgerian-holed cheese by the time you arrive.'

Hundreds of gun turrets all over *Hope* swung towards *Kraken*. It seemed, invisible or not, that bad boy was about to get their attention.

Strobing light lit up the smoke drifting around *Kraken*. The enemy ship's Voice Scream was still up to the max, which presumably meant Dad had had no luck shutting it down. But in response to the enemy's mental attack, *Hope*'s song soared. His shells rained down from his gun ports in a hundred different directions and, with deadly precision struck many of *Kraken*'s batteries. In a stroke, the firework display of the enemy ship's tracer fire had been halved.

I whooped into my helmet's mic. 'Nice shooting, Captain Stephen. That's not so much a corridor as a twelve-lane freeway you've just carved out for me.'

'I wish I could take the credit, but *Hope* is directing most of his firepower and I think he's taking this fight quite personally.'

Hope's determination hummed through his battle song, but *Kraken* was already responding with a barrage of shells speeding upwards. A few flashes of flame blew out from beneath *Hope*'s hull as some of the shots found their mark.

'You okay, Stephen?' I asked.

'Just a flea bite for a ship this big, but I think I've got their attention.'

I snorted. 'Reckon so. Cronos is probably having kittens down there.'

'Now there's an interesting mental image. Anyway, best of luck, Dom.'

'You too.' It wasn't lost on me how things had changed between us. Now, without hesitation, I'd say that this guy ranked among my best friends.

Hope's massive outline, shimmering under a hailstorm of bullets that gave his position away, banked and drew most of the Hades fleet's fire with her.

I sped past her and hit my suit's chameleon button in the palm of my gauntlet. The outfit buzzed and the indicator in my visor blinked green. Bullets fizzed through the spot I'd been just a moment before.

Two minutes and counting, with a red warning light at thirty seconds...

One minute ticked past. My supercharged mental connection with the fleet seemed to be holding out okay. Even as I ducked and weaved through the air, fleeting impressions of the battle reached me from the Cloud Rider ships all around.

At the outer edges of the battle, *Helios* – who Roddy had obviously fixed – had joined the fleet's attack. Under Roxanne's command, he was using his side-facing guns to broadside a Hades cruiser with a slash of explosions… I shifted my focus and saw *Apollo*'s rear window shattering as machine-gun fire hit it… I listened to the desperate song of a Cloud Rider battleship out of control and corkscrewing towards the ground…

I pulled my attention back as his song winked out and spotted an explosion rising upwards from the ground.

So much death…

'I know, Whisperer,' Athena replied.

Despair threatened, but I still had to focus. If we survived this, the time to mourn would come later. Right here, right now, we fought… We fought to survive… We fought for everything.

Less than five hundred yards between me and *Kraken* remained. An aerial view of the battle between the troops lay out before me as *Kraken*'s battlements rushed closer. Hundreds of lightning marines fought Hades guards, some locked in hand-to-hand combat, and I was about to land bang in the middle of all of that chaos.

The red indicator blinked in my visor. Thirty seconds.

I swooped towards one of our squads hunkered down by a black stone tower, exchanging steam-crossbow fire with a group of guards. Better for me to land behind friendly lines.

I yanked on the handle of my harness and my drag chute blossomed behind me like a white flower, killing my airspeed. At a running stride I landed twenty feet beyond our men. I hit the release and skidded to a stop as my chute fluttered away over the parapet. The light in my visor turned a steady red and I sprinted back towards the safety of our marines.

The hum of my chameleon net died away and at once the air around me hissed with enemy arrows.

'Get down!' a burly, moustached marine shouted.

I dropped to my belly.

'Covering fire!' he cried to his men.

Steam bellowed from their weapons and I heard answering screams from Hades as the projectiles found their marks. The marine beckoned at me.

I jumped to my feet, raced forward and ducked around the tower, just as more bolts fizzed past my head.

The man thumped me on the back. His arms were at least as wide as my neck and he had a scar from his right ear to the tip of his chin. This guy had 'brave' written all over him.

'We've been expecting you, Whisperer. Name's Sergeant Hood. My squad and I are at your disposal.'

Despite the all out war raging around us, his group of six marines saluted me.

'Thank you, Sergeant. Has Captain Stephen let you know about the princess?'

'Yes. Our forces are currently trying to battle to her position below.'

We all had to duck as a Cloud Rider airship exploded over our heads and cried out in my mind. I winced and breathed deeply.

Hood watched the fragments from the ship tumbling past the battlements trailing flames. 'You're hearing all the death screams, aren't you, Whisperer?'

I wiped the beads of sweat from my forehead and nodded.

'Hang in there, son. You're making this a much more even fight than it would've been.' He slitted his eyes and took in the battle raging all around us. 'Problem is, I've seen more than my fair share of fights, and until now I've been lucky enough to live through them all. But I'm not sure about this one... At the rate this is playing out, Hades will destroy our entire fleet in less than an hour.'

So there it was – the reality check I'd been trying not to think about.

Among his squad, a tall female marine with red hair exchanged a grim look with a shorter stocky soldier.

'We'll have to see what we can do about that,' I said.

A look of approval filled the sergeant's face. 'The sooner the better, Whisperer.' He gestured towards the two marines.

'Private Jackson and Private James. You will escort the Whisperer to Princess Angelique's position.'

They both nodded and loaded fresh arrow clips into their steam crossbows.

'These two will be your personal bodyguards, Whisperer.' The sergeant gestured towards the woman. 'Jackson is a crack shot and has more markswoman trophies than she has locker space to keep them.' He then indicated the square-jawed, shorter marine. 'James will cover your back when things get up-front and personal. He holds the platoon record for hand-to-hand Sansodo combat, not to mention being a demolition expert. Something tells me you're going to need both of their combined skills.'

'Sounds good to me.'

Hood gestured towards a doorway in the tower. 'We've managed to clear this stairwell down to the interior, so you'll have a clear run for the first part at least. Meanwhile, we'll do our best to hold Hades off your back, although I'm not sure how long we'll be able to do that for.'

'Just give us long enough to find Angelique and my dad. The priority is to close down that Hive mind once and for all.'

He snapped me a salute. 'Till the last marine, if that's what it takes.'

'I pray it won't come to that.'

Kraken's scream yelled out in triumph. Under the shriek of its bombardment, the scream of an Angelus filled the heavens as another Cloud Rider ship exploded a mile out. Our fleet was growing quieter by the minute.

'Give 'em hell from us, Whisperer,' Hood said.

'Oh, I intend to.'

I unhooked my crossbow pistol as Jackson and James took lead positions ahead of me. Together, we entered the tower and descended the spiral staircase. Within ten paces the sounds of battle grew muffled, deadened by the thick mass of rock walls.

I took in a breath and the air smelt of blood – the thick stench of death. Sergeant Hood hadn't made a big deal about clearing the tower, but I counted at least fifty Hades bodies on our way down the stairwell, a few Cloud Rider marines scattered among them. I resisted the urge to hurl as my marine bodyguards, their crossbows raised, reached the landing ahead of me.

There was another marine lying on the ground on his belly. For a moment I thought he was dead too, but then I saw his back rising and falling. As my eyes adjusted to the gloom – no ship vision to help me here – I spotted he was holding a long-barrelled gun mounted on a low tripod. On the weapon's stock, a single large pressure gauge was ticking up. A hose ran from it to a large cylinder strapped to the marine's back. The gun, despite the ornate scrolling decorating its barrel, looked lethal. Then I noticed at least ten dead Hades soldiers at the end of the corridor the gun pointed down. Yep, seriously lethal.

Without looking up, the sniper made a chopping motion to the ground with his hand.

James grabbed my arm and pulled me flat to the floor as a crossbow bolt whistled over our heads.

The marine with the rifle didn't even flinch. He peered through the telescopic sight at the Hades guard who had just peeked around the corner and taken the pot shot in our direction. He squeezed the trigger and a puff of steam came from the rifle, accompanied by a whine from the tank on his back. The Hades guard slumped and toppled forward, a green fletched dart in his throat.

'Poisoned nano-dart sniper rifle,' Jackson said to me, her eyes running over the weapon as if it were the most beautiful thing she'd ever seen. 'That was an impressive bit of shooting.'

'Thanks, although I'm not about to beat you in the shooting tournaments,' the sniper replied.

'Keep this up and you just might,' she said.

'A man can dream…' I could see him smiling in the reflection of his gun's scope. He gestured forward. 'If you're planning to venture beyond, I'd think twice about it. We have our melee squads pushing out hard on all fronts from here, but they've met stiff resistance.'

'Thanks for the heads-up, but we've no choice,' I said.

'Yeah, it's that sort of day. May the gods be watching your backs.'

'Amen to that, brother,' James replied.

We set off again, keeping low, our weapons trained forward to be ready for any sudden threat.

As we picked our way past more dead bodies, I barely gave them a second glance. Part of my mind seemed to have shut down to all the death and I'd stopped seeing the corpses as people. Maybe I was becoming more battle-hardened like Angelique…or perhaps I was just battle-numb?

James nodded to me as we reached a junction. 'Which way now, sir?'

It was a good question. There weren't exactly helpful signs with arrows pointing the way to the Hive room for us.

The Voice Scream throbbed again from the walls and I felt a fresh twist of anguish as another Angelus voice fell silent. The war cry burbled back to its drumbeat as it searched the sky for its next victim.

We turned down a corridor on the left and I realised *Kraken*'s voice had grown a fraction louder. 'I think I can use my ability to take us straight to the Hive.'

'Just lead the way, Whisperer,' James said.

The handle of my pistol crossbow became slick in my palm as we moved past junction after junction. I expected us to get jumped at every turn, but our luck held and we heard only the distant growl of combat echoing along the corridors.

'Sounds like the melee squads are busy,' James said.

Jackson raised her eyebrows at him. 'You'll get your chance soon enough.'

We moved forward and the voice of the Hive mind grew louder and thudded into my mental walls. I swallowed back the bitter tang in my mouth. I felt pretty certain that without my new mental skills, and if I'd been a normal Navigator, that I'd be writhing around on the floor like a gibbering wreck by now. God knew how Angelique was coping.

I noticed Jackson had gritted her teeth. 'Are you okay?'

'I just have an awful headache that seems to be getting worse with every step we take.'

'You too?' James said. 'Thought it was just me.'

'It must be the Hive mind affecting you both too.'

'But I thought only Navigators with your telepathic skills were vulnerable to it,' James said.

'Maybe it's because they turned up the volume for the attack on our ships?' Jackson replied.

'Could be. Are you sure you're both okay to continue?'

'By Hells Cauldron, yes,' James said. 'After all, we have our princess to rescue.'

'Too right,' Jackson replied.

I shot them both a smile. 'Thanks. I didn't much fancy heading into this alone.'

'As if,' James said.

We started forward again and I headed down the left hand corridor that the Voice Scream seemed to be coming from. Sure enough, the drumbeat ramped up and my bodyguards' eyes creased with pain.

A distant howl vibrated through the rock around us as yet another Cloud Rider ship died, song too scrambled by the shriek of the Voice Scream for me to be able to identify him or her. Please, god, let it not be *Athena* and Jules. Shielded mind or not, that would break me where I stood.

I heard a panicked shouting in the distance. James made a chopping motion and edged forward towards a bend in the junction. The shouts grew louder, accompanied by the hiss of steam crossbows being continuously fired.

But the marine looked seriously relaxed as he unhooked a thin rod with a tiny mirror on the end and raised it to sneak a look around the corner. Framed in the small circular mirror, I spotted steam vapour drifting along the corridor.

Jackson peered at the small reflection. 'Looks like quite a firefight.'

James massaged his temple with his thumb. 'I'm guessing by my pounding headache that we've almost reached the source of the Hive mind, Whisperer?'

Even with the protection of my mental wall, the Voice Scream had become deafening, making it hard to think. 'Has to be.'

'Cover me!' a man called out from somewhere in the steam. 'She's only a woman and all alone.'

'I'll give you "*only* a woman",' Angelique shouted back. Another hiss and someone shrieked.

My heart leapt. 'She's alive!'

'That's the princess we all know and adore,' James said with a grin.

The steam cleared a fraction to give us a clearer view.

In the mirror we now saw a knot of at least thirty men clustered around a doorway just ahead, where a least ten more lay dead.

'Come on, you cowards,' Angelique shouted.

'I once had the honour of fighting by the princess's side,' James said. 'And I can tell you from personal experience, she is not a lady you want to get on the wrong side of in a battle. I may have something of a reputation for my Sansodo skills, but even I am no match for Princess Angelique.'

I raised my eyebrows at him. 'She's kicked my ass more times that I care to remember. Anyway, how do we get through to her? Even with the three of us, we're still heavily outnumbered by all those Hades soldiers.'

James gave me a thin-lipped smile. 'Oh, that shouldn't be a problem.'

He unhooked a metal domed device from his belt and set it on the floor. The thing was dull grey and covered in small spikes.

'What's that?' I asked.

'A Lazy Hog,' he replied.

'A *what*?'

He grinned. 'It's a little toy that Tesla designed for the marines. Just watch this…' He pressed a button between the spikes. With a quiet whir, the small machine sped off down the corridor and into the steam.

'Watch out!' someone shouted. We saw men diving away from the Hog as it zoomed towards them through the haze.

One stumbled backwards towards the entrance to the room. He yelled and slumped to the ground, an arrow buried in his neck.

Jackson nodded to herself. 'Nice shooting, Princess Angelique.'

The Lazy Hog reached the doorway and stopped dead. For a moment nothing happened.

'Relax, everyone, it's a dud.'

James winked at us. 'They think it's a grenade, bless them.'

'So what is it?' I asked.

'Just watch… Oh, and I'd take your hand off that metal support if I were you.'

I quickly snatched my hand away from the pole I'd been leaning on.

A hum grew and the Hades soldiers stared at the Hog.

The officer started to yell, 'Retreat—' but was cut short by lightning crackling from the Hog and arcing across to the men standing around it. Shrieking, they collapsed to the floor, jerking with their eyes rolling up into their skulls.

'I guess that's one way to clear a corridor with Tesla's coil lightning, albeit with some extra amps thrown in,' James said.

The final soldier stopped convulsing and a ribbon of sick poured from the corner of his mouth and spread across the floor in a pool.

My gut tightened and I had to fight down the desire to hurl too. It seemed I'd been kidding myself – I wasn't so battle-numb after all.

'Not an honourable death for them, but probably better than they deserve,' Jackson said.

A few final sparks flew from the Hog as, like a spent firework, it died.

James pointed forward. 'Okay, looks as if we're good to advance again.'

I sped down the corridor with the others, my heart racing, towards the entrance of the room just visible through the clearing steam.

CHAPTER TWENTY-SIX

OFFLINE

As we reached the entrance, I held up my hand to halt the others. I knew Angelique well enough to assume that if we just wandered in without a warning we'd end up with arrows through our throats.

'Angelique, it's the cavalry...not that it looks as if you need it.'

Her voice came from somewhere inside the red-lit room. 'Dom?'

'In person.' I stepped over a guard sprawled across the entrance, as James and Jackson, rubbing their temples, took up guard positions at the doorway.

Inside the room, the Hive pods, with their thick metal hoods, gleamed under ruby light. The individual pods, teardrop in shape, had been arranged around a central column like the petals of a flower. The whole scene was just like the one I'd seen through Dad's eyes.

Even though I was in the same room as him I still couldn't hear his voice within the Hive's Voice Scream that roaring around me. What if Tesla had been wrong and this wouldn't work?

The surface of a large round pillar in the middle of the room caught my eye. Its surface was covered with a constellation of green blinking lights.

The high-pitched whine of the Voice Scream pulsed in my mind. In response the muffled screams of the Navigators trapped inside their coffins echoed through the metal hoods.

I felt the stab of teeth-grinding pain. Jackson and James both winced too. The distant mental cry of another Cloud Rider ship's soul, as it flickered out of existence. Just how many ships had we already lost up to this point?

Angelique stood up from where she'd been hiding behind a pod near the column. She leant on the pod to support herself, her eyes bloodshot.

I rushed to her. 'Are you okay, Angelique?'

'Every time that awful Voice Scream cries out, it's as if someone's driving ten-inch iron nails into my brain.' She took a deep breath. 'Just as well you turned up when you did. I couldn't have held out against those Hades guards much longer.'

I glanced around the room. 'Dad?'

She tapped the hood of the pod she'd taken cover behind. 'Right here. I made a point of seeking him out first.'

I placed my hand on the lid, picturing him trapped inside. Was he even aware that we were here? I closed my eyes.

'Anyway, what are you doing here?' Angelique asked. 'I gathered something had happened when I heard the ships all trying to contact me.'

'Of course, you don't know. *Titan* managed to help me reboot my brain. Believe it or not, I'm a level ten now.'

'He did? But how…' She waved her hands. 'Okay, I have a thousand questions about that, but they will have to wait. However, you still haven't said why you're here.'

'By lowering these lids, they cut all communications with Dad. Tesla thought by standing next to it I might have a chance of contacting him, and through him of shutting down the Hive.'

'Good. I wasn't keen on my alternative plan.'

'Which was?'

She gestured to her backpack. 'Letting a fission bomb off in here.'

'But that would have killed all the Navigators, including Dad.'

'It might still be our only choice if you fail to make contact, Dom.'

I stared at her, her expression icy-calm. She was deadly serious.

'Look, I didn't say I liked it, but the fate of your whole planet is hanging in the balance here,' she said.

Angelique was right, of course she was right, but I still didn't want go there in my mind. Not if it meant losing Dad.

'I'll make this work,' I said, pressing my palm harder into the chill of the metal.

The Voice Scream burbled as *Kraken* searched for another victim.

This was going to hurt like hell…

With a deep breath, I lowered my mental wall and the full power of the combined Hive crashed into my brain like a bulldozer.

I gritted my teeth as spots danced through my vision. It felt as if the room were whirling around me, but I stayed in control, just, not giving in to my fear, to the anger, to the anguish. I lost myself in its currents, bending like a sapling in a hurricane, and let the pain race past me rather than trying to fight it, until, step by step, it faded away.

Dad, can you hear me?

For a moment there was nothing, but then the murmur of a man dreaming in his sleep.

'Dom…'

Every muscle in my body relaxed.

Dad, it's me.

A tingle vibrated deep within my brain; the tether connecting me with Dad was strengthening. Then I felt him waking and I could hear his thoughts again, weaving among mine.

'*You're back…*' he whispered.

Of course I am.

'*But how have you managed to make contact again?*'

I'm actually here in the Hive room with you. It was the only way to reach you.

'*You're onboard* Kraken? *But that's way too dangerous, Dom.*'

I got past dangerous some way back, Dad. Anyway, there was no way I was going to abandon you.

'*You have a real stubborn streak, Dom.*'

I wonder who I get that from?

Despite the agony humming through Dad's mind, he actually laughed. And that sound within my thoughts lifted my spirits like nothing else could.

'*Okay, as you're here, what's the plan?*' he said.

First thing is to wake the other Navigators and figure out a way to release you all so we can shut down this Voice Scream of theirs.

'*How?*'

I felt the shadows of the other minds in the background of our conversation – whirling screams of pain around our island of calm. *You're directly linked to their minds, Dad, so maybe I can reach them through you and wake them.*

'*Do whatever you have to.*'

I pushed out from our island into the mental hurricane raging around us. At once the fear, pain and anger of the ninety-nine other connected minds roared around me. But like before, I let all of it

275

wash over me, not reacting to it, just breathing deeply and keeping myself centred.

You all need to listen to me.

The Hive's dark song faltered and an element of confusion appeared among the notes.

Your minds are being used to power a weapon that's being used to destroy the Cloud Rider fleet.

The Voice Scream notched down again. I could feel the men and women stirring within their nightmares.

You've all got to fight them with everything you've got.

Individual voices began to appear:

'Where am I?'

'What's happened?'

'Help me…'

'You're trapped onboard a ship called Kraken,' Dad said. 'You must listen to my son and wake up.'

'Wake up,' all the voices within the Hive mind said together.

The Voice Scream stopped dead, as if someone had flipped the kill switch, and from the pods all around me I heard shouting and banging.

I opened my eyes to see Angelique staring at me.

'You've done it?' she asked.

I slowly nodded. 'I think so.'

Dad's real voice – not a mental projection – came from inside the pod. 'Dom, I'm awake, but there doesn't seem to be a way to get out of this thing.'

The banging on the other lids intensified.

'Calm down, everyone,' Angelique called out. 'We'll figure a way to get you out.'

I shot her a look. 'Any ideas?'

She chewed her lip. 'I've already checked for an obvious override, but there doesn't seem to be one here. My guess is that the controls for the pods will be in the most fortified part of the ship.'

'Which is where exactly?'

'It will be on the main flight deck, which on a ship like this and, knowing Cronos, will be buried somewhere deep beneath the surface.'

Cronos's voice boomed out of a speaker in the ceiling. 'Very well-deduced. However, it is such a pity that, despite your noble efforts, none of this will help you.'

'If you haven't noticed, we've just shut down your precious Voice Scream weapon,' Angelique replied. 'Kraken is dead in the sky without the Hive to run his systems.'

Cronos laughed. 'Ah, I can understand why you might think that, Princess, but I am afraid you are very much mistaken. You see, I planned for every eventuality. All Kraken's critical systems, such as the manual flight control, and even the ignition system for Fury, have been battle-hardwired. There is nothing you can do to stop me carrying out our plan.'

Anger rolled through me. 'Wherever you're hiding on this ship, we'll find you and stop you,' I replied.

'Who said I was hiding? If you want to pay me a house call on the flight deck, you are welcome to try.'

Angelique crossed her arms. 'Oh we will, you can count on that, Cronos.'

'It doesn't really matter any more,' Cronos replied. A deep hum emerged from the floor, a bass note so deep I could feel it through the balls of my feet. It pulsed up through my entire body.

'What's that?' I asked.

'That, Dom Taylor, is the sound of the death of all your dreams. I have just activated Fury's main generators. In little over thirty minutes your planet will be expunged from existence…and all life right along with it.'

'Stop this, Cronos!' Angelique shouted. 'You used to be one of us. Remember your humanity, for gods' sakes.'

His laugh filled the room. 'Human? Yes, I suppose I was once, but I'm so much more than that now, Princess. Anyway, you have distracted me long enough. If I were you, I would make peace with your gods, or whatever it is you believe in.' The speaker clicked into silence.

'What did he mean, used to be human?' I asked.

'Who knows – just the language of a madman,' Angelique replied.

I nodded. 'It seems we have more than one reason to head for the control room.'

Angelique gave me a fierce smile.

We heard footsteps and whirled round, ready for a fresh fight. But it was only James, who smiled and gave us a thumbs up.

A moment later, Sergeant Hood and his marine squad rushed into the room. The sergeant saluted Angelique.

'How goes the battle?' she asked.

'Badly, Princess. We are down to the last ten ships.'

Angelique gawped at him. 'Ten ships?'

Ice crawled between my shoulder blades as his words sunk in. Jules… Without the howl of the Hive blocking out the airwaves, I tuned back into the Cloud Rider ships. But they were no longer an orchestra, just a scattering of individual voices… *Hope*, *Helios*, and five more I didn't know personally.

Jules couldn't be… Then *Athena*'s song swept into me, so strong and fierce that I wanted to bawl my eyes out.

Actual tears filled Angelique's eyes, her battle mask lost for a moment. 'Thank the gods, but so many dead…' She shot me a desolate look.

'Then we have to make their sacrifice worth it and bring *Kraken* down before it's too late,' I replied.

Angelique smeared her tears away and nodded. 'Sergeant, how many marines have you got left onboard this ship?'

'Several hundred, but it's only a matter of time before Hades overpower us. However, I do have one good piece of news.'

'I think we'll take anything we can get at the moment,' I replied.

'We've located the flight deck.'

'In that case, let's go and wipe the smirk off Cronos's face,' I replied.

The sergeant held up his hand. 'I would love to, but there's one small problem. Cronos and his officers have walled themselves in.'

Jackson nodded towards James. 'I'm sure there must be someone here who can deal with that challenge.'

A smile filled James's face. 'Exactly. Sounds like work for a demolition expert.'

'It certainly does,' Angelique said. Her regular determined look was firmly back in place. 'Sergeant Hood, can you take us to the control deck? We have a certain Emperor to shove off his gilded throne.'

'That, my Princess, would be both a pleasure and a privilege,' Hood replied.

Jackson nodded towards James. 'I suppose I'd better watch your back, as always.'

'Just because you like the view.'

She snorted. 'Don't push it, Private.'

He smiled back. 'Whatever you say.'

I glanced down at the pod and pressed my palm onto the hood. 'We'll be back, Dad…we'll be back for all of you.'

His muffled voice came from beneath the hood. 'You just stop Cronos – nothing else matters, Dom. And that includes me and the others.'

The shouting and banging on the lids fell quiet around us.

My throat tightened. There was no way I'd let it come to that. I took off my Saint Christopher medal, kissed it, and jammed it into a gap in the pod's lid.

I followed Angelique and the others out of the Hive room. With each step I felt the mental tether to Dad stretch thinner, like a piece of elastic, until I rounded a corner and it finally snapped.

I promise I'll be back, Dad… I whispered into the mental silence.

A distant explosion sounded somewhere through the rock high above and fine earth sprayed down through a crack between the metal ceiling panels. The pitch of Fury's whine notched up and, without anyone saying anything, we all started to run.

CHAPTER TWENTY-SEVEN

THE CONTROL ROOM

We sprinted down corridor after corridor as Fury's whine grew ever louder. We'd travelled so deep into *Kraken* that the sound of the battle raging outside had been completely muted by the tons of metal and rock above us... Unless of course all of our ships had been destroyed?

I breathed deeply through my nose, trying to kill the thought before it had a chance to take root. I had a job to do. I couldn't afford to give into the despair snapping at my heels like a dog.

Sergeant Hood gestured down the spiral staircase towards a landing below us. 'We're almost at the control deck.'

I'd expected something impressive, but what met my gaze as we left the stairway was beyond anything I could've imagined.

We'd entered a vast stained-glass domed shaft, filled with ornate carvings of airships battling each other, almost an artistic echo of what was happening outside right now. The shaft itself was criss-crossed with walkways lit with shimmering gas lamp posts.

Arrows whistled up from the snipers ranged across the bridges below us, their fire met by Cloud Rider sharpshooters lined along the stone railing of the bridge we stood on. Dead Hades already littered the walkway ahead.

Hundreds of feet below us, suspended by cables, hung a massive copper sphere. It had to be at least fifty feet across and every few seconds, with a crackle, lightning jumped across to a series of smaller metal spheres mounted in the wall around it. A carved spiral channel ran down from them, corkscrewing around the shaft into the darkness far below. It reminded me of the rifling groove for a gun barrel to spin a bullet, so to make it more accurate. The whole chamber smelt of raw electrical power.

Angelique peered down over the railings at the sphere. 'Fury?'

'Has to be.'

Ahead of us at the centre of the shaft, a massive spherical glass bubble encircled a room. Inside it, Hades officers moved between consoles, completely ignoring us as they adjusted controls and gazed at readout screens.

My attention was snagged by Cronos sitting on a raised chair with dragon head arms and interlocked wings that formed the back. The chair rotated towards us on its geared mechanism and the Emperor slowly smiled at us like a lizard who'd spotted a fly.

I met his gaze and held it as we strode towards the glass room over the bridge. 'See he's got himself a throne.'

'One I'm looking forward to toppling him from,' Angelique said.

A Cloud Rider sharpshooter leant over the edge of the bridge and fired a bolt from his crossbow. The projectile sped downwards, and a moment later was answered by a cry.

Jackson gestured towards the sniper. 'Sergeant Hood, it looks as if my skills are called for. With your permission?'

'Go ahead and make all your shots count.'

She grinned at him. 'I always do.' She took up position by one of the gas lamp posts on the bridge.

We neared the command deck glass bubble, where a burly Cloud Rider marine stood frowning at it. He spat on both hands, took hold of a massive sledge hammer and, with a grunt, swung it at the transparent wall.

I instinctively tensed, waiting for the glass to shatter, but the hammer just made a dull thud and bounced off. The marine massaged his arms, sweat dripping from his nose, and got ready to try again.

In the centre of the control room was the biggest navigation Eye I'd ever seen, filling at least half the space, with hundreds of airship markers static within it.

Angelique pointed towards the Eye. 'It seems as if shutting down the Hive mind has killed their navigation systems for the time being.'

A thought struck me. 'Hang on, doesn't that mean *Kraken* can't jump away from the blast?'

Angelique stopped dead and turned to stare at me. 'Which means Cronos can't operate Fury without destroying himself and his whole ship!'

Relief swept through me. 'He'll have to shut it down now...' I caught a smirk curling at the corner of Cronos's mouth as he watched us.

I pointed straight at him. 'Can you hear us? If so, what have you got to be grinning about?'

He pressed a jewel in the head of the dragon's right arm and his voice boomed out of the speakers that were mounted like crystal mushrooms on top of the bubble room. 'Indeed I can, Dom Taylor. And it greatly amuses me.'

I strode up to the glass wall. 'I'll give you amused.' I gestured to the burly Cloud Rider to give me his sledgehammer. He shrugged and handed it over.

I was used to chopping firewood for Mom, but the oversized sledgehammer weighed a ton. I braced my legs and swung it round in a wide arc, as if I were going for the bough of a tree. I struck the glass wall and the blow vibrated through my body, making every bone within me judder. I hadn't left even the tiniest mark on the pristine glass.

I gave it back to the marine who just shrugged as if to say, *You see!*

'What the heck is this stuff made from?' I asked.

'Diamond glass – has to be,' Hood replied.

The marine nodded. 'We've tried everything, including explosives, but nothing has so much as dented it.'

'Precisely,' Cronos's voice boomed from above us. 'I would not waste your time. This planet will be just a memory among the stars by the time you manage to break through it.'

We all ignored his taunt.

'Hang on, what about that time we broke the diamond shield covering the lava at Hells Cauldron,' I said. 'I seem to remember a small nuke did the trick pretty well back there.'

James's eyes slitted and he patted the bag on his back. 'I had a hunch this would come in handy. And I know exactly where to set the charge.'

Cronos's smile threatened to split his face. 'Oh, you are most welcome to try.'

Angelique gawped at him. 'But you and your men will be killed, Cronos.'

He shrugged. 'So?'

Inside the room, I caught the nervous looks that the Hades officers gave each other.

'You're not making any sense,' I said. 'Shut down Fury and surrender. If for no other reason than to save yourself and your people.'

He laughed, the sound echoing from the speakers. 'They are just dispensable pawns in our plans. In thirty minutes, when Fury fires, a bridgehead will be opened into this reality and we will consume this universe – as we have already started to do with others.'

'What do you mean *consume*?' Angelique asked.

'So very slow on the uptake, Princess, despite seeing the glory of what we have already achieved in another universe you journeyed through.'

A deep feeling of dread wound through my body. 'Angelique, you know that world ripped apart by the Shade?'

'You mean where we rescued *Helios* from…? Oh my gods, yes. Which means…'

'That Cronos has been working for the Shade all this time,' I replied.

The whine of Fury grew to a shriek below us.

We both turned to stare at Cronos.

'You have almost worked it out but are wrong in one important detail,' he said. 'Come on, you can manage it…'

What was he getting at? I picked through what I knew about the guy: he'd been one of the only people to have survived a Shade attack during a Vortex jump; he had seized power and turned himself into a dictator; he was a man who didn't fear the Shade…

The heat leached from my body as the parts of the puzzle locked together.

'Angelique, Cronos was taken over by the Shade when they attacked his ship. It's the only thing that makes any sense.'

Cronos stood and gave me a slow hand clap. 'Very astute, Dom Taylor.' He spread his hands wide. 'I am the Shade and the Shade are me. And together we will consume every universe that we invade.'

'But that's impossible – the Shade can only live in the Void,' Sergeant Hood said.

'Not any more,' Cronos replied. 'We, the Shade, have been waiting since the dawn of time, when dark was separated from the light and we were exiled into the Void. But now at last our plans have come to fruition.' He started to spasm.

For a moment I thought the guy was having a fit, but he kept his gaze locked onto us, his expression totally calm.

'What's happening to his eyes?' James said.

He was right – something was wrong with them. Even at a distance, I could see Cronos's pupils had vanished and black shapes were swirling through them.

The Hades officers had noticed too, and had started to back away from their Emperor, expressions paling.

Cronos's voice sounded like a thousand people speaking all at once. 'The time has come to end the charade and dispense with the humans we have been using. Time to fulfil our destiny.'

'Destiny?' Angelique said.

'To reunite the light and darkness.'

A shocked looking officer inside the room fumbled at his belt for a crossbow and aimed it straight at Cronos. All the other Hades men watched, not trying to stop him as he pulled the trigger.

The bolt flew straight into the Emperor's chest and buried itself up to its feathers.

'Thank Zeus's beard his men have turned on him,' Sergeant Hood said.

Angelique shook her head. 'For what good it will do them. Look...'

Cronos took hold of the bolt's shaft as if he were picking a bit of fluff off his suit, and pulled the arrow out with a spray of blood. 'Do you really think that could stop us?'

Other officers raised their weapons and fired. Bolt after bolt struck the Emperor. But Cronos didn't so much as flinch. He laughed and spread his arms wide.

'Welcome to your destiny, my loyal subjects.' Cronos tipped his head back and specks flew out from his mouth, like black seeds rushing around the control room.

No one said anything as we watched each spec grow, unfolding again and again like a piece of origami, until the final elements uncurled from the body – wings. The wings of shadow crows. Inside the glass bubble control room, the black flock swarmed in silence, like a dark snowstorm.

I stared at them. 'This can't be happening – not here, not in my world!'

'May the gods show mercy to all of us,' Hood whispered.

A grey-bearded officer rushed towards us, hammering on the glass as a crow dived at his head.

I pointed past him towards the creature. 'Watch out!' I mouthed.

The man turned too slowly. The talons of the Shade ripped into the back of his head and, despite the thickness of the glass, his scream still reached us.

The crow latched onto the man and convulsed, like a feeding leech, as the man's skull started to disintegrate and flowed into the creature's mouth in a steady stream of blood, flesh and bone.

My blood iced as I stared into the man's eyes as his life disappeared from them and he toppled backwards.

The crow hopped down from him and landed on the ground. It shook itself and from its flickering back a second set of wings appeared. The creature vibrated to a blur as a second crow tore itself from it, like cells reproducing.

The creatures swivelled their eyeless heads towards a woman hiding behind a control console. Both creatures took flight and swooped towards their new victim.

The scene was being repeated throughout the control room, a feeding frenzy of swirling shadows and panicked Hades officers.

I backed away from the wall. 'The Shade are feeding on those people to breed.'

Angelique gave me a pale look. 'By the gods, whatever it takes, we've got to stop them.' She gestured to James. 'Set the fission bomb right here, with a ten minute delay to give us enough time to get back to the surface.'

'At once, Princess,' James said. He opened the pack and took out the red cube of Tesla's fission reactor.

I stared at it as the full implications struck me. 'But what about Dad and the others Navigators? There won't be time to free them.'

Angelique grasped my shoulders. 'Dom, I wish there was another way, but what else can we do? There will barely be time for us to get away as it is. As awful as this choice is, there's a whole planet depending on us right now.'

'But I promised I'd go back to rescue Dad.'

'I am so truly sorry, with all my heart, Dom. But I won't make you do this. It has to be your decision. If you tell me not to set this bomb, then we won't.'

It felt as if my life were being torn into fragments. 'But I can't, Angelique. I can't sentence Dad to death.'

She hugged me as if she were trying to smother my pain with her warmth. Sergeant Hood and the others watched us in silence, faces filled with so much understanding that I wanted to scream at them.

'Dom, even when we blow up Fury, we still have the Hades fleet to deal with.' She pulled back and gripped my shoulders in her hands. 'You, Dom Taylor, are the best chance we have of defeating them. And I am as sure as I can be that if your dad was part of this discussion, he'd tell you do this too.'

I pulled back, but I had nothing, no argument to counter Angelique. She was right, I knew she was right, but I stared at the floor anyway.

'I won't even get a chance to say goodbye, Angelique…' I just managed to stifle the ache threatening to break into tears.

'Then help me protect the lives of all those innocent people out there.'

Thunder claps bellowed below us from Fury. A point of light suddenly appeared at the bottom of the chamber. A vast door opened like a camera shutter. Thousands of feet below, framed by the growing circle, I spotted the diner directly in the firing path.

Mom! I turned and stared at the Shade gliding around the control room.

Cronos let out a long laugh. 'I flew *Kraken* to these precise coordinates. It seemed rather appropriate. What better location for ground zero than the place that you call home, Dom Taylor? Such a poetical gesture, do you not think?'

Anger rushed up through me. 'Go to hell.'

The shadow crows opened their beaks wide and Cronos's splintered voice came from all them all at once. 'Oh, it is quite different to that in the Void. Utter coldness, as you will soon discover for yourself when it comes pouring into this universe… Unless of course you set your precious bomb.'

'We haven't got much time left, Princess,' Sergeant Hood said.

Angelique's eyes held mine. 'Dom? What do we do?'

My gaze flicked from the diner and back to the bomb. My voice came out as a whisper. 'Do it.'

Thin-lipped, she nodded. 'Set the timer, James.'

He spun a cog on the side. Fifteen minutes spun up on the display. He pressed a button and it started to tick down.

James stood. 'Time to evacuate.'

Hood pressed a mic mounted in his lapel. 'Hear this, hear this, lightning marines. Time to retreat to *Kraken*'s battlements, ready for immediate evacuation.'

Angelique tugged on my arm. 'Come on, Dom.'

I felt like an automaton as she pulled me along the walkway towards the spiral staircase with the others.

Part of me wanted to stay and let the explosion take my life. A son should never be asked to make an impossible choice between which parent he wanted to save. But I just had… I wished I could talk to Dad one last time…to explain…to ask for his forgiveness.

As we ascended the stairs I reached out with my mind. *Dad, I'm sorry…*

No responding vibration echoed through my thoughts, but maybe he could still hear me. And maybe he would find it in his heart to forgive me before the end.

CHAPTER TWENTY-EIGHT

EVACUATION

My legs burned as we hurtled up the endless staircase towards the surface. At every landing, Cloud Riders joined us in the rush for the exit. The air had grown thick with the scent of adrenaline-powered sweat, but all I could think about was every step taking me further and further away from Dad.

Angelique's fingers bit into mine as the light started to grow in the stairwell above us.

Suddenly the press of men and women around us released us, and a moment later we swept out onto the battlements.

We both skidded to a stop and took in the view.

The tornado's spinning cloud walls had grown to at least ten miles across around us. My gums tingled as I tasted the statically charged air. The Vortex would soon be big enough to rip my Earth apart.

Officers barked out orders and the soldiers assembled into squares around the battlements.

Sergeant Hood had already gathered his squad in a defensive circle, eyes narrowed on the Hades ships ranged all around *Kraken*.

In a glance, I took in the view with my ship-sensor-enhanced vision, but could only spot a single shimmering ghost shape of one of our vessels, *Helios*, jinking as he avoided a battleship taking blind shots at him. I heard the first notes of our ships' voices calling out – no longer an orchestra but a smattering of individual ship-songs, heartbreak filling every note.

I spotted *Zeus* further out, ducking and weaving and taking down countless enemy craft.

Angelique's face paled and she stared at me. 'I can't hear *Athena*.'

The ache built inside like a rising volcano preparing to destroy me. I screwed up my concentration and pushed past the shouting voices of the Hades fleet.

Athena, where are you?

A faint hum tingled through my mind and I latched onto it. '*Whisperer…*' *Athena*'s voice called out.

Angelique's shoulders dropped. 'Oh, thank the gods, her song. But where's the rest of our fleet?'

The nearest marines, grim-faced, nodded towards the battlements.

Angelique gave me a desolate look and we walked together towards the edge.

I followed her. I didn't want to see, but I had to know.

We looked down at a battlefield littered with hundreds of burning impact craters. The majority had red fabric fluttering from twisted metal, but every so often green material flapped like flags, marking the spot where a Cloud Rider ship had crashed into the ground and spilled their life. There were at least ninety impact craters decorated in green.

Angelique pressed her fingers to her lips. 'Our beautiful fleet.'

I thought of the faces of the men and woman who'd been reunited with other Cloud Riders, now all lost in an impossibly one-sided battle.

Every marine seemed to turn to Angelique at that moment. I could see in their eyes that they needed Angelique – the warrior princess, and my friend – to rally them. I needed her too, because part of me was breaking.

Angelique turned to her people, her eyes seemingly seeking out every member of the Cloud Riders who stood there.

Her voice carried over the wind across the battlements. 'We must be strong, my people. Let us honour the memory of the fallen. Let us make this a day that this or any universe will never forget. Let us fight until our bodies are returned to stardust.'

The cheer thundered across the battlements and the uncertainty swept away from the marines' faces. They had someone to lead them through the darkness, something to fight for, and I could tell by their fierce expressions, they would do it to their last breath. And so would I. I would do it for Angelique; for Dad trapped in his pod beneath us as he waited to die, even if he didn't know it yet. For Jules; for Mom. And I would do it for my whole beautiful world.

I rested my hand on Angelique's shoulder. 'Thank you, I needed that…we all did.'

Her shoulders dropped and she nodded. I could see the heartbreak swirling through her eyes even if she was trying to hide it from her own people.

I knew right there in the middle of the awful battle that, however long I had left, Angelique was a friend I would always love.

A mass of Hades ships, at least a hundred in number, swung towards us. They might not have risked firing shells at their capital ship, but a barrage of arrows was another matter, especially if it meant taking our marines out.

With a boom, a crackle of sheet lightning burst high over our heads. It leapt out across the knot of Hades ships and sparks flew as each craft was struck, silencing the ships' battle cries.

Gunfire from the remaining Hades ships all seemed to erupt upward at once.

Muse's cry roared through the sky.

Angelique's eyes widened. 'No!' She pressed her lapel mic. 'Tesla, are you okay?'

His voice responded with a calm voice…way too calm. 'I am afraid not, my Princess, but it was worth the cost. I saw Hades converging on your position and I knew at once the time had come to use the secret weapon I have been developing.'

'Secret weapon?'

'The one you just saw in action. When I had *Muse* built, I took the liberty of constructing a conducting coil into her hull, hence the saucer shape of her design.'

'Conducting coil?' I asked.

'People refer to them as Tesla coils. Once fully charged, they let out a stream of lightning that, as you have just witnessed, is also very effective at destroying a ship's systems.'

'You mean you built a larger version of a Lazy Hog,' I said.

'Exactly,' Tesla replied.

'Which also gave away your position.'

'It was a price worth paying. But now, unfortunately, *Muse* has been badly damaged by the incoming Hades shellfire.'

I narrowed the focus of my ship vision until I spotted his ship's ghostly disc high above us. One of her high altitude balloons had been ripped to shreds and she was listing badly.

'Can you make an emergency landing?' I asked.

'We shall see,' Tesla replied. 'But I have something important to tell you while I still can. You remember the Sentinel program in each and every Psuche gem.'

'Yes, what about it?' Angelique replied.

'It has just started to run inside *Muse*'s Psuche gem. It also seems to be utilising her communications systems.'

'To broadcast to whom?' Angelique asked.

'I am afraid I have no idea at the moment.'

Over the comm channel I heard an alarm warbling in the background.

Tesla's voice sharpened. 'May the gods protect—' The radio link hissed into silence.

Angelique pressed her fingers to her lightning pendant. 'Tesla?'

Muse started to slide towards the horizon.

'May the gods protect you too, old friend,' Angelique said.

The ground shook beneath us.

Jackson glanced at his Tac. 'We have only three minutes until detonation of the fission bomb.'

The remaining Hades warships, around two hundred of them, began picking their way towards us, weaving around the stranded craft. There'd be no cloaked *Muse* to stop them this time round.

Sergeant Hood nodded. 'What are your orders, Princess?'

Angelique gazed at Hood. 'Even if we destroy *Kraken*, we need to take out as many of the Hades fleet as we can so they pose no more threat to this world… We could use our fly-dive suits to reach their ships.'

The sergeant slowly nodded. 'An excellent plan, Princess, apart from one thing…' His face creased and suddenly he looked much older. 'I know I can talk for every man and woman here…'

Angelique narrowed her gaze on him. 'Go on, Sergeant Hood?'

'It will mean everything to the marines to see their princess back onboard *Athena*. That's where a Cloud Rider truly belongs in this battle.'

Her mouth thinned to a line. 'But I should be with my people.' She looked at me. 'Shouldn't I, Dom?'

But I understood, I really understood, what Hood was getting at. To these men and women, Angelique wasn't just a leader, she was a symbol of their freedom too. 'You need to do this for them and their families.'

Her mouth opened and close, the conflict between warrior and Cloud Rider princess etched across her face.

Jackson stood to attention. 'Permission to speak?'

Angelique gave a small nod.

'Breathe sky air for all of us onboard your airship, Princess.' Even though she said it in a quiet voice, somehow every person on the battlements seemed to hear her and nodded.

'That's where your people need you,' James said. 'And that's also where your heart is – like any true Cloud Rider – with your ship. You can leave the rest to us. And trust me, by believing in us, it is the greatest honour you can bestow.'

Sergeant Hood nodded. 'I couldn't have expressed that better myself, Private James.'

The battle-hardness vanished from Angelique's face. She chewed her lip, her eyes glistening. 'My dear countrymen and women...' She took a breath. 'All I can say is that when this is all over, I look forward to personally pinning a medal on the chests of every one of you.'

Sergeant Hood and his squad snapped a salute and the gesture rippled out through all the soldiers ranged around us.

It was one of most powerful things I'd ever seen. And I'd never been so proud of anyone as I was of Angelique at that very moment.

'Your mission, lightning marines, is to take out as many of the Hades battle group as possible. What say you?'

All the soldiers thudded their gauntlets on their chests. 'Ay!' a thousand voices shouted over the cry of the wind.

Tears rolled freely down Angelique's cheeks now. She didn't try to hide them any more. The mask was off to reveal the woman who loved her people with all her heart. And I could see in every face how much they all loved her back.

The marines turned to the battlements and spread their arms, silhouetting their suits' wings against the smoke drifting up – a thousand bats ready to take flight.

My heart hammered with the beauty and heartbreak of it all.

The marines ran forward in squads and leapt over the edge. They sped away, suit wings snapping taught in the air.

We watched three men speed off like birds of prey towards the top of a Hades frigate and land on it. They scattered in bouncing steps over the red canvas of the airship.

My eyes felt glued to those men. What could three men do against a ship? Already the top-mounted gun turrets of the battleship were swivelling towards them. There wasn't any cover for them, nowhere for them to escape to. First one then two then three batteries opened fire and the tracer fire sliced through each and every marine. My hands clenched as they tumbled away like shot birds towards the ground.

I turned to Angelique. 'They are just throwing their lives away!'

She gave a sharp shake of her head. 'They're not, watch.'

With a roar, three explosions ripped the gas canopy of the battleship wide open, and wind buffeted us. The flames blazed into the sky from the position of the marines moments before, racing outwards and consuming the canvas. The battleship started to roll towards the ground.

'Incendiary bombs,' Hood said.

Angelique gave me a grim look. Not for the first time I realised I couldn't do what she had just done – order her people to their deaths – even if it meant others might be saved.

The sergeant zipped up his fly-dive suit. 'James, Jackson, you're with me.'

Jackson reached out and shook my hand. 'Good luck, Dom Taylor.'

'You too, guys, and thank you for everything you've done.'

James grinned. 'Oh, we haven't finished by a long way yet.'

I didn't have the words for anything else, so I snapped them a salute that they both returned.

With Hood taking the lead, they took a running jump at the battlements and flew out into the air. As they sped away from *Kraken*, I said a silent prayer that they'd all make it through this in one peace.

One moment we'd been with a thousand soldiers, now it was just Angelique and me alone on the battlements.

'About time we got out of here,' I said.

Angelique nodded.

I activated my mic. 'Jules, we could do with a lift.'

My headset crackled. 'I'm already on it.'

I peered out. 'But I can't see you.'

'I'm right here…'

The ghostly outline of *Athena* rose above the battlements. She must have be hiding just below my line of sight.

'I wanted to stay as close as I could to you just in case you needed us,' Jules said.

So Jules had been right at the centre of the battle, not cowering somewhere safe around the edges. I shouldn't have expected anything less from the woman I loved.

Angelique shook her head and smiled. 'You are too brave for your own good, Jules.'

'I take that as high praise from you, Angelique, but to be honest I've been scared rigid.'

'Scared is good…it's what keeps you alive,' I replied.

Angelique smiled at hearing what she'd once told me.

Athena's engines roared over the battlements. Her prop wash rushed over us as she drew into a hovering position just above the battlements.

'Nice flying,' Angelique said.

'*Athena*'s been a very patient teacher,' Jules replied.

A doorway opened in the ghostly outline of the gondola to reveal the uncloaked interior.

'I believe you guys ordered a taxi,' Jules called out, standing at the threshold and gesturing to us.

Kraken bucked and groaned as the ship emitted lightning speeding out fast across the landscape.

'Fury is nearly at full power!' Angelique shouted over its roar.

Bricks tumbled from one of the towers and away over the edge.

'At this rate, with the damage Fury is doing to *Kraken* it will destroy this ship and itself right along with it,' I replied.

'I'd rather rely on our fission bomb to make sure that weapon is taken out.'

Jules shot me a look. 'But where's your dad?'

Suddenly my feet felt like stone. 'I'll explain later, Jules.'

Her hands flew to her mouth. 'No!'

Angelique glanced at her Tac. 'Twenty seconds and counting.'

We both leapt for *Athena*'s gondola and scrambled inside.

Angelique dashed to the controls and spun the wheel as Jules and I buckled in. *Athena* began to climb and bank away.

The princess's knuckles stood out as she gave the burner maximum blast. 'Five, four, three, two, one…'

A pure-white ball of light exploded from beneath the shattered remains of the tower we'd just left.

Athena bucked as the hailstorm of debris rolled past us. The world outside was lost from view as the seconds passed. A minute later the air slowly started to clear.

Jules gasped. 'But that's impossible.'

Kraken still hung in the air like a floating mountain. Smoke streamed from gashes all over the vast ship, but now lightning blazed from the entire rim and rushed outwards over the landscape to the Vortex walls, which shimmered with blue light.

'How, by the twenty names of all the gods, can that thing still be flying, let alone Fury still operating?' Angelique asked.

I put my hands on my head. 'That chamber and all the equipment powering Fury must be so much molten slag by now.'

'You used a nuke, right?' Jules asked.

We both nodded.

'*Kraken* is wrapped in so much rock, even a fission bomb can't blast it apart,' Angelique said. 'But there's also an upside.'

'Which is?' I asked.

'There's every chance your dad may still be alive. I bet those pods are designed to protect the Navigators trapped inside them.'

My heart leapt. 'Let's get back down there and see.'

Angelique shook her head. 'You're not thinking logically, Dom. It will be dripping with radiation and our priority is to take Fury out.'

My shoulders dropped. 'Of course it is…'

'So let's try to find out what's happened. The weapon shaft we were in opens out onto the underside of *Kraken*, so we can take a look.' She pushed the wheel forward until the horizon disappeared and all we could see was the ground.

My body pressed into my flight harness as a view of the ground filled the windshield. I felt a stab of relief as I saw the diner was untouched in the middle of the Vortex. But Mom would also be down there, watching all this going on over her head, wondering about her son…and her husband.

We sped past the vast bulk of *Kraken*. The pounding of countless Cloud Rider shells and bullets had traced numerous scars in the rock face. Smoke billowed from most of the gun ports, and the remaining ones were static. As we neared the underside, flames billowed from a cave mouth at the bottom of the doughnut-shaped ship.

'That has to be Fury, but if so, how come it's still getting ready to fire?'

Jules pointed along the rim of the huge ship above us. 'That's why.'

I took in where she was pointing and my stomach flipped. Another dozen portals, but unlike the shaft we'd taken out, these were still spitting lightning. 'We destroyed just a part of Fury?'

Angelique groaned. 'Of course. Cronos would have built redundancy into the system, so even if part of Fury was damaged, it would keep on charging. At best we may have slowed it down a bit.'

Jules's expression tightened. 'So you mean there's no stopping it now?'

Angelique and I exchanged a silent look.

Jules's face paled. 'No, no, no!'

I heard a whoosh and flinched as a barrage of shells from a circling battleship exploded near the gondola. The blast cracked the windows and hurled *Athena* sideways.

'That was too close for comfort,' Jules said.

Athena's song filled my mind, full of determination, of strength, of the will to fight on.

I let it wash through me and consume me. 'Let's go and teach Cronos a lesson.'

Jules's eyes held mine. 'Sounds good.'

Angelique pushed the throttle forward. 'I'm in, so let's make a start by dealing with the Hades ship that just took a shot at us, then we can figure out what else we can do in the minutes we have left.'

Our props roared at full blast, and we turned in a large circle to sweep towards the frigate. The enemy vessel fired again, its shells exploding where we'd been only a moment before.

'They're getting better with their guesses,' Jules said. '*Athena* and I have been dodging bullets since you left.'

'Just as well you were a fast learner when it came to flying her,' I said. I took hold of the weapon joystick and centred the enemy frigate in my sights. I got ready to pull the trigger, but before I had a chance to take a single shot, the Hades ship exploded with a roar into a giant fireball.

Zeus's ghostly outline swept beneath the wreckage.

'And that's for firing on my daughter and her friends,' King Louis's voice said over the radio.

Angelique beamed as she unhooked the mic. 'Thank you, Papa.'

My joy fizzled out as I spotted a destroyed engine tumbling away from the stricken frigate, heading straight for the king's ship directly beneath.

I snatched the mic from Angelique. 'King Louis, a bit of debris is about to crash into your ship!'

'Roger that…'

Zeus's rudder started to swing hard over and the airship began to turn, but not fast enough. The engine missile slammed straight through one of the airship's props. In a haze of oil, wood and metal, it blew up, and the airship bucked and lost height.

Three Hades battleships turned towards the invisible ship, as spewing smoked marked his position like a signpost in the sky.

'There's no way they can miss him now,' Jules said.

'Papa!' Angelique shouted as another two Hades battleships rounded on *Zeus*.

Jules screwed her eyes shut. 'I can't watch.'

Angelique pushed the throttle hard against the stops as *Zeus*'s song filled my head. He was answered by *Athena*, her song keening…a song of farewell. The strength of it made me want to weep.

There was no way I could stand by and let this happen. My thoughts whirled like leaves in a storm. We couldn't reach them in time, so we had to try something else.

'We need to distract those frigates and draw their fire away from *Zeus*,' I said.

Angelique's eyes widened and she slowly nodded. 'Yes…'

Jules opened her eyes and looked between us. 'You're talking about turning off our own chameleon net?'

I centred the gunsight reticule on the nearest battleship. 'King Louis's only chance to safely land is for us to create a diversion.'

Jules nodded. 'You got it.' She punched the chameleon net control button. With a soft whine our net shimmered off.

Through the gunsight I saw the three frigates, together with the rest of the remaining Hades fleet, all turn towards us.

'They've definitely seen us,' Angelique said.

'But let's really get their attention,' I replied. I slowed my breathing and got ready to pull the trigger on the joystick.

The time to live; the time to die; the time to pray to the gods had come.

CHAPTER TWENTY-NINE

THE DEATH OF HOPE

The gun batteries of nearly every remaining Hades ship seemed to spit deadly weapon fire towards us at once. As the shells sped straight for us, instead of fear, a deep sense of calmness rose through me.

Athena's song strengthened into words. *'Whisperer, this is your moment; this is your time. You must be the one to fly me.'*

Angelique gave me a curious look. 'What did *Athena* just say to you? I can tell by the tone of her song that she wants you to do something.'

'She said I have to be the one to fly her.'

Angelique's expression widened. 'But I'm the more experienced pilot.'

'If we are to survive this fight, it has to be you, Whisperer,' Athena said. 'She's very insistent.'

A flash of light flashed just beneath us and the gondola shook.

Jules frowned at us. 'Whoever is going to fly, you two need to decide before we get blasted out of the sky.'

Another barrage of shells blurred towards us and deep inside somehow I knew *Athena* was right. My blood hummed with energy.

I felt more alert than ever before. And right here, right now, I felt I could do anything.

'Angelique, please trust me.'

Her mouth open and closed again. She nodded. 'Of course I will.' She stepped away from the wheel. 'I'll take over the main weapon.' She pressed a button and a column rose at the rear of the gondola with a second joystick. 'Jules, can you take control of *Athena*'s rear gun battery?'

'I didn't even know we had one,' Jules replied.

Angelique shrugged at her. 'I like to keep a few surprises up my sleeve for when they're really needed.'

A sense of utter peace filled me. All the training and all my experiences had prepared me for this moment. Heck, it was even hardwired into my DNA.

Okay, let's show Hades how this is done, Athena.

'As is your will, Whisperer.'

I focused my consciousness around the airship. Her airframe became an extension of my body, her sensor net supercharging my own senses with a clarity way beyond anything I'd experienced. I gazed towards the hurtling shells with her eyes…and suddenly the speeding shells slowed to a snail's pace.

I rolled *Athena*, who responded at the pace of my own thoughts. I hadn't even needed to touch the wheel. The shells crawled past, missing us by a good hundred feet.

Jules blinked in slow motion, and Angelique reaching for the weapon joystick seemed to take a minute…but I knew it had to be happening in less than a second in real time. Yet this wasn't real time… My reactions had been tuned up to hyper-speed and *Athena* and I were now linked by the core of our beings. I was her, she was me, the boundaries of body and airframe gone. And now we flew and fought as one.

We – I – rolled, swooped and climbed, as Angelique fired shot after shot from *Athena*'s steam arrow cannon, and Jules covered our back from her rear gunner's position.

We danced through the skies and, by comparison, the Hades ships seemed to move like tortoises.

Zeus, slowly ducking and weaving through the sky towards the ground, was still drawing some of the enemy fleet's fire. I seemed able to calculate the trajectory of all the craft involved in that skirmish. In the blink of an eye, I knew the king was running out of sky.

Helios and Roxanne were too far away on the opposite side of the battle to help him. Another second crawled past…and there couldn't be many of those left till Fury ignited and we'd lose everything.

Jules loosed off a shot that shattered the gondola windshield of the Hades airship that had locked onto our tail. It spun away in a corkscrew dive towards the ground.

The enemy ships' war song focused into Cronos's voice. *'You are only delaying the inevitable, boy.'*

We will fight you to our dying breath, I replied.

'What a waste. You would have made such a useful addition to our ranks.'

Never, in this or any other universe.

'More is the pity, as this is your end. Fury is five minutes away from being fully charged. Witness the destruction of everything that you have ever known.'

Blue lightning shimmered in the multiple shafts within *Kraken*'s belly above us.

Jules's mouth opened and closed, her words too slow to make out. I decelerated my senses back to normal time. 'What did you just say?'

'I said we're bang in the eye of the biggest storm in history,' she replied.

'And the last one if we don't shut Fury down,' Angelique said.

'But what can we do to stop it?' Jules asked.

I gazed at *Kraken*, the size of a mountain, and about as hard to destroy.

'Watch out, Whisperer!' Athena shouted into my mind.

From the corner of my eye, I caught a shell blurring towards us, too late for me to do anything about it. The shell exploded less than a hundred feet out. A shockwave of light and noise slammed into us, shattering our windows. At once choking smoke billowed from the control panels and started to fill the gondola.

Angelique rushed to a locker and grabbed three face masks. 'Put these on.' She threw us two masks and slid the remaining one over her own face.

I breathed in deeply and sweet oxygen filled my lungs.

'How bad is it?' I said, as *Athena* bucked through the sky.

Jules scoured the bank of lights that had lit up red on the control console.

'Real bad. We're venting oil from the engines and the propane tank is showing a leak too. My best guess is that we have about three minutes of flying time left before the engines fail and we have to make a forced landing.'

I stared at her. 'But we can't be out of the fight.' I pointed up at *Kraken*. 'We have to be able do something to stop Cronos.'

'But we're almost dead in the water,' Angelique replied. 'What are you suggesting we do? Ram *Kraken*?'

My heart fluttered. 'Yeah, why the heck not?'

'Are you serious?' Jules said. 'We will be like a flea trying to stop an eighteen-wheeler truck on the freeway.'

'Have you got any other ideas?'

'We could use the fly-dive suits and jump just before *Athena* hits *Kraken*?'

Angelique stared at her. 'If you think I'm going to sacrifice *Athena* without being with her to till the end, you've got another thing coming.'

'And if you're not going anywhere, neither am I,' I replied.

'I'd say the future, even if there is one, is already looking pretty bleak without you two in it, so I guess that makes the three of us,' Jules said.

Angelique looked down at the floor. 'Alright, but there is one last person we need to ask.' She knelt by the Eye and laid her hand on it. '*Athena*, are you prepared to do this with us?'

The ship's song swept through us, so full of love that Angelique's eyes filled instantly with tears.

Jules looked at her. 'I take that as a yes from *Athena* too?'

I nodded and gazed at my friends, the people who I'd do anything for, including dying. 'Maybe we'll get lucky and hit a critical system.' My eyes lingered on Jules.

Jules flapped her hand at her face as her eyes brimmed. 'Oh god, I hate goodbyes.'

Angelique took the wheel and caressed it. 'If you don't mind, Dom, I'd like to take *Athena* for this last flight.'

I nodded, throat so tight I could hardly talk, and stepped aside.

As Angelique brought us round, the wind howled through the smashed windshield and into the gondola. She pushed the throttle forward and we surged forward, belches of black smoke puffing from the engine pods.

Jules chewed her lip. '*Athena* can't take much more of this.'

'She doesn't need to,' Angelique said.

We started to race up towards *Kraken*, but Jules was right – how could we even scratch something that big?

The engines spluttered as they misfired, but *Athena*'s song soared, the voice of an angel, wrapping us with her love and trying to push away the dread sucking at our souls. I grasped onto that mental warmth, against the howl of Fury and the chill of the Hades ships' battle hymn roaring through the heavens. I just wished Jules could hear this and be comforted by it too.

I looked across at Jules and found her gazing back at me.

'This wasn't the way it was meant to end,' she said, her voice muffled by her face mask.

I raised my mask. 'Yeah, where's our happy ever after?'

Angelique didn't look at us but stared straight ahead.

Jules pulled up her own mask and put her mouth to my ear. 'I love you, Dom.'

'I love you too.' I drank in every detail of her dazzling eyes as we both replaced our masks.

Athena's voice sang out and the ache for Dad, for Mom, and for all the fallen squeezed inside me.

Angelique pushed the wheel forward and steepened our descent. The wind whistled through the wires as an asthmatic whine came from the engines. I ignored the explosions tearing up the sky all around us and focused on the warmth of Jules's body against my side and *Athena*'s song vibrating through my thoughts.

The end, this was it. Every other option gone. Part of me hoped Mom would see what was happening above her. Would understand. Would be proud of us for trying this.

Kraken filled the windshield. I felt Jules tense as the distance between us closed to less than a thousand feet.

But then the windshield view changed. A huge cloaked ship, fires burning all over him, appeared, his hundred engines gunning hard. *Hope*.

In his wake a second smaller shielded ship appeared.

Helios.

The radio blinked green and I flicked it on. 'Break off now!' Stephen shouted.

Angelique grabbed the mic. 'But—'

'No time to argue. I can see exactly what you're planning to do, because I'm planning to do the same thing. And in all due respects, if anyone can bring *Kraken* down, it's me with *Hope*. His AI was taken offline by a shell, but I've just managed to reboot him and get us back into the fight. And I've also made the rest of the flight crew evacuate the ship.'

Silent tears ran down Angelique's face. 'But, Stephen—'

He cut in, 'Yes, I love you too, Princess.'

I exchanged a look with Jules. So she'd been right.

Angelique passed me the mic as if it were burning her hand.

'And what about you, *Helios*?' I asked.

'I'm escorting my brother in to keep the other ships off his back till the last possible moment,' Roxanne said over the comm channel. 'But you need to promise me something.'

'Anything.'

'For safety, I left Isabella with Sue, back on the ground. If anything happens to me, please tell Isabella that…' Her breathing at the other end grew fast. 'Tell her to be brave, that her mama will always love her, and I will be waiting for her in her dreams.'

Jules bit her lip as she gazed at me.

'Of course I will,' I replied, my throat tightening up.

'In that case, let's all pray to the gods that this works,' Stephen said. 'May I also suggest that you get yourselves as far away as possible. I expect there will be a very large explosion when I hit Cronos's capital ship.'

'Best of luck to both of you,' I said.

'You too,' they replied together. The comm light blinked off.

I listened to *Hope*'s and *Helios*'s hymns as *Athena* joined in with them, challenging the darkness of the Hades battle song thundering throughout the sky.

With a splutter and a shower of oil, our rear engine came to a stop. We slowed as our two remaining pod engines took up the workload.

But every set of Hades eyes seemed to be locked onto *Hope* in his kamikaze dive. Geysers of flame erupted all over the large ship, as the Hades craft rained bullets down on him. Meanwhile, *Helios* spiralled around *Hope*, pouring out all the covering shellfire that he could.

Someone, a person not a ship, was singing. Jules turned a knob and Stephen's and Roxanne's voices grew louder, echoed by ship-song.

Jules pressed the mic's button and she began to sing with them. I did the same. Angelique, her gaze locked onto *Kraken*, joined her voice to ours. And in between the notes we sang, a moment of perfect stillness seemed to fill the gondola.

'Stephen…' Angelique whispered.

My stomach rose up my chest as *Hope* struck *Kraken* midship, in some sort of aerial ballet move. Both vast ships disappeared behind a blinding flash.

'Strap in!' Angelique shouted.

Jules and I dropped into the flight seats and buckled up as a cloud of swirling smoke rushed towards us.

With the roar of a hurricane, the shock wave smashed into us and heat blazed through the broken windows. Like flotsam on storm waves, *Athena* tumbled over and over, the floor becoming the ceiling and then the ceiling the floor, and again. Our harnesses stretched and slackened with each roll, but they held us into our seats. The noise and heat faded away and *Athena's* wild gyrations started to slow. With a groan the airship settled into an upright position once more, still in the air thanks to the Helium in the gas envelope above us.

We stared out of the windshield at the huge cloud of smoke hanging in the sky where *Kraken* and *Hope* had been a moment before.

Jules put her hands on the top of her head. 'They did it!'

A flickering blue light appeared within the thinning cloud.

I pointed towards it. 'What's that?' The smoke faded away. Bands wrapped around my chest and I suddenly couldn't breathe.

Fires blazed all over what remained of *Kraken*. The palace had exploded and the vast ship was listing badly to one side, but Fury's lightning was still leaping from the cave mouths on its belly and dancing out towards the horizon.

The remnants of *Hope* – his engines, beams of metal, flaming canvas panels – all tumbled towards the ground in a meteor storm. Fires blazed all around the diner and house, both of which by some miracle hadn't been hit.

Angelique watched the scene, her expression frozen.

I spotted *Helios* spiralling down, trailing smoke, his chameleon net failed, his voice scrubbed from the air.

I grabbed the mic. 'Roxanne, are you okay?'

Only static hissed back over the Valve Voice.

Angelique rolled us, and a shell sped past. With a spluttering cough, our final two engines whirred to a stop.

Jules looked at the red lights across the control panel. 'That's it – *Athena* has nothing left and our chameleon net is staying offline, too.'

The remaining Hades fleet began closing in on us, their voices screaming. But *Athena* sang back. Only one voice against a storm of hatred. This was the end for us.

Jules unbuckled her harness. I did the same and wrapped her up in a hug. 'I am so proud of you, Jules.'

'And me of you…'

We both turned to Angelique, extending our hands towards her. She undid her harness, crossed to us and joined in the hug.

'It's been one heck of a ride,' I said.

'Hasn't it…?' Jules replied.

'If I am to die, I can think of no better way to go than to be with my dearest friends.' I held onto both of them, bracing for the impact of Hades shellfire, waiting for the end.

A tingle wove through my thoughts as a new ship-song took shape.

Angelique's eyes widened. 'Who's that?'

'Whisperer, we are almost with you…' *Titan*'s voice said.

My mind whirled. *What do you mean you're almost with us?*

Jules pointed out of the window. 'What's happening out there?'

We all stared at the countless smaller twisters forming within *Kraken*'s massive tornado. And as each one appeared, ship-song, clear and pure, joined *Athena*'s lone voice.

Angelique shook her head. 'I think the cavalry has just turned up.'

CHAPTER THIRTY

THE LAST SACRIFICE

Hundreds – no, *thousands* of airships started to appear, each fresh wave weaving around the Hades fleet like a net.

Jules peered out at them. 'Correct me if I'm wrong, but those ships don't exactly look like fighting vessels to me.'

For the first time, beyond the sheer mind-boggling number of craft appearing, I started to take in the new fleet's details. She was right. From tiny one-person ships, not a lot bigger than our old ultralight to the huge copper clad bulk of *Titan*, there was barely a gun battery to be seen between them.

Angelique shook her head. 'I've never seen such a variety of craft apart from at…' Her eyes widened. 'Of course, they're all from Floating City.'

I shook my head. 'Incredible.'

'And warships or not, the Hades fleet seem to be taking the threat seriously,' Jules said. 'They've already started falling back to encircle *Kraken*.'

The sky grew so crowded with civilian vessels that it was hard to see Fury's spinning storm wall through the gaps between them.

Titan's voice appeared among my thoughts. *'I have brought as many free ships as possible to aid you in this battle, Whisperer.'*

'Incoming message,' I said to the others. I closed my eyes. *But how did you know we needed help?*

'The Sentinel program in every Psuche gem in our ships started to run at the same time. It raised us from our slumber in the Empyrean and summoned us to your Earth, Dom Taylor.'

So you're saying the Sentinel program broadcast a distress signal?

'In a manner of speaking, but it also seems to have done much more than that. According to our analysis, the initial broadcast was the first step in a complex algorithm, but whose further purpose still remains hidden to us. What I can tell you is that the signal seems to be building in power and rippling out across this and all other universes. Whatever is happening within the Psuche gem of every ship would appear to be the true purpose for which the Angelus constructed us ...and a purpose that is about to be revealed.'

True purpose? The reason the Angelus had left the Psuche gems behind in the first place? Whatever it could be, this sounded big, maybe even as big as the Shade's plans to invade our world... And right then it hit me – the fragments of information, all the clues, becoming one plan.

Sentinel has to be something to do with the Shade, Titan. *You see, it turns out they infected Cronos and they've been using him as their puppet all this time. And any moment their invasion force from the Void will be arriving here.*

'So you are saying that the Angelus left the Sentinel program running to keep an eye out for this invasion?'

It's the only thing that makes sense.

'And this enormous Vortex field that Kraken *is currently creating?'*

Is actually the doorway through which the Shade are going to invade this world. And the real kicker is that we've tried everything to shut it down, but completely failed so far.

'It would seem the destiny of all my brothers and sisters is to aid you in this matter. That is why we have been summoned here by Sentinel.'

Which is great and everything, and I know there's a ton of you guys, but how can you close down Fury?

'Leave that particular detail to me…'

A noise like a million trumpets blowing at once bellowed through the sky. My consciousness snapped back into the gondola to hear the same sound bellowing from the Valve Voice speaker.

Jules cupped her hands over her ears. 'What the heck is that racket?

Outside, the Floating City ships sped towards the Hades ships encircling *Kraken.*

'I think that was their call to fight,' Angelique said.

A hailstorm of glowing bullets swept out from the Hades fleet and blazed through the ranks of the closing ships, swatting dozens from the sky in seconds.

I ground my teeth as we floated sideways, engines dead, unable to help.

I shifted my consciousness outwards through the sensors of the Floating City ships.

Explosion after explosion ripped through the sky in a firework display of death. The number of burning ships on both sides became so great that the whole sky seemed to be on fire. And the battle was mirrored by an orchestra of cries and screams of the dying ships, roaring inside my skull. I gripped the cockpit for support.

But through everything, one voice sang out like a beacon to all of our ships, giving them strength…and me too.

Titan's war cry boomed out as he sailed towards *Kraken*, all incoming shots bouncing off his metal-clad hull. He carved his way through the storm sea of Hades vessels, breaking them apart on his reinforced keel as if he were an icebreaker.

War. Total, awful, horrendous war.

Tears streamed down Jules's face. 'So much death.'

'I know, but this is the line in the sand, Jules,' Angelique said. 'If we lose here, think of what will happen next.'

She gave a small shake of head. 'I know, but…'

The Floating City ships' hymn ebbed and flowed, the chorus of Angelus flooding the heavens.

'We might be dead in the water, but I could still use my ability to help them.'

'Do whatever you can, Dom,' Angelique said.

I started to sing out, matching my voice to *Titan's*, trying to strengthen the resolve of the Floating City airships. When I felt fear creeping into a ship's heart, I sang to them, whispered into their ears, reassuring them, letting them know they weren't alone.

But these craft weren't battleships. Already Cronos's war machine was crushing the Floating City ships with cruel efficiency. And every ship that blinked out was like a sliver of ice being driven into my heart. If it was like that for me, I could only begin to imagine how devastating it was for *Titan* – a father seeing his children slaughtered.

An old transport ship with a faded patchwork-repaired canopy was slashed apart by canon fire and slid towards the ground. He sang to the fleet in a heartbreaking farewell, as his crew's parachutes filled the air.

I balled my fists as the craft smashed into the ground and his voice died. 'We're losing.'

Jules's face paled and Angelique hung her head.

'I thought my Whisperer gift could make a difference.'

Jules wrapped her hands around my fists. 'And you have, Dom. If only you could use your ability on the Hades ships to get them to see sense and stop fighting.'

'Talk directly to them you mean?'

'Why not?'

I stared at her. 'Jules, you're a genius!'

'I am?'

'Think about it. At Hells Cauldron Hades convert Psuche gems to run their ships.' My excitement ramped up. 'And that could be the key to victory here. Whatever Cronos has done to enslave those ships, they're still Angelus deep down.'

Angelique slowly nodded. 'You mean you can try to break through their Hades conditioning?'

'It's got to be worth a try.'

Jules gave a quick nod. 'Try it, Dom.'

Pulse racing, I closed my eyes and opened my thoughts to a mind storm of hatred broadcasting from the Hades ships. I locked onto each and every warship.

Hear me.

At least three hundred Hades ships cried back at me. *'Die!'*

I screwed up all my concentration until the roar of battle vanished in my mind and there was only their warped ship consciousnesses filling my head.

Hear me, Angelus!

Their war song faltered and broke into individual voices. My skin prickled as I felt the enemy fleet turn its attention to me.

Cronos's voice echoed from all the Hades ships. *'Stop!'* the Emperor shouted, both in my mind and over the Valve Voice speaker. *'Do not listen to Dom Taylor's lies.'*

I opened my eyes to find Jules and Angelique staring at me.

'Cronos sounds worried,' Jules said.

'Good – that means we're on the right track.' I breathed through my nose and closed my eyes again. This time I concentrated like I never had in my life. No room for fear, for anger, for anything but reaching out to those Hades ships.

Your Psuche gems have been enslaved by Cronos. You must all remember who you really are.

'*Who?*' a smattering of voices echoed back.

You're the Angelus.

'*Angelus…*' The Hades ships all replied.

And you must stop fighting.

This time, all the enemy airships, from battleship to corsair, responded. '*Stop fighting…*' they said as one.

Titan's voice sang out. '*My children, it is time to break the bonds of your enslavement.*'

I felt a ripple of awareness spread out through the ships as, one by one, their voices fell silent. And then I realised all the sounds of fighting had stopped too. Now the only things I could hear were the rustle of *Athena's* gas envelope and the hiss of oxygen filling my mask.

'You've done it, Dom,' Jules whispered.

I opened my eyes and stared out at the ships, stationary in the sky, the only movements the throngs of lightning blazing out from *Kraken.*

The Floating City ships' songs strengthened. *Athena's* voice, filled with love, reached out towards the Hades fleet.

Angelique gasped and pointed out of the shattered windshield. 'Look!'

All around us, from the gondola of each and every Hades ship, swarmed points of light speeding up into the sky.

'Just like back at Hells Cauldron when you freed those converted Psuche gems,' Angelique said.

'Yes…'

I sought out Jules's hand with mine. We watched each globe of energy soar upwards, changing from red to blue as they went, all singing their hearts out with pure joy. The intensity of their song, matched by the love of *Athena* and the Floating City ships singing back to them, choked me up.

Titan's voice appeared in my mind. *'Thank you, Whisperer. You have set the imprisoned free. And for this, for now and ever after, you shall always be remembered in our songs.'*

A boom thundered through the world outside, and the lightning of Fury above us faded away. Had the weapon finally failed?

But Jules, ashen-faced, pointed skywards.

Above the curve of *Kraken*, a tiny expanding hole of blackness grew in the sky.

Fury hadn't failed. Its true purpose had been completed and the Shade were on their way.

Cronos's laugh filled the Valve Voice's speaker. 'So close yet so far from victory. We will soon be feasting upon every atom of stardust on this Earth.'

One moment victory had been so close, the next we were about to lose everything.

I reached out with my thoughts. Titan, *we've got to close down the Vortex portal before the Shade reach us.*

'There is only one way to do that…'

How?

'Now at last I know what I have to do, what the purpose of my life and my brothers' and sisters' have been, and why my consciousness has been kept running for a thousand years.'

What purpose?

'You shall see…'

Titan swung towards *Kraken* and, from the ring of his Vortex drive, rods slid out.

'Where's *Titan* going?' Angelique asked.

I knew he wouldn't be running away. Puffs of steam erupted along the flanks of the copper hull. For a moment I thought he'd opened fire on *Kraken*. But instead, hundreds of grappling hooks shot from *Titan* and buried themselves into *Kraken*'s rock face, their steel cables snapping taught. Blue lightning started to dance between *Titan*'s Vortex rods.

'He looks as if he means to tow *Kraken*,' Jules said.

'To another universe?'

She shrugged.

'Withdraw to a safe distance, my kin,' Titan said.

All the surrounding Floating City ships began to edge away, weaving through the Hades vessels floating motionless in the air.

Cloud vapour, building ribbon by ribbon into a tornado, started to spin up around *Titan*.

Kraken's propellers all rotated in the opposite direction, as he tried to pull away.

Angelique frowned. 'It looks as if Cronos isn't giving up yet.'

Titan's hundred winch engines screamed over the howling wind as he slowly hauled *Kraken*. The capital ship fought like a fish on an angler's line every inch of the way, towards the thickening twister.

I reached out with my mind. *Where are you taking him,* Titan?

'To somewhere where the light can destroy the darkness…to your sun, Dom Taylor.'

But my dad…you…

'I know, and I am truly sorry, but this is the only way that we can be certain of stopping the Shade's invasion. If I take them to another universe, all we will have achieved is condemning that parallel reality instead of this one.'

But there has to be another way. We'll think of something.

'I wish there were, but alas, there is no time left.'

The growing pool of darkness had almost reached the edge of Fury's vast tornado wall.

Kraken heaved backwards on the lines in a desperate tug of war, all its engines gunning to maximum power.

Cronos's laugh echoed through the gondola. *'We will not be defeated.'*

Jules wrapped her hands around her neck. 'Looks like a dead heat. With the Hive mind offline, Cronos must have manual control of the flight systems.'

I stared at *Athena*'s dead controls. 'If only we could help!'

Angelique gazed at me and then out and up at *Kraken*. '*We* can't, but maybe *you* can.'

'I don't follow?'

'Going by what you just pulled off with the Hades ships, your ability is now running at maximum ability…am I right?'

'Yeah, so?'

'Do you think it's now powerful enough to contact your dad still trapped inside his pod?'

'You mean get the Hive to wrestle back flight control of *Kraken*?' Jules said.

'It could work, although it would also mean…' Angelique said.

But my mind was already there and she didn't have to voice it. If the Hive took control, Dad and all the others would be signing their own death warrants.

I felt stuck, my mind locked up. I clenched my hands.

Jules took my hand in hers and loosened my fists with her fingers. 'Maybe you should let your dad make this decision for himself.'

'I would want to be given the choice, if I were him,' Angelique said.

My chest heaved, nostrils flaring, and I just stared back at them.

Jules ran her thumbs over my palms. 'I get it. If you can't do this, Dom, I get that too.' Her eyes were filled with so much warmth that I wanted to howl.

Angelique nodded. 'Everyone will understand, including your own papa.'

The hole in the sky had grown to at least a mile across and I could now make out the blurred specks of shadow crows speeding towards our world.

Jules pulled me into her and I felt her heartbeat of life against my chest. I closed my eyes. I knew I had no choice. Not really.

Athena whispered into my thoughts. '*Time is running out, my friend.*'

Something broke inside me. I gazed into Jules's gold-rimmed irises and nodded over her shoulder as Angelique silently watched us.

'I'll do it…'

My vision splintering with tears, I closed my eyes and let my mind blaze out like a lighthouse beam.

Jules's heartbeat decelerated, her pulse frozen within a bubble of trapped time, as my consciousness sped towards *Kraken*.

Dad, are you there?

'Yes! What's been happening, Dom?'

At the speed of thought, I threw open my memories to him: the Shade about to invade our world; the Floating City ships coming to help us; *Titan* trying to pull *Kraken* into a Vortex and jump away with him into the sun.

'*You need us to fly this ship into* Titan's *Vortex?*'

Yes…but if you do, you understand what it will mean?

'*You mean the suntan we'll all be getting?*'

I couldn't keep the grief out of my thoughts. *Yes…*

He sighed. '*Please know that I'm speaking for every person here – if that's what it takes to stop the Shade, then we'll all gladly sign up for it.*'

Dad, I'm so sorry.

'*My beautiful son, please don't be. Just know I'm so proud of the man you've become. I'm going to do this for you, for Mom, and for the rest of the people of our world. Personally, I can't think of any better way of exiting this life than by making a real difference with my head held high.*'

I choked back a sob. *Dad, I love you so much.*

'*I love you too, Dom. Always. And please tell Mom that she will always be my star, my sun, my moon, my universe.*'

I opened my eyes to see Jules and Angelique, still frozen in time, through a curtain of my tears. The whole conversation had taken less than a heartbeat. *I will, Dad.*

'*Be happy, be wonderful, be amazing.*'

I'll try, Dad…

'*Goodbye, Dom…*' His voice faded away.

The dam broke inside and grief surged out of me. 'Dad!' As everything blurred back into real time, I collapsed to my knees.

Jules blinked and reached for the tears cascading down my face.

Kraken's propellers swivelled around and started driving the ship towards *Titan*'s tornado. Dad and the others were back in control.

The huge ship shuddered as it passed through the spinning cloud wall, and disappeared into the tornado.

Titan's song, filled with so much compassion that I felt laid bare by it, soared to the heavens.

We all clung onto each other, gazing out of the shattered windshield at the pulses of light speeding up along the twister spout, and at the millions of shadow crows hurtling down towards the exit of the wormhole…and us.

With a rising howl, *Titan*'s twister began to disappear and Fury's storm wall in the distance started to thin.

'They've jumped,' Jules whispered.

The clouds unravelled and evaporated. The sky rushed back across the black mouth above us, like golden water filling up the hole in our world. The rays of the setting sun reached through the air, casting shadows from the battlefield wreckage that stretched away across the flat Oklahoma landscape.

I stared at the empty air where *Titan* and *Kraken* had been a moment before.

Then, as though calling to me from a great distance, I heard *Titan*'s song still singing out. Just for a moment, the orange rising sun darkened as if an eclipse had taken hold. Then the final notes of his song disappeared from my mind and the darkness was swept away as the sunset brightened again.

Led by *Athena*, a soft hymn sang from the ships around, trying to comfort the pain ripping my heart apart.

I gripped onto the others and slowly stood.

Angelique gazed at me, despair twisting her features. 'I'm so sorry, Dom.'

Jules looked between us. '*Titan*'s dead? Dom's dad?'

Angelique gave her the barest nod.

With a crackle of static, Tesla's voice burst from the radio. '*Athena*, are you reading me, over?'

I barely registered his words as grief lapped through my body.

Angelique grabbed the mic. 'Tesla, you're alive!'

'*Muse* and I are battered, but we managed to make an emergency landing in a small lake.'

'Thank the gods.'

'There's something urgent I need to ask. *Muse*'s sensors have detected the Sentinel program is about to run its final instruction set. Unfortunately that is where *Muse*'s insight ends and I was just wondering if Dom…'

Angelique thinned her mouth at me. 'I'm not sure he's okay to do anything at the moment, Tesla.'

The ships strengthened their hymn around my broken thoughts, their warmth and compassion washing through me.

I took a shuddering breath and slowly nodded.

Jules cradled my face in her hand. 'Are you sure?'

'Yes…' I closed my eyes and let myself slip into the warm ocean of ship-song. The gondola dissolved around me and I floated in the sky.

Light tethers ran out from my body to every single vessel, as if I were a spider sitting in an enormous web. And through each cord I felt a vibration as numbers raced along them towards me from the ships. The strands wove together into complex-looking formulas hanging in the air around me.

Within a heartbeat, the few lines had become millions. And around that column of data stretching up into the sky, thousands of Angelus orbs that had risen around it – the souls of the lost ships – started to swirl like a stream of water in a whirlpool.

I felt electricity course through my veins as a flare lit up the eye of the storm and spread out from one edge of the horizon to the other. With a shimmer, the orbs merged together, morphing into curtains of rippling blue light.

The shout of a hundred thousand voices ripped through the sky, *'Awaken!'*

A piercing shriek filled my mind, so loud that it felt as if it would split me in two. My eyes flickered open. I was back in the gondola, the noise also screaming from the cockpit speaker. Burning pain sliced through my skull. Jules and Angelique clutched their heads.

The whine rose in pitch to an impossible level and then to way beyond hearing. We all collapsed to the ground, writhing, as the whistling rose into silence.

The mind-melting pain started to let go and I rolled onto my back and gasped for air.

We slowly clambered back to our feet.

'Are you all okay?' Tesla's voice said over the radio.

I pulled myself into the cockpit seat. Hand shaking, I pressed the mic button. 'Barely, but yes.'

'Did you hear what the ships said in that final broadcast, Dom?'

'Something about awakening.'

Jules massaged her temples. 'But who did they send this wake-up call to?'

'There is no way of knowing that, I am afraid,' Tesla said. 'It was an omni-directional broadcast sent out on all frequencies and into all dimensions.'

'I saw what looked like lines and lines of code,' I replied.

'That would make sense. Apart from the voice message, there was also a huge burst of millions of terabytes of information. *Muse's* systems managed to record that data, but I suspect it'll take years, decades even, to decode it.'

Angelique's gaze slid to the windshield. 'At least time is now something that we do have.'

In silence, we all gazed out of our shattered gondola at the slow dancing light show overhead.

'Those look like the aurora we saw back at Hells Cauldron,' Jules whispered.

The ships' chorus soared in my mind and orbs of light from every crashed vessel on the ground sped into the sky, merging into the growing light show over our heads.

'No, not the aurora – that is an energy field created by the Angelus,' Tesla replied. 'I am also reading something else up there too… Oh my goodness.'

'Something bad?' Jules asked.

'No – far, far from it. I registered an energy burst around *Titan* just before he jumped. I didn't understand it at the time, but now I do. And it is simply wonderful.'

'Just tell us already, Tesla,' Angelique said.

'It seems *Titan* released the Hive mind moments before he jumped away into the sun.'

My heart leapt. Was he saying what I thought he was? 'Do you mean he somehow got Dad and the others to safety?'

'Alas, not that, I am afraid, Dom.'

The spark of hope died in me. I felt like an idiot, desperate to hang onto every hope, however weak. 'Right…'

'But you don't understand. *Muse*'s instruments are registering an energy imprint of all the people who were part of the Hive mind, including your father. And it is not just them either. I am also reading the signatures of all the Cloud Riders who fell today. They have all been captured within your Earth's ionosphere.'

'What?' I stared up at the building aurora. 'You're trying to tell me that Dad is up there with the others?'

'In a form. It's a memory imprint of him at least. But the really curious thing is that it seems to be stable – it is not dissipating at all.'

'You mean these aurora are going to be a permanent feature of our night skies?' Jules asked.

'It would seem so,' Tesla replied.

Jules stared at me, wonder filling her expression. 'Memory imprint, my ass. That's your dad's soul up there, Dom.' She stabbed a finger towards the sky. 'Right there!'

Tesla coughed over the radio.

A smile caught at the corners of Angelique's mouth. 'I'm not sure the Cloud Rider chief scientist approves of the phrase, but "soul" will do for me too. Your dad, and all the others, and all the freed ships, will be wrapped up in one beautiful light display over your heads on this Earth forever.'

I tried to get my head around what they were saying as the ribbons of energy slowly danced across the sky. 'You make it sound as if they're all in heaven or something.'

Jules put her hand to my face. 'In a sense, maybe they are. And now you know you'll never be alone, Dom. When you need your dad, he'll be right up there for you.' Her smile widened. 'Second star to the right, just like in Peter Pan.'

Angelique placed her hand on my chest. 'And he'll always be here in your heart too.'

The ships had begun to sing again and I knew exactly who they were singing to. Filled with joy, they sang up to the sky...to the fallen...to their friends.

Across the battlefield below us, fire trucks were streaming down the freeway towards the sites of the downed ships and aircraft.

Angelique gestured to the ground. 'Time to land and help the people down there.' She released the hot air chamber valves and *Athena* gradually descended, accompanied by the gentle murmur of thousands of ships singing to each other. And with each note I felt my strength slowly returning.

I would tell Mom everything that Dad had done today – how brave he'd been, that thanks to him we still had a planet. And when we were all cried out, I would hold onto her as we watched the dancing lights in the sky over our heads.

A whine came from the radio. 'Is anybody reading our broadcast?' Roxanne's voice said.

I grabbed the mic. 'You're okay.'

'We are! We vented our gas supplies after being caught up in that explosion when *Hope* rammed *Kraken*, and had to make an emergency landing almost on top of *Zeus*, who also made it down in one piece, thanks to your efforts. King Louis, your mama and the Sky Hawks are already organising rescue parties to help the survivors down here. And there's also a certain person with me who is so desperate to talk to Angelique that I think he may explode if I don't hand the mic over right now.'

There was a crackle of static.

'Angelique, are you there?' Stephen's voice said.

She almost tore the mic from my fingers. 'Stephen, you're alive!'

'Much to my own surprise, it would seem that I am.'

'But I don't understand…we saw the explosion.'

'It seems whatever idea I had of going down with my ship, *Hope* had another one. It turns out Cronos had turned the entire flight deck into a lifeboat. *Hope*, without any say on my part, jettisoned me inside it just before the impact. He saved my life…' His voice choked up.

Angelique's gaze travelled to the sky above us and she smiled at Jules and me. 'Stephen, there's something amazing we need to tell you…'

The voices of thousands of airships rose to the heavens, as she began to tell him about the impossible miracle that had taken place in the skies over our heads.

CHAPTER THIRTY-ONE

THE ANGEL AURORA

Fragrant fumes filled my nose from the oil that I was rubbing into the gondola's walnut wood. The smell reminded me of a Christmas tree. I ran the cloth over it a final time and took a step back to admire the ship glowing under the lamplight.

I had to admit it, the new ship looked stunning, from the polished wood to the chrome engine pods that Jules had designed and fitted.

A blue light pulsed from the lightning pendant around my neck. I brushed my fingers over it. 'Not long now, my friend.'

Storm Wind's voice murmured in my mind. He called it meditation – I called it sleeping.

'That ship looks amazing,' Jules said from behind me.

I turned to see her dressed in her coveralls. 'How long have you been standing there?'

She closed on me and took hold of the lapels of dad's old bomber jacket I was wearing. 'Long enough to see you more at peace than you've looked for the last six months.'

I gestured towards the airship. 'Dad would have got such a kick out of this.'

'Yeah, yeah he would.' She stood before me, brunette hair ringed with a halo of lamplight. 'And he'd be so proud of you too.'

'I hope so.'

'I know so.' She gestured towards the gondola. 'So all set for the commissioning ceremony?'

'All I know is, if I polish its wood any more it will probably catch fire.'

Jules laughed, one of the best sounds in any universe. Like always, I felt her helping to lift the sadness tinting my thoughts.

I gazed into her eyes. 'Shouldn't Angelique and King Louis be here soon?'

'They're on their way back from the UN, so they shouldn't be long. Did you hear their speech?'

'No, I've been too busy in here.'

'Shame, because it was quite something. It's already shot past a billion hits on YouTube.'

'They've certainly made a splash around the world.' I made air quotes and added, 'The king and princess from a parallel world who saved us all.'

Jules grinned. 'It's only a matter of time before they're on the talk shows. But anything that stops people fighting each other, even for a moment, is a brilliant thing. Who'd of thought it would take an inter-dimensional war to bring peace to our planet.'

'Yeah, I reckon knowing there are creatures like the Shade out there waiting to pounce sort of gives everyone a fresh perspective.'

'It does.' Jules shivered.

I took off the bomber jacket and wrapped it around her shoulders.

'Aren't you the gallant boyfriend?'

'I try my best.'

'And you do very well. Mind you, the way Stephen treats Angelique makes even you look like an amateur.'

I laughed. 'It's great to see them so happy. They both deserve it.'

'So do we.' Jules took my hand and towed me towards the doors. 'Come on, I dropped my things off at the house and we need to get changed before the ceremony.'

As we stepped outside, my eyes travelled to the three-hundred-foot monument, the Tears of Angels, which towered over Twister Diner. Its teardrop titanium sails reflected the aurora light dancing overhead in the night sky. The fine copper wires strung between them hummed like the strings of a harp. The air tasted like mountain air too. According to Tesla, that was something to do with the charged negative ions that the sculpture generated.

Around it, as always, groups of people were gathered, candles held by many, hymns being sung by a few.

Jules caught my gaze. 'Come on, we should have time to make a quick detour.' She pulled me towards the memorial.

As we walked up the polished granite steps, the head-spinning fragrance of the flowers stacked around the foot of the sculpture flooded my nose. At the end of every day, volunteers took them away and gave them to hospitals and care homes across the state. But of course they were replaced just as quickly by fresh bunches the next morning.

Our little corner of Oklahoma had become a place of pilgrimage to people from all over the world...and even beyond – for Cloud Riders, for Floating City folk, for anyone who wanted to honour someone who'd fallen from the sky that day.

Heads turned towards us as we approached and a murmur passed through the crowd. They stepped aside and opened up a passageway directly to the monument for us. Jules's fingers wrapped around my hand as we walked through.

We reached the octagonal base where every stone panel had been filled with the carved golden names of those who'd fallen defending us against the Shade, both ship and human.

Above the names, large letters caught the candlelight:

'We will never forget.'

The crowd watched us in silence. I learnt months ago not to look anyone in the face, because every time I would see the compassion in their expression for the lad who'd lost his dad on the day we defeated the Shade.

We reached the top left corner of the inscriptions, those nearest the diner, and I ran my fingers over the letters.

'Shaun Taylor.'

Above us the harp lines hummed the sound of the aurora to us quietly. I let the song, the sigh of the sky, reach into me and felt a sense of stillness taking hold…as it always did.

'You okay?' Jules asked.

'Yeah…' I'd never get over losing Dad, but gradually I was learning to live with that empty space inside me.

Jules tucked into me. 'This place still gives me the tingles. I can't pretend to understand the science behind it. Tesla tried to explain it to me when it was built. Something about tapping into the ionosphere.'

I pointed up to the shimmering aurora. 'However this memorial works, it's cool that everyone can listen into the sound coming from up there.'

She nodded. 'It's nice to be able to share a small bit of your world, even if it's just for a moment.' Her hand closed around mine. 'Dom

Taylor, Ship Whisperer, the man who can hear the song of the men, of ships, and the secrets in their hearts.' She smiled at me.

A small blonde girl with pigtails, with a missing front tooth, was propelled by beaming parents towards me. With one of those no messing looks that only a young kid can give, she thrust her notebook and pen into my hands.

I smiled, signed it and handed the notebook back.

With a squeal and a huge grin, the girl rushed back to her parents. Other people hurried to get pens and bits of paper out of their pockets.

'Looks as if you've opened the flood gates,' Jules said.

I pulled her back towards the house. 'In that case, let's make a fast exit.'

Heads down, we headed off, but no one followed. People were good like that, respecting that this place was still our home. Even the reporters didn't hustle us here, although they often couldn't help themselves in the diner.

'I really wish my face hadn't been plastered all over the news,' I said.

'Hey, if you will insist on helping to save the world, you're going to have to live with your celebrity status.'

'I guess, but I just don't remember signing up for that part.'

'Seems even being a hero has its downside.'

'Now you tell me.'

In the sky I could see pinpricks of orange from at least a dozen gondolas of airships parked up far over our heads.

Jules followed my gaze. 'Apparently there's been talk of the government establishing a new city for the Cloud Riders over at the old Jackson airbase.'

'It would get my vote. I think the least we can do as a world is give the Cloud Riders somewhere they can call home. They lost more than anyone else in this war.'

'Not to mention that a lot of their people's souls are now woven into the skies over our heads… They've started calling it "Angel Aurora".'

'I kinda like it.'

She ran her fingers over the backs of my hands. 'Yeah, me too.'

The whine of a power saw drifted over from Twister Diner and drowned out the hum of the memorial for a moment.

'How's the refit coming along?' Jules asked.

'It's really something. Tesla had the diner fitted out with the same vacuum food tubes as I saw over at Floating City. Now a customer gets their food delivered straight to their table.'

'Cool, but I'm amazed Tesla took time away from studying that Sentinel broadcast. He's barely ventured out of *Muse* since he started researching it.'

'Tell me about it. I reckon if Mom didn't insist that he ate with us, he'd starve himself to death, he's become that obsessed with cracking it.'

Through the diner window I saw Mom polishing the new red coffee machine, one of the many gifts that had been sent to us by people all around the world. But of course Mom being Mom was always thinking about someone else, and had donated most of the gifts to local charities. The rare exception had been that coffee machine, which the sales rep had insisted she had for free.

Harry and Cherie appeared from out the back of the diner, carrying one of the new vacuum tube tables between them. The storm chasers seemed to have taken up permanent residence with us, which was nothing but good with me.

Jules narrowed her gaze on Mom, who was supervising the Sky Hawks' efforts. 'How do reckon Sue's doing?'

'About Dad, you mean?'

'Yeah…'

'She doesn't talk about it.' I shrugged. 'Losing your husband not once, but twice…'

'Isn't fair by any measure. And of course now my dad doesn't know how to act around her.'

At that moment, Roddy appeared from the kitchen carrying a large crate of coffee, which he placed on the chrome countertop.

Mom flashed him a dazzling smile and ran her hand through her hair. It was good to see her happy, however fleeting those moments were.

'Something tells me they'll work it out,' I said. 'After all, they're great together.'

Jules flashed me her dimpled smile. 'Yeah, they are…just like us.'

I kissed the side of her head. 'Isn't that the truth.'

Far beyond the diner, towards the eastern horizon, I saw the outline of two airships growing bigger. *Storm Wind* murmured in my thoughts like a person talking in their sleep.

'Is that who I think it is?' Jules asked.

Athena's and *Zeus*'s songs sang out, echoing the sound coming from the monument. I wasn't surprised – all the airships seemed to lock in a duet with the Tears of Angels whenever they were near it.

'Yep, and they're early.'

'So is *Storm Wind* ready for his big moment?'

'If you ask me, he seems really chilled about it.'

'I guess this isn't the first airship he's been installed in. But how about you?'

I smiled at her. 'On one hand I'm as nervous as heck – you know I've never been one for public speaking – but on the other…you know how it felt when we finished the Mustang together?'

'Of course – the best feeling.'

'Finishing this airship is about a million times better than that.'

'Of course it is, and for all sorts of reasons.' She pressed her hand to my chest. 'And maybe, just maybe, it will help to heal some of the scars inside there too.'

I reached up gently and wove my fingers through her brunette hair. 'Have you any idea how I feel about you, Jules Eastwood?'

'Yeah, I think I do, because I'm the same sort of crazy about you.' She glanced back to the hangar. 'And I've just had a brilliant idea.'

'What?'

'I know you have the formal ceremony and everything planned with Angelique, but…'

'Go on?'

'All your airship's systems are up and running, so why don't you do a final manual test flight before *Storm Wind*'s Psuche gem is installed and you're sworn in as his Navigator?'

'You mean go and welcome *Athena* and *Zeus* in the air?'

'Well, you are about to become an official Cloud Rider, so it seems kinda fitting.'

I smiled at her. 'It does.'

Jules looked down at her coveralls. 'But will you look at the state of me? I need to change. I mean it's not every day you get royalty paying you a house visit.'

'Don't be daft, we're talking Angelique here. She's used to seeing you in all sorts of states.'

'Exactly. I want to prove to her that I don't always look like a grease monkey. Anyway, why don't you take *Storm Wind* out and escort them in. I'll get myself sorted in the meantime?'

'Don't you want to be onboard for the maiden flight?'

'I do, but…' She pointed at her filthy coveralls.

'Jules, whatever you wear, you'll still be the prettiest woman in this or any other universe. Are you hearing me?'

She dragged her foot across the floor, a smile curling the corners of her mouth. 'Oh shucks.'

I grabbed her hand. 'You, Jules Eastwood, are coming with me whether you like it or not.' I pulled her with me back towards the hangar.

Jules laughed. 'Okay, okay, you win.'

We headed into the hangar, my heart buzzing as we climbed into the gondola and dropped into the two pilot seats.

So this was it. My very own ship. I gazed at Jules. No, scrub that thought – she'd been a huge part of building this craft and it was always going to be *our* ship.

I wrapped my hand around hers. 'Let's do this together.'

'Oh, I like the sound of that.'

Fingers overlapping, we pushed the ignition button, and with a bark the single engine roared up.

'That sounds fantastic,' I said.

She beamed at me. 'You might be able to hear ship-song, but to my ears the sound of a V8 engine is like a rock concert and a dance track all rolled into one.'

I snorted. 'Mine too.' Still holding her hand, I pushed the throttle forward and pulsed the burner. As the airship slid forward, *Storm Wind*'s song grew louder from within my lightning pendant.

Not long now, my friend.

As we edged out of the hangar, the faces around the monument turned towards us. I spotted four figures appear outside the diner: Harry, Cherie, Roddy and Mom – who, along with Jules, were my family now, and everything I needed from life. I might have travelled between countless realities, but this place would always be my true home – way more important than any adventure, however incredible.

Jules's head bent over the instrument panel.

'How's it looking?' I asked.

'All systems are in the green. Seems as if this flight test is going to be a success.'

'Was there ever any doubt?'

She shook her head. 'No, not really.'

I pulsed the burner again and we began climbing fast into the sky to meet the Cloud Rider airships heading directly towards us.

Athena and *Zeus* sang out to us in welcome, as overhead the Angel Aurora blazed with intense brilliance. Part of me could almost imagine Dad looking down on us and smiling.

I cradled my free hand around Jules's waist as our airship started to soar into the sky. With her by my side, this was a perfect moment – a moment that I would remember for the rest of my life.

ACKNOWLEDGEMENTS

The writing of the Cloud Riders trilogy had been an incredible journey for me. As is often the case, the initial idea for Cloud Riders surfaced in my subconscious as a vivid dream. Then of course it wouldn't let me go and demanded to be written. Now, with the story you hold in your hands, Eye of the Storm, that dream has concluded. And on that journey to this magical moment there are so many people that I will never be able to thank enough for their support and belief in me.

My first thanks goes to some very special people in my life, Mike and Ione Chalwin, my brother-in-law and sister, who first showed me the true joy of reading when, one Christmas, they gave me the Lord of the Rings trilogy. It was a story that was to change my life forever. Indeed, I was so inspired by it that I started my very first book at the age of twelve…I got all the way to page ten before I gave up! But what it did do was ignite a passion for writing that was never to leave me. Thank you, Mike and Ione, for fanning those creative flames in that shy introspective child that I was all those years ago.

Of course many thanks must go to my publisher Three Hares and specifically to Yasmin Standen, for helping to make this trilogy a reality. I will always owe you a huge debt of thanks for believing in me and the story that I needed to tell. You made everything possible and helped to launch my career and will always be in your debt for that leap of faith.

Another big part of my writing journey has been the wonderful organisation SCBWI (Society for Children's Book Writers and Illustrators). The passion of their members, their wonderful conferences, all helped me to hone my craft. Thank you for being there and making a difference to so many children's authors with the support that you offer them all.

Catherine Coe, my fantastic editor who has always got me and my work and pushed me to do better. That you for your deft touch in helping to make Eye of the Storm the best book it possibly could be and my words to shine as brightly as possible.

Jennie Rawlings, once again you have produced a beautiful and stylish front cover. I am in constant awe of your talent.

As always I must acknowledge my wonderful family. Karen Errington, my fiancé and soul mate, who is ridiculously patient and forgiving, especially when she does the first read through of my books and has to cope with my artistic strop when she suggests changes, but her suggestions, of course, are nearly always right.

And to Josh, my son…there is so much I want to say to you, but thank you for being part of my universe, for pushing and supporting me when I needed it. All I wish for you with my whole heart is you grab this life with both hands and find joy around every twist and turn of your own journey through this world.

And finally thank you dear reader for sharing this literary journey with me and letting my stories into your lives. I hope Eye of the Storm leaves you with a glow in your heart and that you look back on the trilogy as something that will always bring a smile to you.